NOT ANY NORMAL MADNESS

"Has anyone identified the man yet?" Pen asked.

"Not so far. Part of the time he talks like a Lodi man, but the rest is gibberish, crying, and these strange squeakings. He falls out of bed, staggers, writhes on the floor . . . we put him in a private chamber because he disturbed the other men in the ward so. Though since the fever from his parching has eased, it doesn't seem he's infected."

Linatas opened the door to a small chamber with a single cot. A harried-looking orderly was just thrusting a sunburnt young man back into it, who batted clumsily at him and whined.

Des, Sight. Pen stepped within; stopped short. The mystic doubled vision of his demon's view of the world filled his not-eyes. Mind, perhaps. *Oh.*

Bastard's tears, breathed Des. *There's a mess and a half.*

The young man stopped fighting, turned his head. Stared straight at Pen—and Des. He stiffened. Opened his mouth. And screamed and screamed.

Pen hastily backed out of the chamber and slammed the door. His shoulders found the opposite wall, and he fought for breath.

Pen inhaled deeply. A couple of times. "You were right, Master Linatas. That's not any normal madness." Wait, was that a contradictio . . . . s. Your patient has cont . . . . l. "I don't know about . . . . s definitely insane."

BOOKS by LOIS McMASTER BUJOLD

The Vorkosigan Saga

Shards of Honor • *Barrayar*
The Warrior's Apprentice • *The Vor Game*
Cetaganda • *Borders of Infinity*
Brothers in Arms • *Mirror Dance* • *Memory* • *Komarr*
A Civil Campaign • *Diplomatic Immunity*
Captain Vorpatril's Alliance • *Cryoburn*
Gentleman Jole and the Red Queen

Falling Free • *Ethan of Athos*

Omnibus Editions

Miles, Mystery & Mayhem • *Miles, Mutants & Microbes*

World of the Five Gods

The Curse of Chalion • *Paladin of Souls*
The Hallowed Hunt
Penric's Progress • *Penric's Travels* • *Penric's Labors*

The Sharing Knife Tetralogy

Volume 1: Beguilement • *Volume 2: Legacy*
Volume 3: Passage • *Volume 4: Horizon*

The Spirit Ring

ALSO AVAILABLE FROM BAEN BOOKS

The Vorkosigan Companion,
edited by Lillian Stewart Carl and John Helfers

To purchase any of these titles in e-book form, please go to
www.baen.com.

PENRIC'S LABORS

by

LOIS McMASTER BUJOLD

A Baen Books Original

Baen Publishing Enterprises
P.O. Box 1403
Riverdale, NY 10471
www.baen.com

ISBN: 978-1-9821-9303-4

Cover art by Dominic Harman
Map by Ron Miller

First printing, November 2022
First mass market printing, November 2023

Distributed by Simon & Schuster
1230 Avenue of the Americas
New York, NY 10020

Library of Congress Control Number: 2022030079

Printed in the United States of America

10 9 8 7 6 5 4 3 2 1

CONTENTS

MAP vii

INTRODUCTION ix

MASQUERADE IN LODI 1

THE ORPHANS OF RASPAY 133

THE PHYSICIANS OF VILNOC 299

OUTRODUCTION 461

AUTHOR'S NOTE:
A BUJOLD READING-ORDER GUIDE 467

INTRODUCTION

WELCOME to the third collection of Penric & Desdemona tales from the World of the Five Gods. To answer the question new readers will have first: Can these novellas be read before reading the earlier stories? Short answer: Yes.

Which is all one really needs to know. Feel free to turn to the first story now. Like other fantasy or science fiction works, the stories themselves will teach you about their world as you read them.

Longer explanation: I originally conceived these novellas as a linked group of tales each of which would work as a stand-alone, but also be part of a larger developing and interconnected series, much as I found stories about favorite characters at random in the science fiction magazines I read in my youth. Paper magazines used to have very limited space for novellas, which do hog a rather high page count per issue. This left few venues, with restricted editorial needs, for the form. When publishing moved online, especially with indie ebooks, this constraint ended—not only for length, but also content. Earlier in my career, there would not have been many places to sell this length of quirky fantasy tale; now, the virtual shelf space is boundless, resulting in a rich flowering of what was once a sparsely populated category of fiction.

I happily seized these e-advantages for the Penric tales, but corralling them on paper later meant the original floating àla carte scheme needed to be fixed in place. Which presents a special problem in an ongoing live series.

I have always felt free to jump around in my characters' timelines as the story ideas take me, inadvertently leading to many online debates about reading orders. For the first two Penric collections from Baen Books, *Penric's Progress* and *Penric's Travels*, setting the then-extant novellas in internal-chronological order (my usual preference) posed no problems. But I foresaw that if the series went on long enough, further collections wouldn't be able to stick to that. So I'm putting these newer stories in timeline-order within each paper volume, but letting the readers sort out the larger chronology for themselves.

Though not by themselves. We include a Bujold reading-order guide for all my work at the back of this volume. This includes a list of all the Penric & Desdemona tales at the time of this printing. For old readers returning (Welcome back! Five gods guard you on your path!) the reading-order guide should help to slot the new stories into the template already in your heads. New readers may use it as a way to find other stories later.

It's very typical for old readers to earnestly claim my works have to be read in some particular order, and for new readers, stumbling across one in isolation for the first time, to say it worked just fine as a satisfactory read all by itself. I'm inclined to trust the new readers on this point, though I do admit later stories will contain inherent spoilers for earlier ones. But, really, so does their very existence. There is a broad and fuzzy boundary between too many spoilers, and keeping a story's contents so secret no one can decide whether they want to read it or not. Spoiler sensitivity varies so much, this seems another issue best left for individual readers to decide for themselves.

So I'm going to place my remarks on the generation of these tales at the end of this volume, not only to put the hazard of spoilers out of the path, but because discussion of the stories' contents will make much more sense after one has read them. This Outroduction will be found after the end of the third story, and before the reading-order guide.

Happy reading!

—Lois McMaster Bujold
August 2021

MASQUERADE
IN LODI

MASQUERADE IN LODI

THE CURIA CLERK wiped the sweat drop from the tip of his nose before it could fall and blot his page. "What could be worse," he moaned, "than copying out letters in the Lodi midsummer?"

"Cutting up corpses in a Martensbridge midwinter," Penric replied unthinkingly, then pressed his lips closed.

The diligent if overheated clerk paused to stare. "What? You did that? . . . Was it for your magics?" He leaned slightly away, as if suspecting Penric and his resident demon of arcane midnight grave-robbery.

"Anatomy classes for the apprentices at the Mother's hospice," Pen clarified quickly. "Our material was donated by the pious, mainly." Plus the occasional unidentified, unclaimed body passed on by the city guard. The ones fished up from the thawing lake each spring had been the worst, if instructive.

"Oh. I did not know you'd been a medical student, too, Learned Penric."

I was teaching. Pen waved the comment away. This

wasn't a topic he wished to pursue. Or a calling, but that conversation had been firmly concluded back in Martensbridge. The bulwark of a large mountain range now stood between him and his former failings, and he was grateful for it. The dead had not distressed him; the dying had. "It proved one task too many for my hands, and I gave it up."

A silent growl from Desdemona reminded him that self-castigation on this matter had also been firmly forbidden to him, under pain of demonic chiding. Since the bodiless demon that gave him the powers of a Temple sorcerer had been the successive possession of ten different women over two centuries before she'd fallen to Penric, she had chiding down to an art form.

Now, now.

Also nagging, he added.

Behave, or I'll blot your page as well.

Which, as a bored creature of chaos, she was well qualified to effect, in so many ways. His lip twitched, and, oddly cheered, he turned back to the last lines of his translation.

The clerk had a point. Six months ago back in Martensbridge, Pen would have had to burn expensive wood to warm his chambers this much, but the humid reek drifting in through the windows overlooking the canal made Lodi heat more oppressive, when no sea breeze relieved it. His own quill scratched as he converted the last lines of the letter from its original Wealdean into Adriac for the archdivine's eyes, and files, and handed it across to the clerk for copying.

This finished the morning's stack. Which contained

nothing, it had proved, too sensitive or urgent. Done for the day, he trusted.

Busy work, sniffed Des. *Make-work. A waste of our talents.*

Speak for yourself. I find it soothing. Although he looked forward to an afternoon to devote to his own personal projects, including free run of the Temple library, far from fully explored in the four months of his residence in the curial palace. Penric cleaned his quill and stretched.

Tomorrow is the famous Lodi Bastard's Day festival, Des grumbled, *and you want to spend it shut up indoors? The preparations and parties are in full swing!*

So, people will all go out and leave me alone, Pen envisioned in hope. Although tomorrow night, he had social duties in the archdivine's entourage; the ceremonies dedicated to the fifth god were supposed to include a feast and a comic masque, and singing by the Temple-sworn castrati choir that was said to be ethereal. He anticipated that more warmly.

He sorted out those letters and their translations that actually required his superior's personal eyes, and with a cordial nod rose to leave the disposition of the rest to the very senior clerk, who wouldn't have wanted a demon of disorder anywhere near his files anyway. Pen wound his way through halls decorated with fine pious paintings and tapestries—or mostly pious; the previous generations of prelates had possessed a variety of tastes—and down a marble staircase to Archdivine Ogial's private cabinet.

The doorway was open to catch the nonexistent draft.

Pen took it as invitation to rap on the jamb and put his head in. Gray-haired Ogial had surrendered his five-colored robes to the heat and hung them on a wall peg, and sat at his writing table in shirtsleeves. A lay dedicat in a grubby green tabard of the Mother's Order hovered anxiously at his elbow. The lad looked up and gulped as Ogial waved Penric inside.

"The Wealdean letters, Your Grace," Penric murmured, and laid them on the table.

"Ah. Thank you." The archdivine gave them a brief survey, then leaned back and looked at Pen with narrowing eyes. "What were your plans for the day, Learned Penric?"

Note past tense, Pen thought glumly, but mustered, "Any duties you assign, a bit more translation on Learned Ruchia's book, and then the library."

"Hah, I suspected as much." Ogial smiled with a paternal air, legacy of his early training in the Father's Order before he'd risen through the hierarchy to broader duties. "This is your first Bastard's Eve in Lodi, and you are a divine of His Order. You shouldn't miss it. Take the rest of the day off, get out of this musty curia, and see how our city honors your chosen god. But first . . ."

Saw that coming, murmured Des.

"Dedicat Tebi here brings me a request from the chief physician of the Gift of the Sea—the charity hospice for the sailors near the northwest harbor, you know—to send over a Temple sensitive to look at a poor mad fellow who was lately trawled up by some Lodi fishermen. One would think that being lost in the sea for, apparently, several days would be enough to turn anyone's brain, but Master Linatas says he finds something more than medically strange about this one."

Ogial picked up a note and twiddled it in his fingers in Penric's direction. Penric took it gingerly. The crisp writing didn't add much to the archdivine's precis, beyond the nameless patient's guessed age, early twenties, and coloration—caramel skin, curly dark hair, brown eyes—which described half the folk in Adria. The reported drooling, thrashing, and broken speech could denote, well, any number of conditions.

"You are well-fitted to sort out the medical from any uncanny diagnosis, I expect"—the archdivine raised a hand to stem Pen's opening protest—"in a purely advisory capacity, I promise. If the physician's more lurid concerns are misplaced, as such usually are, you can reassure him and be on your way at once."

True, mused Des, unruffled.

You just want the excuse to get out.

Likewise true. So?

Ogial turned to the dedicat. "Tebi, escort Learned Penric here back to your master, with my blessing upon your work. He's new to Lodi, so don't lose him in the back alleys or let him fall into a canal." He added to Penric with a chuckle, "Although if those whites of yours don't end up dunked at least once during the festival, you aren't doing the Bastard's Day right."

Pen managed an appropriate smile at the wit of his senior. And rescuer, he was reminded; the archdivine's prompt offer of employment in his curia had hooked Pen out of Martensbridge the moment the passes had cleared of snow in the spring. His half-bow grew more sincerely grateful. "Very well, Your Grace."

Tebi, dutifully preceding Penric out the door, cast a glance over his shoulder with scarcely lessened alarm. It couldn't be for Pen's vestments, an Adriac design common enough in so large a city—a close linen-white coat, fabric thin for the season, buttoned up the front to a high round collar and skirts open to the calves, handy to don over ordinary clothes. So, presumably, the unease was for the triple loop of braid pinned over Pen's left shoulder, the silver strand with the white and cream marking him as not just a regular divine, but a regulated sorcerer. If he did go out on the town tonight, Pen thought he might leave both items in his clothes chest, and not just for the hazard of the canals.

Pen attempted a friendly return nod, which didn't seem to reassure Tebi much. Pen wasn't averse to his garb buying him easy respect from adults, but he'd never expected it to frighten children. Or at least children schooled in the meanings of Temple trimmings.

We don't need the guide, Des opined as they exited a side door of the curia onto a non-liquid street. *I remember my way around Lodi well enough.*

From near a hundred years ago? Des's previous riders, the courtesan Mira and, come to think, her servant Umelan, had both been long-time residents of the town—then.

Islands don't move that much. Granted bridges rise and fall, and new buildings sprout—they detoured around just such a collection of scaffolding, stone, and shouting workmen—*but I could have landed us at the sailors' hospice all the same. I wonder if they still dub the place Sea Sick? Also, Learned Ruchia visited here more than once, on her assorted missions.* Des's immediate prior possessor, from whom Pen had so unexpectedly inherited the demon and her powers. And knowledge and skills. And opinions. And, yes, memories not his own. Pen wondered if that would ever stop feeling strange.

They angled through narrow shadowed streets and alongside translucent emerald canals, the margins of their enclosing pale stone walls stained dark by the rise and fall of tides. Their warm green scent permeated the air, distinctive but not unpleasant. The route led over five bridges, and through a couple of lively squares colorful with market hawkers, before the opening light and screeching of gulls marked them as coming out by the seaside.

Threading past bollards, quays, docks, a private shipyard—Pen could just glimpse the walls of the big state shipyard beyond, source of Lodi's famous war galleys—they turned into another street and square. A four-story building in warm gray stone flanked a whole side, and the lad led them through the thick wooden doors, one leaf propped open for the day. A porter rose from his stool, identified Tebi at a glance, and waved them on, though his gaze lingered curiously on Penric, who cast him a polite blessing in passing.

On the second floor, past the lair of an apothecary, Tebi knocked on the doorjamb of another writing cabinet: smaller, more cluttered, and less elegantly appointed than that of an archdivine. "Master Linatas?"

The man within turned in his chair, his leathery face

animating at the sight of his messenger. He was a thick-bodied, muscular fellow, salt-and-pepper hair cut in an untidy crop, wearing a practical green smock shabby with wear and washings. The braids of a master physician hung not from his shoulder, but from a brass stand on his desk. "Good, you're back." A glance at Pen, and he lumbered to his feet. He still had to look up, his eyes widening slightly. "Goddess bless us."

Linatas could certainly read braids, so Pen merely said, "I'm Learned Penric. The curia sent me in answer to your request for a sensitive." Pen proffered the note by way of authentication.

Linatas took it back, still staring. "Huh! Are you, hm, Wealdean?"

A deduction from Pen's excessively blond queue and excessively blue eyes, Pen supposed, and his milk-pale scholar's skin. "No, I'm from the cantons."

"Ah, that would account for it. I've met merchants from those mountains, if not quite so, hm. Light. You speak Adriac very well!"

"I've a talent for languages, hence my employment in the curia."

The physician shrugged off Pen's appearance without further comment, thankfully, turning to his more pressing matter. "I suppose it would be fastest to just take you to the poor fellow. I've seen my share of men brought in with exposure, injuries, near-drownings, bad drink, or just too much horror, but this . . . ngh. Come this way. Ah, Tebi, thank you, well done. You can go back to Matron now." The boy nodded and scampered out. Pen followed Linatas up an end staircase to the next floor.

"Has anyone identified the man yet?" Pen asked.

"Not so far. Part of the time he talks like a Lodi man, but the rest is gibberish, crying, and these strange squeakings. He falls out of bed, staggers, writhes on the floor . . . we put him in a private chamber because he disturbed the other men in the ward so. Though since the fever from his parching has eased, it doesn't seem he's infected."

Pen bit his tongue on the impulse to run down the list of symptoms for strokes. He had only one task here, to assure the physician that his patient wasn't suffering from some unlikely curse, vastly more common in tale than in fact. And then he could escape. The familiar smell of a hospice, clean enough but distinctive, was making him just a little belly-sick.

Steady on, soothed Des.

I'm all right.

Uh-huh . . .

Linatas opened the door to a small chamber with a single cot. A harried-looking orderly was just thrusting a sunburnt young man back into it, who batted clumsily at him and whined.

Des, Sight. Pen stepped within; stopped short. The mystic doubled vision of his demon's view of the world filled his not-eyes. Mind, perhaps. *Oh.*

Bastard's tears, breathed Des. *There's a mess and a half.*

Within the sun-scorched fellow thrashed another demon. And not a new-hatched elemental, chaotic and weak, nor even one imprinted by some short-lived animal host. (And all animal hosts were short-lived, once an untutored demon of chaos infested them.) This was a demon of middling density, that had been human once, but then . . .

Des could read off its layers like the rings of a tree. *Elemental. Bird. Bird again. Human—a boy. Murdered, cruelly, young demon riven from him. Human, of no good character, but he didn't get away with his unholy theft for long. Roknari—they put him into the sea. For once, I can't object. Dolphin, quickly sickened. Demon dismasted of its acquired humanity, splintered, left a stub. Another dolphin, grieving—I did not know they could. Sickened again, more slowly. Then it found this fellow. So confused. The dying comforting the drowning . . . He thought he had gone mad when the demon jumped to him, and no wonder. Nightmare hours more in the water, then hands drawing him out, yes-no-yes-no . . .* Pen wasn't sure which of them was shuddering. Well. Both, of course.

The young man stopped fighting, turned his head. Stared straight at Pen—and Des. He stiffened. Opened his mouth. And screamed and screamed. Because Sight cut both ways, when two sorcerers were thrown together.

Pen hastily backed out of the chamber and slammed the door. His shoulders found the opposite wall, and he fought for breath.

Even other Temple demons, tamed and trained, found Des's density frightening. Who knew what this wild thing made of her? Though as the screams trailed off Pen supposed he could imagine it. He was cursed with a much-too-vivid imagination, some days.

Most days, panted Des. *But now, I admit, it's justified.*

Linatas exited after him, eyes round with alarm. "Learned Penric! What is going on? You've turned absolutely green." He pursed his lips. "Which I'd always thought was a figure of speech—shock is more gray, usually. Must be an effect of your coloration."

Pen inhaled deeply. A couple of times. "You were right, Master Linatas. That's not any normal madness." Wait, was that a contradiction in terms? "Er, common madness. Your patient has contracted a demon. From a dolphin, or rather two dolphins. Who had it from a drowning Roknari, who stole it from a servant boy, who had it from, it seems, a couple of ordinary birds who'd scarcely altered the original formless elemental."

"You could tell all *that* from a glance?"

"No, from experience. Quite a lot of experience. You know how that works. Don't you." Pen managed an ironic eyebrow-lift. "Or you wouldn't have called me here, eh?" He straightened. "I don't know about your patient, but that demon is definitely insane."

Linatas was briefly speechless, taking this in. Had he really not expected validation of his half-formed suspicions? He found his footing in practicality. "What . . . should we do for him?"

"Certainly continue to keep him in isolation. That demon will be shedding disorder indiscriminately. Potentially dangerous to people and things around him. And to him." Penric winced an apology in prospect to Des. "It will have to be extracted from him by a dedicated saint of the white god."

This time, thought Des grimly, *no argument*.

Penric knew there was such a saint in Lodi, but not

offhand at which of the scattered chapterhouses of his Order, or other domicile, said holy person might presently be found. It would seem easier to bring the saint here than the madman to the saint, but who knew. "I'll have to ask the archdivine, and make arrangements."

With a few moments to compose himself, Pen's mind was beginning to move again. Unfortunately into proliferating questions, like a dog scattering a flock of pigeons. "Did you speak to the men who brought him in? How long ago was that?"

"Briefly, and two nights ago. Ah, perhaps we should return to my cabinet and sit down for this." Linatas was still looking at his visitor with medical concern, though Pen was sure his color was coming back.

By the time they'd gone back downstairs, Linatas had parked Pen on a stool, pressed a beaker of tepid tea upon him, and watched to make sure he drank, the pigeons began to settle. Bird the first . . .

"Just where was he found, did they say?"

Linatas sat in his chair with an unhappy grunt. "About five leagues out to sea. Too far, really, to be a swimmer carried off by the currents. We guessed he must have been swept or fallen from the deck of a ship, although no returning vessel has so far reported a missing man."

"Was he a sailor, do you think?"

"No. He's very fit, or he wouldn't have survived his ordeal, but he doesn't have the hands of a laborer." Linatas held his up and clenched and unclenched them by way of illustration. "Deckmen's and fishermen's hands are very recognizable."

Working here for long, Linatas would surely have seen many such, right. "An officer? Seems too young."

"Lodi shipmasters apprentice young in their trade, but I think more likely he was a passenger."

Penric glanced down at his own writing callus and ink stains on his fingers. "Any sign of being a clerk or a scholar . . . ?"

"Hm, not strongly marked, no. Perhaps a reluctant writer. When we can make out his speech, it's neither rude nor high." Linatas glanced at Pen with return curiosity. "Why did he scream so when he saw you?"

"Ah, not me. He saw my demon. Desdemona. Here, I'll lend her my mouth, and she can introduce herself. Des? Please be demure, now."

Des grinned; Pen could feel the set of his face change as she took charge. "Demure? Who do you think you're talking to? But I shall be properly polite, as befits a tame Temple servant. How do you do, Master Linatas? Thank you for looking after Pen, who tends not to do it for himself. Ah, perhaps that's demonstration enough, Des," Pen ended this before she decided it would be droll to embarrass him.

Spoilsport. But she settled back, gratified with her brief outing. And acknowledgement.

Linatas's thick eyebrows had climbed. "That . . . was not a jape. Was it?"

"No, though many people think it is." Pen sighed. "You may speak to her directly any time you wish. She hears everything I hear."

". . . She? I mean, demons have no bodies."

"Very long story. About two centuries, so best not

delay for it here. But getting back to your patient. Uh, how much do you know about Temple sorcerers? Or any sorcerers?"

"None have come my way as patients. I've seen them about town on rare occasions, or at ceremonies for their god."

Though if they were not in their whites and braids, Linatas could have passed such men and women unknowing in the market any number of times. For such a rare calling, the Lodi Temple was relatively well-supplied with sorcerers; Pen knew the Mother's Order here had more than one sorcerer-physician in its service, if not at this poorer hospice. Pen's duty directly to the archdivine was outside the usual chapterhouse hierarchy.

"At a minimum, I need to explain how ascendance works, then," said Pen. "As a creature of pure spirit, a demon requires a body of matter to support it in the world of matter. The question then becomes who shall be in charge of that body. A person can either possess or be possessed by their demon—rider or ridden is the usual metaphor—and demons in their untutored state naturally desire control. But as creatures of chaos, most aren't exactly fitted for it. If a wild demon ascends, it's more like being taken over by a destructive, overexcited drunk." *With supernatural powers*.

You were doing all right till that last bit, Des said dryly.

"The other thing you need to know," Pen went on, ignoring the interpolation, "is that elementals, the bits of the Bastard's chaos leaked into the world, all begin as identical blank slates. Their ensuing personalities are acquired from and through their succession of hosts. *Imprinting* is a, hm, not-wrong way to envision it, like ink pressed down from a carved plate. Adding subsequent learning and life experience like any other person, but anyway. So every demon is different from every other demon just as every person is different from every other person, d'you see?" Pen looked up hopefully. This was a key point in his basic-demon-lecture where he often lost his listener to their prior more garbled beliefs. He'd also learned not to try to fit in all the fine points and exceptions at this stage, though the simplifications pained him.

Linatas gave him a *go-on* wave of his hand; if not exactly convinced, seeming willing to wait for it.

"Which brings us back to this demon." Unnamed, much as its possessor, or possessee. "It's very damaged. First, it came into being somewhere in the Roknari archipelago, which is, um, due to the Quadrene heresy not a healthy place for sorcerers or servants of the fifth god generally. The first animals it occupied were a couple of chance-encountered birds, nothing unusual there. But a demon, when its host dies, always tries to move up to a stronger—actually, more complex—host. The now-bird-imprinted spirit next went to a servant boy of maybe ten who, because Quadrene, would have known nothing about what was happening to him nor had any access to help or counsel. But someone else around him, a grown man, I think another servant, figured it out, and coveted what he imagined would be magical powers. Which, in his oppressed state, must have seemed worth the risk. He lured the boy out and secretly murdered him to steal those powers."

Linatas's head went back in surprise. "That's done?"

"It's tried. By the same sort of person who would commit murder and theft anywhere, I suppose. It... generally does not go as the assailant imagines it will." Pen cleared his throat. "His career as a would-be hedge sorcerer was evidently short, but long enough to attract the attention of the Roknari Temple authorities, who have rather different methods than us Quintarians to deal with problem demons. But effective enough in their way. He was put out to sea to drown. This prevents the demon from jumping to any other human. If no other large-enough creature is around in range to possess, the demon, um, well, *dies* is as good a term as any." *Evaporates* was another, but, fine points.

"Except this time, there *was* another creature, a curious dolphin. But when a demon is forced back to a lesser host, the effect on the demon's growing personhood is highly destructive. I've only seen one case where the demoted demon could be saved, afterward, and in that one the demon was unusually stable."

"*Save* a demon?" The *Whyever?* hung implied.

Des seemed a bit offended by the bafflement in Linatas's voice. Pen touched his shoulder braid, and put in on her behalf, "They give us great gifts, if they can be educated, and treated with understanding and respect. Like any other complicated thing of power and danger, which can kill you if misused. A water mill, a sailing ship, a hunting dog, a forge, a foundry—a human being. A pity and a waste when they are ruined."

Linatas, Pen had no doubt, had seen his share of pitiful waste in his line of work. By the twist of his lips, he was following the argument well enough for now.

"This demon seems to have been ruined twice over, once to be sure by its fall from human to animal, but more from its imprinting by the murdering servant. The apparent madness you are seeing in your patient is from moments of ascendance by aspects of this shattered demon. I suspect some of his gibberish is Roknari. I can't guess at the language of dolphins."

"That is the strangest part of all this, to me," said Linatas. "How he was saved by the dying dolphin, if that's what happened."

"Mm, maybe not so odd. Demons are the property, if you like, of the very god of chance and mischance. He looks after them, in His own way. The mark of His white hand seems all over this." And not for the first time, in Pen's experience.

"You're claiming a miracle?" Linatas's voice rose in pitch, as well as volume.

"In a sense. They say the gods are parsimonious, but I think a better term might be opportunistic. Your drowning patient doubtless prayed to any god listening for succor—I certainly would have, in his position—but the Bastard might merely have seen a good chance to recover His demon for proper disposal."

Now Pen was getting That Look, which he won so often when trying to explain his god's peculiar theology. He wasn't spinning fables, blast it. Or at least his was *informed* speculation.

"What I'm beginning to wonder more is how your

fellow was parted from his ship in the first place. Since I don't imagine the god pushed him overboard. Not to mention who he is. Though once he is, ah, de-demoned by the saint, he should come back to his senses fairly quickly, and be able to tell us for himself what happened to him. So that's a set of problems that will solve themselves. The sooner, the better, I suppose."

Pen climbed to his feet. "I'll be back, or send a message. The demon will be struggling to stay on top, but it's possible your fellow may gain ascendance himself from time to time. You may be able to get more out of him then—he'll be speaking Adriac if he does. Probably." He wondered at the advisability of his next caution. It might cast an unfortunate doubt upon his own authority. Nevertheless. "Although demons can lie."

So can humans, muttered Des. *And rather more often*.

Linatas placed a hand on his desk preparatory to rising. "I'll call for Tebi to escort you back to the curia, Learned."

"No need. I know the way now."

"When will you return?" A tinge of anxiety colored Linatas's voice.

"Not sure. But I promise I won't delay. This has become the day's most urgent task."

Quick footsteps sounded from the hallway. A man in a green tabard whom Pen recognized as the orderly from upstairs stuck his head through the doorway, his gaze raking the room. "Not here," he muttered.

"Gnade?" said Linatas. "What's going on?"

"Sorry, sir. The madman got out when I went to empty

the chamber pot. Only a moment—I'm sure he must still be in the building."

"Get Tebi to help you look."

"Right, sir." The orderly galloped off.

But Linatas did not relax back into his chair.

"Has your patient done this before?" asked Pen.

"He rattled around the ward obsessively yesterday, but he was pretty unsteady on his feet. He can't be far." Linatas's worried frown reflected no such certainty.

"Des?" said Pen aloud. "*Is* he still in the hospice?"

A dizzying roll of demonic perception stretched in three dimensions, dotted with the colorful glows of souls still in their bodies. Pen ignored the faint signatures of ghosts, gray and drifting and fading; all such old buildings had them, hospices more than most. The aura of the fractured demon would be a glittering beacon by comparison.

"No," said Desdemona through his mouth. Linatas glanced up sharply. "He's got out. That was fast."

Had Pen and Des triggered this very flight?

Likely, conceded Des. *The demon must have realized we're a danger to it, if not precisely how. That would depend on how much its hosts, past and present, understand Temple procedures. The mad Lodi boy may know more than the Roknari, and either would know more than the dolphins. Or the birds.*

An insane ascendant demon of disorder, loose in Lodi . . . The possibilities were daunting. Pen thought bad words in Wealdean.

Linatas pushed up from his desk.

"I'll help you look," sighed Pen.

❖ ❖ ❖

They quickly found from the porter that the runaway patient had not fled by the front door. Of the three other ground-level doors, two were locked from the inside. That narrowed the choice nicely. Pen, trailed by Linatas and Tebi, stepped out onto a side street and looked up and down. It would have been much too lucky for the man to still be in sight.

"If the demon is being dominated by the dolphins, it might actually try to get back to the sea. If by the one drowned and one near-drowned man, anything but." Pen bit his lip and pointed toward the harbor. "You two take that way. If he's jumped into the water, somebody should have seen him, this time of day. One of you could follow the shore in each direction. Look for a fuss. I'll head into town."

This logical plan was adopted without argument, seeming well to Pen till he came to the first cross-street. He halted in frustration.

"Des, if you were an insane demon, which way would you go?"

The sense of an offended sniff. *I am not insane. And I would do something much cleverer.*

Pen looked upward at the band of blue sky in vague futility.

This won a scoff outright. *As we have several times established, I can't fly, and neither can he.*

Might the distraught boy try to go home, wherever that was? *Would that demon be organized enough to pretend to be him? Well enough to fool people who know him?* It would be the most ready camouflage.

A doubtful pause. *It could submerge, let him take over*

and take them both home. But that would risk not being able to regain ascendancy.

If the mad fellow was indeed a Lodi native, he would know this maze of a town. That knowledge would become increasingly available to the demon as it put down its roots into him, but not instantly. Pen remembered his confusion when he'd first contracted Des—more in the sense of a disease than a legal agreement, though there had certainly been negotiations later.

If, on the other hand, the demon was trying to get as far from the sea as possible, it, he, they had to head for the big causeway from the lagoon city to the mainland. The man had been bathed and shaved and fed in the hospice, but—how far could he bolt dressed only in a loose shirt and trews, barefoot and without money?

This was not getting them forward. He set his teeth and strode right, extending Des's perceptions to the limit of her range. Which was curtailed, in congested places like this, by the many distracting live souls around them. They came to another square where a canal intersected the street, small boats tied up supplying another busy local marketplace, loading and unloading: men, women, and children buying and selling bright vegetables, fruits, flowers, and more miscellaneous goods. The noise in his ears was merely cheerful. The glut in his Sight was near overwhelming.

Des, how can you bear it? All of us together?

A shrug. *I've never known anything else.*

There were good reasons why the very first thing Pen had sought, when this gift of Des's had come to him in full, was how to turn it off again. And it wasn't due to the poor sundered ghosts, much as they'd unnerved him back then. Nowadays, the worst part was when his trained brain started to *diagnose*. He really didn't want to know anymore which random strangers he met were dying.

All of them, eventually, Des observed.

I suppose in two centuries you've earned your long view.

The hard way, aye.

The Lodi madboy must be equally spirit-assaulted about now, if without the fine discernment Pen possessed. This suggested he might seek less peopled places, not that there were many in Lodi. Which pointed back to a break for the mainland, again.

Blast it, they needed to assign their quarry a name. Two names, as there were two agendas in play. He couldn't keep thinking of them as Lodi Madboy and Deranged Demon.

We could nickname them Mad and Dee, like Pen and Des, Des quipped. Pen rolled his eyes.

He circled the area, coming back to the front door of the hospice in time to meet Linatas and Tebi returning from their search of the shore. Alone.

At Pen's anxious look, Linatas shrugged. "No luck our way. Any from yours?"

Pen shook his head. "I covered about half of this island." After centuries of development, Lodi was still cut up into island-based neighborhoods, for all that some had been built out on pilings and dredgings to join up with each other. "Due to the demon, the problem of your patient has shifted from the Mother's Order onto the Bastard's." In other words, into Pen's lap. "He'll be leaking dangers far beyond his madness that can only be handled by a sorcerer or a saint. But please send his description at once to the causeway gate guards to be on watch for him." Which, given the fellow's common appearance, was going to be less than useful, but Pen could only work with what he had. "Tell them not to approach him, but to send a runner to . . ." Pen, ideally, but if he was out combing the city, he would be as hard to locate as his quarry. "Archdivine Ogial's office. Send there too if you learn anything more."

Which meant he needed to report in at the curia next, and warn them of their task as his message depot. Among other things.

Pen bade Linatas farewell with a cursory gesture of blessing, and hurried back over the five bridges. He made the return journey with his Sight at full stretch, just in case. It was like trying to rapidly skim a densely written book where paragraphs kept snagging and tripping his eye. The only thing he needed to discern of passersby was that they did not bear the demon, which was pretty instantly apparent. Unexpectedly exhausting; drawing Des's senses back in when he reached the curia, on the reasonable assumption that Madboy would not have come here, was a relief.

He scuffed up the stairs to the office on the second floor belonging to the archdivine's secretary, Master Bizond. At the doorway, he almost collided with a middle-aged woman in the trim black robe of the Father's Order. The black-and-gray braids of a full divine upon her shoulder were threaded with purple, marking a specialty in law. She carried a stack of papers and documents; reflexively, Pen held the door for her, which won him an abstracted nod of thanks. It inadvertently put her in line ahead of him at Bizond's desk.

Bizond was lean and gray and with the air of a permanent fixture in the curia, like the marble staircases. He looked up at the lawyer with something as close to approval as his stony features could unaccustomedly produce. "Learned Iserne."

The woman nodded crisply. "Here are the copies of the wills and documents for the Vindon lawsuit, together with my precis."

"Oh, good, we were waiting for those." His bony hands darted for them. A pause, while he sifted through in some preliminary assessment.

The woman, evidently feeling her mission discharged, eased back and eyed Pen in mild curiosity. "You are Learned Penric, are you not? Ogial's new sorcerer?"

Pen ducked his head. "Yes, Learned. I believe we have passed each other in the library?" He remembered her, dark-eyed and rather handsome for her age, hurrying in and out of the curial archives. Her glances at him had been neither impolite nor friendly; perhaps just distracted.

"Yes, I've noticed you." People typically did, with his height and eyes and hair. And braids. "Is it true you were court sorcerer to the princess-archdivine of Martensbridge?"

And now the subject of whispered curial gossip, Pen was dryly aware. "Formerly, till she sadly passed last year.

The new royal appointee brought her own sorceress from Easthome, and I was encouraged to seek other employment."

Meaning, pressed hard to take formal oath at the Martensbridge Mother's Order as a full physician-sorcerer, in place of his unofficial service doing, actually, the same thing. But he wasn't discussing *that*. His sideways escape to Lodi had been unexpected even to him.

Pish, said Des. *Ogial leapt at your first note of inquiry. He considers you quite the ornament, you know.* The sense of a smirk. *Ornamental, too.*

The stack of documents was looking as if it might take some time. Shifting from foot to foot, Pen blurted, "I'm sorry to interrupt, Master Bizond, but I have a bit of an emergency."

Bizond's face twitched from annoyance at this disruption of his concentration, to vague alarm at what a full-braid sorcerer of Pen's standing could possibly dub *a bit of an emergency*. His voice took a startled edge. "What?"

Swiftly, Pen gave the gist of his outing to the Gift of the Sea, minus the fine points. "The upshot is, if he hasn't made it across the causeway already, there is an ascendant demon loose in Lodi, riding, in effect, this kidnapped young man."

"This . . . is bad?"

"For the young man, yes. For whoever encounters him, I'm not clear yet. I will of course be going back out to look for him. Meanwhile, I need to know who and where is the saint of Lodi."

"Which one?"

"There's more than one?"

"Three petty saints that I know of in the Father's Order, and six scattered around the Mother's Order. I believe the Daughter's Order has a few as well. The Son's Order does not much run to saints."

"Er, I meant the one of my Order."

Bizond's eyebrows rose in surprise. "You don't know?"

Pen declined to explain how Lodi's demon-eating agent of the white god was someone Des would have preferred not to meet ever, settling on, "I'm new here . . . ?"

"Ah, I suppose. Well, Blessed Chio may likely be found at the chapterhouse and orphanage on the Isle of Gulls. Do you know where that is?"

"Yes," Des replied for both of them.

Pen explained his plan to conscript Bizond's office for his message drop. Bizond, who had grown increasingly nonplussed through all this, didn't protest, though whether due to Pen's logic or his looming Pen wasn't sure. Pen hurried back out, trailed by Iserne's dazed stare and Bizond's mutter of "Five gods preserve us . . . !"

From the bedemoned boy? Pen wondered. *There is only one god for that task.*

I think he meant from you, said Des, too amused as usual.

As he left the curial palace again, Pen wondered whether it would be faster to walk or hail an oarboat. Des sketched a crude map in his head, and advised, *It will have to be a boat. Gulls is too far out for a bridge.*

Right. Pen switched directions to the boat-hire closest to the Temple square, at the edge of the city's central basin. Half-a-dozen narrow boats were pulled up at the dock, loading or offloading passengers: merchants and Temple folk and city officials. All the craft were painted and ornamented according to their owner-boatmen's tastes and notions of what might attract customers. The collective effect was clashingly gaudy: reds, oranges, yellows, greens, blues, some fresh, some weather-faded; stripes, swirls, solids, or carved animal motifs; polished tin or copper inlays glinting.

At the sight of his pale vestments and raised hand, a couple of the boatmen pretended to be looking the other way, but one aging fellow pushed back his hat, grinned, and waved Pen on. Pen stepped down carefully and centrally onto the damp, rocking planks and sank back on the worn cushion provided, which would have been more thoughtful for his lean haunches were it less compacted. He was still grateful to be off his feet for a bit.

"Bless us to avert your god's eye on His Eve, Learned, and where to?" the boatman inquired genially.

Pen dutifully returned a full tally of the gods, touching forehead, mouth, navel, groin, and heart, with a double tap of the back of his thumb to his lips. "The Isle of Gulls, please."

"Visiting the orphans?" The boat wobbled as the boatman pushed them off and out into the waters of the basin.

"The chapterhouse."

The boatman took up his stand at the square stern,

and began to sweep his oar rhythmically back and forth in the squeaking oarlock. Progress was slow but steady, to the musical slapping of the choppy salt waves against the hull. Pen eyed the creaking seams beside his feet, but the tow and tar seemed to be holding, their sun-warmed odor evocative of marine livelihoods. *Keep your chaos to yourself, please, Des.*

Hah.

He gazed out across the basin, sparkling in this bright afternoon, sprinkled with other vessels of all sizes and sorts, moving or moored. A returning convoy of three big-bellied merchant cogs was the most impressive, as their happily shouting crews warped them in to their anchorages, canvas thumping down. Pen would have enjoyed the sight more if he'd been less distracted. Des felt uneasy within him as they bobbed across the waves, like incipient seasickness.

You've been involved in such demon-retrievals more than once before, haven't you, in your career as a Temple demon? Part inquiry, part reassurance. *Poor Learned Tigney, I know about. His affair wasn't that much before my time.*

Agh, yes. That idiot. He preened so when he was first gifted with his demon by the Order, certain he would soon surpass Ruchia and me. We weren't in Martensbridge when his demon ascended and absconded, but we were saddled with the task of tracking them down when we got home. He led us a vile chase across Trigonie. We only caught up with him because he'd stopped too long in a town just over the border of Orbas to pursue an excessive course of carnal pleasures.

The way demons do, Pen put in slyly. When they had the chance, in their stolen, or shared, carnal bodies. Though after ten years together, he was over his embarrassment by Des's enjoyment of his. Mostly.

And men do, Des shot back. *When both surrender to one desire, there are no brakes. If I were not much more balanced*, she continued primly, *I could not have lasted this long. Howsoever, Tigney's demon seemed more addicted to gluttony and sloth than, say, lust and wrath, which fortunately slowed them. Though the pride and envy by which he first fell was all Tigney.*

Pen mused on her list. *So where does greed fit in all this?*

Just middling. Greed is an appetite that looks largely to some imagined or feared future. Ascendant demons are not much known for foresight.

Hm. Pen frowned as they approached the boat landing on the island shore. *So did you bring the saint to Tigney, or him to the saint? It was still old Blessed Broylin of Idau back then, wasn't it?* A creaky and cranky old man when Pen had so memorably met him, until the god had shone through his eyes like a dive into infinite space.

Fifteen years ago, so not as creaky. Though just as cranky. We dragged Tigney back to him.

We need to discuss the mechanics of that.

Less mechanics than force and threat. Ruchia's guards supplied the force; she and I supplied the threat.

Will you be able to overawe this wild demon?

. . . Probably.

Only probably? Pen didn't quite like that hint of

doubt. *It must surely be less powerful than Tigney's was.*

Lack of foresight, remember. Fear can be the opposite of greed that way, shortening one's horizon.

I'd have thought Tigney's demon would have been utterly terrified, knowing exactly what was in store for it.

When terror surpasses all bearing, it can tip over into despair. And a sort of docile lassitude.

A relief of sorts?

Not really.

"You're a quiet one," remarked the boatman as he steered them to their island docking.

Not on the inside of my head. "Sorry. I've a few things on my mind."

The boatman's eyebrows twitched up at the apology. "Busy night coming up for you folks of the fifth god, with the festival and all?"

"I expect so." Though not, in his case, due to the festival.

The boatman chortled. "Don't celebrate so good you dunk that white dress in a canal."

What is this obsession by everyone we meet with my whites and canals?

Des would have smirked if she could. As it was, Pen's lips twitched. *Hopeful anticipation, probably.*

They glided into perfect position at the algae-fringed stone quay. Heartened by his customer's near-smile, the boatman added, "D'you want me to wait for you, Learned?" He named the fee for this restful service as Pen drew up his purse on the cord around his neck and fished out the right coin. He'd been relieved, like most Lodi visitors, that boatmen's rates were set by law and posted on all public landings.

"I'm not sure how long I'll be here." He considered Madboy, who-knew-where doing who-knew-what by now. "But I won't be lingering. Yes, please." He added the half-in-advance coin to the boatman's outstretched leathery palm, then turned to climb the steps.

More remote than its sister city wards, the Isle of Gulls was less built-up, the households scattered across it sparing space for gardens and orchards and useful domestic animals. It gave the place a restful, rural air that Pen discovered he'd missed in the scurry of the Temple precincts in Lodi's heart. The chapterhouse of the Bastard's Order was not hard to find, as a channel was dug from the shore near the landing right up to its walls, and through a water gate presently raised.

When this place was a merchant's mansion, Des reminisced, *he passed his goods in and out that way. When he died childless, he left house and fortune to the Order to build on the orphanage. That was back in Mira's day. We knew it well then, as we'd come out here for patrons on occasion. Mira had the most flamboyant boat, with an awning of silk and liveried oarsmen.* A nostalgic sigh. *It's changed . . .* A century had softened the raw brick; the walls were climbed now by no enemy more dangerous than ivy.

A high wooden gate stood half open to the afternoon, cheery voices floating through it. Pen entered to find two boats pulled up from the terminating pool of the small channel. A motley assortment of children laughed and argued around them, engaged in decorating wherever decorations could be fitted on, ribbons and bannerets and garlands of miscellaneously colored cloth flowers clearly made by little hands. They were benignly supervised by a pair of adults in stained white dedicat's tabards, who looked up in question at Pen's arrival.

"May I help you, sir?" said the man.

Pen supposed he'd better go through proper channels. How did one gain audience with a saint? Should he have tried to send ahead for an appointment? "I'm Learned Penric of the archdivine's curia. I need to speak with the head of the chapterhouse."

"Of course, Learned. Please come this way." With a cautious and deeply curious glance at Pen's left shoulder, the man led off across the trampled yard toward the stately house, two stories high and faced with fine creamy stone, window frames and doors painted russet. "Oh, there he is now."

A distracted-looking man in bleached vestments cut much like Pen's, if more worn and less ink-spattered around the cuffs, and with the badge of his office hanging from a silver chain around his neck, exited the front door and looked around. He spotted Pen at once, his brows drawing together. Pen pegged him for another middle-aged functionary, more administrator than holy man, the backbone of every Order.

They met at the foot of the shallow steps. The dedicat bobbed his head. "Learned Riesta, this is Learned Penric. He says he's come from the curia."

"Oh," said Riesta. His tone seemed more enlightenment than surprise.

"Pardon me for arriving unheralded," Pen began politely, "but I seek an urgent conference with the saint of Lodi, whom I was told resides here."

"Yes, that's right." He continued to peer perplexed at Penric. "Is there something the matter with your Temple demon, Learned Penric?"

"Not at all," Pen assured him hastily, while Des puffed in silent offense. "I was detailed by the archdivine"—yes, given Pen's own deceptively unweathered features, it never hurt to prop his authority—"to deal with another matter, which is going to require the blessed one's attention. Uh, I trust the saint is here?"

"Yes. Blessed Chio awaits you in the garden. I was told to bring you around." Waving his dedicat back to his orphan-supervising, Riesta led off along the flagstone walkway bordering the old mansion.

"The saint knew I was coming?" Disturbingly possible, in the god-touched.

"It seems so," sighed the chapter head, in an oddly put-upon tone. "This was only announced to me a few minutes ago."

The garden might once have been formal, but was given over now to more practical vegetables and fruit trees, tidy as a stitched sampler. A dedicat and a couple of what were probably more orphans knelt weeding on the far side. The only other occupant sat on a bench under an old peach tree, its branches bending with still-green fruit. It was a young woman, barely more than a girl. Her thin white coat, unadorned by any sign of rank, was worn carelessly open over an ordinary faded blue dress. Pen blinked, startled.

You shouldn't be, said Des. *A saint can be anyone at all, you know that. Anyone whose soul gives space for a god to reach into the world....Not sorcerers, naturally.*

The god was not immanent now, or Des would be reacting more violently. As they trod up, Pen studied Chio's exterior appearance.

Dark hair in a simple braid down her back, finished with a white ribbon. Skin a typical Adriac honey. Amber-brown eyes, well-set in a long narrow face with rather a lot of chin and nose. In middle age, her features might still be dubbed handsome, if she were fortunate in her health; in sunken old age, possibly a little scary, but in the flower of youth they remained memorably pleasant. Pen wasn't sure whether to revise her estimated age upward at her well-filled bodice.

No telling, said Des. *Some of us started early—Mira was one. Vasia was another.* She left off, thankfully, without detailing ten different examples of female puberty.

Chio looked up at him with equal attention. "Oh," she said, in a voice of surprise. "You're not quite what I was expecting."

The feeling is mutual. Pen didn't think her narrowing eyes expressed disappointment, but what she was making of him was not obvious.

Riesta performed a brief introduction, ending with, "What's this all about, Learned Penric?"

Pen scratched his ear, marshaled his story, again. Having explained it once already today helped, but Pen suspected Chio's was a very different listening from

Bizond's. He didn't need to recap basic demon lore here, but . . . she couldn't possess Idau's long years of experience, surely.

It's not the saint's experience that matters. It's the god's, said Des. *I don't think we need worry about that part.*

Finishing his tale of the shiplost lad, Pen settled on a tentative, "Have you had to do yet with removing a dangerous demon from a person?"

She shrugged one slim shoulder. "It's mostly been fetching out young elementals from animals. That's how the god first came to me, four years ago—one of the householders on the island thought her cow was sick. Which it would have become, shortly. She was most pleased when I seemed to cure it. A Temple sensitive soon brought me an infested cat, my power was proved—I could have told them so, but who listens to a fourteen-year-old girl? A fuss followed, and then a further parade, well, trickle of elementals, and here I am. Still."

Riesta listened to this with a rather fixed smile.

Chio brightened. "I did get to go to the mainland one time, for a woman who'd caught an elemental from one of her chickens. And once for a horse."

Pen tried not to let his mind be diverted by the picture of a demonic chicken. Des's sojourn in the world had begun with a wild hill mare and a lioness, after all.

I wonder if that woman ate the chicken, as the lioness did the mare? Des mused.

She'd no doubt started out to slaughter it for her table. It would have been a short and enticing, if ultimately unlucky, jump for the demon. Also, how would you tell with a cat . . . ? *Never mind*.

Pen was reminded of the old saw about the recipe for rabbit stew. *First we catch the demon*. "It's my belief that the ascendant demon is still hiding somewhere in Lodi. My next task is to find him. When I accomplish that, I'll wrestle him out here to you." Against the demon's uttermost resistance, no doubt, but Pen would cross that bridge, or boat ride, later. "But I thought I'd best meet and warn you, first. I'm, um, not actually sure how long this retrieval will take, but I trust you will be here?"

She studied him back with disquieting intensity. "No . . ." she said slowly. "I think it will be better if I go with you." Her eyes glinted as she straightened. "Yesss . . . perfect."

Riesta choked. "Blessed, surely not. Town will be riotous tonight. You know you are safer here."

"I'd think the archdivine's own court sorcerer would be worth a dozen guardsmen, don't you?" Her smile seemed a sly challenge: *Deny that, if you dare*.

Pen wondered why Des was suddenly amused.

Chio bounced to her feet. "There, that's settled. I'll just go get my things."

There had been no discussion at all. For one thing, no one had asked *him* if he wanted to take on the escort of this young woman. Saint. *God-vessel*. On the other hand . . . if she were with him when he found Madboy, the god's demon-removal could be performed at once, saving a great many hazardous steps. Hm . . .

Riesta, watching her swiftly receding back, sank to the bench with an *oof*. Pen perched beside him.

"Did the god just speak through her?" Riesta asked Pen plaintively.

No? Yes? "Our god speaks in mysterious ways. Usually maddening riddles, to be frank. So I'd hesitate to say no."

"She *knows* that, you realize." Riesta vented a sigh. "It's not that she's not god-touched. It's not even that she's not all there, but that she's not all . . . here. Sometimes. And at others she's a trammeled and difficult young woman much like any other her age. The trouble is, I'm never sure which one I'm talking to, or is talking to me. When she figured that out, I was never in control again, yet I remained in responsibility."

Pen offered a sympathetic nod. "Did she grow up here in your orphanage?"

"Yes, she was a foundling. Probably bestowed at our gate by one of Lodi's prostitutes. We get a steady supply of such. She seemed an ordinary enough girl, on the quiet side, just fair in her studies—she was supposed to have been apprenticed to a dressmaker, was about to leave us, but then this other thing happened."

"Not the apprenticeship you expected, I take it?"

"Nor anyone else. After the archdivine inspected her, we were ordered to keep her here and give her theological instruction, and hold her at the disposal of the Temple. This . . . has not always gone well."

It finally dawned on Pen that the man's anxiety was not for Chio, but for him. Trying to delicately warn that this girl would lead her escort by the nose if she could, without actually saying anything rude about his saint? Penric considered Des's two centuries of female experience. *Think you can handle her, Des?*

The girl, yes. The saint . . . At least, unlike Riesta here, I will be able to tell which one is talking.

"I think it will be all right," said Pen, more out of hope than experience. "The god wants his demon back. Through her, He may even be able to help speed my search."

"No doubt the god will protect her." Riesta didn't sound all that confident.

With reason. However god-touched, saints were ultimately human beings, frail flesh like any other person. Without which, Pen was reminded, the gods could not reach into the world at all. *The gods do not save us from death. They only catch us when we fall from life.* Pen also translated that as, *Don't lose my saint in a canal!* Fair enough.

A tabarded dedicat ventured up, ostensibly to ask her superior some question about arrangements for tomorrow's festivities; more, Pen suspected, to get a closer peek at the mysterious visitor from the curia. Riesta sent her off for tea. It was served cool and sweetened with honey, along with a plate of grapes, cheese, and bread, for which Pen realized he was ravenously grateful—lunch had been mislaid somewhere in his day's travels.

By the time this refreshment was consumed, they were still waiting for Chio. Pen hoped his boatman was faithful. Although if the fellow had given up and poled off, Pen supposed there would be another one along. The basin was busy this time of day.

At last the saint tripped back, looking suspiciously satisfied with herself. Her braid had been wound up and secured on the back of her head with some fetching hair sticks, cut-glass balls on their ends glittering as she moved. Her white coat was buttoned up to her throat, though a different skirt hem fluttered at her ankles. A lumpy linen bag swung from her hand. Pen eyed it in some bafflement.

"Let's go, then!" she declared.

Pen was willing, though beginning to wonder what they would do when they reached the city shore. He needed a better plan than randomly, or even systematically, continuing to quarter Lodi with his uncanny sense being battered by every soul in it but the one he sought. With old Idau in his mind as the model for a saint, he supposed he'd been vaguely counting on some sage, avuncular advice here at the chapterhouse to direct his steps further. Though if he'd wanted to be led, he now had it—Chio grabbed Pen's hand to drag him off. She walked backward a moment to wave a cheerful farewell to the glum Riesta, who called parental-sounding cautions after her as they made their way around the old mansion.

They were delayed at the gate by an ambush from the children, who demanded Chio inspect and approve their boat-decorating. Pen, taking his cue from her, strove to come up with a few admiring comments as well. It was plain Chio's words were more treasured.

She smiled over her shoulder as they left the walls of the chapterhouse compound. "I used to do that, help decorate the boats every Bastard's Day."

"To be part of the ceremonies tomorrow, I take it?" At her puzzled glance up at him, he added, "I only just arrived in Lodi a few months ago."

"Oh. Yes. All the chapterhouses and orphanages have a boat parade around the canals in honor of the god. Isn't your chapterhouse . . . ?"

"I work directly for the curia, so no."

"The archdivine does come out and bless us at the start."

"Boat races, too?"

An amused smirk, which looked well on her lips. He was beginning to suspect the girl hid more wits than she displayed. "Of course."

Of course. As far as Pen could tell, there was no event in Lodi that was not considered pretext for the population to show off their boats and boat-prowess to each other. High holy days. Low holy days. Weddings. Funerals. Ship-launchings. Guild anniversaries. High appointments in the ducal court or the archdivine's curia. Pen understood that the oarboat races among the more athletic ladies of the bordellos on his god's day were particularly popular with the spectators.

"I was let to ride in the chapterhouse parade twice, when I was younger," Chio went on. "All the children chosen to go get wildly excited about it. If we made ourselves look especially well and clean, we all imagined that someone in the crowd would pick us to go home with them as apprentice or even, highest prize, adoptee. Which did happen sometimes, though not to me." Her smile turned wry. "I was horribly disappointed. But then a better Adopter found me, and I was glad for my sadness in hindsight."

The faintly defiant way her chin rose made Pen wonder if this last statement was quite true.

As they came to the landing, where Pen was relieved to find his boatman still reclining under his broad-brimmed hat, she suddenly asked, "Do you have much money?"

"Er, the archdivine pays me a generous stipend?"

"I mean *on* you."

"Oh. Enough, I suppose. Should I encounter an unexpected expense, I could return to my chambers for more." He wondered if his vestments and braids and high employment would buy him trust for temporary credit. With his tranquil life inside the curia, it wasn't a problem he'd needed to test, yet.

"That's all right, then." She gave a sharp, satisfied nod, making her hair ornaments splinter tiny rainbows.

Unfolding from his paid repose, the boatman tried to not look too amused at Pen's sudden acquisition of a young lady on his arm; their garb hinting, correctly as it happened, at some mutual Temple business. The man handed her down into the boat with no more banter than a few helpful directions. They found their balance and started off again across the basin. The slanting sun painted the busy waters with shimmering liquid gold.

Pen's appreciation of the beauty of the light was undercut by his unease at time getting away from him. Where in Lodi might the deranged demon choose to hide his ridden partner? In some obscure corner? Or in the holy eve crowds, which were going to be out in force tonight?

He turned back to find Chio unbuttoning her pale coat. The dress revealed beneath was much lower-cut across the bodice than the demure maiden's pale blue she'd been wearing earlier, set about with bits of lace and ribbon, and woven in sophisticated dark blue and cream vertical stripes. In fair condition but not new—orphanages often acquired overfine if damaged garments from the wardrobes of wealthy women patrons. Pen wondered if she'd mended it with her own needle, and if she regretted her lost chance at becoming a dressmaker.

She folded the coat and stuffed it into the sack, exchanging it for a holiday half-mask in silk decorated with sequins, a fringe of white and blue feathers lending it visual clout. She held it up to her eyes and grinned at Pen under it. It turned her visage mysterious, older. How alarmed should he be with this transformation? Des remained merely amused, though, so maybe it was all right?

"I was going to wear this dress for my birthday tomorrow," she answered whatever taken-aback look Pen was sporting. The mask came down, and the usual Chio returned. "But if we're off to the Bastard's Eve, I thought I'd start tonight."

"Your birthday is on our god's day? That's supposed to be lucky." Which flavor of luck, good or bad, usually left unspoken.

She shrugged. "It's not that special. All the foundlings who arrive around midsummer without any other identification get assigned the Bastard's Day as their birthday. We always got sweet custards at dinner together anyway."

"Ah," Pen managed.

❖ ❖ ❖

They arrived back at the Temple precinct's boat landing with Penric no more inspired as to his next move. As he helped Chio up the steps, Pen asked, "Does our god give you any clues how we should shape our search?"

She shook her head. "Nothing yet."

Pen was unsurprised; if the god had so much as whispered to her, Des would have reacted, strongly. This was still only Orphan Chio, not Blessed Chio.

"I'd better check in at the curia first, in case any messages have arrived." It was, he supposed, entirely too optimistic to hope for news that their quarry had been captured and was being held for them by the causeway guards.

Ordinary guards could not restrain him, Des noted.

Pen wasn't sure how able that demon and its confused, ridden host would be to fight armed men— Des could make short work of such opponents, if they were not too many—but it had been adept enough to readily escape the hospice. Best not underestimate. Worse, the demon might be careless of the life of its mount, since it could just jump to another host if poor Madboy were, say, run through with a sword. *Ngh*.

Offering his arm to Chio, which she took with a small smile, he chose a different route back to the curia building, his Sight again extended. He realized his mistake as they circled through the main city square, which would take them past the gibbet. To his relief, it was empty, no raucous crowd around it being more entertained than edified by the price of crime.

Nor would it be used tomorrow. There were no

executions on the Bastard's Day: not in reprieve for the condemned, but to grant holiday to the hangmen, one of the many questionable callings that came under the fifth god's cloak. And, in theory, under Pen's care as a seminary-trained divine, but such pastoral duties usually fell to more regular servants of his Order. If they weren't sundered into dwindling ghosts, the souls the executioners sped might go to any god at all, to the frequent confusion of the onlookers.

Ordinary living folk hurrying across the square to duties or dinner pressed upon him hard enough. Chio looked up shrewdly at him, and asked, "Does your Sight hurt you, Learned?"

"Um . . ." He didn't want to admit *Yes* to her. "It's a strain, but bearable." It would be a lot more bearable were it rewarded with some results, but he felt nothing more than too-complicated humanity all the way to the curia doors.

Chio's bright soul could not be the least complex of these, but Des's Sight seemed to slide around her.

Is the god keeping you out?

No, she said shortly. *Would you walk on the edge of a precipice?*

Yes, if I wanted to see over.

Ugh. You canton mountaineers and your heights.

Des's aversion to altitude had been hard-earned, so Pen didn't quibble with her metaphor. Demons were more durable than humans in their fashion, and Pen had become all too familiar with Des's fearlessness, but perhaps the absence of risk should not be mistaken for the presence of fortitude.

Don't be rude. You have your own sources of helpless terror. A thoughtful pause. *In your case, frequently moral rather than mortal, but deadly all the same. Scars on your arms faded yet?*

Yes. Thank you. And my apologies.

That's better.

The ornate colonnade of the curia was flushed dusky pink in the fading light. At Bizond's chamber, they found the senior secretary gone home for the day, his place taken by a night clerk.

"So you are why I'm here," the man sighed, sounding not best pleased to be missing the holiday eve, if resigned. But there were no messages yet. It was too soon to mutter frustrated curses in Wealdean, though Pen was tempted. Chio seized the chance to leave her sack with this trustworthy guardian.

They came back out on the Temple square after a short detour for the saint to inspect the sculptures that graced the main entry, not a little of it war booty. Pen wondered at a world that hanged poor men for thievery, but celebrated great ones.

"Now what?" said Chio, looking around at the growing shadows muted by a still-luminous sky.

Pen rubbed his face, mulling. "Go back to the beginning and start over, I think. To the Gift of the Sea. It would at least put one certain end of the trail in my hand. And Master Linatas might have heard something more." After the threat from Penric and Des had cleared out, could the demon even have slipped back to the place it had been fed and cared for? It seemed unlikely straw-clutching.

Pen chose a different way back to the farther shore of town, which involved seven bridges, not five, and took them down a few darkened alleys that would have been more daunting were Des not the most dangerous thing in them. The paths alongside the canals were better lit, partly by lanterns bobbing along raised up on the sterns of the oarboats busy with transporting holiday-goers in fancy dresses and masks. Laughter as well as light rippled in their wake across the night-silk waters.

With full dark, the more restrained parties had withdrawn indoors to the wealthier houses. *Also the more randy ones*, Des put in. *Mira did so enjoy those, in her day.* Music drifted down from radiant upper windows overlooking the canal paths. But a few canal-side markets had been given over to neighborhood celebrations, young and old combining to set up trestle tables for foodstuffs and booths from local taverns. It was still early enough in the evening that most of the shrieking came from running, overexcited children, but several tables sent up volunteer choruses of hymns, drinking songs, and, at the more inebriated, parodic combinations of the two. The cleverest made Pen grin.

"Oh, gorgeous, grant me a godly kiss from that *mouth*," came a drunken cry from offside. Pen wheeled, preparing to fend off a happy-sounding assault on the saint. Which was how the fellow managed to fall on *him*. Pen dodged fruity wine-breath—this one must have started celebrating well before sundown, the official start of the Bastard's Eve. He gritted his teeth and used the fellow's stumbling momentum to forward him into the nearby canal, where he fell with a mighty splash. His companions, equally drunk but not so amorous, laughed uproariously and lurched to fish him back out.

"Good work, Learned!" one cried in passing, attempting to congratulate him with a shoulder-bump. Pen dodged that, too. He grasped Chio's elbow and drew her back through the crowded square to the less hazardous building-side, sparing a glance to be sure the idiot was retrieved. Some Lodi canals could be waded across, but others were ten, twenty, or more feet deep, and swallowed the careless with tragic consequences. It looked like this was going to remain a comedy.

Chio, at least, was amused, her amber eyes glinting in the lantern light. "Does that happen to you often, Learned Penric?"

"*All the bloody time,*" Pen answered, goaded. He brushed down his coat, which was growing too warm as the humid night failed to cool, and tamped his temper. "It's not worth my effort to get offended. Although I am sometimes put to it when some, er, suitor takes his rejection in bad part. That can get dangerous."

"For you?"

"For him." Or her, but peeved females did not usually resort to physical violence. Poisonous words he could endure.

It was her turn to murmur, "I see," concealing private thoughts. One escaped: "Do your suitors ever succeed?"

"Not that sort." Pen sighed. "And the quiet, bookish types I might actually enjoy talking with are too shy to ask, leaving me only with the others."

She looked around, straightened brightly, and

dragged him to a nearby booth. "Here's a solution. Because we wouldn't want more delay tonight. Buy yourself one."

It boasted a display of holiday masks in a multitude of designs, from cheap and plain to much less cheap. Had that been a saintly order? Or did the girl just want her escort to look more the part of half a couple?

Under the benign gaze of the booth's proprietress, Pen reached for the plainest linen half-mask on the rack. Chio's hand caught his wrist.

"No," she said in a thoughtful tone, "I think this one would suit you better." She handed him a mask molded in the shape of a stern white lion, subtly made and convincing, its price reflecting its art.

Pen knew he'd not told her about the lioness that made up that long-buried layer of his demon. Was this coincidence, or something more unsettling?

In any case he dutifully acquired the mask, to Chio's obvious approval. "Good," she said. "You look more imposing now. There's still the unfair jaw and mouth, but this should deter all but your worst admirers."

He did not escape the square before also purchasing at her demand a posy of fresh white flowers shaped in a bracelet for her slim wrist, stewed meat wrapped in thin pancakes, and candied fruit on sticks. At least they could eat the latter as they walked.

He kept his senses extended as they continued along the canal, sieving the flux of passing souls: on the path, on the waterway, tucked up in the surrounding houses. So many, so heaped. So not-demonic. Searching, walking, eating, and talking all together was very distracting. He kept as far from the bank as he could while still sheltering Chio on his other side.

"Do you have any money?" he thought to ask Chio in turn. "On you, I mean." Should they get separated, she should at least have the price of an oarboat back to the Isle of Gulls. Though if any oarsman would accept her promise, he supposed someone at the chapterhouse would settle up on her arrival.

"Of course not," she said. "The chapterhouse covers all my keep. And my travels, should I have any."

"Doesn't the Temple pay you a stipend?"

"Me?"

"It should. Blessed Broylin of Idau is paid one, I know." Through a different realm's Temple administration, but still.

"Really!" A glance up, then a thoughtful hum. "Do you know how much?"

"Not offhand. He's a retired baker, I believe, so has some money of his own. Any chapterhouse that wants him to travel pays his way, of course, but the stipend is separate. I don't know if it's his age or his calling that makes him uninterested in riches, but he's kept decently."

"I had no idea saints could be *paid*."

"You are, in your way, Temple functionaries, the same as divines or sorcerers." *Well . . . not* quite *the same*, murmured Des. "Your soul may belong to our god, but your body is owed any body's wage."

"No one has ever suggested that before." Her lips pursed in, Pen feared, calculation.

Are we creating chaos, Des?

This one is all your doing, Pen. A pause. *I approve, of course.*

Chio's mask tilted toward him in new curiosity. "Have you had your demon long, Learned Penric?"

"Since age nineteen."

"Huh! That's just a year older than I am now."

"So it was." Had he really been that young?

Yes, sighed Des.

"Ten years ago, now. Odd. It seems longer. A third of my life." And four years a saint made almost a quarter of Chio's short life. He asked in return interest, "Was it lonely for you in the orphanage? After your calling came upon you?"

Her mouth rounded in bemusement, as if no one had asked her that question before. "It was different. My old friends fell off, though everyone was scattering to their apprenticeships by then anyway. Except for Carpa, who is going to be five years old and there forever, poor afflicted girl. But the divines swarmed me. They made me read piles of theology, and I am not bookish. Teaching the orphans to sew or cook is far more fun." She added politely, "No offense to you, Learned Penric."

"None taken. I admit some of those tomes can get, er, turgid."

"Yes, and that's so *wrong.*" She made a face. "I could tell, after a while, which writers *knew* and which ones were reciting by rote. The divines didn't like it when I told them so."

Pen grinned. "I imagine not."

"Do they have the saying in Wealdean about locking the stable door after the horse is stolen?"

"In just those words, yes."

"It was like that. The divines and all those books."

He sobered, remembering that visceral, direct experience of the unimaginably vast that defeated all words. Young, guarded from the world, not bookish, all these Chio might be, but in certain dimensions profoundly not ignorant. "I've told the tale of how I acquired Desdemona at the death of Learned Ruchia so many times, it might as well be a rote recital by now. But when I try to describe what happened with Blessed Broylin . . ."

She smiled into his lengthening silence. "Yes. Exactly that."

They turned the next corner into a narrower street. No canal here, but Pen linked her arm through his to prevent stumbles in the dark. The lack of animal traffic made Lodi streets cleaner than those of inland towns, and the tide carried off most of the rest of the residents' refuse, but not, alas, all.

"Is it lonely being a sorcerer?" she asked abruptly.

"No, because I'm never alone." Reflecting on his past decade of nesting in narrow chambers in other people's palaces, he rethought this. "Although I'm never sure if people are taking my braids as a mark of rank or a plague warning."

She snickered. "I've not actually talked much to the sorcerers, despite my calling. They bring me the elementals and then leave as soon as possible."

He thought of the city gibbet they'd lately passed. "Desdemona once told me it's like watching an execution. For a demon. So I'm not greatly surprised."

"Your demon seems calmer than most."

"We've been through something like this before. Me once, Des two centuries' worth."

She nodded. "Dispatching elementals for the Order had started to feel more like killing chickens for the god's kitchen than anything holy, even leaving out that real chicken. But then there was the horse. Speaking of horses."

"Hypothetical absent horses. I take it this was a real one?"

She waved her free hand in sudden delight. "It was the first demon the god refused to take from me. It was a very good horse, so beloved, trained for parades and for children to ride. And beautiful! The glossiest beast I ever saw. The god sent it back to be raised as a Temple demon, to go to some learned sorcerer-candidate next. Its family was very relieved to be told it could live out its life with them."

"That was remarkably kind of the Order. And wise."

"Your demon must know of this. She's stood at the gate of her riders' deaths for such judgment and been told to go back, what, twelve times you said?"

Pen hadn't said. "That's right." After so many passages, did it feel to Des as if that gate was narrowing upon her?

Yes, she muttered.

Pensive, Chio went on, "I'd always felt the god's sorrow, before, when I did His work. Never His joy. I finally knew what I was here for. I keep hoping for another one like that lovely horse."

"The Order does, too," said Penric. "Though I'm afraid this mad boy's demon isn't going to be one."

No, agreed Des grimly.

The vague scent of canal sewage gave way to a more estuarial tang as they came out at the big northwest harbor. Not many lights here; should he have acquired a linkboy's lantern at the marketplace?

"Can you see in the dark, as sorcerers do?" he thought to ask Chio.

She shook her head. "I see the same as everyone else. Until the god is upon me, and then I see everything. Whether I want to or not."

"Ah."

Helpfully, a bright lamp over the main entry of the hospice guided them in.

The wooden door was half ajar. Raised voices leaked from within. Pen opened it to hand Chio into the spacious vestibule, well-lit by lamps and wall sconces for receiving night emergencies.

The person arguing with the night porter was not some injured or, more likely tonight, wine-sick poor seaman. To Pen's astonishment, it was Learned Iserne. But a very different Iserne than the trim, brisk official he'd met this afternoon. Her black coat was hanging open over her dress, her sleek hair was escaping its pinned-up braids, and her face was drained and distraught. She near-vibrated with tension as she stood before the porter with all the air of a dog about to launch an attack.

She was accompanied by a young man apparently acting as her linkboy, for he held a walking-lantern in uneasy hands. He was dressed as a sober merchant, not a servant, though, in a gray jacket with pleated skirts to

the mid-thigh, tight trousers, and a silver-studded
leather belt for his knife. Lanky, typical Adriac
coloration. His lips were pressed closed in distress, but
he opened them to say, "Perhaps we should come back
tomorrow, Learned Iserne."

She shot him a scorching look that silenced him again,
and returned to the porter: "If Master Linatas is not
here, there must be *someone* who has seen him. Night
staff. Anyone."

Penric thought to pull his lion mask down, turning it
to hang from the back of his neck. Chio kept her mask
tied, pressing his arm and stepping half behind him. It
seemed unlikely this was a sudden attack of shyness, but
who knew. He gave her a reassuring nod and moved
forward, interrupting the scene.

"Good evening. I'm Learned Penric, the Temple
sensitive who was sent to Master Linatas to examine your
mad castaway this afternoon, the one who ran off. I
stopped in to see if he has been found or came back, or
if you had any other word."

Iserne spun and stared at him in surprise. "Learned
Penric! I was just thinking I might try to find you
next."

"What's this all about?"

Iserne waved her expressive hands, but hardly
seemed to know where to begin. A lawyer, at loss for
words?

Her companion gave her a pitying glance, and cut in,
"My name is Aulie Merin. I was riding share on the
spring convoy to Cedonia, shepherding a mixed cargo
for my employer. Learned Iserne's son Ree Richelon was

aboard doing the same for his father. Our ship just returned home to Lodi this afternoon."

He inhaled, as if steeling himself. "I was charged with the heavy task of bearing the news to his family that Ree had been lost overboard in the night. Nearly a week ago, when we were beating up to our last stop in Trigonie. It seems heartless to encourage hope at this point, but . . ." He made a frustrated gesture at Iserne. "The shock. His mother."

"Did you search the water for him?" Pen asked.

Merin shook a regretful head. "Between the time he was last seen in the evening, and the time he was first missed in the morning, the convoy must have made fifty or sixty miles. There was no way."

"Was there a storm?"

"No, the night was clear, though the wind was brisk. No moon, so the deck was very dark."

Demanding a physical description of Merin's lost companion was going to be unhelpful, given Madboy's common looks. Pen had decanted the basics in front of his—maybe mother?—Iserne this afternoon without triggering recognition or alarm. Some hours before this news had arrived, to be sure, shattering her calm belief that her son was safely on his way home to her. Pen doubted the Bastard's Day was strongly celebrated in Iserne's household, as she had taken oath to a very different god, but likely any of her domestic thoughts had been pleasantly bent on a welcome-back dinner or some such thing. Pen had barely noticed Madboy's exterior, although he would recognize his demon-splintered soul at a hundred paces through a stone wall.

Pen turned back to the night porter. "Master Linatas has gone home for the day, you say? He left no messages for me, I take it?"

"That's right, Learned," he replied, relieved to face a less frantic interrogator.

"There must be others who worked directly with the shiplost patient you took in." The other men in the ward he'd so disrupted yesterday could also bear witness, but staff were more likely to handle distraught relatives smoothly. "Is Orderly Gnade still about?"

"I can send upstairs and see." The porter rose to call through one of the archways leading from the entry, to be answered by a young dedicat interrupted swallowing down a snack of bread. The lad scampered off up the stairs willingly enough.

Chio watched, quiet and attentive—aware?—as Pen extended his senses. Through the opposite archway, past closed doors, a few souls moved in a treatment room: a physician, hurting patient, assistant, and some anxious companion. No demons of any kind, so not Pen's affair.

Footsteps scuffing, plural; Pen looked up to find, thankfully, the page leading Gnade down to them.

"Oh," said Gnade, recognizing Penric. "You're the sorcerer fellow who came this afternoon and scared that poor mad boy into running off."

Pen ignored the second half of this, and hoped Iserne would, too. "I gather you've had no further word of him here?"

Gnade shook his head. "We did look, sir."

Pen turned to Iserne, whose slim hands were working in an anxious urge to interject, barely suppressed. "Did

your son Ree have any particular identifying scars or
tattoos, Learned?"

"Not—not when he left home." She looked to Merin.
"Unless he acquired something on the voyage?"

"None I know of."

"What about clothing?" asked Chio, winning a curious
glance from Merin, who had barely given notice to her
till now.

Madboy had been dressed in, hm, a clean but worn
shirt and trews with the look of the charity castoffs
hospices reused for their patients. Pen asked, "He must
have been wearing something when the fishermen
brought him in, yes?"

"Not much," said Gnade, "but what the sea left you're
welcome to examine, to be sure."

He was looking in puzzlement at Iserne, so Pen put
in, "Learned Iserne here may be your patient's mother.
She should see them." Although if Madboy had been
wearing newer garments when he went overboard, that
wasn't going to help either.

Gnade extracted a key from the porter, picked up a
lamp, and motioned them through the left archway. The
four visitors shuffled awkwardly after him, Chio again
hanging back. Her silence masked a close listening, Pen
thought.

Down the corridor, Gnade unlocked a door to what
proved a small storage room, lined with shelving of plain
sanded boards holding a miscellany of clothing and other
possessions parted from their original owners. He set the
lamp on the plank table in the middle and counted down
the shelves. "I think we put them . . . ah, here."

He turned back with a scant pile of cloth and leather smelling of sea damp, and dumped them out. Iserne's companion stood back looking sick, but she dove upon them, hands rapidly sorting. She bit her lip, scowling in disappointment at an anonymous torn pair of trousers, a plain leather belt, the shreds of a shirt, and one stiff, rank sock. Her hand stopped short holding a salt-crusted embroidered handkerchief, and she bent to shove it into the pool of light and spread it out. "This was his. This was *Ree's*."

"Are you sure, ma'am?" asked the orderly. His even tone spoke of due care stemming from experience with upset relatives, rather than disbelief.

"I embroidered it myself. Then he's *alive*!" If Madboy—Ree, Pen corrected his thought—had been raised from the dead in front of them, her eyes could not have glittered more brightly with jubilant tears unshed. Her parted lips caught breath like a woman surfacing from drowning. "Saved from the sea, oh it *is* a miracle! One I didn't even know to pray for!"

If it was, it came with the kind of ambiguous catches for which Pen's god was noted. He cleared his throat. "This puts us very much further forward, but we still need to find him."

Merin looked up from the handkerchief and said plaintively, "I don't understand any of this! I thought the news I'd brought had turned her wits, and I shouldn't let her run off into the night here alone, but what's all this babble of demons and madness?"

"My wits are fine," snapped Iserne. "It's my *world* that's turned upside down."

The god of chaos and mischance, Pen reminded himself. He should know. "The man you lost overboard was found by a bedemoned dolphin, whose demon jumped to him. This is the one part of all this that was probably not an accident. Though you'll have to take my word for that. Ree would have experienced this invasion of his mind as a kind of madness. Maybe his exhaustion from trying to swim made him more susceptible, but in any case, the demon has ascended—possessed him. Long story, but while Temple demons are a benefit to their recipients, this wild one is effectively insane. When the fishermen picked Ree up, I'm sure it seemed he'd lost his reason altogether."

"Five gods." Merin signed himself, looking unnerved. "That's *bizarre*." He turned to Gnade. "Could he even talk?"

"Aye," said Gnade, "but there was no getting any sense out of him. Not even his name."

Merin huffed in horror. "Can he be cured?"

Pen glanced at Iserne, hanging on his words. He returned a firm "Yes," and concealed his gulp. *We'll make it so. Somehow.* "When he's found." He motioned Chio forward. She pushed up her feathered mask, baring her sobered face, and made a curtsey to Iserne, regarding the older woman intently. Less daunted by all these surging maternal emotions than Pen was? Or—odd perception—fascinated by them? Orphan, after all. "This is Blessed Chio, saint of the Bastard's chapterhouse on the Isle of Gulls, and my, er, colleague. When we find Ree, she will"—*eat the demon* maybe didn't sound reassuring.

No lie, muttered Des.

"Draw the demon from him," Pen continued smoothly, "by the grace of the white god. It may take him a while to recover from his physical ordeal and the shock to his mind, but with rest and quiet at home I'm sure he'll be all right in time." He nodded encouragement at Iserne.

Iserne stared at Chio in a surprise that turned to ferocious hope. "Really...?"

"Yes, Learned Iserne," said Chio with earnest politeness—rising to the occasion, or previously schooled by experience in dealing with distraught, confused...clients? Supplicants? Her usual guardians had likely handled the details. "I'll do all I can to help your son."

"Thank the gods."

Thank the white god, technically. But maybe not too soon.

"I'll help you search," Merin volunteered. He grimaced in guilt. "In exchange for the search I did not insist upon a week ago, at sea."

"I as well," said Iserne, her chin rising in determination.

Penric did not need the parade. Or even a linkboy. He temporized, "I think it would better serve if you were to return home, in case your son finds his way there."

Her head went back; her face lit. "Do you think he might?"

"By no means impossible. Ah..." The caution was painful but necessary. "There is a chance his ascended demon might feign to be him. If he does turn up, you should do nothing to alarm him, but secretly send for me at once."

She didn't like that one bit, but he thought she understood.

"Merin here can escort you home. Which is where, by the way?"

"It's not too far. We have a house on the Wealdmen's Canal, which empties out to the harbor between here and the state shipyard."

A decent address; not so elevated as the palaces of the merchant princes lining the main canal of the city, but an abode of hardworking men on the way up, or sometimes down.

"I really want to go with you," Merin told Penric, unhappily.

"Why don't we all escort Learned Iserne home," suggested Chio. "Then we'll know where it is for later."

This sensible compromise was adopted. With strongly worded instructions to the porter to send a message to the curia, regardless of the time, if anything new materialized here at the hospice, Pen led his enlarged party back out into the night.

Iserne's house lipped its canal. They had to circle past it to find a bridge, and then the narrower street that ran up to—Pen wasn't sure whether to think of it as the front or the back door. The dry door. They mounted steps behind Iserne to a second-story entry. The ground-or-canal floor presumably held the merchant husband's goods, with the living spaces above. She had a big iron key in her hand, but the door opened at her pull. "I don't suppose I thought to lock up when I ran out." She grimaced at this carelessness. She must have been going nearly as mad as Madboy in that moment, caught between the shock of grief and the greater shock of lunatic hope.

They entered the hallway to find it lit by dim wall sconces, and the brighter glow of a walking-lantern in the hand of a startled maidservant. Two young women clustered behind her looked equally disconcerted. "Mama," the elder or at least taller, who looked to be about Chio's age, said faintly. "We didn't know where you'd gone out to, or why..."

Best dresses, fetching white bows tied around their necks, and masks in their hands suggested this was not an incipient search party, but the other sort. Iserne had no trouble figuring it out either.

"I leave the house for an hour, and this is what you get up to?" Her voice was sharp, grating with real anger that seemed to take all three aback. These girls, clearly, had not yet been given the news about their brother, either version, before Iserne had rushed back out with her unhappy herald Merin.

"We were only just walking over to the party at the Stork Island chapterhouse," the younger protested. "Taking Bikka, and staying together! The divines of the white god will be there, giving blessings! It's safe!"

"Not that safe," said Iserne between gritted teeth. "And not *now*. I can't deal with any more chaos tonight..." She gripped her disarrayed hair and took a deep breath.

The elder looked up, discovering that there was a divine of the white god standing right in their hallway.

She gaped only briefly at Pen and then Chio before her gaze went to Merin. "Ser Merin, you're back!" And more eagerly, "Is Ree with you? Is he still dealing with Father's cargo, or is he coming?"

Merin winced and gestured helplessly, tossing these unanswerable questions back to Iserne. He did produce a pained smile for the sisters.

"Lonniel, Lepia. Listen." Iserne's serious, strained voice caught both their attentions, their naughty excitement beginning to be quelled by unease. "Your brother is . . ." She faltered on the complexities, retreating to, "Very ill."

The elder—Lonniel?—gasped. "Where is he? Isn't someone bringing him home?" As all pleasure fled from her face, Pen could mark her wondering if *very ill* was a euphemism for *dead*.

Merin, with a glance at their hostess, cut in before Pen could. "He took a blow to the head from, from a crane as we were starting to unload. It seems to have scattered his wits. I think he might have been hallucinating, because he grew very frightened and didn't seem to recognize us. He ran off into the town, and now we're looking for him."

That's impressively glib, murmured Des.

Merchant. I suppose he had to learn to think on his feet. The tale did cover the essentials of the situation, erased of the uncanny and softened for the ears of the innocent.

True, but their mother should have been the one to make that choice, said Des.

He did take his cue from her lead-in.

Iserne's hands closed and opened in frustrated

acceptance of this unasked-for aid. "I'll be waiting up for news, or in case he comes back here," she told the girls. "*You* two go to your beds and stay there." A scowl at the maid Bikka promised there would be another follow-up in her direction later.

With the perilousness of their brother's condition and their mother's upset impressed upon them, the sisters' mouths closed on mutiny, their shoulders slumping.

"I'm going out to search for him," Merin told both sisters, though his tense smile seemed aimed especially at Lonniel. "Even the Temple is lending us its aid, with Learned Penric here." He nodded in Pen's direction.

Lonniel touched her mouth, forming an *oh* at this explanation of their more baffling visitors. Looking over Pen and Chio, she said, "I'm sorry we have interrupted your holy eve with our affairs, Learned, and um—" Pen watched her trying to place Chio, and coming up with the notion they must be a couple out on the town, though uncertain whether the young lady's affections for the evening were paid or gratis. She settled on, "Miss. But please help Ser Merin all you may."

An attempt to straighten out this misconception of Pen's chain of command was not worth the delay, given the saint was merely smiling below her mask. She granted the other girls a friendly nod, returned with slight confusion.

Lepia put in, "But where could he have *gone*, hurt like that?"

"Not far, we hope," Merin told her. "With luck, we should have word by the time you wake in the morning."

Her face scrunched in her effort to imagine where her

injured brother might try to den up. Pen would have liked to tax both sisters for ideas, given they'd probably know, hm, not more but different things of their sibling than even their mother did. Merin, since he was colleague, peer, and apparently family friend of Ree's, would possess yet another set.

But Iserne, reaching the limits of what Pen suspected was long patience, sternly drove the sisters up the stairs under the questionable supervision of their maid. Chio watched them ascend, her expression curiously covetous. A mother's chiding was still caring of a sort. Surely a saint was not subject to ... envy?

As their steps echoed away, Iserne turned back to the entry hall, scrubbing her hands over her face as if to drive out numbness.

"Two hours ago," she told Penric, "I was going out of my mind trying to imagine how I was going to write my husband with the news of the death of our only son. This ... I have no idea how I'm going to write this."

"Where is Ser Richelon?" Pen inquired.

"He travels every year up to the foot of the mountains to deal for timber. We supply some instrument and cabinet makers here in Lodi who have very particular needs. He usually goes later in the summer, but this year is the first that he let Ree take the spring convoy to Cedonia alone." She swallowed distress.

"I think you can safely put off that task till tomorrow," Pen said. "You should have more news by then. Better news, maybe." Risky promise.

"I suppose so." Iserne straightened and exhaled, her eye falling on a pile of objects dropped at the side of the hallway: several cases, a poniard in a tooled scabbard, and some loose clothing. "I could go through these and put them away while I wait. I'm not going to be able to sleep anyway."

"That was everything Ree left in our cabin," Merin told her. "It all fit on the one cart. Your husband's cargo is still aboard the ship, as there was no one to receive it. It will just have to wait there, since all the stevedores have gone off for the holiday by now, but I'll take on that task for you the day after tomorrow, if you wish."

Frowning, she waved away this offer. "I'll send Ripol's clerk."

Ripol? Merchant husband's first name, Pen decided.

She doesn't favor this fellow Merin, Des observed.

A case of beheading the messenger?

Perhaps . . .

Iserne poked at the pile of cases with a tentative toe, possibly considering how much more painful her unpacking would be if their owner had been dead. Pen renewed his resolve to prevent that from becoming so.

"As far as I know," said Merin, "all of Ree's documents and letters of credit from the voyage are safe in there. I'm afraid his purse and money belt were on him when he went over the side. We didn't see either among his other things, later. I thought the belt had dragged him under—he'd had a very successful trip."

Neither item had been in the sad damp pile in the storage room, either, though sticky hands among those that had drawn Ree from the sea and delivered him to the hospice could have taken toll.

"Thank the gods he'd had the sense to drop it, rather

than drown trying to keep it!" Iserne said fervently. "Just the sort of thing idiot brave boys attempt."

Merin offered a crooked smile. "I think my employer would have chastised me roundly for that."

"Hah." The maternal scorn in that syllable could have weighted a cudgel. "More fool he, since he'd have had neither money nor agent, after."

Since Iserne was as anxious as Penric for them to hurry the search, their farewells were brief.

"Blessed Chio." Iserne offered a clumsy curtsey; her supplication could not have been made more plain if she'd fallen to her knees. "The hope of my heart and house is in your god's hands tonight."

"It cannot be misplaced there, Learned." Gravely, Chio pulled her mask altogether off and returned her a full formal blessing, with the extra tap of the back of her thumb to her lips. It was the first trained gesture of their Order Pen had witnessed the girl make—Chio might have been as feral as a young elemental for all that Pen had seen heretofore.

Her face, as they descended the steps to the street again, had shed all its earlier merriment. She drew her mask back on, tightening the ties, as Merin raised his lantern and turned his head back and forth.

"Which way?"

Pen grunted. "I was hoping you might have some ideas. This wild demon, though ascendant, knew nothing of Lodi, so all the local navigation must be coming from Ree. Asking *Where would Ree go when in his right mind?* is probably not useful, but where would a man like him, or you, think to hide if he was in terror for his life?"

Merin blew out his breath. "Gods, what a question." The lantern sank to his side as he cogitated. "Lodi has a thousand alleys, all with corners and cubbies, and then there are all the interiors. Even if you stick to those that are unpeopled this time of night—shops and workshops, warehouses, government offices—probably not them—the central islands are circled by docks and wharves, and then there are all the outlying islands. This seems an impossible hunt."

"Not entirely. I only need to come within about a hundred paces of the demon to sense it, regardless of what walls or alleys or canals lie between." A sharp spike, somewhere in this buffeting phantasmagoria of the town's souls.

"How..." began Merin. "Never mind. But I don't quite understand what you do if we do find him."

Penric shrugged. "Hold Ree down as best I can without doing him injury, then let Blessed Chio call on our god. It should be a quick operation at that point." *I pray.*

"Will he be all right after that?"

"Exhausted, I'm sure." And grateful, Pen trusted. Un-Madboy had better be, after all this chase. "But then we can deliver him home and let Iserne take care of the rest."

"I see. I think." Merin frowned. "It sounds as if Ree was hard-battered by his ordeal in the sea. And the gods know what misadventures he's met since he escaped from the hospice. What happens if he dies before the saint can release him?"

"A greater mess than ever. I mean, over and above what the *dying* part would do to his family. Because the demon would jump to the closest other person it could reach, and we'd have the whole search to do over again, with even less information."

"But not to you? Or to Blessed Chio?" He made a newly nervy half-bow at the girl. "You'd need to be close for this, wouldn't you?"

"We're already occupied. Not sorcerers, not saints, not Wealdean shamans, though I wouldn't expect to encounter any of those in Lodi." Wealdean merchants, yes. "Anyone else in proximity would be at risk." Merin, for example. Really, the man was very much in the way.

"That . . . sounds really bad. Unless someone wanted a demon, I expect." His glance lingered, wondering, on Pen's shoulder braids.

"No one would want this demon," Pen assured him. "Most certainly not the Temple. Even though it would then be taking an imprint of Ree's memories with it overtop, it's still far too crazed to be tamed for any use."

Merin looked properly aghast, thinking this through. "Wait. It would *remember* Ree?"

"The next person it jumped to would. Think of it as like having the ghosts of all its prior possessors haunt your head, although that isn't theologically precise." He added, "And *talking* to you."

You needn't sound so put-upon, sniffed Des. *You enjoy our company.*

You still took some getting used to. The ten of you.

"Do these ghosts remember their deaths?"

"Vividly."

Merin's shoulders twitched in a cringe. "That sounds horrifying."

"One grows used to it."

His thick brows drew in. "Why don't demons go on forever?"

"Saints. And other accidents. There is attrition. Fortunately, or we'd all be up to our necks in them." *Instead of just my neck.* "That said, some can live a very long time, if they're carefully husbanded by my Order. My demon Desdemona is over two hundred years old."

Merin's expression hovered between impressed and appalled.

"Two directions, right or left," Chio prodded. "Pick one." She glanced back up the steps, her mouth pursing. "Needless delay seems much too cruel, right now."

Aye, agreed Des, and Pen was reminded that six of her riders had been mothers. He wondered if any of them had lost children.

In two centuries? We outlived all of them. In a sense.

Oh. I'd never quite thought that through.

Even now, we do not speak of that.

I see.

"Any guidance from your side yet?" Pen asked the saint.

"Not so far."

Of course not.

Pen tried to think what areas of these neighborhoods he'd already covered. He was losing track. Not that Madboy couldn't move about, so maybe it hardly mattered.

Merin pointed. "Left."

Pen shrugged and turned that way, leading them toward the middle of the muddled island neighborhood.

Nothing in Lodi had a regular shape. Maybe he could find the center and spiral outward?

Scanning, walking, and talking at the same time risked stumbling over his own feet, but he asked Merin, "I take it you and Ree were thrown together as cabinmates. Had you known him and his family before?"

"Not as well as I got to know him shipboard. I used to work for one of his father's cousins, before I was hired away as an agent for this voyage, so I had some acquaintance." A longing sigh.

What's he pining for?

What, wasn't it obvious to you in Iserne's entryway?

I was following a great many things back there.

"So you were rivals with Ree, not partners?" Pen asked.

"Friendly rivals this time, yes. We might expect to be partners on some future venture. I'd hoped to work for Ser Richelon, who has a good reputation, but this other opportunity came up first."

Chio enquired slyly, "Does your current employer also have pretty daughters?"

Merin snorted, unoffended by the implication. "No, more's the pity. Among his other defects. Four strapping sons. A hired agent has no chance of moving up in that clan, no matter how hard-working."

Nor of marrying into it, obviously. Certain long-term relationships that came under the Bastard's thumb could be economically similar, one type of close partnership cloaked by another, but Pen hadn't noticed Merin's eye being caught by anyone not female, so far. To his personal relief. Pen favored round girls, given his choice—though not, alas, the otherwise personable Chio. Her *randomly channels a demon-eating god* aspect was too daunting.

Thank you, murmured Des. *One of your infatuations in that direction would have been supremely awkward.*

Pen's lips twitched.

Chio observed to Merin, "I thought you fancied Sera Lonniel, just now."

In the glow of the walking-lantern, Merin's cheeks darkened in a sheepish blush. He ducked his head. "Who wouldn't? Just on marriageable age, respectable house— her parents guard her very closely, though, so it makes her hard for a poor man to court. Ree was—is—will be again, I hope, good company, but on that point he's just as stiff as his learned mother."

Ah. Iserne's distaste illuminated? Rich daughter, poor suitor, a common tale.

Merin's jaw set. "A sufficient fortune of my own could overcome all those barriers, if I can ever gain it."

"Your own family isn't in trade?" said Pen.

"No. I'm from a farming village in the Adriac hinterland. The usual tale, too many siblings, and the younger turned out like stray cats to seek their own fates."

As the seventh and lastborn in his own family, Pen could sympathize. Although his fate had sought him, as nearly as he could tell. Or perhaps his god's left hand.

Pish, said Des. *You would never have been happy in that narrow mountain valley, even as its shabby lord.*

Less even than as its youngest scion, Pen reflected. *I was entirely content to leave those dreary duties to my eldest brother.* Who appeared to be content to have them, so a win all around.

"At least," Chio remarked to Merin, "they didn't drown you like a sack of kittens."

Foundling, right. Unwanted bastards left on the white god's doorstep were the *lucky* ones. The canals of Lodi swallowed many secrets, to be flushed out on the tides.

A flash of bitterness from Merin: "No, they send us to Lodi and let the city destroy us for them."

Penric had read the man as an unhappy soul from the beginning, but this appeared to go deeper than the disaster to his cabinmate that had been dumped on his hands. Right now, though, Pen had other souls to attend to. Too many, everywhere, and all the wrong ones. Still. The trio—four, counting Des—fell silent for a time, pacing along the maze. Pen's feet were starting to hurt.

The alleys grew quieter as people with duties tomorrow, religious or otherwise, drew in for the night. Though Lodi's prostitutes did not seem to be taking their holiday off; they passed a few such squeezed into dark niches actively pursuing their trade. Pen shifted Chio to his other side, but she seemed neither shocked nor afraid.

"Of course not," she murmured at his anxious query. "Those boys are too busy jumping their ladies to jump us. It's the unattached bravos you have to watch out for."

Shrewd girl, Des approved.

Chio glanced over her shoulder at the lewd noises fading in the shadows, and remarked, "Those poor street whores are not so valued by the city. They're harder to squeeze taxes out of than their sisterhoods in the brothels and bordellos. It's said that the levies paid by the ladies of Lodi fund the building of a state galley every year. *I* think those ships should be named for famous courtesans, but they keep naming them after boring old men instead."

Pen was surprised into a bark of laughter, imagining an imposing warship named *Mira of Lodi* gliding over the waves.

It would overawe all rivals, Des assured him smugly.

He sobered, considering Chio's insights. The denizens of the Bastard's orphanages must have a rough view of the backside of the colorful tapestry that was Lodi. Chio might play a sheltered maiden most convincingly, when it suited her, but she was not one. Even without that hidden portal on infinite space she had tucked secretly about her.

They came to a halt at an alley mouth that gave onto another market, illuminated by what table lanterns hadn't run out of oil and the dancing flames of a cresset, its iron basket held up on a post beside the canal landing. Sinuous yellow-orange lines reflecting in the dark water danced back.

The party hosted here had reached the latest stage of devolution: families gone, young and unattached older men getting drunk, drunker, or drunkest, throwing up or pissing into the canal, loud verbal fights with each other edging toward brawls. Those women yet present, some of them as drunk as their partners, were either plying their trade or else just being very bawdy.

Pen would have been content to edge around this mob, but Chio raised her chin and sniffed the lack of breeze. "Ooh. That fellow still has meat sticks for sale. Let's get some. We can eat them as we walk on, and not need to stop."

One of the last remaining vendors apart from the wine booth supervised an iron basin of coals on a tripod, topped with a grille where he turned sizzling skewers. Their smoke might be the only appetizing smell left curling through the damp midnight air. Pen's suddenly watering mouth reminded him that they hadn't eaten for hours, and they would both need their strength if—when—they caught up with Madboy. *Feed the saint* was certainly part of his Temple duties tonight, eh?

He waved an amiable assent to Chio and threaded his way toward the enticing tripod, where he had to wait for the preceding customers.

'Ware cutpurse, murmured Des.

This square being demon-free, Pen had gratefully eased Des's extended senses, but he flared them a little now. The back of his neck crawled in expectation of a very sharp knife slicing the cord of his purse, in preparation for some drunken-seeming collision later where he would be relieved of it. But to his astonishment, the hand rose to his shoulder braids. A butterfly landing upon him would have had no more weight.

Pen was so boggled, he almost gave the man another few seconds just to see if he would succeed in his delicate unpinning operation. He was fairly certain the answer was *yes*.

Sadly, no. Pen reached up, seized the pickpocket's wrist, and turned in one smooth motion, yanking the man forward. A reach, a sorcerer-physician's precise twist to the axillary nerve—not hard enough to snap it, but enough to leave the whole arm limp and stinging.

"Was this a dare or a death-wish?" Pen breathed in the man's ear.

"Dare!" he squeaked. "Pardon, pardon, learned sir! Just a prank! Forgiveness on our god's day!"

No question that this was no prank, but the man's trade—he'd been far too adept for an amateur thief. From the corner of his eye, Pen spotted a couple of his probably-colleagues, who had been watching the show and grinning, retreat hastily into the shadows at this abrupt reversal of fortune. Pen could imagine the conversation that had led up to this—*I wager I can lift the braids right off that skinny sorcerer's shoulder!* If Pen had been any other sort of Temple divine, he likely could have.

Servile, grinning, and terrified, an unsavory combination. Pen took a deep breath to calm himself, and continued his sermon at a whisper's range. "Your hand will be useless for a day. If I chose to take you to a city constable, it would be removed altogether. Consider this foretaste a god-given chance to pray and reflect on your poor choice of callings. Some craft where your fifth mistake won't result in your hand being amputated would be good. You have skill. Use it for better ends."

Pen released his assailant-turned-victim, who backed away bobbing bows and babbling apologies until he could turn and scamper.

Pen sighed. *Do you think my homily will take, Des?*

Hard to say. Impressive try, though. Demonic amusement. *On both your parts.*

Pen wondered if *Don't drink and rob!* would have been more pointed advice. It wasn't as if he didn't have two spare sets of braids in his clothes chest.

He fished his purse from under his coat and shirt, thankful to find it still there, and settled up for three skewers of meat. Aromatic with garlic, otherwise not very identifiable; *browned* sufficed tonight. A stop at the wine booth for something red and redolent to wash it down would delay them, but it was tempting. Toasted sticks in hand, he looked around for Chio and Merin.

They were gone.

He was *puzzled*. Not *alarmed*, Pen told himself and his leaping pulse as he swept the square with his gaze. Chio's showy striped dress should stand out even in flickering shadows. *No luck*. He flashed Des's demonic sense to its fullest range. By now, he could recognize those souls at a distance much as one would recognize the form of a friend seen down the street. Nothing.

He wheeled, checking the square again. The cutpurse and his cronies were gone, naturally enough. He didn't see how they could have taken Chio and Merin with them by force without his or Des's notice in the few moments he'd spent collecting the meat. Nor why, actually.

No, agreed Des. But when a *demon* sounded worried . . .

The canal here had no footpath, lapping right up to the buildings on either side. The sole access was by oarboat at the market landing. Water traffic had thinned out, only a few hardy boatmen still circulating to ferry inebriated customers home.

This market had three dry entries, the alley they'd
come in by, and the other two leading who-knew-
where—just because they started off in one direction
didn't mean they'd continue that way.

Pen picked the wider, cobbled one and trotted down
it, frugally munching his meat skewer. The snack didn't
settle well in his newly nervous stomach, despite his
peckishness. After a hundred paces, the street narrowed
and ended in a close-built ring of houses. A Lodi rat
could have escaped between them, but not a girl in a
party dress and whoever she'd left with. Merin must be
accompanying her, Pen reasoned with himself, his pulse,
and his digestion. Chio could not be completely
unprotected.

I've lost the saint! Envisioning himself explaining this
to Learned Riesta, Pen fought panic. She was only
temporarily mislaid, surely.

Back to the market. Taxing a few bleary men and the
less bleary vendors for witness bore no fruit; the first had
been too drunk and the second too busy keeping them
so. Pen scowled at the time he'd lost and headed into the
final street. In a minute, the first crossing presented him
with the usual three-way dilemma.

Pen halted, thinking of his late father's description of
a dog trying to chase two rabbits. Doomed to catch
neither, in the paternal parable. Increasingly frantic
circling was not the answer. He'd been doing that all
night.

If the pair hadn't been kidnapped, one must have
persuaded the other away. But which? He wouldn't put
some impulsive start past Chio, certainly. Earlier in the

evening, he might have imagined her growing bored
with her stodgy Temple protector and haring off to find
a better party, but not since their sobering encounter
with the distraught Iserne. So she must have had a
reason. A god-inspired reason? Attempting to picture
what, or how, made him want to gibber.

The notion of Merin luring her away from Penric also
left him at a loss. Not slyly divesting a romantic rival of
his prize; he'd shown no hint of being interested in Chio
that way, although it would take a brave man to approach
a saint.

Or the penniless orphan *part accounts for his lack of
ardor,* Des put in.

Would Iserne concur with her? But no, Merin had
been as intent on their pursuit as the rest of them. Pen
had not misread that.

"Des, what do you make of Merin?"

The impression of a doubtful *Hmm. I see souls. I don't
hear their thoughts as you and I hear each other's, you
know that. Handy as that god-like gift would be. He's
upset, but then he would be. More determination than
malice, and more fear than either. Much more fear. For
Ree, and unease at his dangerous situation, I'd thought.*

Thus Merin, regardless of the details of his
motivation, would still be set on finding Ree. So . . .
maybe Pen wasn't chasing two rabbits. Maybe there was
only one, or in any case two going in the same direction.
Where haven't I searched yet?

He reviewed his routes around a mental map of Lodi.
The city was ten times the size of Martensbridge, itself
ten times the size of Pen's mountain home of Greenwell

Town, but he'd chewed through most of it by now. He hadn't covered any of the outlying islands except the Isle of Gulls, though how a penniless madman could contrive to get across the lagoon defeated even Pen's imagination.

I really don't think he'd have tried to swim, said Des. *Dolphin-haunted or not*.

Agreed.

Oh. There was one place Pen hadn't examined; the harbor shore near the hospice, apart from the bits along the route between the hospice and Iserne's house. Because it had already been searched in that first hour by Linatas and Tebi—looking for a madman and a fuss. Could the bedemoned Ree instead have hidden himself from their view in the marine clutter? *Easily*. Pen would have spotted him regardless, but ordinary eyes might not.

Pen swore aloud in Wealdean at this potential miss.

Though if Merin had been seized by some late inspiration of a new place to look for his lost cabinmate, why hadn't he brought the thought to Penric? Pen was liking this less and less. He walked on into the darkness that wasn't dark to him, somewhat vengefully consuming Merin's meat stick. And, in the twenty minutes it took him to backtrack through the stone and water maze to the harbor, Chio's as well, though mainly to free his hand. Her penalty for running off without telling him.

Trying to be systematic, always a challenge in Lodi, Pen angled through to the shoreline on the far side of the hospice and worked his way back up toward the state shipyard. There was a surprising number of souls about in the after-midnight darkness, and not just celebrants staggering home. Sailors slept out on their moored ships. Others denned up in various cubbies and shacks. Pen passed a pair of night watchmen, more looking for fires than criminals though prepared to sound an alarm for either.

One lifted his lantern and frowned at Pen, glimmering gold-white in the pool of light. Seeing a divine's coat and braids, and of the fifth god's Order on His night, he bobbed his head in nervous respect. "Learned sir. You're out late."

"Unfortunately yes. I'm looking for a, uh, sick man who might have come through here. Also for a young couple . . ." Pen described his missing trio, leaving out the lengthy explanation. Which made it all rather mysterious; the watchmen regarded him with misgiving. But they had not seen any of the people Pen was looking for since they'd come on duty at nightfall. Pen left them with a parting blessing anyway, which they accepted with scarcely less worry.

He searched as far as the mouth of the Wealdmen's Canal without luck, then had to circle up it for the bridge. This brought him back down Iserne's street and past her steps. He did not stop in; Des's Sight told him that Ree had not returned here. Lamplight leaked through third-story shutters from the wakeful woman waiting.

Needless delay would be cruelty . . . He would run, if he'd known what way.

Back to the harborside. The next stretch was mainly devoted to the use of Lodi fishermen like the ones who'd first trawled up Madboy. Tackle, festoons of nets drying, crates, fish-traps, and boats small enough to be pulled ashore for the night made a maddening obstacle course through damp sand. A few craft were upside down, waiting repairs or maintenance on their hulls. If Pen hadn't been looking with Des's Sight, he would never have spotted the man tucked beneath one. Not Madboy, not Merin. Fisherman? Vagabond? No . . . *What's wrong with him?*

Quite a lot, said Des uneasily, *but not our affair, surely . . . ?*

Pen knelt and peered into what would be black shadow to anyone else. The fellow breathing in stertorous gasps was neither sleeping nor drunk. He'd taken a plank to the head. Crawled under there himself, or been rolled in? Robbed?

Comprehensively, murmured Des.

He was wearing nothing but his drawers. He might be in his twenties, sailor or merchant or anything, but he didn't look starveling so probably not a street beggar. Pen didn't wonder *Who would rob a beggar?* since the answer was *Anyone with fewer possessions and more desperation*. Wanting clothes, in this case. And a purse? Pen set his teeth, got a grip on clammy ankles, and dragged the fellow out from under the downturned oarboat.

His dark hair was clotted with blood, mostly dry. So, the injury suffered about two hours ago? The profusely bleeding scalp wound had been superficial, the concussion less so. His skull was not fractured, though, and the bleeding seemed to be confined to the outside, fortunately.

Pen could afford a strong dose of general uphill magic against the shock, brain bruising, and blood loss at no more cost than the life of one of the harbor rats, which were ready to hand, skulking in the shadows. It was a wonder none had taken a nibble of the fellow so far. Pen drew breath and called up this most-practiced basic healing skill, trying hard not to think of all the grievous times it had failed him. He wasn't *doing* this anymore, so why was he doing *this* . . . ?

Des made her silence a dry-enough comment.

Pen quelled the shiver of raw mortal memories as order passed out through his hands into the hurting body, trading for slightly greater disorder flowing up into him.

His . . . patient, foundling, emitted a groan. Pen searched around for a splinter of wood, stuck it upright in the sand, and set it alight with a touch. This makeshift candle wouldn't last long, but it didn't need to. When the fellow pried open his sticky eyelids, he would be able to see more than a threatening silhouette looming over him.

He stretched his jaw, raised a hand to his head; a gleam of dark eyes at last shone up. They widened at Pen. "Am I dead?" the man croaked.

He might have been by morning, if the rats had found him. "Happily not."

". . . thought you might be the white god come to collect me. Wondered what I'd done wrong."

"No, just His errand boy."

"Good. M' mother wouldn't have liked that . . ." Fingers poked gingerly through matted, crusty hair.

"You took a bad knock, though," said Pen. "Any idea who gave it to you?" He was getting an unsettling notion about that.

The fellow was momentarily distracted as his wandering hands discovered his near-naked state. He swore. "My good doublet!" Bony feet felt each other. "My good boots! You 'spect to lose your purse, but who steals a man's *breeches*?" A moment later: "Gods, I feel sick . . ." He spasmed; Pen helped him roll over to vomit. There had been a wine party earlier, evidently. "Ohh, Mother of Summer help me . . ."

"I'll bring you to the Gift of the Sea hospice shortly," Pen promised. "As soon as you think you can walk."

A whuff, possibly grateful.

"Did you see who robbed you?" Pen asked again.

"Only f' a moment. 'S coming home up the harbor street about an hour before midnight—what time s'it now?"

"About an hour after, I make it." Not the worst swoon, though such were never good.

"Barefoot young man by himself. Mumbling. Thought he was too drunk to be a danger, didn't pay much mind as he went by. Then I saw stars. The next thing, you." He pushed himself up on one elbow and looked around, wincing and blinking, then sank back with another groan. "Not far from here."

"What did he look like?"

"About my height and size, I guess. A bit younger? Pretty ragged, so it was hard to tell. Not much light."

"Hair?"

"Dark, tangled."

Pen repeated the somewhat useless physical description of Ree Richelon.

The stripped fellow shook his head, then clutched it. "Ow. I . . . maybe?"

Not obviously *Not*, then. Pen passed his hand over the victim. No signs of demonic disruption—he didn't think Madboy understood the theological hazards of magical violence, but perhaps the plank or chunk of spar or whatever had seemed weapon enough.

But if it *had* been Madboy, that meant he'd still been here in the area not two hours ago. Though also that he had amended his purseless and unclothed state, and gained more ability to move about or escape.

Not over the causeway till it opens again at dawn, though, Des put in. *He's trapped in Lodi tonight unless he goes by boat.*

The stolen money would aid that, although not many boats were still moving at this hour, Bastard's Eve or not. Not that he couldn't just seize a small boat, if he was strong enough to drag it to the water by himself. Or simply untie it from a dock, though their owners usually took in their oars for the night to thwart such thefts.

"How much was in your purse?" Pen asked.

It took bashed-man a dizzied moment to follow the question. "Less'n I'd started out with tonight. Never thought I'd be glad to *lose* at play."

"What color was your doublet?"

The man squinted at him in further confusion. "What? . . . Wine-red, I sup'ose. Good cloth. Only second time I'd worn it." He sighed regret.

In a few minutes, Pen was able to urge the man to his

feet, one arm hoisted over Pen's shoulder, though the movement made him shudder with renewed nausea. They staggered along bumping hips up to the paved harbor street, where Pen prepared to retrace his steps, fretting. He'd traded too much time for these ambiguous clues. Though he supposed he qualified as the Bastard's luck tonight to the robbery victim. He'd have to suggest a donation to his Order.

They'd not limped very far when they encountered another pair of night watchmen. Relieved, Pen traded off his foundling to them with instructions to take him to the Gift of the Sea.

"Tell them Learned Penric sent him, and that he may have something to do with a problem I'm working on for them," he instructed the watchmen. "They'll understand. My Order will cover his fees, if it's required."

This last barely reconciled them to their unexpected and out-of-their-way chore; getting the hint, Pen tipped a couple of coins into their palms to assure the concussed fellow's safe arrival. His slurred voice drifted back still mourning his doublet as Pen turned and strode toward the state shipyard.

Despite the cooling night air, he was sweating from his magical exertion. *Magical friction*, Learned Ruchia had dubbed it in her book on fundamentals of sorcery. Which he'd planned to spend the past afternoon continuing to translate into Adriac. He gritted his teeth. "Des, a rat. Or something."

A brief survey. *Over there.* In the black shadow of a drain, a blacker movement. At least it was one of the big, ugly, corpse-chewing harbor rats, and thus not

distressingly cute. The creature squeaked and died as
Pen divested the healing's dregs of disorder into it.
Passing on, Pen tapped his lips with the back of his
thumb in dutiful thanks to his god for the sacrifice of one
of His creatures.

Pen's stride lengthened. Blessed Chio had been out
of his sight for far too long. And while he wouldn't have
minded losing Merin, could the fool have abandoned her
somewhere? *Not good, not good*.

He came to his next check along the harbor street.
Another canal bisected it, a stubby channel leading only
to a small basin ringed by goods sheds and warehouses.
The buildings shouldered tightly together, each with its
own water gate closed and locked for the night. The
water glimmered against their black bulks. He was just
trying to see a way past when Des said tightly, *Found
'em*.

Bastard be thanked! Finally! He whipped his
attention around and followed her Sight.

Three souls: Merin, Chio, and the fractured, pained,
demon-ridden being he'd glimpsed so vividly at the
hospice. This—no, yesterday afternoon, now. All were
together. Distress, anger, and fear were as thick as a fog
around them. *Where . . . ?* They appeared to be within a
warehouse on the opposite side of the pool. And
something bad was going on. The cornered Madboy
attacking the saint? Even Pen could not run across the
water to get to it directly. He'd have to go around.

He could still run. Expecting the road to ring it for
access on the dry side, he snarled in frustration to find it
led on into the city instead. He spotted a narrow passage

between two houses and turned sideways, scuttling through it to the street opposite. This one led back to the harbor and the goods sheds on the farther arc of the basin.

The warehouse's double door was locked, barred from the inside. The only other visible access was a door on the second floor leading onto air, a crane affixed above it for lifting goods up and down. Des could undo locks. Bars were heavier and trickier. Winded, Pen bent to examine the mechanism.

Chio's screech—Pen wasn't sure if it was in fear or rage—moved him instantly to a more brutal approach, magic and a mighty kick combined. Lock, bar, and door burst inward, followed by Pen. He looked wildly around.

Bundles, bales, and lumber blocked his view. An orange glow rose beyond them. Pen caromed through the narrow aisles to an open space for marshaling cargo by the water door. Merin's walking-lantern, sitting on a nearby crate, illuminated a confusing scene.

Merin and Madboy were locked together in a furious scuffle. Not a wonder in itself; with the saint present, the demon was fighting for its life. The disheveled Chio orbited the pair just out of range. Her mask was hanging, her hair was half-down, and a fresh red bruise marred her cheek.

Merin had his belt-knife in hand, gripping a pewter pitcher in the other by way of a makeshift shield. Madboy was armed with a longer poniard, no doubt lifted from the same source as the red doublet, breeches, and boots he now wore.

"You murderer. You cowardly thief," snarled Madboy.

As accusations went, this seemed to Pen oddly turned-around. Steel clanged off pewter.

"Chio!" Merin bellowed desperately. "Do it, do it, you idiot bitch! Hurry!"

She yelled back, "I don't call the god like a dog! He comes when He chooses! I've *explained* that!"

To, or through, tranquil, emptied souls, Pen had thought. Which Chio's wasn't, in this frenzied moment.

Exhaustion and despair can work as well as tranquility, Des put in.

Aye, not those either.

As the wrestling pair turned, Merin's eye fell on Pen. "Oh, gods, *he's* here!"

Not the joy at rescue Pen would have expected; more a voice of loathing. *Mad demon first, mysteries later.*

At least nothing was on fire, yet. This demon seemed slow to deploy even the most basic magics, but maybe dolphins didn't think in terms of arson.

The two fighters sprang apart, gasping for air. Circled for another opening as if revolving on a rope.

As the demon fought his friend Merin, Ree ought to be impeding it as best he could, beyond just the bodily fatigue of his sea ordeal sapping demonic speed and strength. Jerks and feints and stumbles, other hindrances. Instead, the two seemed of one mind, equally intent upon their attacker. *When both surrender to one desire . . .*

This demon likewise should have been attending to its greater threat from the Temple sorcerer, not following its mount's impassioned focus on Merin. It was leaving itself wide open, and Pen did not delay.

Two anatomically expert nerve twists, one to the right

hand and the other to the left leg. The poniard dropped from paralyzed fingers, and Madboy's leg folded under him, dumping him to the floor. He cried out in pain.

Merin lunged for him. Pen lunged faster, wrapping his arms around the man and trapping his knife hand. "That's enough, Merin! It's over. He's down."

Merin wrenched, then went still. After a cautious moment, Pen released him.

"Oh," said Chio in a peeved tone. "*Now* He shows up." She shoved back her hair and braced her spine, as if lifting a burden.

Stepping forward, she placed her hand on Madboy's brow. Pen could track the arrival of the god by the departure of Des, who, with no other escape, curled into a tight, terrified ball inside him. He granted her the retreat, but he wished she wouldn't take most of her perceptions and all of her powers along, leaving Pen disarmed of his magics.

Chio took a deep breath, opened her mouth, and gulped. Pen had just enough Sight left to feel the demon being drawn out of Ree and into her, and on to the god, in a hideous, frantic, spiky stream. Madboy's anguished howl ran down abruptly as his possessor was torn from him, turning into Ree's very human groan.

"Ugh," choked Chio. "That's a bad one. Just awful." She swallowed and swallowed again, as if trying not to throw up.

With all the hours and sweat and shoe leather spent getting Blessed Chio into position for this confrontation, the actual ... miracle, Pen conceded, was the work of a moment. Miracle, murder ... putting-to-dissolution, he supposed. The saint was an executioner who wasn't getting this Bastard's Day off.

A flash in Pen's mind, but not his eyes, a sense of endless vertigo an instant in duration but infinite in depth, and the god departed with His prize, a strange perfume lingering in His wake that might have been a whispered, *Well done, my lovely Child.*

Pen wasn't sure. It hadn't been to his address. He couldn't have withstood any more direct exposure than that. But Chio's plain face shone with a fleeting inner light of heartbreaking beauty. *Numinous*, Pen supposed, was the precise theological term. The word seemed wholly inadequate.

Single-minded again, Ree gaped up in awe at Blessed Chio, swaying on her feet. *"Oh . . . !"* Breathed like a prayer. As it should be.

Merin swung his head back and forth as if expecting Madboy to rise and attack again. Penric knelt to the de-demoned youth, hoping he hadn't hurt him too severely. He knew he hadn't snapped the throbbing nerves, so they should settle down in a while, an hour or a day, he wasn't sure. His back half-turned, his demon not recovered from her brush with the holy, he only barely caught Merin's motion as he raised his knife and dove forward. At *Penric.*

"What—!"

"No!" shrieked Chio, and threw her shoulder forward into Merin as though trying to batter down a door. It unbalanced him enough that his first stab missed, grazing Pen's sleeve instead of plunging into his back. Pen fell to his hands, scrambling.

Eyes white-rimmed, teeth bared, Merin turned to this unexpected hazard from his flank. His knife flashed in the lantern light, gripped for a lethal thrust. Weaponless, Chio whipped her remaining hair stick out of her braid and brandished it. Merin looked at it and scoffed.

Pen regained his feet. *Des, blast it—!* "What are you doing, you lunatic?" he yelled at Merin. Was the man overcome by some blinding battle frenzy, unable to tell friend from foe? He seemed to have gone wilder than Madboy. "This fight is over!" He started forward to again restrain him.

"Not nearly," Merin gasped, and lunged once more at Penric. Pen had only his own speed to evade the blade, and maybe he'd been sitting in libraries too much lately—

Whereupon both combatants discovered that a thin, six-inch-long steel rod, with the full weight of an angry young woman behind it, had quite enough power to go completely through a man's upper arm and tack it to his torso. Unsharpened point or not. Merin yowled and dropped his knife, clawing at the glittering glass knob with his other hand. Chio yelped and retreated as Merin staggered and swung his free arm viciously at her.

At *last*, Des's powers flooded back into Penric. Pen reached out with her magics and twisted *both* of Merin's sciatic nerves, just to be sure. As excruciating agony seized his legs, he flopped to the floor, screaming.

You're late, Pen panted to his demon.

Sorry . . .

"What," Penric began, but doubted he could be heard over Merin's cries echoing off the wooden rafters. He grimaced, bent forward, and touched the man's throat, then had to reach again as he thrashed away. Paralyzing the vocal cords without blocking breath was a delicate task that he wouldn't have dared from any greater distance. The screaming didn't exactly stop, but it grew unvoiced, a wheezing series of gasps.

"That's better," said Chio in a shaken voice.

"Yes," rasped Pen as his ears stopped ringing. He stood catching his breath and his scattered wits.

"I'd wondered why I didn't like him." She touched the red mark on her face. Wait, was that the work of Madboy or Merin? *Until the god is upon me, and then I see everything*, she'd said, and Pen believed her. What inner worlds had she just seen here?

Pen turned to her, his eye taking in Ree as well, who was clumsily sitting up trying to work his numb hand. "But Bastard's teeth, *what* was going on here? No, start with—why did you two run off from me at the marketplace?" He pointed one cautious toe at Merin, squirming and mouthing like a landed fish.

"He suddenly said he'd guessed where Ser Richelon would be hiding," Chio said, vexation coloring her voice. "Then he grabbed me"—she rubbed her forearm; Pen scowled to see young bruises forming up in the pattern of fingerprints—"and bundled me into an oarboat that had just pulled up to let off another passenger. He told the boatman to take us to the harbor. I expected you to follow on with your Sight, so I didn't cry out or protest— I didn't think I needed to. I mean, I wanted to get to the demon, and he was taking me to the demon." She looked around, and asked Ree, "What exactly is this place, Ser

Richelon, and why were you here? Because Ser Merin was right about that part."

Still shaky with pain, Ree gestured distractedly. "This warehouse is shared by my father and my uncle. His cousin, but I call him my uncle. When Merin was employed by him, we both worked here, sometimes. Then he left, and we didn't meet again till we were thrown together on the spring convoy. You two know about that?" He twisted toward Pen. "You're that scary sorcerer from the hospice—of course you must, if you came for me. You and the god. And the . . . saint?"

From the stunned-ox air Ree bore as his gaze returned to Chio, Pen grasped that he'd had an intimate view of his miracle. And of that holy execution. How much had he felt of his ascendant demon's destruction? And had it been release, horror, awe, or all three inextricably mixed?

Des shuddered.

"This felt like a safe place to hide, and I knew how to get in," Ree went on.

Looks like Merin remembered how, too, said Des. *With less destruction to doorways*. Her regret for the front entry was entirely feigned, Pen judged.

"I didn't have much control, but I dreaded the demon getting any nearer to my mother and sisters. Do you know about them? Oh . . ." Ree looked down at his red sleeve in fresh worry, then up at Penric. He quavered, "Learned sir, I think . . . I think I might have killed a man earlier tonight. I know I robbed him."

So, Ree remembered Madboy's acts. This was going to be interesting. "Put your heart at ease," Pen advised him. "The man survived, and will recover. You may even get a chance to return his things." As Ree continued to look distraught, he added, "The Temple, or at least my Order, will know it wasn't you, and will speak on your behalf if it comes to that."

Chio wrinkled her nose. "How do you even *know* that the man . . . never mind."

Ree blew out his breath in a mixture of turmoil and relief. "It was all so confusing till just now. Like the worst fever dream ever." His gaze caught again in wonder on Chio.

"I daresay," said Pen. "Ah—why was Merin trying to kill you?"

"Trying to kill me *again*, rather." Ree's black brows drew down in anger. Wrenching aside from his worship, he glared in Merin's direction. "He'd thrown me off our ship to drown."

"Why?" asked Chio. She didn't sound shocked.

"I'd spotted him stealing his master's funds." His voice heated. "More fool I, I'd thought I could talk him into putting the money back, and then I wouldn't tell anyone, and all would be right again. That's why I took him out on the deck alone in the night. First he tried to bribe me, as if I would—! Then he saw a more certain way to shut me up."

"In the panic of a fight?" asked Pen.

"We did fight, but he knocked me woozy. He was cool enough to take my purse before he tipped me over the side rail, though." His lips tightened in remembered outrage.

"How frugal." *Premeditation enough, I daresay.* "A money belt was mentioned—did he take that too?"

"I kept that locked in a chest in my cabin. I don't

know if he found it later." Ree looked suddenly even more worried. "Its key was in my purse. He knew that."

"If he filched it, it should be discovered in his things when this incident is investigated," Pen suggested. "I don't know about your father, but if it's lost I can promise you your mother won't care."

"You've met my mother?" Ree's eyes sprang wide, and he gasped in new alarm. "Oh gods, they'll have told my family I drowned!" He lurched, trying to rise. "I have to get home!"

Chio knelt to him and made soothing murmurs, patting his shoulder as if he were a restive horse till he settled back, still panting anxiously.

The disjointed tale laid bare Merin's formerly baffling motives, though. Cold greed, and hot fear of being found out. Should fear be added to the list of great sins?

It can do as much harm, I'll grant, said Des.

A stiff voice called from the wrecked doorway, "Hey! What's going on in there?" Wary footsteps resolved into two men in the tabards of the state shipyard—its lords administrative kept a full roster of watchmen in the area, even or perhaps especially on holiday nights, so Pen was less taken aback than they were. One held up a lantern; the other had his short sword out and ready. "We heard screaming."

Well, here's trouble, said Des.

Not necessarily. It all depends on how I play it.

I yield this hand to you, templeman. By all means go be Learned Sir at them.

Chio shrank back beside Ree. Pen stepped forward, saying heartily, "Five gods be thanked you're here!" The sword sank only slightly. Lantern-man put his other hand on the truncheon hung at his hip.

"We interrupted an attempted murder," Pen went on, which didn't seem to reassure them. Leaving aside the question of who had been trying to murder whom when Pen first had come in. Merin had certainly been bent on getting rid of witnesses, but had been blocked by the problem of the demon until the saint had done her deed—Pen had to give him credit for paying attention to his demon-lectures.

The whole growing, teetering pile of lies and crime tonight must have been cobbled together impulsively as Merin tried to work around the unexpected god-gift of Ree's survival and demonic possession. Add *rashness* to his list of defects. If he'd managed to dispatch Ree, would he have gone on to Chio? *Where would he hide the bodies?* was hardly a problem in canal-laced Lodi. The picture made Pen sick. *My Lord Bastard, you trim your timing far too fine.*

For this audience, Pen decided to stick with more recent and clear events. "This man"—he pointed down at Merin— "just made an ill-advised attempt to stab me." True enough. "Ah, permit me to introduce myself. I'm Learned Penric kin Jurald, court sorcerer to Archdivine Ogial."

Ree's eyes widened. So did the watchmen's, though they maintained a properly suspicious stance. In Lodi, Ogial's was a name to conjure with even if one wasn't a sorcerer.

"And this is my colleague and saint of my Order, the Blessed Chio," Pen went on, moving possessively to the girl's side as she rose.

He'd been making headway up to that point, but

received a look of narrow disbelief as they took in the details of the alleged saint: a rumpled young female who might have been a bedraggled festival-goer, prostitute, victim of attempted assault sexual or otherwise, or all of them at once. Chio raised her decided chin and cast them a credible look of disdain in turn. But she shifted closer to Penric.

Ree overcame intense self-consciousness of his stolen garments to offer, "This is my father's warehouse. Ser Ripol Richelon. I'm his son Ree. This man is Aulie Merin, and he's a thief. Among other things."

And if the watchmen construed that the trio had interrupted a robbery in progress, so much the better. Still unable to rise, Merin clutched at his throat and leaked constricted rasps, like a bladder deflating.

"He's bleeding," Sword-man noted of Merin. "Why can't he talk?" Not kneeling to help yet; he kept his eye on Penric.

"Sorcery," said Penric, truthfully. "Which is also why he can't walk right now. I did mention he just tried to knife me. You'll have to fetch a couple of bearers. He'll recover on his own in a while. Take him to whatever you use for a lockup, and keep him there till someone comes from the Temple or the city tomorrow to make it all official." The legal part of this mess should now fall into the hands of authorities who were *not Penric*, so that was a bright spot. Though there would doubtless be testimony required of him later. In writing.

"When he gets his voice back," said Ree bitterly, "I promise he'll use it to lie."

"Folks always do, to us," said Lantern-man. His gimlet

gaze around did not specify who, except that it was likely those who were talking. If the watchmen arrested the wrong parties by mistake, would Learned Iserne come to free them?

She's a property lawyer, Pen.

I'll bet she knows people.

I'll bet she does too.

Pen moved this along in the hopes that assuming his conclusions would overbear further delays. "It's very late, and I have yet to escort the victim to his home and the saint back to the chapterhouse of our Order." And what Riesta would have to say about their dawn return Pen didn't dare guess. "We also need a guard placed on the door till its owner can come arrange repairs. May we leave this in your capable hands?"

Good flattery there, said Des. *Now follow up and bless the crap out of them.*

Pen did so, but thought unshipping his purse and paying in advance for the guard, and a few other details he didn't inquire into too deeply, did more. When he finished he didn't have enough left for boat fare back to the Isle of Gulls.

Borrow it from Iserne, Des suggested. *I imagine she'll be good for it.*

Though by now, he'd have emptied out every last coin just to get Merin safely into a cell. Vastly more efficient and less trouble than, say, chasing the fugitive through Lodi till he pitched into a canal and drowned from the weight of his stolen money belt.

Less satisfying, though, said Des. *Have I mentioned I actually like your overactive imagination?*

Speak for yourself. Bloody-minded demon. Yet the vivid picture of having to pull the rotting bodies of Chio and Ree out of some similar canal, had Merin had his way, drained Pen's thought of ire. Lodi canals were a deal warmer and less preserving than the chill Martensbridge lake.

The watchmen still squinted at them all, but the prospect of transferring the entire mess to the hands of the day shift probably did more to sway them than had Pen's coins and Learned Iserne's name and direction combined. They divided their tasks, one standing sentry and the other trotting off for reinforcements, and Pen seized the chance to slip his party away before yet more questioners arrived and he'd have to go over it all *again*.

Ree's dismasted leg was still not working right, so Pen heaved him up with his arm over his shoulder. He choked down a whimper.

Pen tried to herd the saint ahead of them to the ruined door, but at the last moment she darted back to search out an ornamented hair stick from where it had rolled into a bale. Setting her teeth, she then bent, wrapped her fist around the glass ball of the one still in Merin's arm, and yanked it back out. Blood spattered on the wooden floor as he jerked and whined. Efficiently, she wiped the wet shank on his gray jacket.

Rejoining Pen and Ree, she wound her messy braid back up on her head and pinned it crookedly in place. Ree watched this firm gesture with, apparently, great admiration.

"Good," she said, collecting Merin's walking-lantern as well. "Let's go."

I'm not in charge of this parade anymore, am I, Des,
Pen thought as they limped after the girl.

*You haven't been all night. God-touched, if you didn't
notice. I did.*

. . . Aye.

It was the deadest hour of the night. Even the most
determined celebrants had staggered home, and early
workers were not yet abroad. The lantern, held aloft by
Chio as Pen supported Ree, guttered out of oil before they
reached Iserne's house. The moon served, just high enough
for its pale light to angle down between the close buildings.

Chio glanced over her shoulder. "Your whites make
you glow like a ghost."

"Ghosts are grayer, usually."

"Oh? Not the ones I see."

"Maybe the god gets them fresher?"

Ree's brow wrinkled at this exchange.

As they made the last turn, Pen could see a single
light still burning on the street, suspended from its chain
over Iserne's door. This was one lamp that wasn't going
to be allowed to run out of oil before dawn, he wagered.

"Up we go," he told Ree as they reached the steps,
preparing to hoist, but Ree got more power out of his
one working leg than Pen expected. His intent face
lifted; Pen could feel his body shaking from more than
just painful effort.

Rapid footfalls sounded from inside even as Pen
raised his hand to the lion-faced doorknocker. He
stepped back hastily before his second tap lest they be
bumped back down the steps as the door was flung wide.

"*Ohfivegodsbethankedyou'resafe!*" Pen staggered a bit as Iserne fell on them, or rather on Ree. For a moment, she seemed to have four or six arms, not two, as she alternated between hugging her son, and inspecting him for injuries.

Chio's smile, as she watched this from the side, was secret, tender, and deeply pleased.

"What's wrong with your right arm?" Iserne demanded, taking up Ree's limp hand. She drew back only a little when she finally thought to ask Pen, "Is he all right now?"

Pen didn't think even the wild demon could have impeded this welcome-home. "Yes, thanks to Blessed Chio and our god, he's all himself again."

Iserne exhaled in vast relief.

"I'm afraid the numbness in his arm and his leg is the doing of my sorcery, but we had to hold"—he probably shouldn't use the nickname *Madboy* in front of Ree's mother—"the demon down for the saint to do her work, and it was, of course, resisting us."

"But—what—but come in, come in, all of you." She drew them into her hallway, casting a last look into the darkness. "Is Ser Merin not with you?"

"Not anymore," said Pen. "Long story, which we'll get to in a bit."

"Oh. Good." She shut the door firmly and shot the bolt. Turning back to them, she said to Ree, "Should you lie down? Should I send for a physician? I made you food."

"Learned Penric has some skills as a physician," Chio put in. "I don't think we need another tonight."

Yes, and how much did she know about that? Another private aspect of himself Pen knew he had not discussed. "Ree's few days at the Gift of the Sea helped the worst of his exposure and exhaustion. He could hardly have been delivered into more expert hands for that. The numbness should pass off in a while." Duration prudently unspecified.

"Yes, but what exactly did you *do* to him?" Iserne's scowl was more puzzled than angry, fortunately.

"Let's just say that learning sorcerous healing also teaches everything one could want to know about sorcerous hurting," said Pen. "Two sides of one coin." Which was why sorcerer-physicians were the rarest and most closely overseen of Temple servants. Pen was relieved when Iserne did not follow up with more questions, dismissing Pen and his late craft in favor of her more immediate concerns.

"Food would be good," said Ree. "And sitting. Then lie down. I'm so tired. But oh, Mother, I have so much to tell you. It was all such madness, and I'm still reeling." In truth, as he hung on his rescuer's shoulder, but only the physical part of that was Pen's doing. "Is Father back yet?"

"Not till next week, but I may hurry him with a note."

"Good. There are things he'll need to know, and Uncle Nigus, too."

"I have a meal laid out in the dining room. Please join us, Learned, Blessed." Her attempt to curtsey and beckon them on simultaneously resulted in a sort of hand-waving bob. Pen helped the halting Ree through the indicated archway off the entry hall—his left leg was getting more movement now, good. Chio set the spent lantern and their masks on a side table and followed.

Iserne had not been jesting. Enough fare for ten people was scattered across the Richelon family's dining table. The array was very miscellaneous, everything an invading army of one woman could possibly forage from a kitchen after midnight when she could not rest: ends of cold meat, cheeses, fruit and dried fruit, boiled eggs, cabbage salad, nuts, fresh-baked bread and cakes, custards, jam tarts, restoring herb tea, wines and water.

"So much food," muttered Pen. "How many people was she expecting?"

"I believe it was a prayer," Chio murmured from his other side.

Aye, Des agreed.

As Pen helped Ree into a chair, Iserne scurried to fetch a hand basin and towel, which, along with a sliver of fine white soap, she presented first to Chio, then Pen, then her son. Chio, who'd seated herself on Ree's right, helped his half-working hands with the wash-up.

Ree lifted his good hand toward the darkening bruise on her cheek. "Did I do that? I'm so sorry, Blessed Chio."

She didn't flinch. Shrugging off his apology, she said, "I know it wasn't really you. Anyway, it was Merin's fault for shoving me at you like that. He should have been praying, not cursing."

Iserne seized the chair on Ree's other side, leaving Pen to take the place across. "What's this tale?"

Ree's and Chio's tumbling joint account of the confrontation in the warehouse was understandably both garbled and horrifying, Ree's part not least because, famished, he kept trying to talk with his mouth full. Clarity was not much improved by them working backward, leapfrog fashion, from each of their vantages through the chaotic events of the evening leading up to it. Pen judged Ree was severely editing his hectic experiences spent under his ascendant demon for his mother's ears. He did awkwardly confess about the fellow he'd robbed for the clothing he still wore, drawing in Penric to give what he hoped were soothing reassurances.

"Wait," said Iserne, holding up her hands. "Go back to the beginning. You're saying *Merin* threw you from your ship? It wasn't an accident?"

Her teeth set as Ree disgorged a longer tale of his accusation of Merin and how it had come about, with a lot of names and details of merchant accounts and accounting that Pen did not follow but Iserne evidently did. It was clear Ree was regaining his wits, if not his composure.

"Embezzling. Well, I'm not surprised," she said.

"You're not? I was blindsided," said Ree.

"Plainly, someone should have told you, but Merin was your Uncle Nigus's man and problem, and so Ripol kept out of it. Nigus suspected sticky fingers back when Merin worked for him, but the losses all had other explanations—sly, I gathered—so he didn't think he could prove it in a law court. He solved his problem by recommending Merin on to one of his more bitter rivals. Which I thought as nearly dubious as the original thefts, but I wasn't consulted."

"I'd wondered why you didn't like him flattering Lonniel. I'd thought it was because he was too poor."

She sniffed. "Ripol was that poor when we first married. And a difficult time we had of it, but he met our challenges by working harder. Not by wasting all his cleverness taking dishonest shortcuts." She went on more intently, "But what happened *after* you were thrown into the water?"

Ree looked away, the fatigue underlying his sunburned features growing more marked. "I was so angry, I didn't even think to be frightened at first, till my cries went unheard and the ship sailed out of sight. I could guess which way was east by the moon, as long as it was above the horizon, and by the stars a little. And the sun when dawn came. I didn't think I could make it, but I swam toward the coast as best I could. Slower and slower as I grew tired. Finally it was all I could do to stay afloat. I thought, well, I thought about a lot of things. Things I should have done, and shouldn't have, and all the things I was never going to get to do."

Iserne's hand pressed her lips, and she didn't interrupt. Chio listened with grave interest, head bent toward him.

"The dolphin was the strangest part," Ree went on, "coming up under me in the dawn just when I couldn't swim anymore. I'd never been so close to one before, let alone touched it. Its skin was all slick, cool and firm like wet leather. Except lumpy—I think now the bumps must have been tumors, because some were broken open and infected, and there was a memory of pain, later. Not easy to hang onto, but I swear it waited for me like a good horse. We must have moved slowly toward Adria all that long day. Then it died, and sank from under me, and I thought I had gone mad from fear at last. I can scarcely remember the fishermen, I was so confused by then. We should find them to thank them."

"Oh yes," said Iserne fervently.

"The people from the hospice may be able to identify them for you," Pen suggested. "If someone takes back that concussed fellow's clothes and purse, you could ask then. He's owed thanks of a sort, too, I think."

"Does he know what he owes to you?" Chio asked Pen in curiosity.

All right, it could have been his life, if the rats had been quicker and hungrier, or if Madboy had bashed him harder. Pen waved this away. "He owes me nothing. All in a Bastard's Eve work." Pen's holiday, hah.

Ree looked perturbed at this reminder, and altogether too grateful to his mother when she said, "I'll take on that task tomorrow."

"You're likely the person best suited to make sure there are no repercussions," Pen agreed. "There's going to be enough of a legal tangle with Merin." Pen was glad his Temple duties ended with the demon and the saint, the machineries of justice being the prerogative of the city and a very different god than his own.

A feminine voice, sleepy and miffed, sounded from the archway. "You're having a feast? And you didn't wake me up?" Then a gasp. "*Ree!*"

Pen looked up, and Ree twisted around in his chair, to see Lonniel pick up the skirts of her nightdress and pelt the few steps to her brother's side. Iserne had to lean away as she grabbed him in an excited hug and ran her anxious fingers through his hair in a sisterly echo of his mother's earlier greeting. "How is your head?"

"My head? Much better than it was, now I'm alone in it again."

"It's not broken after all?" she said as her searching fingers found neither lumps nor clotted blood.

"No, that was the other fellow, but Learned Penric says he'll get better."

"What?" They blinked at each other in mirrored confusion.

Penric explained to Ree, "We stopped here earlier, after we first encountered Iserne and Merin searching for you in the hospice. Merin didn't want to mention your near-drowning or the demon, which he'd just found out about himself—Bastard's teeth, that must have come as a shock. Nor tell the truth, for obvious reasons. So he told your sisters that after your ship moored in Lodi you'd run off due to being hit on the head in an unloading accident."

"Son of a bitch," growled Ree. "Whyever did he come here in the first place?"

"To bring the news to your mother of your loss overboard sailing up to the last stop in Trigonie," said Chio. "He claimed he was sent to do so, on account of you two being cabinmates and him knowing your family, but I'll bet he volunteered, to make sure only the right things were said."

Ree's jaw dropped at this outrageousness, echoed by Iserne's affronted huff.

Chio mused on, "You have to admire his nerve, in a

way. To face his murder victim's mother and tell all those smooth lies. I knew he was sweating about it, but I didn't realize why."

"*What?*" shrieked Lonniel.

Her mother, not willing to give up her place, sent her around the table to sit next to Penric as Ree began his tale once more. Wide-eyed, she worked her way through two fruit tarts and a pile of pistachios as he brought his synopsis up from his fall into the sea to the mortal fight in their father's warehouse.

He paused and cleared his throat. "If you were sweet on Merin, I'm sorry."

She made a wry face. "Not especially? He made sheep's-eyes at me, but so do the other young fellows who work for Father and Uncle. I knew he was angry and resentful of anyone with more luck than himself, which to hear him tell it seemed to be most people. I never dreamed he'd take it so far."

"To be fair," said Pen, seminary debate-habits lingering, "I don't think he'd ever planned murder. His main aim seemed to be theft. But when Ree caught him out, things went from bad to worse, each rash impulse struggling to fix the one before it." Pen contemplated this. "Ending with trying to *stab a saint*, which strikes me as epically stupid." He frowned at Chio. "Though the god could not have protected you from a blade, you know."

Her lips curved up. "Of course He could. He sent you."

Pen buried his flattered, horrified grumble in a bite of fig.

"Saint . . . ?" said Lonniel faintly, stopping in mid-chew.

"I was just getting to that part," said Ree, his tired face growing eager as he glanced over at Chio. "It's how the Temple gets rid of demons, you know. Or maybe you don't. I can't say as I really knew, before, just a dim notion that someone from the white god's Order took care of such things."

"That someone would be me, for the archdivineship of Lodi," Chio said, with a tentative smile across the table at Lonniel.

"Uh, had we introduced Blessed Chio to you when we met earlier?" asked Penric. He couldn't remember, in the welter of subsequent events.

"*Blessed* Chio . . . ?" Lonniel shook her head. "No! Nor you either, properly, Learned," she added as an afterthought. "A real sorcerer, come to our house? Nobody tells me *anything* important."

Iserne bit her lip, possibly on a tart reminder that they'd caught the sisters sneaking out the door, not an incident to invite much in the way of confidences.

"My apologies," Pen interjected, before Iserne was pricked into saying anything that might restart some chronic mother-daughter dispute. "Penric kin Jurald, court sorcerer to Archdivine Ogial. And Blessed Chio, my Order's saint residing at the chapterhouse of the Isle of Gulls. I was originally sent by the archdivine to look into the case of the shiplost man brought to the Gift of the Sea, and, well, we have." He gestured at Ree, and by extension at the whole tumultuous night.

Lonniel, her brows scrunching, asked her brother,

"What was it like? Having a demon?" An eye-flick at Pen, as she realized another demon must be sitting next to her. She didn't, quite, edge away.

Ree made a helpless hand-wave. "A horrible fever dream, that went on and on and I couldn't wake up from it. Memories that weren't mine, running through my head. Some terrible—strangling and being strangled all atop, gods that Roknari man was more awful than Merin—some just strange. Moving through the water, weightless and joyful and powerful. Crunching down all those wriggling live fish, ugh. My body walking around Lodi on its own, and I could only watch as it did things I didn't choose. I got all the bruises and hunger just the same. When the god came and took it away . . . I can't . . ." His voice died.

Chio, listening, smiled quietly at that.

He shifted to face her. "You do this over and over? The god comes to you each time?"

She tilted her head. "Whenever the Order brings me another elemental. It's an unsteady supply, but maybe four to six a year."

"It—that experience—must . . . do things. To you." As it just had to Ree?

She considered this in kindly seriousness. "The god . . . enlarges my world?"

Or her soul, Pen suspected. And she confronted this vastness six times a year? One direct encounter—two, now—with his god in Pen's lifetime had been overwhelming enough.

"How can you bear it? That demon was so dreadful."

"That one was very, very bad," she agreed with a sigh.

"With new elementals, caught early, it's more like killing chickens. Uncanny chickens, but still. An unpleasant task I try to make as mercifully quick as possible."

Which meant the one in the warehouse had felt more like hanging a human? Chio did not point this up, so neither did Pen.

"Will you always be a saint?" asked Ree.

"I'm at the god's disposal, not Him at mine. Any time could be the last, I expect."

Pen offered, "I believe the Saint of Idau has served the region around Martensbridge for over thirty years. He's quite aged now, but he's still at it as far as I know." Blessed Broylin's calling must have come upon him in mid-life, Pen realized. That had to be a story, and he regretted not collecting it. But, indeed, sorcerers did not linger around saints to socialize.

Lonniel asked, "Will the Bastard's Order always keep you on the Isle of Gulls? Like . . . like a princess in a tower?"

A more gratifying comparison than *a prisoner in a dungeon*, Pen supposed.

Chio was surprised into a laugh. "I'm sure Learned Riesta—my chapterhouse supervisor—wishes he could. But I'm devotee to the Bastard, not to the Daughter of Spring. I have no religious duty to withdraw from the world. I can have whatever life I can arrange. You said Broylin was a baker, Penric? I wonder whatever happened to that dressmaker . . . Now I'm not a child, I stay on Gulls mainly because I can't afford to take myself elsewhere." She grew thoughtful. "Does Riesta keep me poor on purpose for that?"

"I could not speculate," said Pen, deciding to be diplomatic.

"Maybe it's just his frugal habit," she said, tolerantly. "The orphanage always has too many mouths to feed."

"Can saints marry?" asked Lonniel. Pen approved her avid curiosity, if not her bluntness.

Iserne, alive to the hazards of both, and perhaps to spare Chio awkwardness, answered this one. "I've met two petty saints, judges in the Father's Order, who are married. To each other, which must make for peculiar bed-talk. And one saint-acolyte in the Mother's, whom I encountered when I helped draw up her will some years ago. So yes. About as commonly as other people, I imagine."

"Oh. I was wondering, because of the Bastard's Order. That maybe it wasn't done over there, on account of some, um, courtesy to the god."

"Yes, people in our Order do marry." Penric cleared his throat. "Sorcerers maybe less often. I'm given to understand our demons make us difficult as spouses. Five of Desdemona's—that is, my demon's—prior riders managed somehow, though. All of them were wed before they became sorceresses, come to think. But never two mages to each other. Two chaos demons in one household would be, how to put this, an oversupply of chaos in one place." Or even two chaos demons in one palace, which was how he came to be booted out of Martensbridge.

"What about a sorcerer and a saint?" Lonniel went on, irrepressibly. Pen estimated she was of the age when marriage loomed as her next great life passage, hence this alarming focus.

Her mother rolled her eyes, reproving, "Lonniel."

"No," Des answered aloud firmly, before Pen could speak again.

"Oh. Too bad." Her gaze flicked at her brother as she continued to serenely demolish her pear.

So may a sorcerer and a saint be friends?

Across a table seems all right, Des allowed, sounding bemused at the discovery. *In the same bed would be much too close.*

Well, quite.

"So . . . you would be, um, allowed visitors, Blessed Chio?" said Ree in a tentative tone. "At your chapterhouse?"

Chio lifted one slim shoulder. "If any ever came out to Gulls." She added to Lonniel, "We don't actually have any towers at the orphanage. It might be fun to live in one, if not as a prisoner. There'd be a handsome view of the basin, and the city. Much better than the girls' dormitory, though they gave me my own room in the chapterhouse after my calling came upon me. They needed the dormer bed for the next orphan, I expect."

Lonniel's eyes brightened, and she gestured urgently with her pear core. "Could we come? And visit you?"

Ree's startled glance shifted to his sister. "What a, a good idea."

Des, watching the play, started to silently laugh. *Well, there's a sister who's just earned herself some brotherly love.*

What?

Do keep up, Pen.

Iserne said judiciously, "We could all go out. Ripol will

certainly want to meet and thank Blessed Chio, when he returns."

Lonniel perked up at this offered treat. Ree cast his mother a grateful look.

Is Iserne keeping up, too?

Oh, I think so.

Iserne bestowed a benign smile upon the saint. Upon the unmarried young woman? Both?

"Be warned," said Chio, "Learned Riesta will ask you for donations to the orphanage. He always does, no matter who comes. From the archdivine down to the boatmen."

"Then we'll be in good company," said Iserne, undeterred.

Lonniel bounced in her chair. "Ooh, yes, let's all make a day of it when Papa gets back."

"You'd be very welcome," said Chio. Her expression warmed as it dawned on her that Iserne's offer was not just a social fib, made to be polite and as lightly forgotten, but a real promise. "All of you."

In the tug between admiring Chio, and falling face-first into his plate, Ree's plate was starting to win. They'd all eaten till they couldn't hold more, both Lonniel and Chio demonstrating impressive capacities. What food was left on the table would have to fend for itself, Pen thought muzzily. Ree wasn't the only one for whom the horizontal beckoned. A gray light leaked through the dining chamber's shutters, harbinger of the early midsummer dawn.

"I should escort Blessed Chio back to Gulls," Pen announced to the air generally. And wasn't that going to be awkward at this late hour. He briefly pictured dropping the disheveled girl off at the chapterhouse boat landing like a package and fleeing back across the water, but no, that would be cowardly. The saint had set a daunting example of courage and nerve tonight, so Pen needed to hold up the honor of, of . . . sorcerers, or whatever. *For the Order and the White God!* he imagined declaiming, except that he was fairly certain his god would just laugh at him.

"Oh. Yes, of course." Iserne, too, had to pull herself away from a fascinated study of her young guest. "It's so late it's become early." Her expression softened at her son. "Ree should go to bed, before he needs carrying up in a sack. I can't do that anymore, now he's man-sized."

Ree made a grunt of exhausted agreement, but pulled himself together as Pen and Chio rose. He managed to stand, holding the back of his chair, and offered her a precarious bow. "Blessed Chio. I hope to see you again soon."

She touched her forehead, mouth, navel, groin, and heart in the tally of five-fold benediction, tapped the back of her thumb to her lips, and pressed it to his forehead. "The white god guard you until then."

"He has been. Hasn't He? You would know."

A secret smile, but it might be a secret shared with Ree. "Maybe."

Pen trailed after her into the entryway, like a pilot boat to some homegoing sailing vessel. There followed the confusions of departure, Pen in embarrassment begging Iserne for oarboat fare, his mumbled apologies overborne by her grateful generosity of coins. He could catch up to her next week in the curia and pay her back, he consoled himself.

Iserne gave them careful directions to the nearest public landing at the mouth of the Wealdmen's Canal, where Pen hoped they would find some early, or late, boatman waiting for work. He considered, for about two seconds, saving money by walking, again, all across town to the landing closer to Gulls on the city basin. *No.* The Richelon door closed on the happy fuss of his mother and sister getting Ree aimed up the stairs to his bed, and his unconvincing protests of self-sufficiency.

The rising light was turning the misty shore air to silver as they arrived at the landing, where they found a sleepy and thankfully ungarrulous boatman waiting to start his busy Bastard's Day labors. Pen settled Chio in the forward-facing seat and took the one across from her. The boatman shoved them off with a surge that settled into gentle and soporific rocking.

Pen blinked gritty eyes, and remembered: "Oh. Happy birthday, Blessed Chio. Will you at least get sweet custard, later?"

"I trust so. The chapterhouse does put on a fine Bastard's Day feast, once we have endured Riesta's homilies. The orphans work up good appetites during the afternoon games in the god's honor. Though right now I'm too full to care." She tilted her head back to the warming sky. "Learned Iserne is a generous mother. I wonder if Ree, and Lonniel, and Lepia know how lucky they are."

And Ripol, presumably. Not hard to see who was the strong glue holding that household together.

"They seem an admirable family," Chio went on. "Much the sort I once dreamed of being adopted into. I'm too old for that now." That telling I-don't-care one-shoulder shrug, again.

"It's a family at a late stage," Pen observed idly. "You're seeing the results of many years of labors, not the labor itself. I grew up in a largish family myself, but as the lastborn, I never saw the beginnings either. We children mostly couldn't wait to get away, toward the end." Pen's older brother Drovo, disastrously into a mercenary company. His sisters more naturally passing into marriage, nothing fatal there, yet. The eldest Rolsch stuck forever at the core, though as baron he presumably had compensations pleasing to him. Penric . . . well. He'd always been the odd duck.

Swan, by now, suggested Des. *Look, you're even garbed in white feathers.*

Seriously smudged and ruffled, after the past night. White was a terrible choice of emblematic color for a god of chaos.

Reminded of his sisters, it occurred to Pen there was another way for a young woman to acquire a family, very traditional indeed. But surely merchant clans did not approve portionless brides? The richer orphanages did sometimes bestow modest dowries upon their girls, he'd heard, though more often the houses were pressed just to come up with apprenticeship fees. It might be unkind to put such a notion into Chio's head.

He offered instead, "The princess-archdivine once quipped to me that our friends are what the gods give us to make up for our families." In one of their more wine-mellowed late-night chats—though he suspected the hallow kings of the Weald experienced family on a whole different level.

Not that different, said Des, and how did she know?

Chio, at least, smiled at Pen's imported joke.

Her orphan state wasn't a problem he could fix by any sorcery of his. That was a task for their god's hand, perhaps. Though one needed to be *cautious* in prayers to the Bastard.

Oh, come, Des scoffed. *What makes you think His hand wasn't stirring this pot all night? And possibly before then. I don't think you need to say a word.*

Parsimony, or opportunism? Why not both . . . ?

I'd bet on Ree, myself. Young. Energetic. Grateful . . .

There's no tower to rescue this princess from, Pen pointed out.

The lad seems resourceful. He might build one just to rescue her from it.

Hah.

Pen wished Chio well in any case. Whatever that *well* turned out to be.

Chio sat up and pointed out across the glinting waters. "Ooh, look! The boats are starting to come in for the Bastard's Day procession."

Pen followed her line. Either a big oarboat or a small galley, five oars on a side, sculled along overtaking them. It was painted, or freshly repainted, in white, with scrolling decorations of silver or more likely tin feigning silver, festooned with garlands and flowers, pennants flirting with the air.

"That's the boat from the Glass Island chapterhouse,"

Chio identified it. She waved wildly at its occupants, who waved back. A grinning woman at the rail, taking in Pen's vestments, tossed them a shouted blessing and a circlet of white flowers, which fell short and landed in the water. Chio made their boatman swerve aside. Pen grabbed the thwart as their boat wobbled when she leaned over to pluck it out and shake it off. She plopped it atop her head, where it sat askew.

"Are there orphan boats from Glass Island, too?" Pen asked, looking around for such. The decorated flotilla of small vessels following the chapterhouse craft seemed to be a miscellaneous lot, but children were only thinly scattered among their passengers.

"No, Glass doesn't have an orphanage."

"I never thought to ask. Are you supposed to be in the procession today?" As an honored saint now, not displayed as hopeful human wares. If so, Pen was going to be delivering her late for it, oops.

"Mm, no, the five Orders here tend to keep all their saints very private. The Father's and the Mother's people, I know, so that they won't get pestered to distraction by supplicants. My task is too specialized to draw supplicants, except those who *really* need me. Who are generally guided in." Her grin flickered. "Like you."

Pen wasn't sure but what *blundered* might be a better term than *guided*, for his Bastard's Eve.

"You have fine weather for the procession, this morning," Pen allowed. The lagoon's soft air felt good on his face, though by noon they'd all be seeking shade.

"It's usually so at midsummer," the boatman put in, the first he'd interrupted—though he had been, inescapably, listening. Slow to wake up, maybe; Pen sympathized. But everyone was allowed to comment on the weather, everywhere, as far as Pen had observed. "Sometimes there's wind. The equinoxes are more chancy. I row for the Father's procession at winter solstice. Chilly, and properly somber if there's mist. Your hands get chapped." He nodded and, evidently satisfied to have said his piece, went back to his rhythmic sweeping.

Five gods, five major festivals; the Bastard's Day always taking over Mother's Midsummer in Quintarian lands. The three other holy days that fell exactly between the solstices and equinoxes found alternate excuses for their celebrations.

The Quadrenes tuck our god's intercalary day in at Father's Midwinter, Des remarked, *because they imagine it keeps Him under better control. It's considered a day of ill luck, for fasting and prayer, where no one goes out or starts any new enterprise.* A pause for consideration, or perhaps memory, for she added, *Young Umelan always found it very boring.*

Pen squinted and yawned. The boatman likely wouldn't be too startled if his passenger curled up on the bottom of his boat and started snoring. He had to have ferried home plenty of exhausted holiday-goers over the years, if none quite this late, nor from a night this strange.

Chio had fallen silent, studying the shifting cityscape as they reached the central basin. Fatigue seemed to be gaining on her at last, though not as much as on Pen. He didn't often meet anyone who made him feel quite so old.

The sense of a snort from Des, which he prudently ignored.

It occurred to Pen, watching Chio trail a meditative hand in the water, that there was one aspect of her night's saintly labors she had entirely talked around at the Richelons' table. And that his duty to her as a divine of their shared Order extended beyond merely acting as her guardsman. Even if she'd handed him back as much defending as he'd given to her, which was a trifle embarrassing.

She has the god's guidance, Pen. Why would she need yours?

Cogent question, but . . . *Let's find out*.

It took him a moment or two to decide how to start.

"When I was nineteen, and feckless, and knew almost nothing yet about my new calling as a sorcerer, it never even crossed my mind to wonder what distress disposing of Des would have caused old Broylin. He was presented to me as already an authority, an immovable fixture in the world, like a mountain. He seemed surprised when the god refused my demon, but not . . . not unhappy. I just assumed he'd seen many and worse. I know of one for certain—a renegade Temple demon, which must have become a full person by the time it was recalled and destroyed by the god." Des's memories of Tigney's ascendant demon were fraught enough, shared only reluctantly with Pen.

Chio shook the droplets off her hand and turned toward him. "You're a noticing sort of man, Learned Penric. In ways Riesta can't be, I guess."

Pen opened a conceding palm. "Yes."

A little silence. Then, "In a way," Chio said, "I'm glad this one was such an awful mess. At least there wasn't doubt, atop the other ugliness of my task. If that was a birthday gift to me from the god, well . . . it's not as if I can give it back."

"Good is not always the same thing as nice, they say." He studied her tired young face in the light of the sun, now topping the city and piercing the watery silver air with rose-gold. It would be a fine fair day, and hot. "Are you going to be all right?"

"I . . . will be." She puffed a faint laugh, adding, "You're the first to ever ask me that, at one of these duties. Everyone asked it of that chicken-woman, after I freed her, but not of me. Not even me. Her elemental hadn't been in her long enough to pick up more than a trace of humanity. It was like erasing a shadow. This . . . wasn't like that. *Full person*, yes. Very full." Her eyes sought the passing shoreline. "The god grieved for the fate of His creature."

Did her hands feel stained with that fate? "It was seven lives deep, by my count, however short some were, and had grown dark and twisted. I don't think any other rider could have healed it by that stage. Not even by all our god's contriving."

"This, I saw." She turned back to him. "Your demon is much, much deeper, but not dark. She glows, like colored lanterns in a vast winding cavern."

Des had been seeing nothing in that moment of demon-destruction, like a child hiding its head under a blanket from night terrors. But if Chio had been watching over the white god's shoulder, nothing would have been hidden from her. It was probably well such moments were short, so that the gods could return their saints to the world still sane. Mostly.

Chio's curious look across at Pen grew grave, unblinking. "What do you grieve for so hard, Learned?"

Oh. So it wasn't just Des that she'd seen into, or Merin and Ree.

He shrugged in discomfort. "In time, most of us become orphans, it turns out. The princess-archdivine had been like a second mother to me. And as great a loss, last year." As that bereavement had fallen bare months before the death of his first mother, Pen supposed he had an exact-enough standard of comparison, though he wasn't sure such a balance-scale made any sense, really.

Chio rocked back, absorbing this. Then leaned forward. "That wasn't all, I think?"

Pen made a face, starting to pass this off as nothing more, nothing much. But Chio seemed not the person for lies this morning, neither as saint nor as young woman. Not when he'd just been demanding truths from her.

He took a breath, for resolution. "I had been working hard to make a new career as a Temple physician-sorcerer, to please all who had cared for me. It wasn't that I was not good at it. That would have made it so much easier to quit. Not a failure of skills, but of . . . character, perhaps." He averted Des's beginning fulmination with a hasty, "Or maybe just a mismatch between soul and calling. Serious mismatch. It broke something."

Your heart, I thought, said Des. Her dry tone robbed

the comment of mawkishness. *And I was there. So don't try to tell me lies, either. It was your error in the first place, for imagining you had to save every patient brought before you. . . . Not that you didn't try.*

The failed physician, and the uncanny executioner . . . Chio, he thought, might understand that futile feeling of lives, and deaths, slipping through a grasp oddly well. *Oh.*

Pen rubbed at his forearms, nervously. "I really don't care to speak of it."

"I see that," said Chio. Her head tilted in a concentration upon him that Pen found unnerving. ". . . I believe your demon isn't the only creature our god wishes to keep in this world."

"This . . . I . . . already know. Received that message very clear. On a hillside above Martensbridge, one morning last fall. Which is why I never made it to my investiture ceremony in the Mother's Order that noon."

If you had succeeded in cutting your bloody arms off, you'd have taken me with you, you know, Des grumped. *As I pointed out at the time, but you weren't listening to much of anything by then. Certainly not reason.*

Yes. I apologize. There won't be a repeat.

Best not be. The sense of a peeved *Harumph!* concealing . . . much. Love, Pen suspected.

"And so I'm here," Pen concluded. Whether in Lodi or the world he left unsaid.

"And so you are." A determined nod, as if Chio might share her very considerable spine with him—another birthday gift that could not be turned down. "I'm glad of it."

At the mouth of the main canal, across the basin, the holy procession was assembling. Chio exclaimed, pointing out the archdivine's fancy barge being brought out for the blessing: two stacked rows of oarsmen, bunting and flags, the tiny, glittering figures of prelates and functionaries all in their best finery. Sweet sounds from musicians and a choir on an upper deck carried clearly across the water. Pen wagered he could have elbowed his way to a place aboard if he'd been over there this morning, although by now he thought he'd rather elbow into his bed. Gull Island's orphan floats had presumably already rowed off to join in. He was so fascinated by the shining spectacle, he only turned around when the oarboat swung in for their landing.

Where he discovered that Iserne had not been the only parent up all night waiting for the return of a lost one. Learned Riesta, his back bowed and elbows propped on his knees, sat on the edge of the jetty with his legs dangling over, head nodding.

His face jerked up as their hull scraped against the stone. "Chio!" He scrambled to his feet to march down the water-stairs, hands reaching to help her out of the boat. Pen was left to fend for his own balance, not to mention pay the oarsman.

It was that last addition of the damp flower crown, listing drunkenly atop her head, that pushed Chio's appearance over the line from *disheveled* to *debauched*, Pen decided as he turned and climbed the steps to join them. And her muted grin. His own bleary, squinting eyes and numb face probably just looked wine-sick. In neither case a reassuring sight for an anxious guardian.

"Where have you two *been* all night?" Riesta demanded. His tone was more strangled than thundering.

"Oh, Learned Penric brought me the most splendid Bastard's Eve ever!" Chio told him cheerily. "We walked all over town to the market parties, ate festival food, tracked down the ascendant demon, rescued its rider, and captured a murderer. And I hear Learned Penric revived a robbery victim and reformed a cutpurse, though even the god wasn't entirely sure that last was going to stick." Her sly grin widened as she capped this with, "Also I met a very nice boy, together with his family."

Was she *teasing* the poor man? And not for the first time, judging by his exasperated sigh. "*Chio . . .*"

Pen was acquiring new insight into the relationship between the stodgy Temple functionary and his saint, to be sure. He might have to reclassify Riesta from *forbidding* to *beleaguered*. It was revealing that he didn't even bother to tax Penric on the alarming progression of the night's events. Nor to generate the sorts of wild accusations of him that a girl missing all night might be expected to foster in a paternal mind, which Pen had been braced to counter.

Nor did he offer the least hint that he deemed she could be lying to him, despite her provoking summary. Interesting . . .

Pen thought to add, "There will probably be a city magistrate's inquiry about the murderer, but not until tomorrow. If they want more than the saint's testimony, send them on to me at the curia."

Riesta did not look as if this news helped.

Chio patted Riesta's arm in a consolatory fashion. "I'll give you a proper report on the demon for the Order's files later, I promise. Right now I want a wash-up and a nap."

"Well," he said, testiness overborne, "Well, see you do . . ."

Penric walked beside them as they started up the path beside the access canal to the chapterhouse, feeling vaguely that as escort he was obliged to at least see the young lady to her door.

Riesta eyed him sideways. "You survived, I see."

He meant the question ironically, but Pen thought of how close Merin's knife had come. The nick on his arm had dried; the bloodstain on his sleeve could be treated later. He answered less ironically, "Barely. But it seems I had a good protector."

Chio smirked, fiddling with the feathered mask dangling from her hand.

"It was a miracle my whites avoided the canals all night," he added. Not that this had saved them—they would still require extensive laundry and repairs.

Chio made a moue, and stopped, the two men perforce with her. "You sound so disappointed, Learned Penric. Is there no one to uphold the reputation of Lodi and our lord of chaos? We should give the god an offering on His day. Hand me your mask."

Pen did so, confused. Or stupid with fatigue, whichever.

She turned him to face her, adjusting his stance. He was just opening his mouth to inquire her meaning when she placed both hands on his chest and gave him a vigorous shove. Over the cut-stone bank and into the waters, backward, with a vast splash. His surprised yelp cut off with a gargle.

Spluttering up through clinging weeds, he found his feet, to discover the water here was only chest-deep.

Des! Why didn't you defend us?

This has to be the cleanest canal we've passed all night. Besides, how is a mere demon to stand up to the will of a saint?

You feign demure *badly, you know.* Or else she was still smug over that *vast, lamplit cavern* compliment, and had switched sides.

Never, she promised him. *Are you awake now? Invigorated? Cheered up . . . ?*

Pen looked up to find Chio's laughing face, and Riesta's resigned one, leaning over the bank. The hands that had pushed him in now extended to help him out. . . . And wasn't that a fitting metaphor for their god.

Helplessly, he laughed back, and took them.

THE ORPHANS
OF RASPAY

THE ORPHANS
OF RASPAY

THE SICKENING *crunch* threw Penric out of his coffin-sized bunk and onto the deck of his scarcely larger cabin, and from deep sleep into frantically confused consciousness in the same moment. Blackness all around him; he called up his dark-sight from his demon Desdemona without thought, though there was nothing new to see in this narrow space. Everything that could move had been tied down in the last day, as the ship had pitched and rolled its way through an unexpected tempest that had blown them, well, he hoped the crew knew where, because he certainly did not.

The horrible motions and the groaning of the ship's timbers had tamed, which explained how he'd finally fallen asleep despite his nausea and alarm. It did not explain the shouts and cries coming from outside, in a more terrified tenor than the workmanlike bellows of the crew manhandling the ship through the storm. Had they run onto rocks?

Des, what's happening out there?

Her reply was terse. *Pirates.*

In the middle of the night? . . . How could two ships even *find* each other in such murk?

It's morning, she replied. *Apart from that, unhappy chance, I expect.*

Pirates were a known hazard all along the coasts and islands, but more to the north than the south where Pen's ship should have been, just a day or two out from Vilnoc and home. Curse it, he wanted to be *there*. Not dealing with *this*.

He was a Temple sorcerer, possessing the most potent chaos demon he knew of. Long before he'd stepped aboard this modest cargo carrier in Trigonie, he had imagined any number of clever magical defenses against such evil attacks, subtle enough not to reveal his nature and calling to the men on either vessel. He now realized that he had always pictured pirates happening on a bright afternoon, in quiet seas, with a good long time to see the villains *coming*.

Sorcerers, and the chaos demons that gave them their powers, were considered bad luck on a ship, and many captains would not take them aboard at all. Mild-mannered Temple scholar or no, Penric thus routinely traveled incognito when he was forced to take a sea passage. Pirates, he expected, would give even shorter shrift to the hazard of him: roughly the distance from the thwart to the heaving water.

Oh, yes, agreed Des grimly. Who, with her two centuries of experiences, knew the risks firsthand. Pen fought against the panicked memories flooding his mind from one of her unluckier prior possessors. He had plenty of current panic on his plate to attend to.

Because mixed among the voices crying in Adriac and Cedonian out there, he heard shouts in Roknari. Pen rubbed his sleep-numbed face and scrambled up, listening harder.

No seamen loved sorcerers, but the Roknari heretics, who abjured the fifth god Whom Penric served as a seminary-trained divine, considered all who worshipped Him an abomination, to be either forcibly converted to their foursquare faith, or inventively executed. Not that Pen *worshipped* his god exactly; their relationship was more complicated than that. Pirates, Pen tried to encourage himself, were unlikely to be passionate about the fine points of theology. On the other hand, they were a superstitious lot. If there was anything more likely than his sorcery to result in him being summarily tossed overboard, with or without torture first—

Attempted torture, Des put in with a snarl.

—it was certainly Pen's calling as a divine of the white god. Both of which would be revealed by his possessions: the garb of his Order, his Temple braids, the letters and documents he carried, all packed away tight in a sealed chest stuffed under his bunk. Plus the three ancient scrolls he'd picked up in Trigonie, which he hadn't even had a chance to read through yet, let alone translate, of which pirates were unlikely to recognize the value at all. He shuddered.

Turning, he knocked open the tiny port at the back of his cabin in the stern of the ship, admitting a leaden illumination. He didn't think his shoulders would squeeze through, nor had he the least desire to anticipate their assailants' murderous actions by throwing *himself* overboard, but, holding his wooden case up to the aperture, he thought it just might fit. Still he hesitated.

Des, impatiently, ran a line of hot disorder around under the lid, sealing it more firmly. *It's more likely to float than we are. Get* rid *of it.*

Thuds like sledgehammer blows against his locked door made him flinch and shove it through. *Lord god Bastard, Fifth and White, if ever you loved me, let this find me again somehow.* More prayer than spell, surely. Too much noise to hear a splash, though the cries out on the ship were dying away.

Who had won? was a question answered by the brutish banging. As the door burst inward he turned and fell to his knees, something between supplication, surrender, and the thought that if the pirate came in swinging, his aim would be too high.

Pen blinked in the dingy gray light framing the hammerer's broad shoulders, and reminded himself that he could see out better than the man could see in. Confirmed at once when the pirate said, in a voice of surprise, "A woman?"

For once, Penric did not rush to correct this annoying misapprehension, though Des muttered, *Being female's not as much help as you'd think.* Electrum hair shining in a mussed queue, blue eyes, fine features, a lean build that might at a glance be mistaken for slender; the error had been made before. His pale coloration, common in the mountainous cantons where he'd been born, was rare here in the lands of Cedonia, Adria, and the Carpagamon islands surrounding this sea. In any case, the man did not at once try to bash in his blond head.

Which allowed Pen time to fling up his convincingly ink-stained hands and cry in common Adriac, "I'm a scribe!" The *Don't hurt me, I'm valuable! And harmless!* was implied, if the fellow wasn't too drunk on violence to care.

If he was, Pen readied a disabling attack on his nerves, regretting, not for the first time, the theological, no, divine proscription upon using Des's magic to kill. Directly. Not that it would help much even if Pen could slay them all, because then what? He was lost on the sea in a ship no single man, even a trained sailor, could manage by himself. If only he could stay alive until they reached some shore, although preferably not in the Roknar Archipelago, it would be a different tale.

. . . What a strange moment he had come to that he was *wishing* for slavers.

The hammer man grabbed him by the shoulder and dragged him through the cabin door and out onto the still-rolling deck, though waves were no longer washing up on it. As his knees scraped the boards, Pen was glad he'd worn tunic and trousers to bed, though he was sorry his feet were bare. The gloom of his cabin gave way to a steely dawn, the ashy lid of the clouds, directionless, matched by the slate of the sea. A second fellow leaned around his comrade to stare at their catch.

"No, it's a man," the door-breaker corrected himself, in a tone of disappointment. Pen kept his beseeching hands raised, hoping this discovery wouldn't just result in the hammer swinging around for a blow. "Of a sort."

"Father's balls and Mother's tits," the second man swore, rudely. In Adriac, they were both speaking an island dialect of Adriac, so where had those Roknari shouts come from? Penric's own ship's crew had mostly spoken Cedonian, and he wasn't hearing them anymore. "If that skinny arse was ten years younger, it'd fetch a *fortune*."

Twenty years, Pen thought irritably. It didn't take much of a stretch to manage an authentic quaver: "Spare my hands!" Along with eyesight, hands were a scribe's main tool and value. He wasn't going to even *suggest* his eyes.

"Hah. Behave, or we'll cut 'em off," the hammer man threatened, fulfilling Pen's assessment. He bent and undid Pen's belt, shoved the belt-knife sheath into his own trouser band, and efficiently used the leather strap to hitch Pen's wrists painfully behind his back. Pen barely mourned the loss of the knife, slim and sharp— more for mending quills than sticking into people. Stripped naked, he'd still be the least disarmed man on this vessel.

Vessels, he emended, finally getting a chance to look around.

The pirate ship was smaller and slimmer than the cargo coaster, jammed up with its starboard bow grappled to the coaster's midships. One mast to their two, yet probably faster, given that most of the coaster's sails were lashed down to deal with the storm, its hull lumbering with a bulk lading of timber and cheap ceramics. Their attacker wasn't a military oarship, anyway, nor some government-appointed privateer. It had the grubby look of a typical all-trades Carpagamon-islands build, suitable for a bit of fishing, a bit of transport . . . a bit of opportunistic theft and lucrative kidnapping. Not the sort of arrogant venture that seized valuables from some rich merchanter, then sank the target and its passengers to be done with the trouble. Granted, such ships were much better defended. Pen found himself hoping for more-frugal pirates.

Still-wet blood smeared the damp deck here and there, but no dead bodies. Valueless corpses already stripped and tossed overboard? Up at the bow, the survivors of the crew, which by Des's head count and to Pen's relief seemed to be most of them, were being shoved together and secured by a larger and presumably more vicious group of attackers.

His census was not done. Pen sighed inwardly and thought, *Des, Sight*.

A couple of fresh ghosts, still bearing the crisp if colorless forms of life and agitated by their deaths, whirled around the deck. Pen could not tell which sides they had been on. He mentally readied a prayer for their succor, though even as he watched one was drawn up and away to the *Elsewhere* by its god—the Father, Pen judged by a wintry tinge that he almost expected to trail a gust of snow in the damp, warm air. The other spirit seemed more lost.

The Bastard was, among many other things, the god of leftovers, last home to all the souls that no other of the Five would take. Criminals, executioners, orphans, whores, bastards, sorcerers, some artists and musicians, those with odd loves, and, yes, pirates. (On the whole, Pen much preferred to deal with prostitutes, with whom he got along *fine*.) Theologically, a divine of the Bastard was obliged to care for them all. He didn't have to *like* them all, fortunately. Just fulfill his duties to them, if no one else could.

The dead could be sundered from the gods in two— no, three ways. A soul might refuse the union, through fear or hate or despair. Rarely, a soul might be so rank and spoiled from the sins of its life that even the Bastard wouldn't take it. Or a soul might become mazed in that brief liminal space between life and the life beyond: looking back too hard to look forward, disoriented and confused, or trapped by uncanny events—Penric had untangled a few of those, memorably.

There was nothing especially uncanny about this darting ghost. He seemed to be a bandy-legged youth, late teens or early twenties, wearing the memory of the clothes he'd just died in: a sailor's trousers and tunic that might have come from either crew. It was disorientation and despair that mired him here, in Pen's reasonably practiced diagnosis.

Pen was already on his knees, though his hands, tied behind his back, could not sign the tally of the gods. He could tap his fingers to his thumb, and did, mutely naming a deity for each digit. He dared not speak the prayers for the dead aloud, revealing his calling to his captors. But such eulogies were mainly for mourners. Silent speech would do for the gods. And for the dead.

The ghost drew near as he began to unwind the words

in his head, his tongue moving behind closed lips. More a warm-up than anything else yet, till he could guess what this snag was. The boy just looked bewildered. Pen switched from Adriac to the Cedonian language and started again. Still no dice. The boy's attention tightened as it dawned on him that Pen was the only person here who could *see* him. Though Pen could not hear him; the bodiless mouth pushed no sounds through the air. But its shapings gave Pen the clue he sought.

Pen switched to Roknari. His Roknari accent was a little archaic, Des had informed him, though intelligible to those commanding either the high or the vile versions of the language. *Ah. He's a Roknari Quadrene.* Refused by the Father of Winter or the Son of Autumn, the preferred and expected gods, so presumably one of the pirates. *What are you?* the boy's wide eyes cried, taking in the peculiar spiritual aura of the blond stranger who held a demon. Which with Des, Pen knew, likely looked fathoms deep.

"If you were going to hold to your foursquare faith," Pen found himself whispering aloud, "you should have picked a different line of work. Or the other way around. Too late now. The white god invites you—though not for long."

Pen could feel, though not see, never see, that huge Presence, somewhere on the other side of the air. So could Des, for she retreated within him, muttering, *I wish at least you wouldn't* bait *Them.*

Not my doing, Des. Death opened a door to the gods as nothing else could—except for saints, Pen supposed, which he certainly was not. The gods in turn were the only force that could destroy chaos demons, once they had anchored themselves in some living being, hence Des's swallowed fear.

Sometimes, Des, I actually have to do the job I vowed to do. Though not for the Temple.

Yes, yes . . . she grumbled, but—valiantly, Pen thought—held her powers available to him in the teeth of this divine gale. She had grown worlds better at this in the thirteen years he'd held her. Confident in his protection?

"It will be all right," Pen told the boy, on exactly no evidence. Pen wasn't sure if staring fiercely at people until they believed him was a skill of divines or of dissemblers, or if there was a difference. Point was, someone who'd let other people tell him what to think all his young life might need permission to change even at the last gasp. And this one wasn't going to get more chances now to grow into his gods, was he? "It will be very well. Five gods bless you on your journey."

Do they? the distraught boy mouthed.

"Yes," said Pen. "Though only one holds out His hand, I promise His grip is sure, and will not drop you into any imagined hell."

Into strangeness, yes; Pen had seen hints enough of the strangeness of the world on the other side of reality. One of his seminary masters had argued that it was as impossible to truly grasp as for a child still in the womb to imagine its breathing life beyond the pains of birth. Pen still meditated occasionally and uneasily on that metaphor.

Pen wanted a year to instruct, to counter whatever

lies the Quadrene teachers had instilled in the youth that were dividing him from his choosing-if-not-chosen god, but neither of them was going to get it. Yet . . . whatever Pen had so clumsily said and done, it must have been enough to tilt the necessary moment of assent, since ghost and Presence disappeared abruptly from his Sight.

Pen didn't even get a holy pat on the head for his pains. This wasn't saint-work. Pen hadn't, couldn't, channel a god; he was otherwise already inhabited. Arguing with a human on the god's behalf, now, that he might do. He let the visions go with a huff of relief.

The respite was short-lived. He'd taken his attention away from the world of matter for a little too long. Evidently thinking his captive had been gibbering in hysteria, hammer-man slapped Pen's face, fortunately with his open hand and not his weapon—which in the seeping light turned out to be a rusty old Cedonian army-issue war hammer, Pen noted dizzily—and grabbed him by the scruff of his tunic to drag him along the deck. Pen let himself be dragged, trying to reorient himself.

"What have you got yourself there?" another rough voice asked.

"White rabbit." The grip shook Pen, cruelly amused. "Says he's a scribe. What d'you want done with him?"

"Could be a prize. Or dinner. Drop him in the small hold with the other virgins."

"Is that safe?"

A thick hand checked the security of Pen's looped belt, lifting his arms up in ways they weren't meant to bend. Pen yelped, wishing he were acting. "What's he going to do with his hands tied behind his back? We'll deal with him later."

Safe for who? Pen wondered as he was hoisted over the rail by his two finders and flung down onto the deck of the other ship. He had a quick, swinging impression of mast and boom, spars and ropes; then a heavy wooden lattice set in the deck was heaved out of the way, and he was chucked into a dark, square hole. Feet first, thankfully.

He plummeted only a little more than his own height, but without his arms for balance he landed crookedly and fell sideways to smack into a bulkhead, then flop to the floor. He lay for a moment catching his breath as the lattice thudded back into place overhead, a black weave set with graying squares. The dark smelled of old timber and tar, fish and rancid oil, spilled stale wine, with a more recent overlay of piss and sour vomit. He'd been in worse oubliettes, though not lately.

More importantly, he wasn't alone.

. . . Or less alone than he usually wasn't. He had only to want his dark-sight, and it was there, stripping away the shadow. *Thank you, Des*.

Any time. Her curiosity seemed equal to his own; her alarm, now their captors were out of hammer range and the soul-harvesting gods had decamped, less.

Grunting, Pen heaved himself upright and rested one shoulder against the bulkhead. In the corner of the space, as far from him as they could creep—which was only about six feet—two small figures cowered.

Oh. Children. Pen started to ease to the opposite corner, realized it was the designated chamber pot, and stayed where he was. Des, at his wisp of thought, unloosed the straps around his wrists, and he retrieved and redonned his belt. He propped his back against the wall more comfortably, stretching out his long legs, and took stock.

Two girls. Perhaps ten and eight? Sisters, possibly, though resemblances were hard to gauge from youth-rounded features. Their clothing was ordinary, calf-length tunics with dyed braided belt ties, simple but carefully sewn; little jackets, leather sandals. His summation of their medical state was reflexive, still hard to resist for all that he had disavowed the calling of physician. They were parched, bruised, tense, hungry; but without broken bones, cuts, or deeper hurts. *It could be worse.*

It still could.

Pen licked his own dry lips, gentled his voice. Tried Adriac. "Well, hello there, you two."

They flinched and clamped each other tighter, staring wildly at him.

Cedonian. "I won't hurt you." Still no help. He repeated his greeting in Darthacan, and then Ibran, which won a twitch. All right, one more . . .

"Hello, there." Adding the endings in high Roknari that suggested *teacher to student*, he continued, "My name is Master Penric. My rank is scribe. What are your names?"

Their frozen grips upon each other scarcely slackened, though as the silence stretched the older proffered, a bit convulsively, "I can write. A little."

A social effort? Claiming value for herself? In any

case, the brave venture into speech should be rewarded. "That's very good."

Not to be outdone, the smaller one put in, "I can draw."

Sisters, no doubt of it. Pen's lips twitched up in a smile that wasn't even false. "So what should I call you?"

The older swallowed and said, "My name is Lencia Corva."

"I'm Seuka," said the younger, frowned, and added, "Corva."

Seuka was a Roknari name, Lencia was Ibran, and Corva . . . Corva was interesting. Their accents were revealing; not the pure Roknari of the Archipelago, but the melodious variant of the Roknari princedoms that capped the great peninsula of Ibra on its northern shore. The girls did manage the polite endings that placed Pen's claimed rank as higher than their own. A Roknari princeling would have addressed a scribe as a servant. Or, Pen was grimly reminded, as a slave.

In the growing light from the grating, Pen noted cropped brown curls on the older one's head; tighter, redder curls on the other's, their springy unruliness prisoned by a grubby ribbon at her nape. Lightish eyes on each, though he could not make out the color quite yet. Both skinny, but not starved despite recent hunger.

"Did the pirates get you, too?" asked Lencia.

"I'm afraid so." Pen leaned his head, which unsurprisingly ached, back against the wooden bulkhead. "I was sick from the storm, and then I was asleep. I was supposed to be sailing to Vilnoc in Orbas." He wondered if it would reassure them to mention the wife who awaited him there, with luck not-yet-anxiously. *No*. He would keep Nikys, and every other vulnerability, clutched tight to his chest for now. Though tossing out these little verbal breadcrumbs as though trying to attract birds seemed to be fruitful.

"We were going to find Papa in Lodi," said Lencia. "But then everything went wrong."

"He was *supposed* to be in Agenno, but he wasn't," said Seuka, sounding peeved.

Agenno was a major port on the coast of Carpagamo, near the border of Saone; about the halfway point in the eight hundred east-west miles that separated the Ibran peninsula and Lodi. These girls were farther from their birthplace than Pen was from his.

Hm, said Des. *A hundred years ago, "Corva" was an Ibran nickname for a whore. Crow-girl. Not wholly rude. Doesn't exactly square with a papa. I suppose it could have become a surname since then . . .*

"Master Corva of Lodi, then?" Pen led on.

"No, our papa is Master Ubi Getaf," said Lencia, with earnest precision. "He's a merchant from Zagosur."

Which was the royal capital of Ibra, and its main entrepôt.

"Taspeig wrote to him after Mama died, but the letter just came back saying he'd gone trading to Agenno. So Taspeig tried to take us there, but at the factor's post they said he'd gone on to Lodi, and she wouldn't go any farther."

Taspeig was another Roknari name, by derivation at least. "Was she a relative?"

Seuka shook her head, the wad of curls moving with

it. "No, she was Mama's servant. We don't have any relatives. Mama said that's 'cause she was an orphan."

Pen had a distinct sense of his boots sinking into a bog, deeper and deeper.

"Papa gave Mama a little house in Raspay," Seuka went on. "I liked it there. We slept out on the porch above the back garden when it was hot. But the landlord said we couldn't stay there by ourselves without Mama."

Raspay was a modest port town in the princedom of Jokona, on the western side of the peninsula, right. A merchant based in Zagosur might easily make it the terminus of some personal coastal trade route. "Did your papa have no family in Zagosur?"

Lencia scowled. "Too much. He has a wife and children there. He wouldn't ever take us to meet them, and Mama said *she* didn't know, and we weren't to pester."

She being, presumably, the legitimate wife. Some such women were tolerant of husbandly by-blows. Most were not. So if not orphans outright, the sisters were half-orphans for certain; bastards by Ibran law, and by Jokonan as well if the second wife wasn't official.

And, of course, they were here. As he was. Was propinquity a theological hazard?

"So, Jokona," sighed Pen. "Are you Quadrenes or Quintarians?"

They tensed, looking anxiously at each other. "Which are you?" said Lencia after a cautious moment.

"Quintarian," said Pen firmly. "Very common in my country." Countries, he supposed. He had traveled far from the cold cantons in late years.

Two sets of narrow shoulders relaxed. "Papa is

Quintarian," Lencia offered. "Mama said we could be Quintarian at home, but had to be Quadrene outside. So . . . I don't know . . . partly?"

Pen spared a moment of fresh loathing for the sectarian idiocy that made even children afraid.

Well. A trained divine and sorcerer seemed a generous gift to fellow wards of the white god, here in this hold. Though surely any other decent adult would have taken up responsibility for the helpless . . .

The gods are parsimonious, murmured Des, slyly quoting his own text back at him. A slight sense of preening.

So it seems. Just once, Pen thought glumly, he'd like to *get* an answer to prayers, instead of being *delivered* as one.

And where are we going now? If his bodiless demon had possessed any eyes but his own, Pen thought they'd be crinkled in amusement.

Lodi. Evidently. He could feel the new weight dropping onto his shoulders like baggage onto a packhorse. *Somehow.*

Clunks and clanks vibrated through the bulkhead, and the thumps of footfalls. Calls in Adriac and Roknari filtered down through the grating—bellowed orders and acknowledgements, not screams. The ship surged sideways, evidently unmooring from the cargo coaster. Flapping canvas snapped taut, and the ship heeled in response.

Des, what can you make out? It was past time to take a wider survey of his situation and what resources he had.

They seem to have split their crew. Taking the coaster whole as a prize, I daresay. I imagine they will travel in convoy to whatever port they use to sell off their captives and goods.

Which port was an important question. In times of war, combatants on all sides would haul captured enemies home to be ransomed or enslaved, depending on their rank. But though conflict among the realms bounding this sea was endemic, Pen hadn't heard rumor of any open warfare this season. Their pirates seemed to be strictly a venture of commerce, homegrown.

The blend of languages in the crew was telling. Adriac-speaking Carpagamo wrestled with the Roknari for hegemony over the long chain of mountainous islands that ran north and swung around to the east, with a gap of open sea before the Archipelago proper. The islands closest to the mainland were held firmly by Carpagamo, though sometimes Adria or Darthaca muscled in. The islands at the looping tip were usually held by some Roknari prince. In between was a debatable stretch that went back and forth, or was left as a neutral buffer if times were peaceful. This mixed lot of sailors had to be from one of the often-brutalized buffer islands, and Pen could only wish Quadrenes and Quintarians could be so cooperative for better ends.

Umelan, Desdemona's—eventual—sixth human possessor, had been a war victim, kidnapped from her Archipelago island home by a Darthacan military raid and sold south to Lodi. Continentals captured by the Roknari were sold north to the Archipelago. In both directions, the scheme worked the same way to tame captives, separating them from families, communities, languages and religions, dropping them down off-balance in strange friendless places. There they would have no choice but to cooperate in the theft of their labor, while working to scrape together what funds they could to buy their way out, or hope to be granted freedom as an act of charity by their bond-holders. Umelan had received such a boon in the will of Des's fifth possessor, the courtesan Mira of Lodi. The receipt of Mira's demon at her death had been less planned.

Umelan's experiences were a century out of date, and in general Pen did not enjoy dipping into her unhappy memories, or, worse, having them invade his dreams, but she was a resource of information better than any scroll. Place her in the plus column.

(A sour snort, he thought, from that one-twelfth layer of Desdemona that was Umelan. He mentally offered her a humble salute in return. She had, after all, gifted him with her language, for all that he had refined his command subsequently by his own studies.)

A buffer-island port would host small merchants and traders from all over, so captives might be sold either north or south. The coaster's men and Penric would be earmarked for north. It was a coin toss whether being enslaved on the galleys or in the mines was more lethal, but either was to be vigorously avoided. Female captives commonly were given over to the same domestic duties they would have been performing at home: spinning, weaving, gardening, cleaning, cooking, childcare. Childbearing. What fate was planned for these Jokonan girls was a puzzle, though the fact that they were being kept separate and relatively unharmed was probably not due to kindness.

In any case, the need to rid themselves quickly of their perishable prizes, plus the division of their crew, meant that the islander pirates would be heading straight for port. Pen could not hope for some new clash to turn out the other way and lead to his rescue.

"Is your papa a rich merchant?" he asked the Corva sisters. "Do you think he would ransom you, if word were taken to him in Lodi?" If Master Getaf was still in Lodi, among other uncertainties. But promise of a ransom greater than their sale price as slaves could be a major protection for them. Possibly safer than hooking up with a displaced sorcerer on the run.

They looked at each other in surprise, so this wasn't a thought they'd already had. Hm.

"I . . . maybe not *very* rich," said Lencia.

"He brought us presents," Seuka offered, in an equally hesitant tone.

And had housed a long-time mistress, but unless Master Getaf kept a family in every port, maybe just the one. Hold the ransom notion aside for now.

Trying to offload our baggage already? murmured Des.

Trying to think sensibly. This hasn't been a good morning.

I could sink this ship in five minutes.

I know you could. Please refrain, at least till we're on dry land. Pen considered this. *I might let you have it then.*

For a present? Des was amused, contemplating this chance at chaos.

You are not my mistress. Thankfully. For all that she

was the permanent extra party in his marriage bed, and any other. Thank all the gods for tolerant, wise Nikys. He tried not to think too much about Nikys, because the worry would make him frantic and stupid.

There were enough other distractions. He cast a "Pardon me, please," over his shoulder at the girls, and turned to hunch over the latrine corner. Some seepage at the hold's seams had reduced the liquid level, which was why the pitching of the ship hadn't spread it all over the floor, but still, ugh. *Let's do something about this mess. What's underneath?*

. . . Bilges and ballast.

Too bad it wasn't pirate hammocks. *Open us some drainage. Quietly.*

Des applied some chaos, Penric supplied some order, or at least aim, and a ragged hole in the deck dropped out. Aware of his audience, he relieved himself as discreetly as he could.

Sanitation improved, he supposed the next problem he could actually address was clean drinking water. Which was a trivial task, except for the lack of a cup. With the air so damp he could spin water off his fingers, catching the trickle in his mouth or other receptacle, but that created the problem of concealing his magic from his hold-mates. He had no idea what wild tales they had imbibed about sorcerers in Quadrene lands, when Quintarians weren't much better informed, but there was a decided possibility that their first response to his gifts would be panic.

Are there other prisoners aboard? he asked Des.

The dizzying doubled vision of her demonic

perceptions came to him as though they were his own, and Pen wondered if he would someday no longer be able tell them apart. The boundary between his will and her magic was already invisible whenever he was in too much of a hurry to take care to distinguish.

Another hold, aft, held half-a-dozen distressed people, some injured. Not from Pen's ship; aside from him, the captured crew had been kept aboard their own vessel. The pirate ship's own crew was scarcely more numerous than their prisoners at this point, though they must have started out with a crowd of rowdies to be sure of outnumbering their targets. His coaster would appear to have been the second ship seized on this venture, stretching the brigands' reserves.

"How long have you two been in here?" Pen asked the Corva sisters. "What ship were you on, and where was it taken? It couldn't have been a large one." Lions might bring down great oxen, but feral dogs had to scrape a living from rabbits, mice, and carrion.

Lencia shook her head. "Taspeig set us on a big ship at Agenno, that was supposed to go all the way to Lodi, but it had to put in at another port on account of woodworm. So we found a littler ship that meant to go there, that would take us on the promise that Papa would pay. Except some other passenger paid them to go north to some island first, and that's where the pirates came."

Opportunistic chance, or might that rich-seeming passenger have been a stalking horse, selecting a bite-sized target and leading it into ambush? If so, that was one clever son of a bitch Pen might attend to later himself, if he could.

"The captain fought, but he was killed"—Seuka shivered, looking sickened—"and the rest surrendered pretty quick."

"That was . . . six days ago?" said Lencia uncertainly, swallowing. "And then there was the storm. I don't know where we are now."

"You two have been having quite an adventure," said Pen, trying to sound friendly without encouraging the teary breakdown that evoking these memories threatened.

Lencia scowled. "I don't think I like adventure."

"I have to agree," said Pen, offering a wry grin. He rubbed his nape under his queue, rose, and stepped into the stretched blocks of sunlight now angling through the grid. The clouds were clearing, or else they had sailed out of their cover. The sisters both stared up at him, lips parting.

The easterly slant of the light shafts was obvious at this hour; the ship was therefore heading roughly north, allowances made for tacking against the wind or currents. Not a surprise. Pen tried shouting upward in common Adriac, "Hoi! We need some drinking water down here! And food!" As long as he was at it. "Hoi!" He would rather drink the remarkably pure water Des produced than anything that came out of a ship's cask, but it might come with a cup he could purloin, to share.

Pen hastily tucked his hands behind his back, as if still bound, when a face loomed at the grating. Its stubble might be on either a Carpagamon with a recent beard-trim or a Roknari who'd missed his chance to shave. The conundrum wasn't solved when the fellow merely grunted, but in a little while a stick of hard bread was dropped down through the grating, followed by a leather water bottle with, blessing, a wooden cup tied to it by a rawhide cord.

This was evidently the routine method for sustaining the prisoners, for neither girl looked startled, but Lencia pounced on the bread as it bounced off the deck, then glared up at Pen in fright as if she imagined him snatching it from her. He secured the water bottle instead, to her clear dismay.

"You two can share the bread," he said with an easy smile. "I daresay I've eaten more recently than you." This wouldn't be a charity he could afford for long, given Des's drain on his body, but it served to set the tone. He sat down across from them with the water bottle, freed the cup, popped the cork, and tested a taste. Every bit as murky and vile as he'd posited, ugh. Knees bent up for a shield, he set about some sleight of hand, concealing the trickle into the cup from the air. Seuka watched him, licking dry lips. Her eyes widened in surprise when he handed the first cupful across to her. She guzzled hastily, then hesitated partway down and glanced at Lencia.

"You can drink up. There's more," said Pen, and she promptly did. He alternated handing the cup across to each sister till they stopped reaching, hoping that they wouldn't notice they'd each drunk more than the bottle could hold. Overheating from the exertion, he finished with a cupful for himself and laid the leather skin aside. Maybe he could use its noxious contents later for flushing the latrine corner.

A sound of gnawing, like rats at a wainscoting, filled the hold for a while as the two girls divided the dry bread. While they were working at it, he leaned his head back against the bulkhead, closed his eyes, and took a quick survey of the number of actual rats lurking aboard. Hm, only a few. Destroying vermin was an allowable and efficient sink for Des's chaos when uphill magic, creating order, produced, as always, a greater amount of disorder to dump. Somewhere. Or he could pass out from the fever generated, usually not helpful. Downhill destructive magic was less costly. . . . Albeit not on a ship in the middle of a trackless sea. Pen opened his eyes to find both girls staring at him again, though no longer in fear. More like fascination.

Seuka pointed to the patches of light falling on the deck, squaring up as the sun climbed toward noon and the sky turned blue. "Sit over there," she commanded him.

"I'm not cold," he said, a trifle confused.

"No, it's . . ." She waved her hands around her head, and pointed to his. "Do it again."

His brief bafflement was alleviated when Des chuckled, *It's your hair, Pen. Works on females of all ages*.

Nikys likewise, he was reminded, who'd made him grow out his queue to twice its former length, so it wasn't as if he could complain at this attention. He scooted over to a sun patch and sat cross-legged, wryly angling for the best backlight. *It's not magic, curse it*.

Hey, it enchanted us, the first time we ever looked up at you on that dismal roadside in the cantons. Where Ruchia, Des's latest prior possessor, had lain dying.

I thought it was mainly the decided lack of other volunteers, he grumbled. *I was a skinny, spotty, awkward youth.*

Who took our hand and said Yes to us. And to our god.

That had been an unexpected codicil. But the corners of his lips edged up in memory regardless.

His stray smile emboldened the girls, or maybe they were revitalized by the food and water. In this better light, he saw their eyes were a bright coppery brown, suggesting a measure of Roknari blood. They inched closer to him across the boards. "Can I touch it?" said Seuka, already stretching out a small hand.

"Yes, go ahead," Pen sighed, wrapping his arms around his bent-up knees and propping his forehead on them. For his privacy and theirs, equally. Touching quickly turned to finger-combing, as one hand became two and then four, and his hair tie was made away with. Then, inevitably, braiding. And rebraiding, because of course everyone wanted a turn.

Somewhere, there was an important boundary between calming their fears, and keeping enough respect that they would obey his orders in an emergency instantly and without question. He wished he knew where it fell. Though as pacification ploys went, letting them groom him like a pony cost only a little of his dignity.

And it's rather soothing, Des observed.

Hush. But his eyes were slipping closed as his head grew heavier.

He jerked upright before he started snoring, though not before he started drooling. Rubbing at the wet patch on his trouser knee, he said, "That's enough, now," and retreated to his propping bulkhead. His handmaids frowned at him in disappointment, but shuffled back to their own claimed corner.

"When I was being dragged aboard," he began again, "I caught a glimpse of another hold, aft." And he needn't mention that this survey had not been with his eyes. "It had six prisoners in it. Not sailors. Are they other passengers from your ship?"

"Maybe?" said Lencia. "There was only our ship taken, and then yours."

"Are they all right?" asked Seuka, freshly apprehensive.

"Alive, at least. There was an old couple, roughed up. A fellow who seemed to be with them had a broken arm."

Lencia nodded. "He's their son. He tried to defend them, but the pirate hit him with his hammer. It made a horrible sound."

Ah, the war hammer again; it must be a favorite of its wielder. The son, himself middle-aged, was lucky it wasn't his skull broken. In any case, not three people Pen could count on in a fight, or to help sail the ship.

"Another middle-aged man, portly."

"That was the merchant from Adria," said Seuka. "He was nice. We asked him if he'd ever met Papa, but he said no." She vented a glum sigh.

"Another older man, skinny. Dyspeptic ... um, grouchy," Pen amended his bookish vocabulary, and they brightened with recognition.

Probably an effect of his worms, murmured Des.

Well, there's some more vermin for you, in a pinch.

An impression of a tongue stuck out in disgust.

"Oh, Pozeni," said Lencia. "The captain told us he was a scribe from Carpagamo, but as the pirates were grabbing him he was crying that he was a divine of the Father, and they'd better watch out."

"So . . . which was the true tale? Do you know?"

Lencia wrinkled her nose. "I think he was a scribe, and was just trying not to be murdered."

"Fair enough." Pozeni might be fit enough to help sail the ship; probably not a hand for a brawl, if it came to that. "There was one other man. Cut up, feverish, weak from blood loss."

"Yes, he was the other Adriac merchant. Partner to the fat fellow, I think. He tried to fight." Lencia hunched at the brutal memory. "He held them off for a little, but then they got him down and were really mad. I thought they'd killed him."

Pen had been disoriented in the moment, but his own quick surrender was beginning to seem a tad craven to his own eyes.

Not to mine, put in Des. *Even your lumpish army brother-in-law is in favor of living to fight another day*.

And it was a measure of . . . something, that Pen could actually *wish* for Adelis Arisaydia to hand. Though *What would Adelis do?* was likely not a very useful model for Pen.

In any case, with the exception of the scribe it was plain the occupants of the other hold were mature persons of property, poor prospects as slaves but promising for ransom. No doubt why they were sequestered together. So they didn't need rescuing exactly; they would be invited to rescue themselves, at a cost painful in purse rather than body.

Pen considered whose name he might cry for ransom. Not Duke Jurgo; that would suggest too high a price. General Arisaydia likewise, besides being much too near to Nikys. His best bet was the archdivine of Orbas, who had sent him despite his protests on this ill-fated errand in the first place and thus deserved the debt. Well . . . all right, the archdivine of Trigonie's request for the loan of Penric to examine a potential candidate for Temple sorcerer had been a legitimate call upon Pen's skills. The dozen administrative chores both archdivines tacked on *As long as you're going to be there, eh?* had been more irksome.

Pen could easily feign to be a favored scribe in his home curia; his name should be enough to alert his superior to his ploy. Maybe? It was a delicate balance, to suggest a ransom high enough to outweigh his profit as a slave, without running up the total as high as it could go. . . . Which led him in turn to muse upon just what price *would* make his ransomers choke. What was his value to Orbas?

Less than my value in *Orbas*.

Besides, the Temple was always running on a tight budget.

These Jokonan sisters lay outside all such calculations. Pen wondered if he could attach them to his own bill, *One stray scribe, plus two orphan wards of my Order.* It would be tricky to claim the three of them as a set to whatever middlemen bid on them, when the pirates knew very well they were not.

The day dragged. Twice more scant provisions were
dropped down: some hard barley bread, an oddly
generous portion of dried apricots that Pen recognized
as filched from his own former ship's stores. The edges
taken off their appetites, the girls thought to offer back
a portion for their new hold-mate, which due to the
hungry ache in his head Pen now accepted. The leather
bottle was raised and lowered refilled. In the dark bilges
below, a stray rat quietly died as the price of Pen's pure
water shared around.

When the light dwindled, Pen, in place of any too-
revealing anecdotes about himself, dredged up some
dimly remembered nursery tales from the cantons,
figuring that at least they might be new to his Jokonan
audience. Translated into Roknari terms on the wing,
some of them came out a little oddly, but they seemed
to work nonetheless. The girls ended up creeping close
to the cadences of his voice and finally falling asleep in
a huddle with one head pillowed on each of his not-well-
padded thighs. Which left Pen again leaning back
propped by the bulkhead, speculating that with Des's
aid, rotting out some boards and breaking through the
wall was possible, but pointless as long as they were still
at sea.

Children, he reflected as he shifted uncomfortably,
trying not to dislodge them because surely sleep was a
good restorative, attached themselves much too easily to
any friendly-seeming adult. Though his persona as a
timid scribe did not seem hard to maintain—for all that
he walked through the world trailing a discreet cloud of
destruction and death as the price of his magic, Pen had

never felt less lethal. *Tally: innocent rats, one; murderous slaver pirates, zero*. He rolled his shoulders and tried to doze.

The sun was climbing toward noon next day when the shifting of the ship betrayed more frequent tacking. Feet thumped overhead, and calls. Pen added a few new terms of ship slang to his vocabulary in two tongues. A rattle of stays and lines, the whooshing thuds of folding canvas, odd groans as ropes and timbers took up slack. *Docking*, murmured Des, relieved. The ship rocked one last time and came to a halt too still to be a mere heaving-to, motionless, blessedly motionless.

Port, five gods be thanked. Maybe.

At length, the grid was heaved up, a rope ladder lowered, and the prisoners were invited to climb out of their noisome hole. Pen made sure the sisters went up safely first, then followed close. He squinted around in the hazy warm air.

Their ship had been tied to a stone-and-piling pier, one of a pair jutting from a rambling shore settlement. Out in the tidy harbor created by a low headland, a few fishing boats were moored, and some larger vessels including, disturbingly, a galley with a long row of oar slots; too broad to be a war vessel, but certainly of Roknari build. The dry green slopes cradling the town rose up to rugged mountains, their spines not high enough to bear snow.

The lay of the light told Pen they were on the eastern side of the sea from Cedonia, therefore on a Carpagamon island, or buffer island. As soon as he discovered the name of the place, he could affix it on the map in his head. But . . . it gave him some of the same problems of escape as a ship, except that Des couldn't accidentally sink it.

A couple of the crewmen were looking back out to the horizon, hands shading their eyes, scowling. "Where are the bloody fools?" muttered one. "I thought they'd got ahead of us."

They were one ship, Pen realized. Not two in convoy. His coaster appeared to be missing. Separated in the night, and then . . . ? It didn't look as though the pirates knew, either.

The disheveled prisoners from the other hold were being prodded off across the gangplank. No one had bothered to chain them together, and little wonder. An elderly woman limped between two men scarcely steadier on their feet. A lanky, lugubrious fellow hobbled feverishly, held upright by his very stout companion— the Adriac merchant partners. A last skinny man, presumably the scribe-or-divine the girls had named Pozeni, whined in their wake, protesting to his supremely uninterested guards, one of whom poked at his backside with a short sword and grinned when he yelped.

A pirate dubiously regarded Pen, fit by contrast. "You going to give us any trouble, pretty boy?"

Pen shrugged. "Where's the point? I can't swim back to Orbas."

"True enough." The man smirked, swinging his truncheon to his shoulder and tapping jauntily, then gestured him after the others.

One Corva sister grabbed Pen's hand fore and the other aft as they made their way over the unstable gangplank. He kept hold of them as they veered onto the dock, and they kept hold of him, though Seuka switched her tight grip to his tunic hem. The stout merchant glanced back at them in curiosity. In a few moments the echoing boards underfoot gave way to solid ground at last. Its vague rocking, Pen reassured himself, was an illusion fostered by his time at sea.

Now? murmured Des. *You promised.*

I did, Pen allowed. He'd diverted them both during the fitful night by working out the details, and this needed to be done before they were marched out of range.

Under his guidance, Des ran a line of deep rot through the hull along the starboard side of the keel, bow to stern. On the port side nearest the dock, they unraveled slivers high up on all the stays that held the mainmast in place, leaving a few delicate threads pulled taut. To make sure, Pen ran a thin layer of rot half-through the mast itself, at what he hoped would be the most destructive height. The galley on this ship was rudimentary, a mere sand table under an awning, aft, with coals banked. The supports on one side of the table gave way, spilling sand and hot embers onto the deck. The awning puffed alight.

Truly, nothing increased disorder as efficiently as fire. Pen bit his lip and did not look back.

"Stay close to me if you can," Pen told his small clinging companions. "Let me do the talking. If we do get separated, I'll find you somehow." He hoped this pledge would not turn out to be hollow.

They trudged up the shore to what was obviously, despite this being a pirate haven, a customs shed. Did even pirates not escape taxation? It was a long, low building with a wooden roof, not the more usual stucco and tile, and Pen wondered if it was built of old ship timbers. As the party of prisoners was being chivvied through the door, the first cry of alarm rose from the dock behind.

The man whom Pen took to be the captain, by his age and the way he'd been issuing orders, swiveled around, and he cursed in surprise. "*Now* what . . . !" He glared at the rising plume of smoke, calling, "Totch, get them recorded. Figure the port fees and the guild charges. You two, come with me," and sprinted back down the slope, followed by two of the three guards.

Which might have made a good opportunity for Pen to try a daring escape, except for his baggage. He grimaced and let himself and his charges be prodded by truncheon-man Totch into the shed, blinking as his eyes adjusted to the reduced light. The air inside was hot and close, with a faint reek of stale urine, old blood, and stressed sweat.

The bare space had only a dirt floor, though a few benches were shoved up against one wall. The fat fellow escorted his injured comrade at once to one of these, helping him to gingerly sit, and the old woman was settled on another by her husband and son. A long table with a few stools occupied the other side of the room, though only one stool was currently in use. Despite his rough garb, the islander who sat there ordering his quills and paper had the air of every customs clerk Penric had ever encountered: middle-aged, ink-stained, underpaid and unimpressed. A couple of big armed men, flanking him, took in the new arrivals with experienced eyes, then drifted back to lean more comfortably against the wall.

"Totch." The clerk waved greeting at the pirate Pen guessed was the first mate. "Is this your whole catch? Falun is in port. He'll be disappointed."

"Aye, I saw his galley." Totch looked over his bedraggled prisoners. "This lot is mostly for ransom. We've two more prize ships coming later, with a fair number of fit men. We were separated from the first a week ago in a storm. The other . . . should be here. Soon." Pen thought he sounded uneasy in this claim.

"Well, let's get started." The clerk, whose rustic Adriac accent matched his beard, motioned Pen and his hangers-on forward. Pen moved without truncheon-prodding.

The clerk poised his quill. "Name?"

"Penric kin Jurald."

The clerk hesitated; Pen helpfully spelled it out for him. Because in case word did get back to Orbas, he wanted it to be recognized.

"Age?"

"Thirty-two."

The clerk snorted. "Good try, but it won't save your tail if someone wants to buy it, Blue-eyes. What's your real age?"

"Thirty-two," Pen repeated patiently. "Many people misestimate me." *And let's keep it that way*.

The clerk shook his head and wrote down *twenty-two*. Pen didn't bother pursuing the argument.

"Family?"

"None to speak of. My parents died some time ago. Back in the cantons." The latter part of which was perfectly true. The inquiry, of course, was to flush out some gauge of how much ransom might be squeezed out of relatives, so many captives lied. As he was doing, by omission.

"Ah." The clerk pursed his lips in satisfaction at the explanation of Pen's alien name and coloring. "Profession?"

"Scribe. I work for the curia of the archdivine of Orbas, in Vilnoc." True in a sense. "I'll be crying ransom to the curia. Also for my nieces." He let his hands rest on the shoulders of the two girls, who, speaking no Adriac, had hunched closer to him in worry. He hoped this gave his new claim an authentic air. "Keep us together. My ransom will cover all."

"Not up to me. Though I'd think the curia of Orbas could buy a new clerk for a lot less than that."

"I'm very good at my job."

"Howsoever. And those two?" The clerk eyed the girls, who didn't look much like Pen, in jaded suspicion.

"Lencia and Seuka Corva." They both looked up at the sounds of their names. "Daughters of my late half-sister." Yes, as he and the dead prostitute were both children of the white god, perhaps siblings in faith. "She'd been lost to the family for a long time, then word of her fate turned up in Jokona. I've only just found her girls. They don't speak any Adriac."

"Jokonan, are they?" The clerk raised his brows. "You speak Roknari?"

"A little."

The clerk made a pleased note. "Anything else?"

"Well, Wealdean, of course. My mother tongue." Pen realized he might be inadvertently running up his price, but after giving his real birthplace he had to admit to that. Literate translators were much sought-after, slave or free, so the rest of his learning had best stay unmentioned.

"Really? Was her tongue silver? I'd have guessed you were a fancy Lodi lad. Or a Lodi fancy lad. But you must speak and write Cedonian, to work in Orbas."

"Well, yes, that too."

Another note. "Huh. You may be able to save your own tail."

"I plan to." Pen bit back tarter remarks. True or not.

Thankfully, the clerk waved him away before he could tangle himself further, and called up the next prisoners. Pen towed the girls to the freed bench and settled them close.

"Call me Uncle Penric from here on out," he whispered to them in Roknari. "I've claimed your mother was my half-sister, and that I've just found you. It may or may not help keep us together, but it seems the best gamble."

"Would slavers care about that?" said Lencia doubtfully.

Young apparently did not mean ignorant. "No, but they care about ransoms."

"Oh." She pressed her lips together, looking reassured. Seuka stared at him as if he had just performed some amazing magical trick. . . . Which he could, but Bastard's tears, not here.

I like these girls, Des remarked cheerily. *Let's keep them.*

At least as far as Vilnoc. Yes, any search for their elusive papa was best performed from the safety of home, at leisure. Preferably by letter—Pen had friends and colleagues in Lodi he might draw upon—because once he stepped ashore he was determined not to leave his and Nikys's neat little house again even if dragged by ox-team. He had ways of dropping an ox-team . . .

But not an archdivine, Des observed. *Or a duke.*

Or a god. Pen sighed concession. Although if the merchant Getaf was found, he might be persuaded to reimburse the curia for the expenditure on his children's behalf, soothing the comptroller.

The aged family disposed of, the stout Adriac merchant came up next to speak for his friend and beg clean water and medical care, only to be told he had to wait for their next destination, and the less trouble he gave, the sooner they would be taken there. Pen had to wonder what quality of physicians might be found in this backwater. Pirates and fishermen both were prone to dire injuries, though, so perhaps the local devotees of the Mother's Order had practice.

The skinny fellow then proceeded to argue for considerations due to his claimed status as a divine of the Father's Order, which Pen doubted and the clerk did not care about. It only ended when the captain rolled back in, soot-smudged and irritated. Regrettably, it seemed he and his crew had managed to put out the galley fire. That was all right. Pen could wait.

The prisoners were all collected again by the pirates

and the armed port-shed guards, to be led on a march
up into town. The captain was briefly interrupted by a
trio of tough-looking, tattooed townswomen demanding
to know where their husbands were, evidently among his
crew detailed to bring in the prize ships, to whom he
gave temporizing excuses that plainly did not please
them. Escaping this hazard, he managed to escort his . . .
catch, a revealing term Pen thought, to another large
building, this in the more usual whitewashed stucco of
the islands. Thick-walled, it was cool and shadowed
when they stepped within.

Pen hadn't been sure whether to expect a prison or
an auction block, but this seemed neither. The front
room was spacious and paved with a smooth cement, a
set of stairs at one end leading to the upper story.
Dormitories, I wager, murmured Des. Other passages
led off it to who knew what, though presumably
including a kitchen, because some trestle tables were
folded against a wall, and a few benches were scattered
about. Holding place, then. It seemed underfilled with
only Pen's party. Did it not hold people for long?
Although two more ships' worth of unhappy sailors were
yet expected.

Maybe there was some more secure prison for violent
captives. How big was this island? Might there be wild
areas where a runaway could conceal himself, or other
towns or villages with boats? The sea discouraged Pen,
but a trained sailor might view it as more road than moat.

It appeared the ransom candidates were to be cared-
for, after a rudimentary fashion. First, the guards herded
them all out to a small closed courtyard, where they were

permitted a wash and drink at a wall-spigot that emptied into a trough, draining from there away to a channel under the wall. Their several days crowded in a hold no larger than what Pen had shared with the Corva sisters had broken down any bodily reticence among them, so the men stripped to wash well, sharing around the chunk of coarse soap provided, and the rinse bucket. Pen resignedly bore the covert stares from all alike that he won during this. The chance to scour off the ship-stink was worth it.

The old woman washed by halves, everyone politely ignoring the inadequacy of her old husband's attempt to shield her modesty by interposing his filthy shirt held out as a screen. Pen in turn prevailed upon her to help him with the girls' much-needed ablutions. Pen grimaced to don his dirty clothes again, but he supposed everyone else's changes were on their prior ship as well. Would such personal effects be returned when the ship came in, or just be stolen? He didn't hold out much hope for his own.

While this was going on, an islander midwife with a green sash around her tunic, cursory salute to the Mother's Order, appeared with a kit to attend to the cut-up Adriac merchant, whose name was Aloro, and the old couple's son with the broken forearm. The arm needed to be rebroken and reset, in Pen's view, but instead received some horsing around that left it scarcely improved and the son fainting. The midwife at least provided him with a sling. She cleaned and bandaged Aloro's sword cuts, several on his arms and a longer gash across his torso. The little ordeal left the man supine and gasping, clutching his fearful friend Arditi's sweating hand till the plump pink flesh bunched white. The wounds were red and ugly with infection, healing barely holding its own.

Don't mix in, muttered Des, uneasy at Pen's restive, reflexive evaluations. *At least till we're sure we can afford it*. Nevertheless, under the guise of assisting the midwife, Pen did manage to slip the injuries a general boost of uphill magic, his reserve from the chaos planted on the ship not yet leaked away.

Back in the main room, an islander man and woman appeared and conscripted the few able-bodied, headed by Pen, to set up the trestles and help carry food from the kitchen: plain but wholesome fare of flat bread, cheese, olives and sardines in oil, dried figs, and heavily watered wine. Pen was amused when the captives begged "Learned Pozeni," in his capacity as a divine of the Father, to bless the meal. This he managed to passably do, which incidentally revealed by the return tally signs that all those present were Quintarian or chose to appear so—apart from the Jokonan girls, who, adrift on the unfamiliar speech, sat mute and motionless. The food was abundant enough that Pen had no need to exert himself to make sure his "nieces" received their share. So, they were not to be starved into submission.

Upon inquiry, Pen delivered a tale to their tablemates, in urbane Lodi Adriac, about encountering the sought sisters by wildest chance in the pirate hold, surely a blessing of the white god. This dramatic and unlikely fiction was accepted wide-eyed by the old woman, and with narrower skepticism by the rest. Pen wished he could be as sure the mystical assertion was untrue. In return he was gifted with the unlucky travelers' own tales, none remarkably different from what he had already construed.

By the time they cleared the trestles, the relaxation induced by the wash and the meal had Pen swaying on his feet, hoping to be led to those dormitories soon. Both the ease and the hope evaporated abruptly when the pirate captain, whose name Pen had learned was Valbyn, returned, trailed by the port clerk with the sheaf of his pages in hand. Totch with his truncheon tagged along. Two new men, one with an attendant servant, followed them in through the door.

The shorter, sturdier newcomer had dark hair and eyes. The tunic, trousers, and leather shoes he wore might have belonged to any active merchant around this sea, but the rings on his hands were heavy gold, and his sleeveless coat, its embroidered hem swinging at his knees, was richly dyed in a dark red. The younger man who dogged him, carrying a writing box, had similar height and coloration, if more humble dress. They might or might not be related, but they both looked very Darthacan.

Pen's guess was confirmed when the older murmured in that tongue, "Watch out for these islanders. The port officials won't hesitate to collude with the free captains to foist off any rubbish they can't saddle on their Roknari neighbors." The younger man nodded earnestly.

The taller, leaner arrival had skin sun-burnished to a gleaming bronze, possibly enhanced with a touch of oil. His reddish-bronze hair was bound up in a complicated braid around his head, a few artful ringlets allowed to dangle at his temples. A wide-cut sleeveless tunic fell to his ankles, allowing him to sensibly dispense with trousers in this heat. The bleached cloth was caught up at his waist by a belt, studded with colored gleams that might be jewels or glass, supporting a long dagger in a tooled scabbard. Good leather sandals, well broken-in, protected his feet. Like his Darthacan counterpart's, the garb seemed everyday working dress for an established trader, suggesting neither man felt need here to impress anyone.

The two exchanged familiar, measured chin-ducks. "Captain Falun," said the Darthacan. "Good to see you well," receiving in return a slightly dry, "Master Marle. I trust your last business prospered." Both in thickly accented but serviceable trade Adriac, establishing the language of the hour, and the hint that neither was privy to the other's tongue.

"Tolerably, tolerably," said the swarthy Marle. "Yourself?"

"The sea was kind to us, last voyage."

"Always a blessing." The Darthacan, who had to be Quintarian, politely did not suggest from which god.

"Aye," agreed the Quadrene captain, as politely not quibbling.

Signaling business, not theology, was to be the order of the day. Really, Pen was relieved.

The house servants brought out two chairs graced with cushions for the important guests. Customers? Totch, waving his truncheon more in gesture than threat, had the captives drag over their benches to the near wall and seat themselves, instructing them to line up in a row and keep their mouths shut, and maybe they'd get some good news.

Doubt that, murmured Des.

Mm, thought Pen back. He whispered in Roknari to the intimidated girls, who'd tucked themselves up one on each side of him, "I think one of those men might be here about ransoms. Be quiet and wait, till I find out what's happening."

They both nodded trustingly. Pen concealed his wince at their baseless faith in him.

The Darthacan and the port clerk put their heads together over the entry papers. The assistant opened his writing box and set up to take notes. Captain Falun, Captain Valbyn following, rose and wandered over to the array of captives.

Falun sniffed in disapproval at the old couple. He made their middle-aged son unship his swollen, empurpled arm from the sling and hold it out; pressing long, strong fingers down it, at which the man choked back a cry of pain, he frowned at Valbyn and said in Roknari, "You've damaged this one beyond my use. *That's* never going to heal straight."

Valbyn shrugged. "Marle will take the family whole, then."

"Marle is welcome to them." Falun looked over the somewhat younger pair of Adriac merchants with equal doubt. Or feigned doubt, Pen realized, likely the first moves in some delicate dance around prices. "Same problem with this fellow. Looks feverish to me. Would he even last the trip home to Rathnatta?" He touched a palm to Aloro's forehead; the man jerked back. Pen thought the merchant might be catching a few words of the Roknari, and all of the interplay.

So the dapper Falun was a Rathnattan, specifically; that semi-independent princedom being either the northernmost large island of the Carpagamon chain or the westernmost of the Archipelago, depending on how the map was divided in any given year.

"You could likely sweat the fat off of this one," Valbyn remarked with a nod of his head at the partner Arditi, supporting Aloro as he sagged on the bench.

"Or he would drop at his oar of an apoplexy." Both trader and pirate were haggling in a low dialect of Roknari, with the special endings and honorifics left out, fluid and quick. Pen suspected Falun, at least, could rise to court Roknari at need.

Falun moved on to the skinny Carpagamon. "Really, Valbyn. Can't you do better?"

"He says he's a divine of the Father."

"And you believe him?"

"Doesn't matter to me. If it's true, Marle will scrape his ransom out of the Temple somehow."

Falun stepped along to the next bench. His gaze skipped approvingly over the girls, then rose to Pen and stopped. "Oh." He gave the exclamation a musical lilt, amused and inquiring.

Valbyn suppressed a smirk. "Aye. Claims he's a scribe in the curia of Orbas."

Falun caught up Pen's hands—Pen, pretending to less command of Roknari than he actually possessed, set his teeth and did not resist—and looked them over. "That, I will believe. Daughter's blessings, those are beautiful."

"Goes with the rest of him, wouldn't you agree?"

Falun stared fascinated into Pen's face. "Where are those *eyes* from? I've never seen the like."

"The cantons, he claims. But no family left there. He's relying on the curia for his ransom."

"Seems optimistic." Falun released his hold and stepped back. For once, he did not offer some price-suppressing disparagement. Pen considered coughing in a consumptive manner, but his mouth was too dry.

No matter, said Des. *We can deal with him later. In so many ways*.

Des's prior rider Learned Ruchia had been a sometime-spy, Pen was reminded, if a generation ago in another country. Perhaps that was how Des had learned to listen prick-eared and not interrupt a flow of useful information.

"He claims these Jokonan girls are his nieces," the pirate captain put in.

The Corva sisters, who for a change could understand most of what was being said despite the local accents, both nodded tremulously and gripped Pen's hands as if rescuing them.

"Seems unlikely," said Falun. "Weren't they from two different ships? What does he hope to gain by the tale?"

"Good question, since as far as I know they first met yesterday at dawn, when we slung him into their hold. Future concubines?"

"Or present ones, given some men's tastes. I suppose they'd be grateful." He eyed Pen in new speculation.

Later, Pen schooled himself. *I will take him apart in ways he cannot even* imagine.

Oh come, said Des. *It's a logical speculation from his point of view. Surely you've learned that much about the world by now.*

Bloody-minded demon. Though Des, through some of her less fortunate riders' earlier lives, not only knew the worst of the world but had experienced a nasty share of it. He chose wisdom and let the point rest.

The sisters, insulted on Pen's behalf, were looking mulishly at the Rathnattan trader. Which meant they, too, knew more about the world than was comfortable. He gripped their hands back, silently urging silence.

A call in trade Adriac of "All right," from Marle interrupted this. "I'm ready."

Falun stepped back, and Marle stepped up and joined him, looking unenthusiastically over the captives. Although he blinked when he came to Pen, and pursed his lips in speculation at the sisters.

Falun swept a hand down the row, and said to his colleague, or rival, "You can have that lot, for all of me. I'll take those three." He tapped a finger toward Pen and the sisters.

"Not so fast," said Captain Valbyn. "You'll need to outbid Master Marle."

"What have you calculated for them?" Falun asked, and Marle obligingly extracted the relevant paper from his scribe and showed his arithmetic. Falun frowned. "I'd like a closer look at the blond lad."

Valbyn's lips stretched in a piratical smile. "Very well. Let's take him into a better light."

At truncheon-prod, Pen let himself be marched back out to the little water-court. There, Valbyn shoved him into the full sunlight and made him turn around. Slight gasps from both flesh-merchants made Pen realize the pirate hadn't been easing his captive's discomfiture by setting the examination in private, but rather, was trying to boost his price.

"Make him take off his tunic," said Falun, an order which Valbyn translated. Pen complied. Falun walked around him making muted noises like a man inspecting a horse. A palm to Pen's jaw did not quite result in a perusal of his teeth. Instead, Falun said in Roknari, "He's not *cut*, is he? He's so smooth!"

One of Des's little tricks made shaving as trivial a task as wiping a cloth over his face; maybe he shouldn't have slipped it past during the recent wash-up . . .

Valbyn, switching back to Falun's tongue, offered, "No, look at his build."

Eunuchs emasculated at a very young age did grow differently, though the one cut man Pen knew as a friend, of sorts, had met his fate well after puberty, and was indistinguishable in outline from any other slim, fit assassin of forty. Except, yes, for his beardlessness.

Falun yanked Pen's trousers down to briefly check, nearly losing his, well, not life, but perhaps permanent use of that arm. The Rathnattan grinned at Pen's angry hiss. Stepping back, he let Pen put himself to rights without further molestation.

"He's been quite docile, so far," Valbyn pointed out.

"Maybe." Falun's bright eyes narrowed at Pen. "If not, it wouldn't be my problem. How many languages do you say he writes?"

"Adriac, Cedonian, whatever benighted tongue they

speak beyond the great mountains where he came from, and he even has a start on Roknari."

"Oh?"

"I've seen him whispering to those Jokonan girls. They seem to understand him."

"Quintarian, I suppose."

"Must be."

Falun smirked at Pen and switched back to trade Adriac. "So you think the demon-god will answer your prayers, Sea-eyes?"

Sadly, no. I think the demon-god employs me to answer them for Him. Lazy Bastard.

Des snickered unhelpfully.

Pen managed a shrug in reply to Falun. Some Quintarians with a deep religious calling might risk martyrdom, proclaiming their faith in the teeth of such mockery. Pen thought if his god wanted him martyred, He could bloody do it without Pen's help.

Good, murmured Des. *Keep that view*.

Marle had looked annoyed at being walled off from this dickering by the language barrier, but Pen thought he had followed the play well enough.

They all shuffled back to the main room. The Corva girls looked up anxiously. Pen rejoined them on their bench.

Falun wheeled to study Pen one more time, pursing his lips, then said to Valbyn in trade Adriac, "I'll take him." He named a price in Rathnatta silver ryols that caused the pirate to break into a broad smile, and Marle to frown.

"Master Marle . . . ?" said Valbyn in a leading tone. "Do you care to bid again?"

Marle groused, "The curia of Orbas won't match that for a scribe, no matter how dainty his hands."

Pen cleared his throat. "They might go up a little," he offered. "For the three of us."

"I already calculated for that." Marle eyed the trio on the bench. "And what price are those girls without him? I misdoubt Orbas will ransom *them*. I daresay his curia has never even heard of them. Subtract the scribe, and the girls become near-worthless."

"Not so," said Falun equably. "One can always sell girls somewhere. Though if you don't want them, as a matter of piety I'll take them along and spare them a Quintarian fate."

The two bidders regarded each other, Marle scowling, Falun smiling faintly.

Valbyn gritted his teeth at the impasse, clearly not wishing to displease either customer, then brightened. "A compromise, then. Why don't you each take one. At a slave-girl's price."

Falun's brows flicked up. "That suits me well enough."

"Mm . . ." said Marle at this lesser consolation. "Not ideal, but it will do."

Valbyn nodded in satisfaction. "Done."

Pen shot to his feet. "No! We have to stay together!" *I promised . . .*

Totch advanced, truncheon brandished. Valbyn, still in a pleased mood, waved him back. "Now, don't damage Captain Falun's merchandise." While Pen stood fuming, trying to think, he added, "So which of you wants which?"

"The elder," both men said together.

Valbyn vented a long-suffering sigh, and drew a coin from his pocket. He motioned the port clerk over, saying, "Toss it."

The port clerk, who looked like a man who wanted to get home to his dinner, took it without comment, flipped it in the air and caught it, and slapped his other hand down over it.

"Call it," Valbyn said, gesturing to Marle.

After a slight hesitation, Marle said, "Heads."

The port clerk lifted his hand, revealing the reverse of the coin. Marle grimaced.

"Very good, hearty sirs," said Valbyn, retrieving his coin before the port clerk could pocket it. "Shall we settle up?"

Pen stood stiff and fuming. Des murmured uneasily, *Now, don't start a scene here that we can't finish. We aren't leaving harbor on that galley anyway, are we?*

If I have my way, that galley's *not leaving this harbor.*

Unusual, that his chaos demon should be the one restraining him. It was normally the other way around. More than one battle had been started by mistake, to no one's plan, but yes, if he was declaring a one-sorcerer-war on a pirate haven, it would likely go better with a little advance thought.

"When will you be taking them?" the port clerk asked Falun.

The Rathnattan waved a hand expansively. "They may as well stay here for tonight. I'll wait to sail with a full load, for my profit. What else do you think will make port this week besides Valbyn's prizes?"

"Captain Garnasvik may send back something. He left here a few days before Valbyn."

"Mm. Let's hope he finds fair winds."

Let's not, thought Pen. He sank back on the bench between the sisters.

Lencia tugged at him in worry. "What just happened?"

He didn't want to induce panic and tears, but he daren't lie. He lowered his head and voice. "Nothing is going to happen right away. We'll all be staying here together for tonight, maybe for several days. The Rathnattan slave-trader thinks he's bought me and you. The Darthacan ransom-broker thinks he's bought Seuka. They're both wrong. We're going to do something else."

"What?" said Seuka, looking at him big-eyed.

"It's a secret," he managed after a choked moment. *Even from me, apparently.*

Des, charitably, refrained from laughing at him, but he sensed it was a struggle.

The bargaining conclave broke up. After a final accounting consultation with the port clerk, Falun took his leave, as did Valbyn. Marle and his scribe ushered the folk to be ransomed to the trestle table, settling them down for a more detailed examination of their hopes and resources. The port clerk lingered for this, evidently with an eye to collecting accurate head fees in due course.

Pen and the Jokonan girls were left to their own devices. The armed port guard who'd sat himself on a stool by the door discouraged any premature attempts to exit. Pen, swaying on his feet after several nights of disrupted sleep, not to mention his disrupted life, took

the girls upstairs to seek bunks in the dormitories. They
discovered two long rooms lined with sailors' hammocks,
and also a smaller chamber with actual beds. The slit
windows were too narrow even for Pen to turn sideways
and slip through, but they overlooked the harbor.

The girls, even more exhausted than he was after their
long ordeal, went straight for one straw-stuffed mattress
and flopped down together. Pen kept them awake just
long enough to divest their sandals. Another bed,
motionless and so much more enticing than a bare hold
despite the stiff straw-bits poking through the not-very-
clean cloth, called to him, but he returned to the window
to stare out into the evening light for a few minutes.

Every tactical plan needed to start with an accurate
survey of the terrain, or so Adelis had remarked. And a
keen evaluation of the physically possible. Some poetic
epics extolled heroism in warriors; Adelis the actual
soldier put his faith in logistics, Pen had noted. Not that
Pen could see much terrain from here, the bulk of the
town being in the opposite direction, but by shifting
back and forth he was able to take in most of the
waterfront. Out on the headland, a ruined fortress was
in process of being rebuilt. Pen wasn't sure of the
rationale for this, since plainly the stronghold had not
held before.

He was about to give up seeking inspiration from the
view and also flop down, when Des said, *Ooh, look.
Something's finally happening down there.* Pen glanced
back to the harbor.

At the long dock, Valbyn's ship was starting to list
sideways. The slow creep, stretching the mooring lines,

converted to a sudden lunge as the first big patch of the hull near the keel gave way. The water pouring into the bilges overstressed the rest of the weakened boards— Pen could hear the muffled cracking propagating even from here. As yet more water roared in, a mooring line pulled its cleat out of the dock, then another did the same. The mainmast snapped abruptly, taking boom, furled sails, and a mess of ropes over the side. The ship rolled and sank till it hit the rocky sand of the harbor bottom with a peculiar grinding noise. Screams and cries wafted up faintly from the shore.

Pen's lips peeled back in something like a grin, only not so nice.

Oh, my, said Des, preening. *Isn't that lovely.*

Yes, there go all Valbyn's profits. And for an added bonus, the wreck would take out a quarter of the port's docking capacity for quite some time to come. Removing that hopeless carcass was going to be a costly undertaking for someone. His glee was muted by the reflection that it would likely be done with slave labor.

This moment of great, admittedly *great*, personal satisfaction did not exactly solve the underlying problems. Sinking every ship in the harbor would leave no way for *Pen* to get off this benighted island.

Still . . . and Pen wasn't sure if the thought was his or Des's, *who here should next be gifted with an amazing run of bad luck?*

Pen rolled over in the night on his lumpy mattress, reaching muzzily for the warm softness of Nikys. *Ah. No.* He crossed his arms tightly over his chest, wanting her in his embrace but assuredly not wishing her here. Wishing himself there was a separate matter.

His wife didn't know when he'd left Trigonie, nor on what ship. He'd sent no message because he'd expected to be home before it could arrive. So she couldn't yet be worried about him, he told himself, couldn't be in distress, for all that he hoped she missed him in a more general way.

And me, Des put in, diverted by this upwelling of pining.

And you, Pen conceded. After a rocky beginning, Nikys had come to enjoy his resident demon. His mother-in-law even seemed to take Des as a *crony*, which had led to some very odd conversations of a sort Pen was sure few husbands were privy to.

So Nikys was safe in Vilnoc. She sallied forth daily the short distance to Duke Jurgo's household as lady-in-waiting to his daughter, which, since the girl was eight, combined the duties of companion and governess. The palace always sent a sturdy page to escort her home in the evening, there to enjoy the protection of her mother, their few servants, and at present her brother Adelis, back after the Grabyat expedition and also in attendance upon the duke.

. . . Pen still thought Nikys's garrisoning would be improved by the addition of one Temple sorcerer.

He suspected she thought so, too. Although she bit back any complaints, Nikys had grown tenser at the increasing frequency of Pen's outlying errands, for all that each success had raised his standing in Temple and court.

Well, of course, said Des. *She thinks the reason she never got a child from her first husband was because he was kept so long away from her bed on his military assignments. . . . Or at least, she hopes that's the reason. Naturally she's afraid of the same thing happening with you.*

Right down to the tragic conclusion? Pen certainly meant to spare her a second premature widowhood. As for making the other lapse up to her, pursuing it was the pleasantest task imaginable. . . . He trusted his demon's leaking chaos magic wasn't interfering in conception.

It can, but I promise you it's not, Des soothed him. *You haven't been married that long. You merely need a few more months. You should know that, physician.*

Not a physician. I set down that calling.

Hah. Once she is with child, the duke will do her a favor by sending you off to do his bidding. You are going to be just like all those medical students who diagnose themselves with every rare fatal malady they've just learned about. When the time comes, mark you, I am not going to let you terrorize her with all your lurid worries.

He had to smile at the vision. Des was probably just being optimistic in order to buoy him, here in this dark near-prison so far from home, but he granted he was a little heartened.

A rustling and a huff came from the cot next to his, and a whisper in Roknari, "Are you awake?"

Not meant for Pen's ears, he realized as Lencia mumbled in irritation to her sister, "I am now. Go back to sleep."

"Can't."

"Well, stop wriggling around. And quit kicking me."

"M'not."

"Are too."

A sigh. Then, "I miss Mama. I want to go *home*. I *want* Mama."

"Don't talk about it," chided Lencia, hunching as if hit. "It just makes it worse."

"It wasn't s'pposed to be like this. Why didn't Papa *come*?"

"You saw he never got the letter. He probably doesn't even know about Mama yet."

"Maybe . . . maybe he came to Raspay after we left. And is following us."

"Well, if he did, he won't find us now. We aren't anywhere we meant to be."

A brooding silence, and a defeated whisper, of, "Yes, I know . . . I just . . . don't want it to be so."

A reluctant, conceding hum. "Me, too, Seuka."

After a while, another whisper: "So what are we going to *do*? Mama died, Papa didn't come, Taspeig left us . . . that poor sea captain was killed . . ." A shudder.

Had that slaughter happened in front of the girls' eyes?

"I don't know. Stop wanting grown-ups to fix things, maybe. It hasn't worked so far."

"Should we try to run away together?"

"I . . . maybe. I don't know. That might be worse. If anyone on this island caught us, they'd probably give us back, and then we'd be beaten. Or maybe they'd just make us be slaves in a poorer house."

"At least we'd be with each other."

"Only until one of us was sold. Or both of us."

A voiceless *mm*, like a dog's plaint. "What about Master Penric? He said . . . uh, I'm not really sure what he said."

A shifting of attention to the nearby cot where Pen lay. He kept his eyes closed and his breathing steady, and refrained from moving.

"I couldn't figure it out either. I suppose he was just blustering, the way fellows do."

"But he seems kind. And smart. He keeps trying to help people."

"I don't think kind is much help against pirates."

"He's pretty enough to be a crow-boy." Seuka considered this. "Or maybe when he was younger, before he became a scribe."

"It looked like that Rathnattan captain who bought him thought so too."

"Does . . . do you think Master Penric realized? Should we warn him?"

"Don't know. Mama says"—a hiccough—"said, crow-boys are worse-treated than street whores. I'm not so sure about scribes." A hesitation. "Anyway, what could he do if we did? He doesn't look very strong."

"The captain was plenty strong, and the pirates still hacked him to bits." A gulp. No, two gulps, confirming Pen's speculation. "Maybe smart would work better. If it was on our side."

"No one is on our side, Seuka."

A long exhalation. "I s'ppose not."

"Go to *sleep*." Lencia started to turn over, but then,

reluctantly, rolled back and hugged her sister close like some bony, awkward, unhappy cloth doll.

The two fell back to sleep before Pen did.

Pen woke at dawn and slipped quietly out of their room, careful not to rouse the girls or the old couple and the injured Aloro, who'd taken the other two beds last night while the less crippled were delegated to the dormitory hammocks. Pen drifted down to the kitchen just in time to intercept the house servants arriving to prepare breakfast.

There, for the price of some volunteer labor and charm, he deftly extracted a deal of potentially useful information. The older woman in charge, her lame brother, and a niece proved chatty, interested in the friendly scribe from far away over icy mountains they would likely never see. Pen paid for their tales with a few vivid word-pictures of his birthplace that left him a trifle homesick.

The island, he'd learned yesterday, was Lantihera, an Old Cedonian name hinting at its deeper history; it had once been a possession of the empire, which explained the antique remnant of water system in the back court. More immediately useful, the name had finally placed it on Pen's mental map of the region. The servants' recent personal and local anecdotes were also revealing.

This unprisonlike building was dedicated to ransom candidates, the injured, and the meek. The port— meaning the town, Lanti Harbor or just Lanti for short—was its owner and the little clan's employers. Their work here was seasonal; both pirates and their prey were driven from the sea by the storms that plagued it in winter, the tempest Pen's ship had suffered being an untimely fluke.

Summer was actually, the cook explained to Pen, the quiet time in town, when most of the ships and their crews were out. The rowdies drank and gamed and whored their way through winter, arriving at spring dead broke, if not just plain dead, and ready to raid again. Given the hazards of their trade, Pen was not entirely sure this approach to life was irrational, though the cook spared a nod of admiration for the few notable sailors prudent or successful enough to retire rich, at least by local standards.

A more secure prison for the able-bodied men slated for slavery lay at the other end of the harbor, owned by the guild of fifteen pirate captains who divided control of the port uneasily with the town council. In either location, captives were kept for as short a time as possible before shifting their risks to the flesh-merchants who carried them away. Making Lanti less a slave market than a wholesale warehouse, with people shuffled off in bulk shiploads.

Really, Pen mused, if the Lanti pirates only captured people and goods for their own use, the island would soon be saturated, and the trade would dwindle. It was the middlemen buying the booty and the captives for coin who made the demand bottomless. Pen wasn't sure which half of the traffic he disliked most. Perhaps he didn't have to choose a hierarchy. Lowerarchy?

Slavery was not practiced in the austere cantons, though there remained the question of the continuous export of its men in the mercenary companies, so railed against by the Temple. At least such fellows bartered themselves. During a few historical famines, starving farmers had sold their children to the merchants who came over the mountains from the north for the purpose, events long remembered and resented. Pen wondered what lives the young starvelings had all found in the warmer countries, and if he'd ever met any of their descendants unawares.

All very fascinating, scholar-man, said Des, *but if you want more of the gruesome details, ask Umelan. I don't see need to repeat her experiences in this life. Pray attend to the practical. I can't get off this island without you.*

Yes, yes. Pen smiled as he lifted a tray of bread and olives to carry into the main room, which made the startled cook smile back in quizzical echo.

After settling the girls—who had been thrown into a brief panic by awakening to his absence, and Pen wasn't entirely sure if they'd worried for themselves or for him—overseeing their breakfasts, and working up a little more goodwill in the kitchen, Pen explored the building. An armed guard who seemed more a dozing porter sat outside the front door; even less picket impeded Pen from going out the back way, though he refrained for the moment. The only reading matter he found was an abandoned sheaf of old accounts, which even he was not desperate enough to secure for later. At the end of the upstairs corridor, he discovered a ladder leading to the flat roof, and ascended.

No guards up here; the distances to the nearest other

rooftops, too far even for a sailor to jump, made an effective moat of air. The drop straight down to the cobbled streets and flagged courtyard invited leg-breaking. More enticing was an odd tower Pen recognized after a puzzled moment as part of a mast and its crow's nest salvaged from some ship, set up to be a lookout. Yielding to the urge to climb, he lodged himself in its basket fifteen feet above the roof. Not a bad perch—when it was standing still. He imagined it swinging back and forth in high seas; Des, who loathed heights, whimpered at the vision.

He surveyed the town, which the cook had said held some eight thousand souls. Closely crowded stone, stucco, and whitewash in the central sections tailed off to scattered mudbrick, stucco, and thatch on the uninviting hills up behind it. Across the town, diagonally upslope, a dome topped a six-sided stone building not much higher than its neighbors—an old Quintarian temple built in the Cedonian style. A Quadrene temple must also be tucked somewhere, but its architecture was less obvious to Pen's eye.

The snowless mountains would not store water against summer drought. Fishing, not farming, was likely the mainstay of the island people. Piracy was a logical extension of the land's dearth.

He turned back to the sea, glittering in the morning light, deceptively serene. Vilnoc and home lay some two-hundred-fifty miles to the southwest from this spot. It was about four hundred miles south to Lodi and then Trigonie whence, hah, he had started. Three hundred miles north and east, entirely the wrong way, would find

Rathnatta-to-be-avoided. Less than two hundred miles straight across, due west, would strike the coast of Cedonia. Currents and cross-winds aside, it was a *country*. Even the rankest amateur navigator could not miss it. Turn left and keep the coast in sight, and eventually one must come to the border of Orbas.

Steal a small boat? That would have been a tempting thought, before Pen's experience of the tempest. Pen had sailed such nimble craft on canton lakes, and even those limpid waters could drown the unwary in storms. Pen and two children in anything he could handle by himself? He might bet his own life on the weather holding fair, but theirs? Were they naïve enough to follow him into that danger?

Bribing a local fisherman to ferry them across would require the man to take them on credit, on Pen's bare word that he would be paid on arrival in Orbas. Finding someone that kindly and credulous on this island seemed improbable. Pen also suspected that while for the pirates stealing from others was all in a day's work, that insouciance did not apply to anyone caught stealing from them. The fisherman's risks could be much sharper than merely that of losing his labor, up to losing his head. Hm.

The Darthacan broker Marle would own, or have passage on, some seaworthy ship heading in the right direction, and have Seuka already with him. Could Pen sneak himself and Lencia aboard, stow away until it was too late to turn around? The news that Pen was sometime-court-sorcerer to the duke of Orbas would catch the man's greed; his sailors might be more inclined to throw Pen overboard. Embarking in any ship that Pen did not himself control bore the same risk.

He'd better find out more about Marle. And Falun. So much depended on which of their flesh-brokers first filled his quota and sailed, and how soon.

Contemplating the sunlit scene, he realized that every possible course of action he might evolve converged to the same point, the absolute need for a boat. *So what I require is the shortest route to one*.

And here came a new one, furling sails and sliding into the harbor. Its draft was shallow enough that it could warp in to the unblocked pier on the farther end of the harbor, where half-a-dozen men came out to catch and loop lines and pull it to a halt. A sturdy gangplank was thrown across to the dock and its deck grew busy, with crew, stevedores, and wharf rats combining to carry off cargo like a line of ants. The line terminated in another customs shed, where Pen was fairly sure harried port clerks took inventory for the town's cut, and perhaps the further divisions among captain's guild, officers, and crew. Some of the nearby buildings must be warehouses for the pirates' ill-gotten cargos. The goods seemed too miscellaneous, the unloading too random and raucous, to be the work of some prudent merchant. Was the ship a pirate's prize? Lencia's and Seuka's first ship, perchance?

Pen's guess was confirmed when a group of men in manacles was marshaled on the deck and marched across the gangplank in chained pairs. Some much more alert-seeming guards than Pen had yet encountered prodded them along at sword's point. Squinting into the salt-hazed distance, Pen counted about thirty heads. They were paraded not to that pier's customs shed, but to a more squat and solid building farther up the shore; they disappeared within. The sturdier slave prison, no doubt, and now Pen knew just where it was.

So, there was a ship. And over there was a crew. All Pen needed to do was bring them back together. Des could go through locks, chains, and manacles like so much paper. And his rescuees would be *grateful* to Penric, a coin he might actually bargain with.

Ooh, said Des. *I fancy that plan.*

Pen wasn't sure if that meant she thought it was the best plan, or just the one that would leave the most chaos in its wake.

No reason it can't be both, she protested.

"*There* you are," called a peeved young voice from below him.

Pen looked down. The Corva sisters stood looking up in vexation.

"You'll get sunburned," reproved Lencia, and "I want to climb, too!" cried Seuka.

Seuka matched actions to words, and Pen's breath hitched when she nearly slipped while stretching for the pegs spaced for a sailor. By the time he'd mustered squeaks of caution, she'd joined him, eeling into the basket. Lencia jittered a moment before swarming up after her. Well, Pen wasn't a heavy man. Their crammed platform probably wouldn't break, though it creaked ominously.

"You can see everything from here!" said Seuka, who likely seldom had an advantage of height.

There was no reason for them to be left as disoriented as he'd been. Pen repeated his little tutorial on regional geography, arm out in a long explanatory sweep. They seemed especially interested in the route to Lodi. Lencia's gloomy glance east, back toward distant Jokona, was blocked by the hills behind.

Lencia repeated her fears for Pen's pale skin in this sun, and Pen let her bid him somewhat imperiously back indoors. He then bethought of a way to divert them from all their anxieties with those otherwise-useless old accounts. Gathering the papers, he led them back to the kitchen where, under the amused eye of the cook, he showed them how to make a serviceable ink with stove soot, water, egg yolk, and a bit of honey, and shape the ends of twigs from the firewood to make writing sticks. At this point, the cook ran them and their mess out, so Pen set up again at a trestle table.

Pen started with a list of useful words in Adriac and Cedonian, and soon had the sisters, heads down and biting their lips charmingly, printing them in two alphabets. They sopped up the new vocabulary with the enviable speed of the young. Seuka drifted from the lesson by drawing a quite recognizable menagerie of a horse, rabbit, dog, and cat, so Pen showed her the words for them as well. He finished by teaching them to recite a short girls' bedtime prayer to the Mother and Daughter, common in both its Adriac and Cedonian versions. This made a useful preamble to easing them back upstairs for the nap in the heat of the late afternoon that was customary in these summer countries for children and adults alike.

He figured he'd be glad of having taken it himself, come midnight.

The rest of the day passed quietly, with another dinner, and the captives left to putter around the building but not, of course, leave. Under the guise of checking his bandages, Penric managed to slip the feverish Aloro another general boost of uphill magic against infection, leaving the merchant feeling mysteriously eased. "I'm told I have gentle hands," Pen misdirected this attention.

Unlike everyone else in the chamber later that night, the Corva sisters slept the enviably solid sleep of youth. Lencia, Pen was able to wake in the deep dark with a shake to her shoulder and a whispered, "Follow me." Seuka he had to carry out to the hallway, easing the door shut behind them.

"What?" said Seuka drowsily, as he poured her onto her feet.

"Here, hold your sandals and be very quiet. We're leaving."

"I can't even see where I'm stepping," complained Lencia. "How can you?"

The hallway was indeed black, although not to Pen. "I have very good night vision. It's, um, the blue eyes."

"Oh."

"Just take my hands."

They followed him to the stairs in blurry obedience, yawning. Pen had been of two minds about this. Leaving them more-or-less safely here while he scouted the situation risked problems in coming back to collect them, if events went well and fast, not to mention having to get out of the building unobserved twice. Taking them along would expose them to unknown dangers along his route. Neither choice seemed good.

He padded barefoot down the stairs and stopped short, getting his hips bumped by his followers.

There was not one guard as there had been earlier in the day, posted outside the closed front door on a stool, but two, sitting cross-legged on the floor inside the entry. In the light of a candlestick, they were passing the time dicing with each other for, apparently, olive pits, judging by the little arrays before each. They both looked up with unalarmed interest at Pen and the girls.

"Why are you folks stirring?" the elder inquired.

"Cook said she'd leave a bite for my nieces," Pen blurted the first plausible tale that came to mind. He half-raised his hands, each gripped by a sister, to exhibit the supporting nieces. "They've had a hungry time of it."

"Huh!" said the younger guard. "She never leaves *us* anything! How do you get the love?"

The older guard snorted. "Look at him. You need to ask? Women!"

Pen turned toward the kitchen. To his intense dismay, the guards rose and followed them.

The pantry was locked, but fell open quietly to Pen's hand. The older guard set his candlestick down on the scarred kitchen table and went to check the back door. It was firmly bolted, to his evident satisfaction. He returned to thump down on a stool, amiably gesturing the girls to the bench, where they were joined by the younger guard.

Pen rummaged in the pantry, bringing back a bag of figs, a pot of olives, and half of a small wheel of cheese wrapped in cloth. Inviting themselves to the impromptu repast, the guards passed the food around; the younger pulled his wicked belt knife and sliced cheese for his tablemates, kindly handing chunks across to the girls first. The girls both watched Pen big-eyed.

"Oh, look," said Pen hollowly. "Here's the wine." He lifted the jug and plunked it in front of the men. Could he get them drunk enough to pass out?

The younger waved it away. "We don't drink on duty." The elder nodded, though he looked regretful. And possibly a touch resentful of his partner's rectitude. The ban did not seem to apply to the food, each saving their olive pits aside.

The guards then proceeded to *chat*, asking Pen and the girls leading questions about their travels and lives somewhere other than this island. Pen diverted attention from his immediate background by repeating some of his childhood stories about snowy mountains that had fascinated the cook, and which also engrossed the Corva girls. Lencia produced a pared version of their own misadventures, remembering to claim Pen as their mother's long-lost half-brother, so miraculously found. Pen didn't think the bemused guards believed it either.

Evidently, talking to their prisoners in the night watch was a better entertainment for these islanders than dicing for olive pits, and one they'd diverted themselves with before, because they traded back some striking tales from other captives. Rather slyly, the older guard threw in a few descriptions of prior ill-fated escape attempts, variously and sometimes violently thwarted.

Pen was learning a lot about the lives of night-guards in Lanti, but valuable darkness was slipping past outside. He suspected the pair would cheerfully gossip till dawn and the arrival of the kitchen crew, along with all the other hazards of a new day. If Captain Falun decided, tomorrow, that the captured sailors would fill his hold and thus he could sail at once, Pen didn't want to still be here having to navigate twisty new challenges.

Maybe he should have devised some way to lower them all down from the roof despite the height.

Really, said Des, sharing his growing exasperation with this sociable delay. *Those girls are light and young, they would have bounced* . . .

Pen found himself actually missing his distant eunuch friend, Surakos, and whatever dozen subtle poisons and drugs he would doubtless have successfully concealed about his person. Not to mention that his sale price would probably have topped Pen's own by half. Pen wasn't sure if wishing pirates on Surakos was any more evil than wishing the eunuch on pirates. But the memory of those apothecarial skills did allow him to settle on a course of action at last.

About time, growled Des.

Pen would have preferred to have been touching the guards' heads for this delicate work, but didn't expect they would let him get so near without some violent fending-off. If they continued to sit still, he might manage it safely enough from across the table. He held himself in a moment of unbreathing concentration, called up his full Sight, and ghosted his magic deep into each one's ears, there to gently stroke the interior surfaces of the tiny looping labyrinths in their encasements of bone that seemed to control balance. When he'd been studying medicine back in Martensbridge, injuries and infections in that mysterious organ and their ghastly vertiginous effects had been fascinating problems brought to him for magical healing. It worked just as well in reverse.

Both men's eyes widened, then squinched in nausea. They swayed in their seats, reaching out for support from the table and missing. The aborted motions made it all worse, and they tumbled from their perches onto the kitchen floor. The elder opened his mouth to bellow, but vomited instead. The girls, startled, jumped to their feet.

"Hurry, help me find things to tie them up," Pen diverted them before they could panic.

The younger guard managed to get up as far as his knees before flopping helplessly down again. His cry came out a heartbreaking moan.

"Sorry, sorry," said Pen under his breath, as he hastened around the kitchen looking for strong bindings. A washing line coiled at the bottom of the pantry would do. Hands tied behind backs, feet bound together and hitched to hands, snapping of cords to the right lengths with a touch of chaos. It was a bit redundant—Pen didn't think either man would be walking again for a while— but convincing, which was what he needed. A major value of his magic as a defense lay in its continued secrecy. Once his enemies knew what they were dealing with, they would be much more effectively on guard.

Pen hunkered down by the distressed men's heads. "The poison won't kill you," he told them. "You won't need an antidote. You'll just need to wait out the sick. It will help to lie very still with your eyes closed." He added after an inspired moment, "And don't try to talk or cry out. That would make it worse."

Ungrateful glares, fair enough.

Pen considered, doubtfully, the inadvisability of gagging a vomiting person versus the risks of their shouting for help. Of course, the only people in the building who could hear them were Pen's fellow prisoners still sleeping upstairs. If any woke, and came down, would they be foolish enough to untie the guards? He wanted at least till sunup for a lead-time. Maybe leave a note?

Just go, snapped Des.

Pen nodded and started to shepherd the girls to the back door, the bolt quietly shearing off beneath his concealing hand. At the last moment, he darted back to kneel over the younger guard.

"You really need to get yourself off this dreadful island while you still can," he advised the youth, while helping himself to his sandals and donning them. Pen's long toes stuck out over the soles, but the other guard's boots were even shorter. "Before the life here ruins you. Adria would do. Go to Lodi, and present yourself to my friend Learned Iserne in the curia of the archdivine. Tell her Penric recommended you. She can find you some decent work that doesn't rest on theft, kidnapping, murder and rapine."

A pie-eyed groan was his only reply. Pen patted the young fellow encouragingly on the shoulder and hurried out after the Corva girls.

Wary of taking a wrong turn in the narrow, crooked streets of Lanti, Pen hugged the harbor shore. The sisters kept a good grip on him. Very few lights relieved the darkness: a mere slice of setting moon, and the lanterns glimmering above the doors of a scattering of inns or brothels that faced the waters. A pair of drunken men making their way home paid them no heed at all. The night air was cool and moist, thick with the dubious smells of the port, fish and salt and tar and dung.

As he led the girls around occasional piles of drying nets and other boat gear, Penric meditated upon rats. Quite by chance, he had lately hit upon a way of brushing light chaos across one spot in the backs of their little rat brains that had dropped them into deep sleep instead of killing them. Sometimes he could repeat the effect. Sometimes the poor creatures just died. Helvia, one of the two prior physician-sorceresses who had possessed Des, had failed to see the value of producing well-slept rats, but Amberein, the other, had been intrigued. She had once treated, with indifferent success, a man who had been brought to her afflicted with sudden, uncontrolled sleeping. That the two effects shared a cause, making the trick extendable to humans, was a plausible guess.

When he reached home again, he must cultivate some Vilnoc knacker to let him experiment on his stock of larger beasts. Because if Pen could work out how to do that to *people* without killing them, it might replace his cruder and more painful tricks, more reliably.

And then practice, because chances were that enemies wouldn't agreeably hold still while he felt their heads, one by one. More likely he'd find himself facing a whole gang of rowdies trying to murder him, and, thus, jumping about erratically. . . . The alternative of never leaving his house and Nikys again seemed ever more attractive.

Meanwhile, he supposed he had better go back to his proven standby of roughing up the big sciatic or axillary nerves, inducing pain so excruciating that the victim could not move. And if he misjudged the force and snapped a nerve, at least it would only cripple, not kill.

The whisper—and not from Des—that some men deserved death, he did his best to ignore. Even as a learned divine, it was not his place to judge men's souls. The gods in Their time would do so without fail, and with much fuller knowledge.

Lencia, whose face had been tight since they'd left the ransom house, finally asked, "What did you do to those men?"

"Drugged their olives," Pen offered. He added after a fraught silence, "Not ours, of course." He trusted that questions like *how?* and *when?* would take further reflection that no one would have time for. *You didn't witness magic, no, of course not.*

"Oh."

The bulk of the slave prison loomed at last. Pen led the girls into the nearest side street till he found a niche between two houses, and tucked them into it.

"Lie up here and wait till I come back," he murmured. "I'm not sure how long this is going to take. But if it works, you'll see some activity starting on the pier."

"What if you don't come back?" whispered Seuka.

"If I haven't returned for you by daylight . . . sneak back to the ransom house. At least they'll feed you there."

Doubtful silence greeted this. He ruffled each of their heads, mute goodwill in lieu of lies, and slipped away into the darkness.

Now it grew tricky, as he'd need to scout and act in the same pass. He began by circling the building, one hand tracing the scabrous stucco, all Des's senses extended. Old ghosts were common in old buildings, sundered souls drifting down into oblivion, but this place seemed to harbor more than its share. He brushed his hand, pointlessly, at one vague shape that pulsed in front of his face like some smoky jellyfish. It had dwindled far past the point of being able to assent to any god; Pen had no means canny or uncanny to affect it. And vice versa, he supposed. *Yes*, agreed Des, *so best attend to what we can do something about.*

On the prison wall above, a few high, iron-barred windows would be susceptible to rusting the rods. At the back, steps led down in shadows to a heavy door with a sturdy lock and a wooden bar, which likely gave onto whatever holding cells lay within. Pen silently unlocked it, unshipped the bar from its clamps, and set it aside, just in case. A higher section of the building, jutting out parallel to the shore, might house administrative offices, unpeopled now. Pen edged around it to the main front door facing the sea and the pier a hundred paces off, where the prize ship creaked sleepily in the lapping of the harbor waves.

Rather more than the thirty sailors Pen had seen enter earlier lay inside; perhaps forty? Residue of an earlier catch? Most dozing, some awake and in pain, none happy. The front doors, also reached by a few steps down, were double, of iron-bound oak so old it might have been iron itself. All susceptible to the three kinds of fire at Pen's command: rot, rust, and flame. But the ornate iron lock was presently unlatched. Pen lifted the handle quietly and slipped inside.

No vestibule; the door opened onto a wide front room. To his right was an archway and stairs up to the record-keeping section. Directly ahead lay a locked, barred door to the prison proper. To his left, four men sat around a table under the light of an oil lantern suspended from a roof beam. Passing the dull night playing cards, plainly. Pen blinked his dark-accustomed eyes at the yellow glare.

They twisted around on their stools at his entry, curious but unalarmed when they saw he was alone. The wine carafe seemed mainly there to make their water safer to drink, because they did not look in the least inebriated. One fellow was older, stringy and grizzled. Two were big rowdies. A fourth was a skinny youth. Sergeant, muscle, and runner, Pen pegged them.

Without the girls to safeguard from sudden violence, this time Pen wasn't stopping to chat.

The sergeant had barely laid his cards face-down

upon the table and opened his mouth as Pen began to methodically disable the squad. The muscle-men appeared the most alarming, but Pen thought the runner, who could race for reinforcements, was his greatest hazard. One, two, three, four around the table Pen blasted each sciatic nerve with strong chaos, barely short of a severing. He was halfway around again for the work on the opposite legs before the sergeant, rising with a frown, yelped and stumbled to his knees. While the rest attempted to leap up but instead discovered the sabotage coming from their own limbs, Pen made a third pass, stinging the big nerves to their tongues. It wouldn't silence them altogether, but it would certainly muffle their pained noises.

On a ledge above the corner fireplace, unlit in this heat, sat a box of tallow candles. Pen snatched it up. One of the burly guards, now trying to crawl across the floor, made a valiant but futile lunge at Pen's ankles as he skipped past. A couple of key rings strung with iron keys hung from pegs beside the inner door. Pen grabbed them down, hanging the rings on his left arm like clanking bracelets. He boosted the door bar out of its brackets, scowled at the overabundant choice of keys, shrugged, and popped the lock without the mechanical aid.

Stepping down into the deeper darkness beyond, Pen found a central corridor with stone walls, a couple of locked doors on each side. Two chambers on the right, unoccupied. A longer chamber on the left housed the present prisoners. Pen picked a candle out of the box, lit it with a thought, unlocked the nearest door with another—fire and unlocking were among his and Des's oldest magics, and he half-smiled in memory—and nudged it open with his knee. He rocked back at the stench that rolled out.

This is an old Cedonian prison. Doesn't it have drains?

Aye, Des reported after a moment. *There's one down at the end. Meant to be kept rinsed with buckets of seawater. Blocked, unfortunately. I doubt it's been cleaned out since the pirates took over.*

Or since the Cedonians left. Pen took a shallow breath and stepped through.

He raised his smoking candle high, less to see than to illuminate himself for his soon-to-be audience. A few gleams reflected back out of the shadows from widened eyes or bits of metal. Men lay scattered up the length of the chamber on the bare stone floor. They were secured by a miscellany of means, some manacled together at the wrists, some in leg irons, some with hands thrust through locked boards. A brief recoil rippled through them, then a slight, threatening surge forward as they realized the intruder was alone.

To prevent unfortunate misunderstandings, Pen quickly shouted in trade Adriac, "I've come to get you out of here! Your ship is still tied at the pier, and there's only a night watch. You'll be able to retake it together!"

Men stirred, neighbors waking others. Pen bent quickly to the nearest manacled pair and slipped their chains loose. He handed them the keys and the candles. "Start freeing the rest." He stood and shouted again, "Who are the ship's officers?"

A thickset man with a nasty green bruise on his

forehead climbed to his feet and staggered forward, holding out his hands trapped in a plank. Before the light redoubled as the first pair shared flame from one candle to another, Pen passed his hand discreetly over the lock and let the man drop the device from his wrists.

"I'm the first mate of the *Autumn's Heart*," he said in a strained voice. "Captain's killed. Who in the Bastard's hell are you?"

"Out of it, I assure you," said, well, maybe Des. Pen cleared his throat and continued, "Was yours the ship taken on its way to Lodi last week, carrying the two young Jokonan girls?"

"Aye . . ." The man hesitated, squinting with increasing bewilderment at Pen. "Do you know what happened to them?"

"They were . . . given into my care." Pen didn't venture to say by whom. Or Whom. "I'll explain it all later. Right now, there are four guards in the front room who need to be tied up before they, uh, start moving again. You'll find a supply of things you can use for weapons out there as well—at least, there was a pile of gleanings in the corner that looked promising."

A number of men interned here were injured, mostly roughed up like the mate, but some cut or with broken bones. *Don't get distracted by them now*, growled Des. *You can fool with them later, once we're at sea.*

Right. But Pen added to the chamber, "Let the hale help the halt!"

Movement rumbled through the candle-shot shadows as the men began sorting themselves out. If they were mostly one ship's crew, they must already be used to working together under dangerous conditions, or so Pen hoped. He turned back to the first mate.

"Once I get you to your vessel, I want you to take me and my nieces—uh, that is, those Jokonan girls—to Vilnoc. There will be some reward for delivering us there. After that, you'll be free to go where you will."

"It's not even my ship. I suppose it belongs to the captain's widow, now. And I've lost all our lading!"

Upset people tended to get tangled in the most useless details, sometimes. "You might be able to make a new start on trade goods in Vilnoc, before returning the ship to the widow. She'll want the news as soon as may be—better saddened than endlessly uncertain. Main thing is you have this one chance to get you and your shipmates off of Lantihera. Because I've met the Rathnattan here who is buying galley slaves, and trust me, you don't want to fall into his hands."

That seemed to focus the man. He nodded grimly.

While this was going on, another sailor had come up: rangy, skin a sun-darkened bronze, ragged and stubbled. An equally bronzed and scruffy younger man followed him. Everyone in here smelled like a privy, there was no helping that, but they seemed to have been soaking up the fumes for longer.

"What are they saying?" Rangy asked his partner in Roknari.

"Something about Vilnoc. Or Rathnatta, I'm not sure."

"We don't want to go to Vilnoc!"

Penric turned and shifted smoothly to low Roknari. "And who might you be, sir?"

The man grabbed his tunic sleeve. "You can speak!"

"And listen. How did you come here?"

"I'm just a poor fisherman of Astwyk." Another island up the Carpagamon chain, Pen dimly recalled. "They took my boat! It was all I had!" Remembered distress pushed him close to weeping. "Why us? It was just a poor boat! And some fish!"

Pen wondered if he'd be less outraged over richer targets. "The prizes were your persons. Pirates will raid anywhere for those, poor boats or poor villages, as long as they are ill-defended and easy. Like plucking the fruit that hangs lowest on the tree."

"But what's this about Vilnoc?"

"I've come to free you, and we are going to flee to Vilnoc." Assuming his conclusion, but if Pen assumed it firmly enough, he hoped it would stick. "Once we're all protected there, everything else can be sorted out."

"What am I to do in Vilnoc without my boat, without a single coin? We'd just be sold into debt-bondage!"

Debt-bondage was considerably easier to escape than slavery; indeed, most people who fell into it expected it to be temporary. Some were wrong, of course, either death overtaking them before they repurchased or outlived their contracts, or, if they found themselves in a comfortable situation, just settling down reconciled to their reduced status. But Pen could entirely understand the lack of allure.

"If it will reassure you, I can give you my personal guarantee that will not happen." A certainty beyond Pen's own purse; at that point he might have to start calling in favors.

"Who are you to promise that?"

"A man who would make a very bad galley slave."

Which was certainly a believable assertion. The fisherman fell back to confer in his own tongue with the rest of his stolen ship's crew.

Some of the sailors reappeared, dragging in the half-paralyzed and disarmed guards from the front room. One of them took the chance to get in a few retaliatory kicks. Pen's hand landed on his shoulder. "That's not necessary. You can tie them up. Or just lock them in here when we leave."

The man swore and turned on him, brows lowered, beginning to snap something; but then fell silent, stepping uneasily away.

A sailor pulled one of his comrades, clanking, up to the first mate. "None of these keys work!"

Pen sighed and bent to the leg irons. "Let me try. Ah, there." The bolts fell into his hand. The comrade shook the shackles free. All three men goggled at him as he rose.

"How did you do that?" asked the sailor.

"There's a trick to it," Pen said vaguely. "It's a puzzle. Like that one with the bent nails." Which had repeatedly defeated him as a child, as he recalled. *Not anymore.* He smirked to himself.

The three said nothing, instead hurrying away to join their fellows who were filing out to marshal their foray in the corridor and the front room. But the first mate frowned back at Pen, and from somewhere in the chamber echoed an unwanted whisper of *Sorcery! He's a sorcerer!*

The mob of them were too noisy to fit Pen's notion of a night raid, but with luck things would go swiftly. The most able-bodied shouldered up to the front ranks, with the injured, mostly helping each other, trailing after. The nervous but determined first mate took the natural lead, or was thrust into it. He had surrendered rather than die before, Pen recalled, but perhaps his unpleasant experiences since had stiffened his backbone.

The Astwyk fisherman meanwhile gathered up his own crew at the far end of the corridor, preparing to escape out the back way, presumably to search for his own beloved boat. Pen didn't think that the surest bet, but provided they didn't impede his own escape he wasn't going to argue with the man. Chaos worked in any direction.

The sailors from the *Autumn's Heart* poured out of the prison and moved off in the dark like a big mumbling caterpillar, more shuffling than charging. But the distance to the pier was short and downslope, and they picked up momentum despite themselves.

Pen hung back till he was sure they'd reached their ship. The wharf guards seemed fire-watch rather than soldiers, and were swiftly overborne by numbers. Pen heard muffled cries and a couple of splashes as bodies hit the water, then the reassuring thump of feet upon a deck, followed by more confidently nautical barked orders.

Pen turned and ran for the side street.

The girls were still where he'd concealed them, thankfully. They hadn't wandered off or even fallen asleep again, but instead waited in a worried huddle.

Their breaths hitched as he dashed up, but they didn't recoil or yelp, so presumably they could at least recognize his height and pale hair in the gloom. They rose at his panted, "Come on. Time to go! Run."

They did their best, but Pen's legs were undeniably longer. He tugged them down the street in little leaps, like young deer. "Where are we going, Master Penric?" gasped Seuka.

"I've secured us a ship. It will take us to my home in Vilnoc." If it got away from the dock swiftly enough to outrun pirate reinforcements from shore that would surely be coming along soon, when the noises from the prison and pier were finally noticed.

The sailors already had one jib-sail up, stretching out to catch the gentle land breeze and bestow the first steering-way. A couple of figures scurried along the edge of the pier, casting off lines. "Hurry!" called someone from the thwart, peering landward toward the prison and Pen. "I can see him coming back!" Leaving the lines to trail in the water, the figures pelted from the dock and galloped up the gangplank, which swung and scraped as the ship started moving.

"Hey!" yowled Pen. "Hold! We're here!"

A pair of sailors *looked right at him* and yanked the gangplank inboard. The ship eased away from the pier, the black water below widening. Already it was farther than Pen could jump, and certainly farther than he could toss the sisters, even one at time. *Crow-girls don't fly . . .* And neither could sorcerers.

"What are you idiots *doing*?" Pen screamed after them.

The first mate hung over the rail, looking unconvincingly apologetic. "I'm sorry! But we cannot be having with a sorcerer aboard. You'd bring us bad luck for sure!"

I'll show you bad luck. I could still sink you from here, you know! Pen, gasping in breathlessness and outrage, barely kept the threat from escaping his tongue. Or, more effectively, from his seething mind.

A couple of seamen stood at the rail beside their leader and made averting holy signs at him.

Pen's return signs were a lot less holy. "You ignorant, ungrateful, selfish sons-of-bitches!" As he stamped along the pier in parallel to their retreat, a torrent of long-unused Wealdean broke from his lips. It was a wonderful language for obscenities, guttural, blunt, and inventively coarse. Wealdean invective had *weight*. It blew his audience back from their rail in brief alarm, but, alas, had no other effect. Even that was lost as the mate cuffed his comrades and sent them to help raise more canvas. At the bow, a spinnaker was haled upward and bellied out, sliding the ship silently away into the night waters.

Pen, halted by the pier's end, bellowed after it, "Bastard's *teeth* I hate sailors!"

He was overheated and dripping with sweat, partly from the run but mostly from using too much magic, too fast. Too carelessly. Too obviously. *Obviously*.

The Corva girls, Pen discovered as he wheeled, were hunched together staring at him in deep dismay.

He hardly needed his dark-sight, raking the shoreline, to spot more trouble on its way. The wavering torches wcrc clue enough. He switched to Roknari. "We have to get off this pier and hide. If they don't see us, chances are they'll think we escaped on that ship, which will buy us time. There's no going back to the ransom house now."

Because if the sisters took refuge there, they would presumably be separated according to the original sales agreement, one sent north, one south, despite the missing Penric. How angry, and at whom, was Falun going to be to discover he'd been sold a false scribe? It occurred to Pen, belatedly, that the revelation of his true calling might protect him from being carried off on Falun's ship. What would happen instead was extremely unclear.

"Are you really an evil sorcerer?" whispered Seuka. And when had she learned to understand that word in Adriac?

Pen rubbed his face in exasperation. "I am really a *Temple* sorcerer. Very tame. Learned Penric. Divine of the white god, graduate almost with honors of the great seminary at Rosehall which . . . you've never heard of, right, never mind. If I were an *evil* sorcerer, I would have sunk those thankless Adriac scum-suckers." Or set the ship on fire. That would have been gratifying. And spectacular. A lesson all around worth half-a-dozen sermons. He'd missed a teaching opportunity.

Now, now, I was quite impressed with your restraint, murmured Des. *Perhaps the white god knew what He was doing after all when He gifted me to you.*

I'm glad someone did, Pen fumed.

"Weren't you casting a spell?" said Lencia.

"It *sounded* like magic words . . ." said Seuka warily.

Better awkward questions than screaming and running, Pen supposed.

"Only cursing in the ordinary way. In Wealdean. Which is an entirely unmagical language, I assure you. Magic doesn't work like that." Grabbing and dragging them wasn't a good choice just now. Pen waved his hands attempting to herd them instead. "Move, move! The pirates are coming." Beleaguered, he added, "I'll explain all about it once we get somewhere safe." *Temporarily safe*.

It appeared they were marginally more afraid of pirates than of sorcerers, or else wildly curious about him, because they turned to stumble off the pier at last. Pen led right, angling away from the shore. As they plunged into the deeper shadows of the narrow streets, the sisters reluctantly took Pen's hands again. It wasn't as if they had anyone else's hands to take.

Where are you guiding us now? inquired Des.

To that Quintarian temple we saw from the crow's nest. It should be somewhere on this side of town, uphill. Help me navigate.

To be sure, but if you are thinking of taking refuge there, you may be optimistic. For all we know it's been reconsecrated as Quadrene. Or turned into a warehouse.

If the latter, so much the better. I just need a place to think. Again. Two good plans, ransom and mass escape, had turned to wet paper in his hands because other people wouldn't be sensible. Maybe he needed a plan that didn't rely on other people. Or being sensible.

They only had to backtrack from blind alleys twice before they came out on the narrow square fronting the temple. It featured a fountain serving the nearby streets, running feebly. Dawn nipped their heels, the sky above the eastern hills growing steely, as Pen led the way under the temple's front portico. A lantern hook dangled, but no lantern hung on it. Brought in at night for fear of theft? Pen snorted at the irony and tested the lock on the double doors. It did not give way easily, though more due to corrosion than complexity. No people inside right now. He slid through, motioned the girls after him, and eased the door shut.

Not a warehouse, at least. Pen counted five altars, one against each wall, and breathed relief, laced with stale incense, for Des's other pessimism disproved. A modest clerestory between the shallow dome and the walls, an oculus above, and narrow arched windows over each altar would shed light—in the daytime. The fire on the holy plinth in the center had burned to cold ash, overdue for raking and relighting. Someone was slipshod, or else firewood was excessively dear, here. Or both.

"Is this a safe place?" said Lencia, her voice tinged with doubt.

"For the next hour or so, probably. Until they open up for the day."

Musty prayer rugs and cushions were stacked beside each altar, ready for use by supplicants. Pen pulled some from the Bastard's niche and piled them three high on the stone floor before it, placing the cushions for pillows. "Here. You can at least lie down and rest for a bit while I look around."

"Is that all right with the god?" said Seuka. "I've never been in a *Quintarian* temple before . . ."

"It's not so very different," said Pen, then realized he'd never been in a Quadrene temple, either. *Four-fifths true*, Des assured him. "As for the white god, I have something of an arrangement with Him." A sometimes-dubious arrangement, but certainly intimate enough to share bedding. Whether this temple's keepers would agree was yet to be explored.

The girls settled, but did not lie down, frowning at him through the shadows. Pen didn't think they could make out much more than a smudge of his face and gleam of eyes and hair. Well, and his smell, drying sweat and filthy clothes, but everyone shared that. Maybe they should have taken yesterday afternoon for laundry instead of language lessons.

"So, um," began Lencia. "How long have you been a sorcerer?" A very grownup conversation opener, apart from the slight quaver in her voice. A ten-year-old terrified orphan, trying to be the grownup, right. Pen bit his lip and simplified.

"Since age nineteen. I was riding down the road near my home and chanced upon a traveling Temple sorceress, elderly, who had suffered heart failure. I stopped to help, but she was dying. A creature of spirit, like a demon—or a human soul, for that matter—cannot exist in the world of matter without a body of matter to support it. Finding me agreeable, the demon jumped to me." *And my future was wholly changed.*

Improved, I trust, murmured Des.

Don't fish for praise. But Pen had to suppress a smile.

"You were *possessed* by a *demon*?" whispered Seuka in shock.

"Are you still?" added Lencia, a little swifter at the implications. She edged back on her rug, though not as far as the hard stone.

"No, I took possession of the demon. And consequently its magic. That made me a sorcerer. Who's in charge is a very important distinction. We call it the demon ascending when it's the other way around. And then actual Temple sorcerers and saints have to go iron things out." This was not the time or place to go into those messy details, Pen sensed. "After that I trained to be a divine. It's usually the reverse order, a person trains before the Temple gifts them a demon, but our case was an emergency. She's like a voice in my head." *Who argues with me.* Best leave out the twelve-fold complications of that, too.

"Your demon's a *girl*?" gasped Seuka.

"Mm, in a sense. Her name is Desdemona."

Given the tight lips and wide eyes of his audience, this wasn't helping.

"She gets along very well with my wife," Pen offered in his demon's support. "Which is good, because it can be a bit like being married to two different people living in the same body."

Lencia's mouth fell open. "You're *married*?" By her tone, his possessing a wife was even more startling than his possessing a demon. Well, in this case perhaps he was the one possessed, and delighted to be so. *Keep simplifying.*

"Yes, we live in a little house in Orbas, together with her mother. Some men don't get along with their mothers-in-law, but we're quite taken with each other. It's nice there." Or was, before he was sent off on a fool's errand and *captured by pirates*. And the sooner he remedied that, the better. He wasn't sure if the girls were actually finding this spate of domestic detail comforting. "I really do serve the archdivine of Orbas. Who lends me to Duke Jurgo, if there's a problem he wishes to set me to. I can get on with my own studies in between, so that works out. But under it all, always, I work for the white god." *Will or nil*. "Who is the protector of orphans, in Quintarian theology." He waited a few moments for this broad hint to sink in.

The wariness did not ease. Pen soldiered on. "So, I've told you all about me. Tell me something more about your mother." *Jedula Corva*, they had let slip her name during those long hours in the pirate-ship hold. "Was she a secret Quintarian? Which god signed her at her funeral?" Both the girls' parents had prayed for their safety, he had no doubt, but only one had certainly met a god face-to-face. Once.

A jerk, a flinch; an increase, not a decrease, in tension. Lencia swallowed and said, "The demon god isn't allowed to sign at a Quadrene funeral."

"A fifth of the time, that ought to be a problem. How do the Quadrene divines in Jokona prevent the white god's sign from being received?"

"He doesn't have a fish," said Seuka, with an everybody-knows-that shrug.

Aye, said Des cheerily. *Fiddle the actions of the funeral animals, which granted is easier when it's four fish swimming in a tub and the divine calling interpretations. Or, if they can't do that, feign the soul is sundered. They'll only admit the truth if they are very annoyed with the deceased or their family.*

Which Pen had heard of, yes. *Quadrenes must believe they are up to their knees in ghosts.* He wondered how offended he should bother to be on behalf of the Bastard, given that the god and His assenting souls danced away together quite beyond the reach of any human chicanery. It was only the living bereaved who were shortchanged.... Or relieved, he supposed.

Coin toss, agreed Des. *Even in Quintarian lands.*

But Pen was after more particular information. *Let them tell what they know.*

"She was signed by the fish of the Mother of Summer," Lencia said at last. "The divine said. On account of her being a mother. But . . ." She trailed off, guarded.

Seuka, less discreet, announced sturdily, "But that wasn't what she told *us*."

Pen leaned his back against the Bastard's altar table, the gritty flagstones cool under his haunches, and pretended to be relaxed. "Oh . . . ? And what did she tell you, and when?"

The gloom of the chamber was receding as the sky paled over the dome's oculus. The two girls looked at each other as if for permission or encouragement, then Lencia said, "She was very feverish."

Memories were slippery stuff, but some were stickier than others. Pen still remembered unwanted vivid details from his own father's feverish deathbed, and that was getting on for two decades ago. So he didn't think it pointless to ask, "What precisely did she say?"

Seuka frowned. "She had Taspeig bring us in. She couldn't breathe very well."

The scene plainly rising behind her pinching eyes, Lencia continued, "She said, 'You're going to be all right. I've been bargaining with my body all my life, why not my soul? I've given you into his hands in exchange.' And then she choked for a while, and Taspeig held her up to drink, and she said, 'Best coin I've ever been offered, from a more reliable client.' And then she choked some more, and waved her hand, and Taspeig sent us out."

"We didn't know she was going to die that night," said Seuka, gulping a little. "Afterward, I thought she meant one of her regular fellows was going to adopt us. But that didn't happen."

"She didn't say a name," said Lencia. "Taspeig said she didn't to her, either."

It would be strange even for a feverish woman to entrust an oral will to two children who couldn't possibly effect it. A servant was a barely better witness. The crow-woman appeared to have managed a decent independent life for herself and her children, by the standards of her trade; not the glamor and riches of a high-class courtesan like Mira of Lodi, but not the degradation of the streets, nor even the protection of a brothel at the cost of autonomy. But their own little house had been rented, and there could not have been much else left to them or the girls would have been snapped up by someone in Jokona. And probably stripped of their bequests in short order.

What a bold courtesan! murmured Des, sounding impressed. *Even Mira never bargained with a god!*

If there's a coin that moves the gods, I'd like to know it.
You already do. Her soul, of course.

You think she threatened to sunder herself? Pen's breath drew sharply in. The words hadn't sounded like a woman in despair, but any soul might deny the gods that much. And some women were known to make fantastically heroic self-sacrifices for their children.

Not at all. I think there was another goddess standing near her bedside, bidding for her. For the Bastard to slip one of His best-beloved out from under the nose of the Mother of Summer at such an auction? He might promise much.

The gods, Pen was reminded yet again, didn't value people by the same measures people did. The great-souled and the great saints weren't found only among great men, or even very often so. Of course, the humble were more numerous to start with. Would it be possible to do some sort of holy head-count, and determine if blessedness was evenly distributed? Maybe not; the high were much better recorded than the low. Maybe no merely human eyes were fit to see why the god had so valued this daughter of His.

But in trying to guess why these two sisters seemed so prized that the god of mischance would dump one of his own sorcerers into their hold, maybe Pen had been looking in the wrong direction. *Not destiny, but heritage.*

An appalled grin threatened to stretch his mouth. *What, so the white god has drunk up His chosen soul like a merrymaker at a tavern, and rolled out leaving me to pay His bill?*

It was a rude way to think about the gods, but the

Bastard could be a very rude god. And, truly, the gods could do nothing in the world of matter except through beings of matter. A doctrinal point Pen had constantly to explain to people trying to pray for good weather or no earthquakes, who never listened, he'd finally decided, because they didn't want it to be so. The gods did not control the weather. Or the world. Or souls.

But death, oh, they own *that.*

Pen made the five-fold tally of the gods, touching forehead, mouth, navel, groin, and hand spread over his heart, then raised his fist to tap the back of his thumb twice against his lips—the thumb and the tongue being both the special symbols of the white god, for good or ill depending on one's beliefs. "Your Jokonan divine lied," he told the girls. "I think that Jedula of Raspay went into the hands of her white god as heart-high as the betrothed at a wedding feast. And found great comfort there. The rest," he sighed, "is up to us."

Pen wasn't sure if the girls took this in as faith or just as proof he was benignly mad.

But, "Oh," said Lencia, and Seuka swallowed, looking as near to tears as he'd yet seen her. Was it from their mother that they'd learned not to weep in the face of fear?

Fear is easy. Joy is hard, said Des.

Mm.

Pen levered himself to his feet. His overstrained body had stiffened while he sat, but this listening had been worth it. "I need to find a better place to hide you before people begin stirring. I'll be back shortly."

❖ ❖ ❖

A door in the wall next to the Bastard's altar led to the back premises. Pen slipped through and found himself under a short colonnade. To the left, a high gate led out. Ahead lay not so much a temple complex as a temple simplex, a typical rectangular stone building around a central court which had its own small fountain, presently dry. Stairs and a wooden gallery served a course of upper rooms.

Residents? Pen asked Des.

Only three right now, upstairs sleeping.

There should have been rather more, even for a small neighborhood temple. Pen took a quick circuit under the gallery. A room for the divine to change his robes, an office and library, a kitchen along the back, refectory, storerooms, a lecture room converted to a lumber room . . . that last seemed the best bet for a temporary den, or else an unused room upstairs.

Pen returned to the colonnade and checked beyond the gate. A stable for the sacred animals was built against the outer wall, with a low, slanting roof. The old timbers were sturdy and elaborately carved. New repairs were crude. The long shed seemed currently underpopulated, with a pen of chickens, a couple of nanny goats, and a dozing donkey flopped in its straw. The menagerie seemed less hallowed than practical, not that it couldn't be both.

Pen returned to the temple hall. His breath caught and his steps quickened as he heard a voice grumbling, "Who left this door unlocked? . . . Hey! You street rats can't sleep in here!"

Dawn light leaked through the oculus, the arched

windows, and, now, the front door, shoved wide. A
fellow—townsman or peasant, hard to tell by his plain
garb—stood beside the fire plinth with his hands on his
hips. He bore a rack on his back holding a bundle of
trimmed branches, which he doffed and swung down to
the floor. He opened his mouth to shout again at the
trespassers, but his jaw hung slack as Penric came up
beside the girls, who were pushing themselves up from
their rugs, sleepiness warring with fright.

The wood-carrier stepped back, his hand going to the
knife at his belt. Pen could see the calculation on his face
as he attempted to average the threat: tall strange man,
danger; small children, not. And Pen bore no visible
weapons; better. The firmness returned to his spine.

"You can't sleep in here. Off with you quick, now, and
I'll say no more." His strong island Adriac accent went
with his sawed-off, sturdy island build.

Pen suppressed his frustrated curses and let the
cultured tones of Lodi infuse his own voice. "But I have
quite a lot to say. To begin with, who are you?" Temple
servant, obviously, to be bringing in the morning's
firewood for the plinth. Or the kitchen, as might be.

The man's face pinched in suspicion. "Brother
Godino. I run this place, as much as it gets run."

"I need to speak with the divine."

"You already are. As much as there is one."

Pen's brows rose. "This temple has no trained divine?
Or acolyte?"

"It did. Once." Godino scowled at him, and as an
afterthought extended the glare to the girls.

Pen hesitated. Would this work? "I am Learned

Penric of Orbas. I claim sanctuary in this temple, by the gods' sacred aspects and the rights of my vows, for myself and my wards."

Godino clutched his hair and vented a horrible huff of a laugh. "Oh, gods. You're escaped slaves, aren't you."

"Escaped I'll grant you. Slaves, not yet."

"And so they all say. D'you think you're the first to try this? There is no sanctuary to be had here from the Guild. They go where they want and do what they want, and when they come to drag you back out, I *might* be lucky to only get a beating for having seen you and not cried 'ware at once."

"I don't think it would go like that." *At first.* Though if his enemies brought enough men, even a sorcerer would be overwhelmed, so that was a situation to avoid; he could agree with Godino there. "But the pirates believe we escaped on a ship last night. If you hid us, there would be no reason for them to come searching. We could evade notice for quite a long time."

"And then what?"

"And then you could send a message for help by Temple courier, and someone would arrive to take us off your hands."

"Aye, whisking you off on a magic bird, no doubt, and leaving me here to take the brunt of the Guild's anger? Setting aside there's no courier here either. If you're that much of a somebody, you can ransom yourself and leave me out of it."

"I"—Pen scratched his head—"may have peeved the pirates, a bit. I'd rather not count on ransom."

Godino stepped back and pointed at the door, his hand shaking. "*Out!*"

Penric cleared his throat and said diffidently, "I, ah, hadn't been going to mention this, but I also happen to be the court sorcerer of the duke of Orbas." Well, on occasion, but this did seem to be a moment to raise his repute. "I really do think you will find it in your best interests to help us."

Godino choked on a laugh. "Good one, Lodi fancy-boy. You're no more a sorcerer than you are a divine. *Out!*"

Des . . . ?

Oh yes.

Pen held out his arm dramatically aimed at the plinth and snapped his fingers.

A gout of flame whooshed up seven feet in the air, with a brief roar like an angry lioness.

Godino leaped back uttering an oath. The girls scrambled onto the same mat and clutched each other in voiceless alarm, laced with bug-eyed fascination. The stagecraft was unnecessary for lighting the fire, except perhaps under Godino. With very little charcoal in the ashes to feed upon, the flames died down quickly, but Penric thought the point had been made.

"I am a Temple scholar and learned divine," Penric intoned, "graduate of great Rosehall and chosen of the white god, and I am here to relight your holy fire. One way or another. By sorcery if necessary." He gathered himself and a memory of one of the more daunting sermons of his experience, and thundered, "*Do you understand?*"

Penric thought Godino understood he'd been trapped

between murderous pirates and a wrathful sorcerer, and the pirates might be more numerous but the sorcerer was *right here*.

"*Yes*," he squeaked, wide-eyed. His glance shifted toward the door.

"And don't try to flee, either," said Penric. "You can't outrun magic." Well, he could, but Pen felt no obligation to explain how. He strolled forward, feeling something between gratified and mildly ill. Bullying a Temple servant was so much easier than bullying pirates. For real villains, mere threats would not suffice, and then things would grow ugly. Uglier. But he needed to get this man under control, and quickly, or their sole advantage left from last night's debacle would be lost.

"Hide us now," said Pen persuasively. "You can always betray us later. . . . Or try to."

The edged smirk he sent with this made Godino flinch. Pen could see the moment the man gave in by the shrinking of his shoulders. Godino set his teeth on something that might have been a prayer or the reverse, and muttered, "Come this way, then. Keep quiet. The fewer who know of you here the better."

The girls had been following this only with their gazes, shifting anxiously from one terse speaker to the other. Pen urged them to their feet, repeating the order for quiet in Roknari. Meek mice, he thought, had not been that lively pair's role at home before their world had caved in, but they had surely learned it in the past weeks. Lencia grasping Seuka's hand, they practically tiptoed in Godino's wake, wary of yet another untrusted stranger in an unrelenting parade.

He led them up the gallery stairs and into what looked to be a disused temple guest room, containing two narrow beds, a washstand, an old chest, and tattered rugs. Some moth-eaten hangings were piled in one corner; a decent-enough commode chair with chamber pot was tucked in another. The thinness of the dust suggested months rather than years between cleanings, but it still made Lencia sneeze.

Pen stepped around their guide to examine the high window secured with a carved wooden lattice. Wide enough for Pen and, if necessary, his charges to slip through, and overlooking the stable roof; an acceptable escape route, good. Any attempt to lock them in would also be futile, not that Pen was going to point this out. Though Pen suspected Godino would actually be glad for them to bolt, as promptly as possible.

Godino closed the door softly before he spoke again. "You can stay here for the moment. People will be about soon, so don't make noise. We have a funeral this morning."

"Oh? Who for?" Pen hoped he hadn't left any corpses in his wake last night attributable to his magic.

If there were, we'd have known it, said Des grimly. *True.*

"Grandmother from down the street. There'll be a lot of relatives."

Life, and death, Pen was reminded, went on quite aside from pirates. "Do you conduct it?"

"Aye . . . I picked up how by watching Learned Bocali before me. The gods don't seem to mind." He regarded his visitor with new suspicion, as if he expected some sacramental critique.

Given that Pen looked and smelled neither learned nor divine just now, Pen supposed it must be the convincing Lodi accent. He just said, "I expect not." And added, "The children should have clean water first, though. Food when you can. Then we need to talk."

"Huh." With this dubious monosyllable, the templeman retreated.

He returned in a few minutes to tap almost inaudibly on the chamber door, wordlessly handing in a water jug. Pen murmured thanks, and turned back to take stock of his revised set of problems. Again.

"Are we safe?" asked Seuka.

Pen rubbed his tired face and answered honestly, "Not till we reach Vilnoc. But I don't think we can do better right now."

The girls had only had a couple of hours of rest last night, and Penric none. When he'd watered them, had them wash up a bit, and tucked them into one cot, a yawning young head at each end and bare feet tangling, they quickly recaptured the sleep they had almost managed in the temple hall. Pen, lying down tensely on the other cot, envied them for that.

Could they do better for a hiding place? On his own, Pen could probably have gone to ground in his choice of a dozen different holes, feigning any of a dozen different roles. As it was ... maybe not. By training and habit, temples felt like refuge to Pen, though it was true that the gods were no more present at Their altars than They were everywhere else. *Nor less, I suppose.* Temples were for the convenience, and perhaps concentration of mind, of their human builders. Pen by his rank also usually had the silent backing of a formal Temple hierarchy that appeared to be lacking here; Godino seemed a very slim reed to lean upon.

Despite his doubts, his exhausted body apparently decided this place was safe enough, because Pen couldn't tell when he slipped into sleep.

He came awake abruptly when the door squeaked open, shooting up in his cot with a gasp, gathering Des the way some men might reach for a sword. *Right here, Pen.* But it was only Godino, returning with a basket on his arm. Alone, not shoved forward by some gang of murderous pirate rowdies. The room was dim, but the angle of the dusty sunbeams and bright patterns of light splashing on the rugs from the latticed window suggested it was a little past noon.

"Food," said Godino gruffly, setting down the basket on the washstand. He stood back and stared at Pen as if afraid he might set something on fire again.

"Thank you," said Pen, sitting up on the edge of his bed as his heartbeat slowed. He investigated the contents, finding flat bread rounds, olives forever, cheese, some of those dried fish planks that people around here thought were food, and, blessedly, boiled eggs. The basket also harbored a jug of red wine and four clay beakers; the number was explained when Godino pulled up two stools, sat on one, and conscripted the other for a table. Maybe Pen wasn't the only man who wanted to talk?

Pen's shaky reserves, drained by last night's exertions, voted for eating first. He peeled an egg and popped it into his mouth while Godino watered wine for two. The templeman cast a glance at the still-sleeping girls and lowered his voice to a murmur.

"There was gossip at the services about the escape of a ship named the *Autumn's Hand* last night. Some say the crew was freed by a poisoner. Some said it was a magician, cloaking himself in smoke and light, casting terrible spells. Some think it wasn't either, just the guards making excuses for themselves for being overpowered. Which given they're bound to be punished, seemed pretty likely." Godino regarded him steadily, and not for the first time Pen wished Des's skills extended to mind-reading.

"And which do you think?" mumbled Pen around a mouthful of bread and cheese.

"If you hadn't shown up here, I'd have guessed the last, too."

Pen cleared his voice with a swallow of watered wine. "Any suggestion the pirates are still looking for this magical smoky poisoner here on Lantihera?"

"Not so far," Godino admitted grudgingly.

"How reliable is your gossip?"

"Some in the neighborhood work for the Guild, one way or another. Lots of folks, really, all over Lanti Harbor, since the rovers are the ones with the money to hire. Not just as crew or rowdies, either, or taverners, but decent work like boat carpentry or ship chandlers."

"How did the pirates come to control this island?"

Godino shrugged. "There were always a few put in here, to offload their goods or captives, and resupply. Smugglers as well. When Carpagamo kept a garrison here, they regulated them and collected the port fees. Rathnatta the same, whenever one of the princes held us.

"Then about ten, fifteen years ago Carpagamo had one of its wars with Adria, and withdrew their men for work closer to home. Usually that's a signal for Rathnatta to move in, but they were having their own war just then among three brother-princes for succession to their dead father's seat. And that's when the pirates ganged together and set up their own conclave."

"Did no one on the island resist this?"

"Eh. Better the rovers should work in one crew than fight each other all over town and make a wreck of the place. And with no taxes being paid to either Carpagamo or Rathnatta, money was less tight, profits rose, and more pirates came. Before we knew it, the town belonged to them, either by coin or by the sword." Godino sighed. "At some point I expect either Carpagamo or Rathnatta will remember us, and muscle back in. No one's much looking forward to that, either."

"Hm . . . ?"

"When Carpagamo's here, the Quadrenes suffer. When it's Rathnatta, it's us Quintarians. At least the Guild makes sure any preying on the local girls gets paid for." Godino frowned at the sleeping sisters. "And the pirates leave both temples alone, pretty much. Unless someone does something really stupid, like trying to hide runaway captives." His mouth tightened.

"You said this temple once had a divine. Was he under the rule of the archdivine of Carpagamo? Did he leave with the garrison?"

"He wouldn't. Later, I wish't he had." Godino stared at his sandals. "I started here as a boy groom, looking after the holy animals. We had some really nice ones, then. I rose to head groom pretty quickly. After the Guild moved in, some escaped captives came one night to beg sanctuary in the temple just like you did. Learned Bocali stood right there in the portico and told the Guildmen that if they wanted the supplicants, they'd have to go through him.

"So they did. It was a short fight, since he had no weapon but a brass candlestick. Our acolyte was struck down trying to defend the altar treasures, which the rowdies said they were taking for a fine."

The current altar gear, candle- and incense-holders and oil lamps, had all been cheap pottery, Pen realized when he thought back.

"Theirs were the first two funerals I ever conducted by myself, next day, for lack of anyone else. And then I just . . . kept on. Since people didn't stop being born or needing ease or dying. Carpagamo Temple never came back for us, never sent anyone else out"—he looked briefly as though he wanted to spit—"and Rathnatta, well, I sure don't wish for them."

Pen massaged the back of his neck, which was tight and aching. "I see." Godino might be an unlettered man, Pen thought, but he was neither stupid nor unobservant. Nor unfaithful. Just . . . vastly overmatched. It sounded as though he'd been eyewitness to the bloody murders, too, which clearly had left a deep impression.

Pen's glance at the other cot discovered both girls with their eyes open, listening worriedly to the baffling

Adriac. He told them in Roknari, "Brother Godino has brought us some food. It's after noon, so time to get up. Try not to thump too much."

There followed a few minutes of Pen's increasingly practiced overseeing of their morning wash-up, and getting them properly fed. He was able to foist off all the fish planks on them, since apparently people ate something similar in seaside Raspay, thus acquiring an unearned air of generosity whilst snitching most of the boiled eggs. Godino sat in watchful silence. Pen thought he followed the gist of the murmured Roknari.

Pen supplied him with a brief synopsis of the sisters' misadventures, leaving out his own theological speculations or mention of his magic. "Helping smuggle us aboard some ship bound for Vilnoc or even Lodi would get us out of your temple about as quickly as anything," Pen finished, invitingly.

Godino's "Mm," in reply was unenthusiastic, but not at once negative. With a last injunction to stay quiet, he took himself off to his further temple duties.

More exploration of the harbor town and its other possibilities must wait till dark, Pen conceded, however anxious he was to do *something*, because this island wasn't going to sail itself to Vilnoc. Soft-voiced language lessons in Cedonian filled some time, till his captive pupils grew mulish.

Then he hit upon letting Des tell stories in Roknari. Not only had six of her ten human riders once been mothers, even Pen hadn't heard all of her two-century stock of memories despite thirteen years of bearing her. Gloomy Umelan in particular was cheered to be called upon. Her clever efforts even won some halting wonder-tales from Jokona in return, which Pen happily stored up. This served much better, as the sun-splashes crept across the floor.

For all of you children, I think, Des murmured fondly. Pen couldn't muster reproof.

After three days trapped in this gentler prison, Pen was growing quietly frantic. A few covert visits to the temple's tiny library provided scant diversion. *Library* was a grandiose description to start with, as it consisted of two scantly filled bookcases sagging against the wall in the old divine's study. When the pirates had ransacked the place, they had carried off anything with fine leather or gilded bindings that might be sold for a high price, leaving only ratty codices protected by thin planks or waxed cloth sewn together with twine, and some tattered scrolls.

Shabby coverings did not necessarily mean that no rare treasure lay hidden within, as Pen was reminded by the example of Jedula Corva, so as he waited for Godino to find help he leafed through every one of them. Despite his diligence he unearthed no sign of his perpetually sought prize of some lost work on sorcery that would teach him more about his craft than he and Des already knew.

Aye, that would be rare indeed, mused Des.

It *could not possibly* be the case that he was—they were—already the most knowledgeable sorcerer-demon pair alive in the world today.

Someone must be, Des pointed out logically.

It can't be me. I still have so many questions!

At least he was able to carry back a couple of simple books written for children in Adriac, and a pair in Cedonian and Roknari, to his young chamber-mates. The well-worn copies were left over from the period when the previous acolyte had taught neighborhood children in the lecture hall, Pen guessed, being religious tales and saints' legends. Some should be lively enough to divert the girls, he hoped, and give point to the language lessons with which, for want of better entertainment, he filled their waking time.

They were probably starting to wonder if he really was a dull scribe, and the alarming *sorcerer* part a self-serving lie like Pozeni's claim to be a divine. He'd so far resisted their urgings to show them some magic, apart from lighting the night-candle, too convenient a skill to forgo. Well, and demonstrating how he'd supplied them with water in the hold, which rendered them gratifyingly wide-eyed. Especially when he followed it up by producing little hailstones, which they held and marveled at and, inevitably, sucked into their mouths and crunched on, grinning.

Benign little tricks, not scary at all. *If you don't think them through.* He could as easily induce an ice ball to form inside a lung, or a testicle. Or, more helpfully, in a tumor, true. But not in a brain, because that would kill at once, laying Des open to repossession by her god. Thus the subtleties of his skills.

Godino's temple kept a cache of donated used garments to be redonated to those in need; Pen supposed he and the girls qualified. It did allow him to cover everyone and then sneak out to the fountain square at night to wash their reeking clothes, a task made easier by a few of Des's surprisingly large stock of small domestic magics. *Well, really, Pen. Ten women. How do you imagine we would not think of these possibilities?* Once he'd learned to access them, he'd found her aids had made his Order's choice of white robes for their learned divines much more manageable. He was starting to miss those robes, and everything that went with them.

Godino brought food and drink faithfully, yes, and bits of news which suggested Pen and his charges were not suspected to still be on this island. But he was inventively elusive about his failure to secure some trusted boatman to ferry them to Vilnoc, or—Pen was getting less fussy— *anywhere* on the opposite coast from which they could at least walk to Vilnoc. Pen began to wonder if Godino was trying to wait them out, induce them to leave on their own from sheer frustration without him ever having to stand up to the menacing sorcerer. Or the menacing pirates. That Pen could perfectly understand his point of view did not make it any less maddening.

The girls, too, grew restive in the enforced quiet, slowly recovering at least physically from their ordeal. Which, really, had begun with their mother's last illness and hadn't let up yet.

On the fourth night, Pen gritted his teeth and slipped out to make a new survey of the harbor.

In the deep dark, the crooked streets of Lanti were deserted by its timid or sober residents, which left only the other sort abroad. Pen had picked out tunic and trousers in a muddled green dye from Godino's stores, and let the girls knot his hair at his nape and tie a black headcloth over it, so at least he didn't glow like the moon in the shadows. As he neared the shore, both Des's Sight and dark-sight allowed him to avoid the late carousers reeling home, and more disturbing sullen shapes curled up in passageways. Not appearing weak to their hungry eyes would fend off the latter, but not being seen at all was better.

He dodged around the warehouses and the customs shed. A cargo-loading crane on heavy wooden wheels was drawn up near the pier by the prison, and Pen quietly climbed it for a better vantage.

Two new ships had arrived and tied up, though whether they were pirates, prizes, or merchants was unclear. The prison was already repopulated, though, and there were a few more guards around it, so at least one vessel must be a prize. In addition to the fire-watch patrolling the shore, crew lingered on board, keeping night-lanterns glimmering orange by the gangplanks. Falun's galley still rode at anchor out in the harbor, so the Rathnattan slaver evidently hadn't filled his quota yet.

I would dearly love to sink that thing, Pen sighed.

I'm for it, Des agreed cheerfully. *Now?*

Tempting. But there might be prisoners chained belowdecks, so it wasn't simply a matter of deploying his favorite sabotages from here. He'd have to swim out, climb aboard, and somehow free them first, multiplying his risks. Not least that of revealing the continuing presence of a sorcerer in Lanti, triggering a serious hunt for him. One ship mysteriously sinking in perfect calm could be put down to any number of causes. Two would start to look decidedly odd.

And the escaping prisoners would still be trapped on this island with their angry captors. Pen was disinclined to sacrifice them for a diversion he did not need.

You're no fun, said Des. If amiably.

He slid down from his perch and slunk off among the piles of fishing gear, nets, and rowboats scattered along the curving strand. Most of the rowboats were meant to ferry crews out to the larger boats at anchor, or fish in the harbor on calm days, and many of them would need at least two strong men to shove them off the sand when the tide was low. A handful of the vessels now moored to buoys out on the lapping water were single-masted craft meant for small crews, so, not impossible; although the smallest craft Pen had ever sailed in on Cedonian seas had carried a crew of three. Hauling up a heavy sail by himself would be a challenge, even with the aid of two wiry girls, though there was a chance there might be some sort of crank for the task.

Could the Corva sisters swim? Most people couldn't, not even, to Pen's surprise, many sailors. The girls would not be very buoyant to tow, though Pen thought he could do it in a pinch.

A splash out on the harbor waters made him flinch, and he peered with both Sight and dark-sight. The inky surface rippled in repeated waves, a faint satin gleam flicking above it. *Ah. Dolphins.* A pod of four or five, it looked like, rolling after one another in pursuit of fish.

Pen wondered if his shamanic persuasion skills, which

worked on other animals, would work on dolphins. Or would the blood he would shed in the water as the price of that style of magic just attract sharks? . . . Would the persuasion work on sharks? It would be awkward to find out the hard way that it didn't.

Dolphins would be slippery creatures to try to cling to, hard for him, maybe impossible for the girls. So would it be feasible to hitch a dolphin or dolphins to a small boat? How would one devise such a harness? Some sort of yoke or padded ring that would be comfortable for the animal and efficient to get on and off . . . ?

Only you, Pen, said Des, exasperated.

Regretfully, Pen laid the alluring picture of a team of dolphins towing them home to Vilnoc aside for later experimentation, along with his narcoleptic rats. Or only for some dire emergency.

Very unlikely emergency. You are supposed to be selecting a ship to steal, remember?

He hunkered down and studied the inventory. He imagined that the three smallest boats put in and out irregularly about their tasks, but they seemed day-vessels, so likely they were always here at night. One way or another, there should be a boat for him.

He would give Godino one more day to produce better help. If nothing was forthcoming, tomorrow night might be time to take his chances on the unforgiving sea. . . . Their chances. He grimaced and rose to slither back to the temple.

The next afternoon, the skies clouded and the wind blew up. Pen found the ladder to the roof and crept around the ledge beneath the clerestory to the top of the portico, lying prone to look out. The height gave him a wide view of both town and harbor. Small boats were hurrying back to their moorings, men rowing ashore with their half-day's catch. Graying wind-waves grew white tops, spume flying from them.

All right, *dead calm* likely wouldn't be helpful for escape either, however much Pen fancied it, but this was too much of a good thing. Pen hissed through his teeth much like the wind, and returned to their hiding-chamber.

He took care to avoid being seen by the temple's few servants, which Godino had described as a groom, a cook-scullion, and a local lad who played acolyte to his divine, equally untutored but valiant in assisting him. Neighborhood women, Pen understood, took it in turns to come to clean and arrange what few flowers or other graces the altars received, before and after ceremonies. Pen and the girls were instructed to lie very low and quiet during the rites.

That night, the rain rattled the window lattice in gusts. Pen cursed in Wealdean, rolled over, and went back to sleep.

The delay was repaid to him the next day when Godino slipped in to announce he had secured a willing ferryman.

"Safe and secret?" asked Pen.

Godino shrugged. "Jato, I trust. He vouches for his crew."

"You did let him know there will be some reward to

compensate them for their risks when we reach Vilnoc?"
And, with luck, something to send back to Godino.

"Of course. They aren't fellows who can afford charity.
Or defiance, so if the risks come down on them, the
reward won't be much use. Keep that in mind, Learned."

True enough, so Pen didn't quibble. "How soon can
we leave?"

"On tomorrow afternoon's tide."

"In broad daylight?" Pen frowned.

"It will be the busiest time. And look less suspicious
than putting out at night."

"Hm, I suppose." However uncertain Godino's
selection was, it still had to be better than Pen trying to
find a boatman blind, with no local knowledge. "I trust
you have not told him I'm a sorcerer."

"He wouldn't have agreed to take you if I had."

"What did you tell him?"

"That you were a man who wanted to go in secret to
Vilnoc."

"Not that we were escaped captives?"

"No, not that either, for the same reason, though I
don't doubt he figures something smells. But if you think
that him pleading he didn't know would save him from
Guild reprisals, you're more optimistic than either of us."

Godino offloaded their lunch and swapped out their
chamber pot. Pen wondered how private the man had
really managed to keep his unwanted guests from the
other temple servants. The non-arrival of some gang of
rowdies to recapture them—well, try to—was the only
clue Pen had, though it did suggest the temple people
were either very loyal, or still in ignorance.

I approve of ignorance, Des commented. *It cannot fuel betrayal.*

"What did Brother Godino say?" Lencia asked anxiously when the door had closed behind the man.

"He was talking about boats, wasn't he?" said tense Seuka, sitting up. "Did he get us a boat to go on?"

"Yes, and boatmen," replied Pen. "I was preparing to steal one two nights ago, but this is safer. Bigger." And without a novice at the tiller. "Plus I won't have to deprive some poor honest fisherman of his livelihood. There are few enough honest men on Lantihera."

He wondered if he should try to arm the sisters. Knives of a size they could handle wouldn't be much use against a war hammer, even in trained hands. Their thin safety lay in their sale value, which was not high. It wouldn't take much resistance for an assailant to decide they weren't worth the aggravation and move on to easy murders. Pirates quite preferred weak opponents. Still . . . "Shall I try to get you some belt knives from Godino?"

"Yes!" said Seuka.

But Lencia looked at him more coolly. "You don't have one."

"It was taken from me the first day. I usually used it for shaping quills."

"Knives would be better than nothing," she conceded.

Pen was by no means sure. But it might make them feel better, and so just that hair less likely to panic in a tight moment. "I'll see what I can get."

Pen continued to think out loud while sharing around the flatbread and goat cheese. "Packing won't be a problem. Nor water, though we'd best keep that trick out of sight of our crew. It might be well to persuade Godino to give us a little food for the voyage. Which should be short." His heart clenched in the hope he'd been strangling since his capture as too distracting. "We could be home in as little as three days."

He'd only lived a year in Vilnoc, so he wasn't really homesick for the town. It was their narrow house, or rather, its occupants—Nikys, her mother Idrene, yes, even her brother Adelis. He wasn't sure if he'd made them his family, or they'd made him theirs, but either way, they were the new and unanticipated anchor for his life's wandering vessel.

The girls were giving him their wary looks again, reminding him that this proposed destination wasn't home to them, but rather, another alien way station in their uprooted existences. Just another strange place where strange grownups would be disposing of their lives, more benevolently than slavers but giving them as little choice.

Pen launched into a description of his house, and its back courtyard common with its row, his quiet, book-rich study, and of Nikys and Idrene, with the notion of giving the sisters a share of his hope. Though their questions led promptly away, through his account of Nikys's charge who was just Seuka's age, to a description of the high ducal household. This seemed to fascinate them more, as if it were a wonder-tale like the ones they'd been sharing the other day. Pen could remember feeling that way as a lad, reading stories of brave nobles in faraway places, though any lingering wonder had been stripped out of him by close service to three successive courts. He did not hurry to disillusion them.

Soon after noon the next day, Godino sent his servants on errands and conducted Pen and the girls to the side entry by the stable. His friend—or so Pen hoped—Jato was leaning against the gatepost with his burly arms crossed, scuffing his sandal in the dirt. The red-brick tone of his sunburn suggested Cedonian ancestry, set off by black hair and beard trimmed short. He wore the common garb of a common sailor, sleeveless shirt and calf-length trousers, sash and belt and knife. He glanced up frowning as they approached.

Pen had attempted to reduce his excessive recognizability by tying his queue in a knot again, and topping his pale head with a worn and stained straw hat. And slouching. He wore the local muddled greens, for whatever use that was. The girls, after a long debate over Godino's proffered cast-offs, had dressed themselves as boys. Lencia's dark curls barely went into a queue, and Seuka's ruddy tangle had needed to be forcibly restrained, but altogether they made a passable pair of street rats, hardly worth anyone's second glance. Certainly they little resembled an escaped Lodi scribe and his two nieces.

Jato looked them over. "Vilnoc, eh?"

Pen touched his hat brim. "If you will. You'll be paid as soon after our safe arrival as I can arrange it."

"Huh." Without further comment, Jato pushed off from the gatepost and motioned them after him. Godino closed his gate with a noisy sigh of relief. Under Jato's eyes Pen couldn't sign a grateful formal blessing as befitted a learned divine, but he thought it, tapping his fingers and hoping the gods would know.

The girls started to reach for Penric's hands, but then caught themselves and strode out at his sides more boy-like, fists clenched near their new-old belt knives. He gave them both approving nods and followed Jato in equal silence into the winding streets, not letting his stride lengthen unduly. He could hardly wait to get off this island.

Be on your guard now more than ever, came a murmuring in his head that Pen recognized as Umelan, and not just by her Archipelago idiom. *There remains that very common way to slay a sorcerer by luring him into a boat with promises of succor or pleasure or transport, sailing out some miles, and then throwing him overboard and sailing off before he drowns and his demon jumps. It was how my clan tried to kill me, after Mira's death in Lodi both released and bound me.* The keening grief of that long-ago betrayal still resonated in her bodiless voice. *I, too, had thought I was going home.*

I am advised, Pen promised her. Almost the only way to kill a sorcerer of any experience was by subterfuge and surprise, really. But Jato, at least, didn't flinch from him, bore no tension suggesting he planned such an ambush, showed no more caution than expected toward any chancy passenger.

The passersby, at this hour, were largely women and servants going to or from the markets, or carrying water jars, who gave them only enough notice to gauge their harmlessness. At length, they debouched from the alleys about midway between the two piers.

Beside a heavy rowboat drawn up on the sand, four men waited, idly leaning against the thwart or crouching in its thin shade. They stood up, and one waved, as Jato and his tail trod down to them.

They shuffled to a halt, Jato looking over his crew. "Where're the other two?"

"They said they'd be along soon," replied the man who'd waved. They looked a typical array of Lanti seamen, dressed like their captain, with a mixed range of skin and hair color, leathery rather than bulky, none as tall as Pen. The crewman looked off tensely up the shore. Too tensely.

Pen followed his glance and thought Wealdean words. Apparently, he wasn't even going to have to wait till they were at sea for betrayal.

A dozen men trotted toward them. All but two wore the tabards of the port guards, and were erratically armed with short swords, long knives, a couple of pikes, two crossbows and two short bows. Had that wave been a signal? By Jato's jerk and curse, this delegation was a surprise to him too, and to three of the four other men at his side.

It wasn't hard to follow the logic. If his crewmen followed Jato, they might be rewarded later in Vilnoc, but if they betrayed him here, they would be rewarded right now, more certainly and with less effort. In addition to whatever bounty the Guild offered for the return of escaped slaves, if Jato came to a bad end because of this they might even expect to receive his ship as a prize.

"Stay behind me and stick tight," Pen told the girls,

who, watching in horror, hardly needed the instruction. "Things are about to get messy."

The port guards spread out, expecting sensible surrender in the face of the odds. Jato and two of his three loyalists drew together, although the other stepped back with his hands raised, glumly anticipating events.

One thing was plain. While clearly someone had figured out Pen's party were fugitive captives, no one had yet realized he was also the sorcerer who had blasted through the prison the night the *Autumn's Hand* had escaped. Or they would have brought a couple of hundred rowdies to try to take him, not just a dozen.

The guard leader stepped forward. "Give it up, Jato," he advised genially. "You can't fight us all. Besides, we know where you den up."

By Jato's flinch, Pen wondered if the man had a family.

Bastard's *teeth* but Pen was getting tired of this. And tired in general, and homesick, and *angry. You know . . .* he thought to Des. *Let's just get started.*

Something like a purr sounded in the back of his mind. Did lionesses purr?

No, smirked Des. *But chaos demons might.*

Almost perfunctorily, Pen snapped the four bowstrings. Distance weapons summarily disposed of, next most dangerous were the pikes and their bearers, then the swords and knives. And fists and boots. With enemies this numerous, efficiency was going to be required. No time for pretty tricks. The magic to destroy all those weapons would be an unaffordable drain. That left the wielders. *But not for long.*

Pen began picking out and ruffling big sciatic nerves, hard, starting with the nearest men. His victims discovered this the first time they started to step forward, and instead fell or staggered, shrieking in surprise and pain. It took a minute of close concentration to work through the entire dozen.

A gasp of surprise brought his attention around. Jato's eyes were rimmed white. "You're that sorcerer!"

No denying it now. "Well, yes, but no danger to you. We can still escape." Pen gave the rowboat a shove. It didn't budge. "The four of us, plus me, should still manage to sail. Hurry!"

Jato did hurry—choosing to pelt away along the sand, trailed by his remaining men.

"Bastard piss on you for cowards!" Pen yelled after them, uselessly.

He wheeled, urgently surveying the harbor for other, smaller boats, and smaller rowboats to get out to them. The three likely candidates he'd picked out the other night were gone fishing or whatever, their owners making good use of this bright sailing day, their ferries tethered out at the moorings awaiting their return. Nothing else lay within immediate rowing or even swimming distance, though a couple more full-sized probably-pirate ships had recently arrived to drop anchor and await their turn at the loaded piers.

A yelp from behind him and Lencia's scream of "Seuka!" whipped him around again.

Pen had overlooked one man, the crewman who had made to surrender first. For whatever reason, he'd chosen to grab up Seuka and start running for the town.

Seizing the potential reward? Planning to offer her to the Guild as an apology in hopes of gaining a pardon? Saving her from the evil sorcerer? Pen couldn't guess, but the son of a bitch was *fast*, even with Seuka struggling and kicking in his grip.

Worse, Lencia had started running after them.

"Lencia, stop!" Pen cried at her, and was unsurprisingly ignored. "*Sunder* it!" He clenched his teeth and sprinted in pursuit, his straw hat blowing off.

The kidnapper, or rescuer, angled up through the shore clutter. Pen overtook Lencia, her legs churning and her face set in a determined grimace, and did not stop. Moving targets were harder to hit with the delicate but so-effective internal disruptions, and this fellow was no exception. Furious as Pen was, he wasn't furious enough to risk death and Des.

He didn't have to. About the time the crewman swung in past the warehouse near the prison-side customs shed, Seuka finally managed to get a hand on her belt knife, draw it, and poke at her captor. He barked more in surprise than pain, but flung her aside reflexively. She slammed into the whitewashed wall and slid down. The fellow started to reach for her again, but then looked over his shoulder at Pen wrathfully closing upon him, jolted in fear, abandoned his prize, and just ran.

Pen let him go. He stopped, gasping, by Seuka, who was sitting up shakily not-crying.

"Are you all right?"

"Yes," she sniffled, breathlessly. No broken bones, at least, as there might have been. Bruises would show later.

Lencia arrived in their wake, also winded and not-crying, or at least denying the smears evaporating on her flushed cheeks. "Seuka, you idiot! Why did you let him grab you?"

"I didn't *let* him. He just did!"

Pen turned back to survey what was happening on the beach. Quite a lot, regrettably, as people hurried to and away from the men he'd left in moaning heaps near Jato's rowboat. The hunt would be up in minutes, and this time, he suspected, they would not repeat the mistake of trying to take him on with insufficient numbers.

Better give them something else to worry about.

Des, what do you make of the contents of this warehouse?

Crammed. Bolts of cloth, piles of clothes, furniture, all sorts of miscellaneous thievings. Plaster floor but wooden roof. The impression of an edged smile. *Very dry.*

Do it.

Yes, Penric, love.

He braced one arm against the wall and leaned, enduring the ripple of heat that even the most downhill of magics generated in his body. And this was going to be very downhill indeed.

Enough. Let the white god's fire do its own work. An offering to make up for that cold temple plinth.

Right. Saving room for dessert, my lord.

A grin snaked over his face. Des only used his old title when she was exceptionally pleased with him.

"On your feet, now," he told Seuka, giving her a hand up. She rose easily, so thin and light. No wonder her would-be stealer had made good time. "Follow me. Let's go around the back of this building." Temporarily out of sight from the shore, though more than one person must have seen where they'd run to.

They skated along the side facing the town, passing a locked double door. Pen kicked it open in passing to provide a better draft for his soon-to-be furnace. He paused at the corner. From the next building over, the customs shed, a few men ran off to investigate the uproar going on down by Jato's rowboat. Pen led the girls past the rearward side of the long shed, trailing his hand over the planks, feeling each little back-blow of heat, *magical friction* Learned Ruchia had dubbed it. Dry wood indeed.

Next over was the prison. A half-dozen guards on the roof were gathered gazing out under the flats of their hands, also toward the shore. Pen considered efficiencies. *Moving fast* wasn't going to be useful for much longer, but he thought he might squeeze one more foray out of it.

Leaving the sisters next to a building that would shortly be ablaze wouldn't do, so he took their hands to prevent straying and had them hunker down by the corner of the prison, holding his finger to his lips to enjoin silence. He walked around to the back entry where, this time, two guards were posted, leaning against the stone wall but otherwise alert. Reaching for their short swords, they both pushed off and scowled at Pen's smile as he approached with both his hands held out empty. For a moment, poised to react, they were usefully still.

Lingual nerves, sciatic nerves, axillary nerves, brush,

brush, brush, and they were down, choking and writhing. He stepped around them and down the steps, lifted the bar, and popped the bolt. A quick jog down the dark central corridor left every lock hanging open. He pushed his head into the main prison, just as full of unhappy men as it had been the other night, and was there no *end* to this trade, and called in Adriac, "The rear doors are open. What you do with that fact is up to you."

He hurried back out to where the girls stood staring down in shocked fascination at the guards he'd dropped.

"Was *that* a magic spell?" asked Lencia.

"No. Well, not technically. I really don't think of anything other than a shamanic persuasion or geas as a *spell*, exactly." They scrunched their brows at him, disbelievingly. "I'll teach you the distinctions sometime if you're interested, when we get home. But first we have to get home. *This* way."

They continued on from the prison. Pen did not look back as the first hoarse voices reached the back doors and grew louder, fearfully marveling. Some of those men might die in this escape attempt, but . . . not by his hand.

You can't save everyone, Pen, Des consoled him.

Yes. I learned that well back in Martensbridge. I am not likely to forget.

He was flushed with heat, sweat trickling down his neck and back. The next building seemed to be a run-down taverna. A couple of servants idling by its back door stared at him and the girls as they trotted past, but did not attempt to impede them, their attention seized by the outflux of men from the prison. They hastily darted back inside and barred their door, shouting warnings. Pen led the girls around the far side of the dingy building to where he could again get a view of the harbor.

The crane he'd climbed the other day had been moved out to the pier, probably by an ox team, and was engaged in either loading or unloading one of the ships. The stevedores had dropped their work and were shouting and pointing back up the shore toward the warehouse and customs shed, from which dark gray smoke was now billowing, its nose-stinging acridity already penetrating the soft salt air. Most of them abandoned the pier and jogged off toward the fires. Pen expected some sort of bucket brigade from the sea would soon be organized. He didn't think they'd be able to save either building, but they were welcome to try.

His feet were still planted on this bloody island. *Ships. Boats. Rowboats. Rafts, barrels, anything.*

Out in the harbor beyond the pier, Falun's galley still sat. Pen hadn't had much luck with the gratitude of freed prisoners up to now, but being chained in the hold of such a ship must surely concentrate the mind. Given the choice of rowing to Rathnatta and slavery, or Vilnoc and freedom, surely he wouldn't have to apply much persuasion . . . ? He could probably swim out that far, but—

"Do you see any rowboats at all?" Pen asked the girls, squinting.

Lencia stood on tiptoe. "There! In the shadows under the pier."

"Ah. Yes. Well, it's our rowboat now. Come on!"

In the clash between terror and excitement, excitement must be winning, for they followed him all-eagerness, laughing a bit wildly. They slid down and clambered awkwardly over the stones at the shaded base of the jetty. The boat's painter was hitched to a rusty iron ring driven into one of the big boulders. Pen waded without hesitation into the murky water laced with tan foam. It wasn't cold by his standards—in the *cantons*, you could drive a horse and sleigh across *properly* cold water—but it was cooler than his body, and drew dangerous heat from his blood. He ducked his head for good measure, then shoved the boat around close enough for the girls to tumble in.

Oars lay tucked under the thwarts. Pen was more surprised by their presence than he would have been by their absence, at this point. He might have swum ahead towing the boat by its rope, he supposed, much like his imagined dolphin, but it would have been slow going. He unhitched the knot, heaved a leg inboard, and shoved off, flopping down into the damp bottom where he lay wheezing for a moment.

The girls must have been in a rowboat before—well, Raspay was a port town—because they earnestly pulled up the heavy oars and managed to get their pins seated in their oarlocks without dropping one overboard. Then they looked to Pen.

"Where are we going?" asked Lencia. "We can't row to Vilnoc."

"Alas, no. Just out to that galley." Pen gestured. "You boys can row if you want."

"Oh!" Seuka grinned in delight, and the two hastily

arranged themselves on one seat, an oar each. They pulled with reasonable coordination, and the boat began to slowly move alongside the ship docked on this side, its hull rising up like a wooden wall.

A head and shoulders leaned over the top of this bulwark. "Hey!" shouted the silhouette. "What are you doing?"

Good question. Pen wished he knew the answer. He crawled over to the side of their boat, propped his chin on the thwart, and considered the passing hull. Running a dual line of rot along it just below the waterline for several yards as they rowed by seemed almost routine, but he wasn't above trying anything. He wasn't sure if he was about to sink a pirate, a prize, or a legitimate merchant, and at this point scarcely cared.

Des *giggled*. She was getting dangerously excited much like the girls, but he couldn't bleed off her nervous energy with rowing.

As they came out into the sunlight and the view widened, he rolled over on his back and studied the rigging of the ship tied up on the far side of the dock. Almost out of range, he snapped stays and started a couple of fires in the rolled-up sails. "The Bastard's blessings upon you all," he murmured, and bit his thumb at them.

Lencia gave him a chary look. Seuka, intent upon her rowing, just sucked her lip in concentration.

Pen considered his next plan. It was probable that most of Falun's crew were enjoying time ashore, though some might be engaged with provisioning. Prisoners, even if chained, required some guards. He was getting very practiced with guards, but that was no invitation to get careless. He was also hot and ragged and worried, with red anger pulsing treacherously through his veins, but dwelling on any of those things was no help. He hoisted himself upright and squinted at the galley.

"I think I see climbing netting hanging over the port side. Row over that way."

They passed not far from another vessel at anchor, clearly a rich pirate by its sleek lines and three masts prepared to carry a wide burden of sails for speed. Some crewmen hung on its landward-side rail, pointing and goggling at the clawing blazes ashore, the flames a strange transparent orange in the bright daylight, the air above them shimmering. Pen systematically snapped every stay within his range, igniting the rigging as it collapsed. Cries turned to screams.

There *was* crew aboard the galley, ah, for they, too, had collected on the starboard side to watch the inexplicable disaster progress. Visible smoke was finally rising from the pier. The hull Pen had perforated was starting to list, ever so gently, outward.

Two boys and a man plodding along in a little rowboat passed unremarked, with all this show going on.

"Isn't this Captain Falun's slave galley?" asked Lencia apprehensively as they slid into the shade of its far side.

"Ayup," said Pen, discarding his wet, worn, stolen sandals as slippery and useless. He sat up and prepared to reach for the netting.

"Isn't that *dangerous*?"

"Probably," sighed Pen. "I think I'm getting used to it." He looked up past the line of oar ports, back at the girls. "Stay here a few paces off, and be ready to row away if they start to come for you."

They looked at each other. "Without you?" said Seuka in a tentative voice.

"If necessary."

Lencia cocked her head at him, and said in a remarkably dry tone for a ten-year-old, "To where?"

Pen stared around the disrupted harbor. "I'll... return."

"You'd better," said Seuka, with determination.

Pen swung up onto the coarse rope weave and flashed a grin over his shoulder. "I thought I was the evil sorcerer."

Lencia shot back, "Yes, but you're *our* evil sorcerer."

"Ah." Pen hung a moment, liminally, letting that claim settle into his bones. It made him feel oddly fond. "Yes. I think that must be so."

Seuka nodded firmly. "So don't you get hacked up, either."

"I'll do all I can." He hesitated, then corrected that to, "All we can." Because whatever he was heading into, he wasn't going alone. He tapped his lips with his thumb, felt for toeholds, and pushed himself up the side.

I told you I liked those girls, said Des smugly.

You were right. He paused just before mounting the deck. *Sight.* No souls immediately nearby, though that didn't mean someone farther off couldn't be looking this way. He rolled silently over the rail and crouched barefoot, taking his bearings.

He was on a kind of walkway between the rail and one of the two low sheds or cabins that filled the deck fore and aft on either side of the mainmast. This galley was square-rigged in an older style, though with a smaller mast toward the bow for some sort of jib sail that had the air of a later addition. Somewhere, there must be hatches down to holds . . . there. He edged around the cabin, found the dark square in the deck, and slithered down something like a lethal cross between a stairway and a ladder.

Headroom was scant, he found out by barking his scalp. This space seemed devoted to cargo and crew quarters, judging by the hammocks tucked here and there. Down again. This was the oar deck, oval beams of sunlight from the ports dotting the deck and benches in a row, the glimmer of wave reflections dancing over the low ceiling, a surprising lack of stench. And one more descent, into unrelieved shadow; his dark-sight came up without thought, laying his surroundings bare. *This* was the hold for Falun's lucrative human cargo. Pen could tell by the long rows of leg irons bolted to the hull braces.

Empty. Falun hadn't loaded on yet.

Bastard blast it, I could have sunk this accursed ship the other night!

Pen fell to his knees in something not quite a prayer. *Lord god Bastard, I dedicate this day to you. I hope you are suitably amused. In fact, you can have this whole detestable week . . .*

Apart from two sisters waiting in hope for him out on the water. Pen was keeping that godly gift. That being so, falling over in a lump of rage and despair and drumming his heels on the deck like some uncannily dangerous two-year-old was not an option.

Preferably not, murmured Des. *You know we old mothers have tricks for dealing with such tantrums.*

I'd rather not find out.

He sighed and clambered back to his feet, and up the ladder-stairs. No prisoner-crew to conscript. A ship too big for him to sail. What next?

If you start pining after those dolphins again, said Des, *I'm going to slap you.*

Pen's lips twitched up despite everything. *What, I think it's a* grand *idea...*

Pen stepped up into the light to discover that what was next was Captain Falun exiting the door from the aft cabin and stopping short, staring at him in astonishment. "You!"

Pen scratched his scalp, damp and sticky and itchy with seawater. "You know," he said conversationally in high Roknari—the mode of scholar to servant was nicely insulting—"I've been having an extraordinarily aggravating day. You probably shouldn't *add* to it."

Falun didn't listen, of course. People seldom did. Instead he started back and drew a sharp cutlass from a rack on the cabin wall, turned, and lunged at Pen.

Pen sheared the complex conglomeration of nerves in his armpit clean in half. Falun's arm fell limply and hung at his side, the cutlass falling from suddenly lifeless fingers to clatter on the deck. "*What...?*" He stumbled, unbalanced, the arm swinging from his shoulder like a heavy sack, confusingly painless.

He'd never be lifting a sword again. Or a spoon.

"I could do the same thing to the nerves from your eyes, you know," Pen informed him. "It wouldn't even be theologically forbidden."

For all his dapper air, Falun didn't keep captive slaves

in line, or control the rowdies who kept them in line for him, by being kindly or slow. He bellowed and bent and grabbed for the cutlass with his working hand. Pen danced back from the rising slash and scraped Falun's sciatic nerves good and hard, and then he went down and didn't get up.

The noise, of course, drew his crew away from the distractions at the railing, plus a servant-or-slave from the cabin, and then Pen was put to putting all of *them* down. Fortunately, there were only half-a-dozen men aboard at present, and their mystification at what was happening gave Pen a marginal advantage which he used to the full.

He surveyed the resultant heap of humanity, flopping around at his feet like a catch of fish. He *could* shove them all overboard into the harbor to drown like a betrayed sorcerer. He could. At least physically. Theologically borderline, such murders, hurrying souls unripe to their gods.

Instead he stepped over the groaning bodies to the base of the mainmast and looked up. A line of pegs for gripping, a crow's nest at the top. Des whimpered.

Yes, yes. The ship is barely rocking. Endure, love. He stretched and climbed, realizing about halfway up just how exhausted he was when his arms started shaking. Des whimpered some more, but he made it up to the bare perch of the lookout without falling, wrapped his legs around the last of the mast, and clung.

He first checked for the Corva sisters in their rowboat. There they were, still bobbing about in the shade of the galley. He waved. They waved back, upturned faces puzzled but reassured.

Next, he swiveled around to observe the shore.

Goodness, said Des. One might take the remark for surprise, but to Pen it sounded more like glee.

Three columns of black smoke boiled skyward, blending in the upper air, one from the warehouse, one from the customs shed, and one from the pier. The two docked ships and their pier were all afire now. Well, one ship was having a conflict between rising water and descending flames. Pen wasn't sure if fire or water would win, but it was plain the ship was going to lose. In all three locations, people had given up running around yelling and hauling buckets, and just stood back in little groups watching in morbid consternation.

The rich pirate ship nearby was not faring fortunately either, or else was coming along quite well depending on one's point of view. Pen thought it was lovely, and so, by her approving hum, did Des. The fire had spread from the collapsed rigging to the deck and below, and the sailors were in process of abandoning it, crowded into a teetering rowboat or swimming with the aid of planks or spars tossed overboard.

Pen studied his trail of chaos. *We aren't going to be welcome back in Lanti, are we.*

Shouldn't think it, no, agreed Des.

That's fine. I didn't like the town anyway.

Pen blew out his breath and started looking around the harbor for something, anything, that floated, had a sail, and was smaller than a whale. They now possessed a rowboat to get to it, so they were that much to the good after all this effort. With all his running, had he only succeeded in running them into a blind alley?

A wink of light and flash of color at the broad harbor

mouth drew his attention away from the spectacle of the shore, and he swung around and squinted.

It was a galley. The color had been a sail being furled, the light a reflection off the long double bank of wet oars as they rose and dipped, turning the ship in toward the town. Another Roknari slaver? No, too narrow, too swift . . .

That's a war galley, said Des. She couldn't sit bolt upright in alarm, but Pen could rise for both of them, standing on the support and peering out under the edge of his hand.

No . . . not a war galley . . . One, two, three . . . six, with others occluded behind, seven, nine, ten . . . A couple of fat freight cogs sailed after, the nautical equivalent of a baggage train. The Carpagamons finally coming to reclaim their island? Some Rathnattan prince doing the same? The ships were actually more in the Cedonian style of current naval architecture.

A breath of breeze in the mild afternoon blew the lead ship's pennants out straight.

. . . What was half the duke of Orbas's fleet doing *here*?

And, oh yes, Pen recognized the commander's banner. Nikys had painstakingly and lovingly sewn it for her dear brother, after all.

General Adelis Arisaydia, scourge of the Rusylli and pride and terror of his troops. Pride because terror, Pen gathered, because soldiers thought like that.

He sat with his mouth hanging open and watched in stunned fascination as the Orban fleet paraded into Lanti Harbor.

❖ ❖ ❖

In another moment, Pen overcame his paralysis and scrambled down the mast so fast it made Des yip. He pounded across the deck, leaping the groaning, swearing bodies who had not yet begun to find their feet, and thrust his head over the rail.

"Lencia! Seuka! Come get me, quickly!"

Alarmed, the girls rowed near as Pen swung out onto the netting and dropped into the boat, making it dip and pitch. "I'll take the oars now."

"Are they after you?" asked Seuka, with a fierce look up at Falun's galley.

"No, but I need to catch my brother-in-law."

"What?" said Lencia, giving up her seat to Pen's urgency. ". . . You have a brother-in-law?"

"Yes, and he's here. Somehow." The boat surged as Pen dug in the oars. He only had time to blast a few fist-sized patches of rot below Falun's waterline in passing, which did not nearly relieve his feelings.

As they rounded the slaver, Pen glanced over his shoulder and tried to select a course that would intercept the flagship. Unfairly, Adelis had far more oars than he did, but then the general—or was he appointed an admiral for this venture?—also had a boat measured in tons. Many tons. With great momentum, and a bronze rostrum that could rip through enemy hulls even faster than Pen could.

And, if those ships were full of his seasoned Rusylli-campaign veterans, he led a gang of brutes who could eat pirate rowdies for lunch, and possibly intended to.

As the two vessels converged, Pen stood up on his knees on his seat, shouted, and waved frantically.

Lookouts observed, conferred; in a moment, a broad, tough, familiar figure in an army cuirass of boiled leather plates and a thrown-back red cloak came to the rail, saw him, and called orders over his shoulder. After a moment, all the churning oars rose in unison and paused. Men hurried, and a climbing net was flung over the bow ahead of the oar banks.

Pen rowed faster, the ship slowed, and he managed to bump the rowboat into the right spot. "Grab on!" he yelled at the girls, who reached for the netting. They didn't quite match speed before they were pulled out right over the thwart; Pen hastily followed, ready to lunge or if necessary dive for a falling young body, but they clung on and climbed. The rowboat thunked off the hull and spun away, and Pen spared a hope its poor owner would eventually find it.

Many strong arms reached down to pull them up and inboard, and Pen in turn. "Ah!" Clutching the rail, he hauled himself to his feet and looked around.

Boots clumped across the deck, and Adelis stood before him, hands on his hips, shaking his head in exasperation. "There you are. Why am I not even surprised?"

"However did you know where to find me?"

"I thought the columns of smoke were a good guide."

"Well, yes, but—" Pen became aware of the sisters shrinking to his sides, staring in fear at Adelis.

Pen didn't find Adelis in the least fearful, but then, he was used to him. Muscular build, Cedonian brick-colored skin, black hair in a military cut, clean shaved, all very normal up to the top half of his face. There, severe red and white burn scars framed his eyes in a pattern like an owl's feathers. His irises were a strange deep garnet color, glowing like coals under the black mantel of his eyebrows when the light caught them. Pen knew every inch of that face, since he'd healed it after the murderous boiling acid that had been meant to steal Adelis's sight permanently. That Adelis had smoothly refitted both miraculous recovery and horrifying scars into support of his commander's reputation was all Adelis, though.

Pen granted the effect was a bit shocking when one first encountered it. He didn't think his brother-in-law would enjoy little girls screaming at the sight of him, though, so he hurried his introductions, first in Roknari, of which Adelis had a good working grasp.

"Lencia, Seuka, this is my wife's twin brother, General Adelis Arisaydia." Pen made his voice deliberately cheerful, by way of guidance. "He serves the duke of Orbas, as Nikys and I do."

Well, not quite the same way, suggested Adelis's eyebrow twitch.

Switching to Cedonian, "Adelis, this is Lencia and Seuka Corva, late of Raspay, orphans and wards of my Order. And so of me, for the moment. I haven't been able to teach them much Cedonian yet, though we're working on it."

"Ah," said Adelis. He looked down wryly at the sisters. In passable low Roknari, he said, "Welcome to my flagship the *Eye of Orbas*, Lencia and Seuka Corva. How did you come to meet our Penric?"

"He . . . dropped from the sky?" Seuka offered hesitantly.

"The pirates threw him into the hold where we were prisoners," Lencia clarified this. "Then we were all brought to Lantihera and sold, and we've been trying to get away ever since."

"It's a long tale that I can tell later," said Pen. The merest glance confirmed Adelis had his hands full right now, from the anxious officers clustered around him like bees tending their queen to the trail of ships following on their stern, signal flags flapping. "But—how did you chance to come to Lantihera? Do you mean to conquer the island?"

"Brother of Autumn avert, no." Adelis tapped his fist over his heart in unironic prayer. "It's much too far from Orbas's coast to defend, and has no strategic value to us. Quite the reverse. We don't need to let them know that, though." A sardonic jerk of his head toward the burning waterfront. "But the Lanti pirates have been annoying Orbas for some time. Yours was the third Orban ship captured this year, and they lately raided a village on Pulpi." One of the dukedom's few coastal islands. "Duke Jurgo was fed up, so he sent me to persuade them to stop."

Along with a couple thousands of his friends, evidently.

"He granted me discretion as to how. Extracting you, which I figured for the trickiest part, is unexpectedly accomplished. And razing the town in revenge for you seems . . . redundant. Is that chaos all your doing?"

"More or less." Penric rubbed his tired, smoke-stung, itching eyes. "It's been a bad day."

"I see that." Adelis tilted his head, lightened his tone. "And do I also find you well, Madame Desdemona?"

"Yes, indeed, General," said Des through Pen's mouth, which he politely yielded to her. "I'm having a delightful outing."

A scimitar glint slipped across Adelis's mouth. Initially appalled, Adelis had only gradually become reconciled to Penric's demon, but lately he'd begun to treat her as a sort of invisible sister-in-law. It was their shared bloody-mindedness that had finally broken the ice, Pen decided.

"But," said Penric. "How did you even know I was here?"

Adelis snorted. "First was that ship you'd boarded in Trigonie, which sailed into Vilnoc complaining of their mishandling. Its crew had retaken it in the night, and it probably arrived not long after you reached Lantihera—though the description of their missing passenger took about a day to reach anyone who actually knew what you were. Next was your travel-box, which some fishermen had hauled up in their nets and couldn't get open, so brought to Nikys. Who did not react well." Adelis grimaced. "Third was an Adriac merchanter with damaged water casks and a lurid tale of their escape in which you featured almost, but not quite, unrecognizably. Once is happenstance. Twice is coincidence. Three times begins to seem like a message to be ignored at one's peril." He cleared his throat. "And Nikys, of course. Very upset. Also to be ignored at one's peril."

"Oh," said Penric. Warmed. Disturbed, but also warmed.

Adelis rubbed the back of his neck and huffed. "Fishing you out of the harbor first upends my tactical plans. Not that they aren't always. Eh, but I think I can do something interesting with this." He didn't look very discommoded.

He motioned over a beardless young officer and detailed him to escort Penric and the Corva sisters to his own cabin. "Get them whatever they need."

The lad led Penric and his charges off, picking their way over the deck. Adelis, gesturing, was the brief center of a new flurry, men departing this way and that, more signal flags urgently rising. Handling ships, Pen reflected, seemed a much more complicated matter than sinking them. But at least he seemed unlikely to be tossed overboard from this one.

Adelis's cabin, tucked down in a corner by the stern, proved an even smaller closet than the coffin on Pen's first ship. It did feature a solid bunk, not a hammock, which was soon put to use with its fold-down board as table for the basin and wash-water the aide brought at Pen's earnest request, plus food or at least rations. Pen gave the girls their pick and then, famished to the point of tremors, snacked on olives, rather stale bread rounds, dried fruit, cheese curds, more olives, and even ate his fish plank.

He and Des personally supplied much purer drinking water all around, worth the heat-price, taming the harsh red army wine. Everyone frugally shared basin, soap chunk, and washrag, and Pen sacrificed the last of the limited ewer of cask-water to lather and rinse his crusting hair.

Clean sailors' tunics, belted with braided cord, made

neat modest dresses for the girls, though they made it plain they meant to preserve their boys' togs as precious plunder. Pen did not miss the tunic and trousers he'd been captured in, not new to start with and last seen much worse for wear, but he wondered how soon the girls would realize the sack of food and clothes they had lost when attacked on the beach included the last work of their mother's hands.

About to redon, with distaste, the damp, muddled-green cast-offs, Pen was startled when the aide brought out and handed him a neat bundle of his own clothes from Vilnoc.

"Madame Nikys sent them with the general," the young officer informed him proudly. "She had great faith in him."

Fine linen drawers. Slim tan trousers. The summer tunic of his rank and Order: sleeveless pale linen, its high neck supported by the silver-plated torc that was the only uncomfortable bit of it. Split down the sides from the hips, it fell to his calves in two panels, slits and hems weighted with a band embroidered with a frieze of creatures sacred to the Bastard in Orbas: rats and crows, gulls and hill vultures, some ambiguous insects, all much more endearing than in real life. It was cinched with a braided sash intertwining white and cream, proclaiming his rank as a senior divine, and its third strand of silver marking, or perhaps warning of, his status as a Temple sorcerer.

Every stitch of it lovingly spun, woven, and sewn by Nikys. Putting it on was like easing into her embrace. It also allowed him to slip in a small lesson in Quintarian theology to the girls, intrigued by its meaningful details but mostly taken with the cavorting needlework creatures.

His rank and calling seemed to settle again on his shoulders with his garb; not inwardly, whence it never strayed, but certainly outwardly, judging by the way the aide stepped back half a pace in new respect. Or possibly caution.

Good, purred Des. *About time we received our due*.

No furious fighting had erupted outside, obviously. Pen had heard the rattle of the ship's stone anchor being let down a while ago, the very opposite of rowing like mad to ram some doomed target. Had there been any left.

Adelis, he shortly learned when they ventured back out onto the deck, had gone ashore for a parley with whatever quorum of the Guild and the town council could be hastily gathered. He'd trailed an honor guard of a few hundred sturdy, heavily armed soldiers. The rest of the fleet hovered on the water, temporarily quiescent but alert. Any lesser Lanti vessels had scattered away like frightened ducks.

Pen hung on the landward rail. The port was in utter disarray. Five ships sunk at their moorings—Falun's galley now lay on its side, waterlogged—three still smoldering, the remains of one pier falling in blackened chunks into the water, a major segment of the waterfront burnt to the ground; really, the work the Orban fleet had come to do was already near-complete. With half its ships and captains out to sea, the Guild was in no position to offer resistance. They had apparently leapt on the offer of a negotiation.

While waiting for developments, Pen persuaded the aide to conduct the girls and himself on a tour of the war galley. Adelis had shown him around its fascinating complexity once before, a few months ago when it was in dock for winter maintenance in Vilnoc's navy yard, so not a few of the men recognized their general's templeman relative, compelling Pen to return salutes with a polite tally sign and blessing. The rowers idling at their benches were military volunteers, no slaves here, and they and the soldiers seemed inclined to take Pen as more mascot than threat, along with his wards, who amused them. Although a number of the men, returning from a visit to the railing to study their erstwhile target of Lanti, cast him unsettled looks.

Adelis never believed in wasting time, so Penric was not too surprised to see him rowed back out to the *Eye of Orbas* at sunset. The faint Adelis-smirk on his face as he climbed back up the netting indicated the general was in a good mood, which seemed to hearten his welcoming men. Pen felt more cautious about that, but he didn't get an explanation till they were sitting down for dinner together.

Beneath a hooped canopy that sheltered a portion of the stern, illuminated by hanging lanterns, they perched cross-legged on cushions and were brought an onboard picnic, a cut above the lunch rations. The girls settled close at Pen's feet. Pen topped up Adelis's wine, not over-watered, and prodded him for his report from shore.

Adelis grinned and held his news hostage for Pen's tale first. Pen started with the dawn attack, though with a short doubling-back to complain of the archdivine of Trigonie whose delays had put Pen on that ship in the first place. He left out mentions of his brushes with the gods, though the bemused narrowing of Adelis's red-sparking eyes suggested he observed the lacunae. The collapses of Pen's first plan for ransom, and his second for the prison escape, he detailed but briefly; Pen thought it unnecessary of Adelis to laugh like a drain at the picture of Pen left swearing on the dock. Then a synopsis of their sojourn in the temple.

"Are you planning to attack Lanti Town?" Pen asked.

"Not at present," said Adelis.

"Because there are good people here as well as ill." Pen reflected on all he'd met, Jato, Godino, the friendly cook, the Mother's midwife, and on and on.

"The gods may be able to sort the just from the unjust soul by soul. I'm afraid armies must treat them in batches."

"Mm," Pen half-conceded. "I wonder if poor Godino remains safe. An attempt at rescue might just draw attention to him where there was none before."

"Possibly. If your Brother Godino is a man of sense he'll have taken to the hills by now."

"So I hope." Pen finished with the tersest description he could manage of his past day, which nonetheless made Adelis's eyebrows climb.

"You know, my offer to you to attend upon my army as an irregular auxiliary still stands," said Adelis, leadingly.

"And so does my refusal," Pen sighed.

It was an old argument. Adelis did not pursue it, turning instead to drawing more of their version of events from the Corva sisters. His efforts at kindliness were more labored than his Roknari, but the girls seemed to take them for sincere.

"The *parley*, Adelis," said Pen, when Adelis finished diverting himself with this.

"Ah, yes, that. I have wrangled a treaty from the Guild of Lantihera."

Pen blinked. "To what end?"

"An agreement to leave Orbas, its islands, and its shipping alone."

"Do you think they'll honor it?"

"For a season, perhaps. I've slipped a few agents ashore to watch for their inevitable lapse. Next time we can return in less of a scramble. Or, better, induce the Carpagamons to do so."

"You didn't look as if you were scrambling. Quite formidable."

"Learned, you have no idea what a miracle of logistics you observe before you. If it weren't for the sea maneuvers I'd talked Jurgo into, and which were supposed to take place next week, we wouldn't have sailed out of Vilnoc for another month."

"I daresay. So . . . a treaty in exchange for not invading Lantihera, which you weren't going to do in the first place?" No wonder Adelis had looked smug.

"I sweetened the pot by offering to not grant my fleet three days of shore leave."

"There's a difference between that and sacking the town?"

"Not much. The council took my point. You were a more fundamental bone of contention. To the tune of thirty thousand silver ryols."

Pen gasped, appalled. "That's a prince's ransom! Or, wait, no, were they demanding reparations . . . ?"

Adelis stared, then laughed. "Ah, no, Penric! I wouldn't have offered a copper for that. No, that's what they're paying *us* to not leave you here."

Des crowed with delight.

Penric just . . . drank.

The Orban fleet sailed on the morning tide, right after the coin chests were delivered.

Pen leaned on the stern rail with Adelis and watched the island recede behind them. That dwindling was the most desirable sight he could imagine.

"What will you do with my, my anti-ransom?" Pen asked him.

"It will be split. Part will be divided among my troops, to compensate them for the sad lack of loot from the sad lack of battle. The rest to Jurgo, to help pay for this sea-holiday."

"Maneuvers," corrected Pen. "Just a more realistic sort."

"That is an argument I will store up."

"Don't forget the share to the Temple."

"I'll leave that accounting to the duke."

Pen snickered. Sails raised, oars shipped, the breeze moved them for free, and in the right direction. White-and-gray harbor gulls swooped and shrieked in their wake, an unmelodic hymn to their recessional. The bold scavenger birds were considered creatures of the Bastard in these seas, he was reminded.

"It doesn't do any good, you know," Pen said at last.

"All those ships and goods I destroyed were stolen in the first place. The Lanti pirates will just return to their trade with their efforts redoubled, to make up their losses."

"I expect so," said Adelis. "We could still turn back and raze the town." Pen was not entirely sure that was an idle jest. "Before they finish rebuilding that old Carpagamon fortress would actually be a good time."

Pen waved an averting hand. "I don't know what would stop the raiders altogether. The middle-merchants who buy the goods and people are as much a part of the system as the pirates, and the ones they sell them to even more so, and more diffuse and harder to attack. Being nearly everybody." Pen brooded. "The *cantons* manage without slavery."

"And are also very poor, you say."

"Mm." Pen could not altogether deny this. "Not that poor. We do well enough."

Adelis offered, "The Darthacans, I'm told, are building ships and warships off their far east coast that are all-sail, and don't require rowers. The rougher seas there have sunk more galleys than battles ever did, so that makes sense to me. If those designs do indeed prove superior, the time of galley slaves may come to an end without the need for virtuous canton austerity."

"But not in mines. Or the demand for concubines and servants." Scullions and scribes alike.

"I can't help you there. Not my trade. Pray to your gods, Learned."

"The gods take almost all who do not refuse them, slave or free. I'm not sure they see a difference between one form of human misery and another. They don't think the way we do. Soul by soul, as you say."

Adelis's black brows flicked up, perhaps at the disquiet of standing next to a man who could plausibly claim *any idea* of how the gods thought. "Thieves will still pursue other forms of treasure that they cannot otherwise earn, or just raid for mad bravado. And soldiers will still be called upon to put them down. I don't foresee an end to either of our trades in my lifetime."

"Nor mine, I suppose. Trade or lifetime." Pen turned to lean his back against the rail and study the Corva sisters, presently cross-legged on the other side of the stern being taught knots by a friendly sailor.

Adelis followed his glance, and asked with an odd diffidence, "Are those two god-touched, do you know?"

Because Pen could tell, being in an oblique chaotic sense god-touched himself?

Adelis went on, "They seem to have suffered the most extraordinary mix of chance and mischance, ill-luck and luck. Of which the most extraordinary was having you dropped atop them. Your god's white hand at work?"

"I wish I knew," sighed Pen. "Not one single thing that has happened requires an extraordinary explanation. It's just the, hm, accumulation." He pursed his lips. "I hope I get a chance to delve further into their mystery."

"If you do, pray share it." Adelis pushed off the rail, called away by some officer wanting his commander's attention. "If you can."

"Aye," said Penric.

EPILOGUE

AS MUCH AS PEN liked his upstairs study overlooking the shared well-court, he had to admit it grew close on a hot Vilnoc summer morning. So he'd moved the girls' language lesson down to the back pergola, its plank table and benches shaded by grape leaves, the surrounding pots of kitchen herbs lending a pleasantly rustic effect. The concentration of practicing Cedonian letters with slate and chalk had given way, in the languid warmth, to learning a few children's Temple hymns instead. Pen thought the rhythm, rhyme, and refrains did more, faster, to fix words in young brains than dry readings or recitations, not that the latter didn't have their place.

And he was able, without drudgery, to slip in the needed repetition by trying for harmony, his light baritone blending agreeably, he hoped, with the girls' sopranos. Curiously, Seuka's voice held to the key better than Lencia's; he fancied Lencia's busy mind was trying too hard. Still straining to be both lost mother and father to their truncated family, when being big sister seemed task enough to Pen.

Their rudimentary choir practice was interrupted by Nikys, rapping on a pergola support and smiling, so presumably not because she was being maddened by the noise. "Penric, we have a visitor."

He looked up and past her shoulder. The man

hovering anxiously there was middle-aged, middle-sized, sturdy rather than stout. He wore ordinary dress of tunic, belt, and trousers, if well-made, and sensible sandals in this weather. His hair and beard were dark with a smattering of gray, his skin not Cedonian-brick but a paler warm tan that might have come from anywhere along the continent's more eastward coasts. Pen pegged it as Ibra by the familiar letter clutched tightly in his hand, and the girls' reactions.

"Papa!" shrieked Lencia; after an uncertain moment—it had been, what, over a year since they'd last seen the man—Seuka followed her bolt around the table.

He dropped to his knees and opened his arms to receive them, embracing them both at once, hard. "Ah," he huffed, dampening eyes closing in a grimace caught between joy and pain. In Ibran, he muttered, "Ah, so it's all true . . ."

"Master Ubi Getaf, I take it," said Pen, rising to greet this welcome, if sudden, apparition. The letter being abused in that thick fist was the one he'd written to Learned Iserne in Lodi, three weeks ago when they'd first reached Vilnoc, tightly summarizing his late adventures and begging her help in finding the wandering merchant. She had followed through splendidly, it seemed.

"Learned Penric?" said Getaf, less surely. He clambered to his feet and, both his hands being occupied by his clinging offspring, ducked his head at Penric. He continued in halting Cedonian, "I understand I have much to thank you for in rescuing my children."

Pen returned in smooth Ibran, "It was no more than any decent adult would have done, under the circumstances."

Well, perhaps a little *more*, murmured Des, amused.

He would wait a while, Pen decided, to introduce Des.

Getaf's head went back as he parsed Pen's regional Ibran accent. "You . . . are from Brajar . . . ?"

"No, but my language teacher was, long ago." *And I thank you for it, Learned Aulia*, he thought to that layer of Des that was the Brajaran templewoman, who had once received Des from the dying Umelan like the baton in some mortal relay.

Getaf accepted this with another nod, too distracted to be curious. The girls dragged him to a bench, both trying to tell all their tale at once in a mixture of Roknari, which he seemed to speak well, and a little Ibran. He sat heavily, his head swinging back and forth like a man trying to follow some fast-moving ball game, or perhaps a bear befuddled by bees.

Nikys folded her arms and leaned back against the pergola post, listening in understandable bafflement, as she had some Roknari but no Ibran. But Pen thought she followed the emotions perfectly well, and approved. He pulled out his bench and motioned her to his side, where they sat, her soft thigh in its draped linen pressing companionably against his lean one. *Don't you dare disappear on me like that again* he received in a language more fundamental than any that tripped from his tongue. He grasped her plump hand and returned an equally silent, *Aye, Madame Owl.*

He murmured to her, "Does Getaf seem an upright fellow to you?"

Equally intent on the reunion playing out, Nikys murmured back, "Look at the girls. Such unhesitating gladness goes beyond just relief at a familiar face, I think."

Thanks in great part to Nikys the sisters were clean; shining hair neatly bound in braids and colored ties; fed, if not to sleekness, at least to the point that their natural skinniness no longer looked sunken with stress; and dressed in a superior grade of hand-me-downs that Nikys had begged from the duchess's household. Penric was pleased that they were able to present the pair to their papa in such good order, as though he were again a student offering some especially well-done work to one of his seminary masters. He hoped he'd get a good mark.

Getaf's expression sobered as the girls worked their way back to the tale of their mother's death, the details all new to him since Pen's letter had devoted only a clause about *died from illness in Raspay* to the root calamity.

"I am so sorry," he told them. "I'd heard nothing of this. When the prince of Jokona's border clash with Ibra closed his coasts to Zagosur trade, I thought to wait it out with a venture west. The Zagosur factor should have forwarded your letter to me, not returned it. And Taspeig should most certainly have accompanied you all the way to Lodi, not abandoned you at Agenno, although . . . although that might not have helped."

"She was very tired and cranky by then," Lencia offered in excuse. "We all were. And I think she was running out of money."

"Still. Still."

Seuka raised her face. "Are you going to take us home now, Papa?"

Getaf hesitated, too palpably. Where was home for these sisters now, really? Raspay seemed as abandoned behind them as any sunken ship, with not even a floating spar left to cling to.

Lencia, as ever the more alert to the difficulties, put in, "Or at least take us along with you?"

That was a, hm, not-bad picture, of living like young apprentices trailing a master trader and learning the world, as many such men made their sons. And sometimes daughters.

Getaf rubbed his forehead, frowning into his lap. "That presents certain problems, which I must take thought for. I can't take you back to Zagosur. Which, I suppose, was never home for you anyway. But I won't leave you without succor; that, I promise." He looked across at Pen and switched to Cedonian. "Learned Penric, may I speak with you in private for a moment?"

Pen and Nikys glanced at each other. Nikys rose, saying kindly, "Lencia, Seuka, can you come help me fetch food and drink for your papa?"

Lencia frowned, and Seuka's lower lip stuck out, wary of the risk of people arranging their lives without their say-so. Penric sympathized, but construed there might be personal matters Getaf didn't wish to share with them. As well, Nikys could seize this chance for a candid conference with his daughters. Pen nodded brightly at them, and they let themselves be shuffled off, only dragging their sandaled feet a little.

Getaf watched them disappear into the house, then

lowered his voice and said in Ibran, "May I take it they were not worse abused by the pirates?"

"You may. Apparently due to their higher sale value as virgins. Which, er, they have retained."

Getaf nodded in relief. Then paused, mustering his words. "Your friend Learned Iserne caught up with me just in time in Lodi. I'd finished amassing my trade goods there, and in another week I would have been on my way back to Zagosur." He chewed his lip. "I don't think it wise to try to take Lencia and Seuka to my household there. My wife holds all in firm hands, very reliable manager, has nurtured our own children near to maturity, with a useful web of in-laws, but . . . I don't think she would make them very welcome. They deserve better than grudging care, and because of my business I would not be much there to provide a balancing weight."

"I gather Madame Getaf does not know about your mistress?" Or had Jedula Corva been more in the nature of a second wife?

Getaf shook his head. "And I'd prefer to keep it that way. Given there is nothing left in Raspay to argue about."

"Understandable . . ."

"Jedula was an anchor to me, but to the extent I'd thought about anything happening to her and not me, I assumed I would pay Taspeig to care for the girls, in their house as before. I can't see taking them back to Taspeig now, given her unreliable behavior in Agenno. Anyway, I expect she has gone on to find some other life for herself. And the status of half-Quintarian orphans in Raspay, even if they're not destitute, is not happy."

"So I've heard."

Getaf stared into his hands, cradled between his knees, then looked up at Pen more keenly. "What can you tell me about the Bastard's Order here in Vilnoc? Is it well run?"

Pen's brows rose. "The orphanage is as decent as it can manage. Chronically short of funds and staff, like most such places, but its people are very dedicated."

Getaf waved this aside. "No, no. I'd take our chances in Zagosur before I'd leave the girls in an orphanage. Spare those resources for the truly needy. I'm thinking about the chapterhouse itself. Lencia and especially Seuka are a little young to be placed as dowered dedicats to the Order, but . . . perhaps you have some influence there?"

"Huh." Pen folded his arms on the plank table. "There's an interesting notion."

"A good chapterhouse might assume their care and education at a higher level than an orphanage can provide, and keep them together if their dower-contract so instructed. And . . . and for the first time in their lives, their birth-status might make them more, not less, welcomed. Um—where have they been staying in Vilnoc till now? Your letter was unclear on that point." He pressed the wrinkled paper out on the table in a nervous gesture.

"Oh, sorry. They've been staying here. I suppose you can think of my house as a branch of the Order, irregular senior member as I am."

Getaf looked up in hesitation. "Do you think you . . . ? Would your wife . . . ?"

Pen felt his way forward, sharing Getaf's uncertainty.

Nikys had been nothing but generous to the lost girls, but was it right to pledge her labor into an indefinite future when a perfectly good parent had turned up after all, willing to do his part? Even more central, what was the optimum opportunity for Lencia and Seuka?

"I . . . actually think the chapterhouse would make a better regular domicile for them," Pen said slowly, "given the erratic nature of my own duties, and also those of Nikys and Adelis. And there would be more kinds of people around to teach and train them, not to mention a supply of energetic young fellow-dedicats to befriend. But, really, this need not be either-or. It's only a short walk from here. Looking in on each other would be an easy task."

Lord Bastard, is this your intent? Pen would pray to his god for guidance, but he never did get any back when he did that, so he supposed he must use his own judgment. Though capturing two such bright souls for His Order must surely be an acceptable offering.

Getaf said wistfully, "Do they seem to like Vilnoc?"

"So far as I can tell. Though any place must seem better than Lantihera, or whatever slavery would have followed."

A wry, conceding nod. "I could make sure my travels extend toward Lodi again. And visit, from time to time." Left unspoken were the hazards of his own trade—Pen was put in mind of Aloro and Arditi, and hoped they'd made it back alive to Adria.

"Well, then, I suggest you put the proposal to your daughters, and discover what they think of it. I see no impediment from this end."

Getaf's stiff shoulders eased at this reassurance. "It could be well. It might be very well."

"It might." Pen pulled his queue around—Seuka had insisted on her turn to braid, this morning—and fiddled with it, perhaps not concealing his nosiness as much as he'd wish. "Do you think their mother would approve?"

An aching sort of shrug at this reminder of grief. "I can only pray so. But if they flourish, then yes. It was all she ever wanted for her girls, their wellbeing."

"How did you two come to meet?" Which wasn't really the question. But *How did you two come to form a bond that could not even be broken by death?* seemed too intimate a query for an hour's acquaintance.

A brief smile. "Through her work, of course. When I was first trying to set up trade in Raspay, what, fifteen years ago now. I moved from being her regular client to her exclusive client whenever I prospered enough for it, which . . . wasn't all the time, to my frustration. But we made do. Sometimes, she was my temporary factor, when I could afford no other assistance."

Which also sounded far more like a merchant's wife than his mistress. Well, apart from her side-jobs.

"Was she very young and beautiful, back then?"

Getaf waved an indifferent hand. "Only a little younger than me—granted, I was younger then, too. Well-looking enough, as one must be for her trade. But she made the best of herself through tidiness and health, not by the unearned gift that's the blessing and curse of those born beautiful." He flicked a shrewd glance at Pen, which Pen pretended not to notice.

Getaf's expression softened. "But she was the most

endlessly kind person I have ever met, of any sex or sort.
Her fearless caring terrified me at times. She would take
in strays, you know, others of her profession who had run
into rotten situations of one sort and another. Especially
the young ones, who had grown no slyness or deceit by
which to defend themselves. I lost count of the number
of secret Quintarians and ill-treated whores and crow-
lads I smuggled out of Raspay with me as servants, to
release in some port of Ibra in the hopes they might find
a safer life. A few escaped Quintarian slaves, too—now,
that was a dangerous game all around. I much preferred
to just buy out the battered ones at Jedula's direction,
when I could afford it. Better for my poor heart."

Penric blinked at this new picture. "Did Lencia and
Seuka know all this was going on?"

"I don't think so, or only the tip of it, when Jedula hid
someone sick or injured in our house. She would
certainly have misdirected or sworn the girls to silence,
in those cases. But for the most part she took great care
to keep them ignorant of those activities. Because even
as shunned as they were in Raspay, they still had a few
young friends, if only the children of others in their
mother's trade. And there would have been no
controlling their chatter."

"I see."

Oh, my, agreed Des.

For the first time, the hidden bud of Jedula Corva's
relationship with her god seemed to unfold its secrets
before Pen's eye like a blooming flower. Beloved, god-
touched, great-souled . . . a saint, even? The true sort,
who moved through the world as silently as fishes,

unnoticed by carnal eyes that focused only on outward domination and display. Never on a small woman in a small town, being *kind*. Soul by soul.

And her faithful lieutenant, it seemed. Pen studied the unprepossessing, middle-aged merchant, sitting oblivious to these reflections, anew.

Getaf sighed. "I suppose Jedula spoiled me for any other woman. Any other person, really. My life is going to be much . . . duller, now." His grimace didn't much resemble the buffering smile he evidently intended.

God-touched at least, then. Pen recognized that particular bereft longing left when a great Presence became a great absence. That heartbroken loss only known to those who, at some perilous apogee, had *almost* grasped that inchoate, indescribable essence.

The gods make it up to us at the end, I suppose. For some, that was a long and tedious wait.

A bustle at the house door; Nikys and the girls bearing trays of cool lemon-water and tasty pastries. Pen amazed the company and amused himself by generating balls of ice for their drinks. He also took this peaceable opportunity to introduce Des; they were successful at not disturbing his visitor too much. The diversion gave time to settle his own upended mind, anyway.

Getaf, who was, Pen mused, a successful trader and therefore negotiator, pitched his proposal to his daughters over the meal. Pen tried to maintain a neutral mien while this was going on, but he supposed his broad smile betrayed him when the girls leaped on his invitation to give the family a personal tour of the chapterhouse that afternoon, to examine what they were being offered more closely. Getaf definitely approved of that mercantile due diligence. Even when the sisters' caginess was a transparent effort not to sadden him by appearing too eager to leave his protection.

The agreement between an Order and the parents or guardians of a young dedicat fell somewhere between a dower and an apprenticeship; Getaf, apparently experienced with both sorts of contracts, ironed out the details with the Bastard's chapterhouse within two days. Waiving the age requirements, upon examination of the matter by the chapter head, was routine enough to scarcely need Pen's clout. Children so placed would, upon their majority, have the choice of regularizing their oaths to full membership, or leaving for a lay life. Pen had no idea which Lencia and Seuka would then choose, and finally decided it was not his task to guess so many years ahead.

Good, said Des. *You borrow enough trouble already you'd need a counting-house to keep your ledger.*

Pen, Nikys, and Getaf together escorted the sisters to their new home. The girls had taken to Nikys—as who would not?—and Nikys to them reciprocally. They all helped haul their few belongings through the chapterhouse's back courtyard up to their narrow room, which had a glassed casement overlooking the town and the valley that wound up into the hills behind it. Also a wardrobe, a pair of chests, a washstand with its paraphernalia, an inviting bookshelf—Pen approved— and two beds, one on either side; Seuka promptly sat and bounced on hers, consideringly. Lencia stared around in both curiosity and trepidation, but Pen fancied the first was winning.

Then it was time to see Getaf off in turn. The man was plainly torn between concern for Lencia and Seuka, and worrying about what might be happening to his year's worth of work waiting in a Lodi warehouse. And Jedula Corva's daughters, Pen was reminded, were not Getaf's only children that he had left to hope and the care of others while he journeyed, though he tactfully did not speak much of his other family in Zagosur.

It was a short walk from the chapterhouse to Vilnoc's harbor. The skies had regained the deep blue of summer, and the gulls flashed almost painfully white against it. There were hugs, there were tears, there were probably futile admonishments against the risks of life in Vilnoc and on ships. Then the merchant pressed his coin into the hand of the oarsman and was rowed out to his waiting vessel. Getaf climbed the net and waved one last time before the crew urged him out of their way.

"Will he be safe?" fretted Seuka. All too aware, now, not just of the hazards of the world, but of the fragility of grownups.

"The storm season is over in these waters," said Penric. "And I don't think pirates will be attacking ships under Orban flags again so soon. He's as safe as anyone alive and moving in the world can be."

Nikys put in, "We can stop at the Vilnoc temple and pray for him, if you like."

Lencia looked down at her sandals, up at Penric. "Does it help?"

"For a certainty...only at the very end of all

journeys," said Penric, his god-sworn honesty wrestling down more soothing platitudes. "But at least there we don't travel alone."

Lencia, after a sober moment, nodded.

They turned into the city's streets. Bumping companionably between Penric, Des, and Nikys, the Corva sisters climbed undaunted.

THE PHYSICIANS
OF VILNOC

DEDICATION

For all the practitioners through the long, long
history of medicine who tried the wildest experiments,
often failed, sometimes succeeded, and helped
make our world.

"The gods have no hands in this world but ours.
If we fail Them, where then can They turn?"
—Ingrey kin Wolfcliff, *The Hallowed Hunt*

THE PHYSICIANS OF VILNOC

❦

WITH FOUR PERSONS in three bodies competing for one infant, Penric mused, it was a wonder his new daughter Florina was ever allowed to touch her cradle. He tickled her cheek with one long, ink-stained finger, and smiled as she smacked her tender lips and turned her head.

"Give her over, Penric," said his mother-in-law, Idrene, genially. "Or is that Desdemona doing the doting?"

"It's me," said Penric. "Novice fathers are allowed to dote, too. And Des is actually only about two-twelfths baby-mad."

"True," put in his resident demon Desdemona, necessarily speaking through Pen's mouth as she shared his body—the sole way such a being of spirit could maintain itself in the world of matter. *Parasitical* was not the right term, as she gifted him with his powers as a Temple sorcerer in return. *Renter* was not just, either. *Rider and ridden* was the most common metaphor, with the implication that an out-of-control chaos demon could reverse the position of power if the rider-sorcerer was weak or careless. Penric usually settled on *person*, which was both conveniently vague, and had the bonus of gratifying Des.

Desdemona gossiped on, "Litikone and the physician Helvia were always the baby-fanciers among us. Amberein and Aulia preferred children able to talk. Ruchia and Mira were indifferent to the nursery set. And Rogaska disliked everyone equally, regardless of age." Not the full tally of ten women (and the lioness and the mare) whom Des had occupied and been imprinted by over the span of her two centuries in the world, but Idrene nodded understanding, while also taking the opportunity of Pen's distraction to swoop in and snitch the sleepy Florina from his grasp.

"I don't recall the old general as doting," Idrene remarked, securing her grandchild on her shoulder and patting her fondly. "More daunted, really. Which is odd, considering how fearless he was about army affairs. But then, like you and Nikys, he'd waited a long time for his firstborns."

"Thirty-three is not old," asserted Penric. Well, not for him. Maybe for first-time-mother Nikys who, after a childless prior marriage ending in a premature widowhood, had feared herself barren. "Nikys's papa was, what, fifty when she and Adelis were born?"

"Around that. There, there, little Florie," Idrene cooed as the infant stirred and daintily burped. "I'm glad you and Nikys gifted her with that name. My Florina would have been so honored."

Pen had been surprised to learn, upon his first acquaintance with Idrene, how cordial the much younger concubine's relationship with her husband's first wife had been, free of the bitter rivalry and jealousy reputed to be more common in such situations. Entirely to his benefit, as Nikys's upbringing in that household had possibly prepared his wife for the complexities of living with two-personed Penric. Idrene as well, come to think.

"I'll hold out for *Llewyn* next time," sighed Pen.

Idrene's dark eyes crinkled in amusement. Even on the high side of fifty, she was still a handsome woman, straight-backed, with warm dark copper Cedonian skin and black hair like her daughter, though her curls were salted with silver. "Next time, eh? I like the sound of that, but what if it's a boy? I can't always tell if those bewildering Wealdean names you favor are for boys, or girls, or both."

"My late princess-archdivine back in Martensbridge was a woman, but in fact that name could go to either sex. So I'm prepared regardless."

Through Penric's open study door, a knock echoed faintly from the street-side entry downstairs. He relaxed as he heard their housemaid Lin answering it.

Idrene, by contrast, raised her head with the perky alertness of a cat sighting a mouse. "Is that Adelis's voice?"

"Sounds like it," agreed Pen as a low rumble, too distant to make out the words, wafted up through the atrium. *Yes*, confirmed Des, whose demonic senses left her in even less doubt than Idrene's maternal ones.

"Oh, Nikys will want to know. Where is she?"

"Setting up her loom in her workroom." Which had been how he'd managed to capture Florina, briefly.

"I'll tell her," said Idrene, marching out still holding her prize. "You can go down."

"Adelis more likely came to see you two than me," Pen protested. But, abandoning the mess of correspondence on his writing table that he'd been ignoring in favor of his much more fascinating daughter, he rose amiably and went to descend the gallery stairs. The stone-paved atrium in this leased row house was scarcely wider than the hallways in the wooden houses of Pen's home country, but it served to let in light and air. And rain, which Pen had needed to grow used to, as it rather violated his notions of indoors versus outdoors. Snow, in the duchy of Orbas, was not a hazard.

The sturdy front door gave directly onto the street. Penric did not keep a porter to guard it, as the knowledge that the house belonged to a sorcerer was usually enough to buffer unwanted intrusion.

Lin ducked her head at him as he strode up. "Learned, General Arisaydia is here. But he refuses to come in!"

"Hm?" Pen poked his head out his doorway.

His brother-in-law, dressed in standard-issue tunic, trousers, and boots, but dispensing with his leather cuirass and the red cloak of his rank on this warm summer day, hovered at the base of the few steps gripping the reins of his horse. A younger man, aide or groom, stood holding the reins of two more, army-saddled likewise.

"Adelis, pray enter. Nikys and Idrene will be glad to see you. Your niece is awake, by the way."

Adelis made an unexpected averting gesture, and said, "No!"

". . . What?"

"I mustn't come inside," Adelis went on, looking very determined about it. Adelis being capable of impressive stubbornness, Pen didn't argue.

"In a hurry, are you?"

"Yes. I need you to ride out to the fort and look at something. Now."

Pen blinked, taken aback at this vehemence. The post that the young general commanded for the duke of Orbas lay about a mile inland from the town of Vilnoc's own walls, up the valley and overlooking the main road west. It had once stood closer, Pen understood, centuries back when Orbas had been a province of the Cedonian Empire, and before the port had followed the slowly silting river mouth downstream. Duke Jurgo tried to maintain most of a legion there when at residence in his summer capital, although his main defensive interest lay on the harbor side with his navy. With several thousand men and camp followers, the fort was almost an outlying town in its own right.

Adelis would hardly be consulting Penric, with such urgency at that, on military affairs. This left something theological, unlikely; something to do with a translation problem, possible in light of his scholar's command of languages; or some suspected magical problem, usually mistaken but, rarely, real, and thus interesting. Or . . .

"A number of my men have contracted a strange fever."

Or that. Yes. Agh. "Don't you have army physicians for such? Experienced with camp dysentery and so on?"

"It's not that. Anyway, we keep our barracks and wells and latrines clean, and our rations fresh. My physicians can't identify it. A couple have come *down* with it, and some of the orderlies, too."

"You know I do not practice medicine," said Pen stiffly. "Anymore."

Adelis made a swipe of his fist, dismissing Pen's aversions. "Four men died last night. *More* men. Six in the previous few days."

Pen hesitated. "How long has this been going on?"

"Ten days for certain. How long before that, no one is quite sure. But it's recent, it's spreading, and it is much more lethal than dysentery."

"Who survives it?"

Adelis scowled. "It may be too early to tell."

That does not sound good, observed Des.

Truly. Any virulent disease that infected the fort was sure to jump to the port, and that included Pen's front door, and the human treasures behind it. Adelis standing well away from that same door told its own tale.

"I'll fetch my case," sighed Penric.

He returned upstairs to the bedchamber that he shared with Nikys and, now, Florina's cradle. The case containing the tools of his third, no, fourth trade—after learned divine, sorcerer, and scholar—rested in a chest out of sight and preferably out of mind, but should he want them at all, they were of finer make than army-issue. He shucked off the comfortable, threadbare old tunic he'd been sluffing about the house in this morning, and donned his second-best summer vestments for a divine of the Bastard's Order.

Slim tan trousers. Sleeveless cream tunic split at the hips falling to panels fore and aft his knees, hems decorated with a frieze of embroidered holy animals; secured by the sash at his waist with a silver cord in its braid denoting, or warning of, his calling as a sorcerer. He left the silver-plated torc for the tunic's high collar with his first-best togs, reserved for court ceremonies and holy days, in the chest.

He stuffed his old clothes, along with a change of smallclothes, into a sack. He hoped he wouldn't need to be gone overnight, or longer, but one never knew. He could borrow clean army garb from Adelis in a pinch, but any trousers would fall hopelessly short of his ankles.

Upon reflection, he wrapped his long blond queue in a knot at his nape, fastening it firmly. He didn't need it falling forward and trailing through the messes sick men leaked. He was just finishing this task when Nikys hurried in.

"Penric! What's going on?"

"Your brother wants to drag me out to his fort to see some of his men who've come down ill." Pen decided not to mention the death count.

"He knows better than to tax you with that sort of task." Her frown deepened. "Which means this is something out of the ordinary, doesn't it." Swift deduction, not question.

"Well, I won't find out till I—and Des—take a look at

it. I'm rather counting on Des." Who had much longer experience than he did.

Entering his arms, Nikys took a deep breath, pleasantly ample to hold—Pen allowed himself a moment of covert appreciation. "Then I'll count on her as well." She laced her hands around his narrow waist in turn. "Don't let him get in over his head, Des."

"I'll do my best, love," said Des through Penric's mouth.

One of the many delights of his delightful wife was the ease she had developed in telling them apart, and she nodded without confusion. "How long will you two be gone?"

"Not sure," said Pen. "An hour, a day, a week? I may need to intern myself for a bit before I come back here."

"It's that contagious?" Her deep brown eyes widened, looking up at him in alarm.

"Mm, perhaps not for me. I didn't contract tertiary fever during my year in Adria, and it's endemic there. I haven't even caught a cold since I came to the Cedonian peninsula." Being knocked on the head and tossed into a bottle dungeon or suffering magical attack from that out-of-control Patos sorcerer did not count as diseases, and Des had healed him of those injuries, too. But Nikys, nursing, was indivisible from their infant daughter in terms of exposure to anything chancy. He was confident she'd share his caution.

"So don't fret if you don't hear from me. It just means Adelis is keeping me busy."

"Humph. Don't let him treat you like one of his army mules, or I'll have his ears."

He kissed away her sisterly scowl, following up with kisses to her elusive dimples—ah, there, much better—and reluctantly took his leave.

Adelis kept them to a swift trot on the short ride, impeding conversation, just as well. He was a tactician, not a physician. His army medics would inform Pen of the messy details soon enough, in their mutual language of the healing arts.

Penric had only been out to the fort once before, for Duke Jurgo's ceremony honoring his new general upon his successful return from the campaign against the incurring Rusylli. Devised to impress the assembled troops, no doubt, but Pen suspected Adelis had been more gratified by his witnessing family, small though it was: Idrene and Nikys and, yes, Pen and Des.

The fort spread over a low hill, with much less elevation than the castle-crowned crags of Pen's home country, but then, the old Cedonian military engineers had always been keen to assure access to water in these hotter lands. They'd made up for it by digging a large fossa around the extensive perimeter, a ditch that had to be periodically cleared of silt, debris, and villagers trying to build right up to the walls.

They clopped across the drawbridge and through the main gate with its flanking stone towers. Inside, they dismounted and handed the horses off to the aide, who towed them away to the cavalry stables. The elite mounted troops and couriers lodged with their beloved beasts on this side of the fort, along with most of the workshops, the smithy, stores, and the armory, though the bulk of the remounts and draft animals were pastured down by the river. Adelis led Pen through to the open central space, more than courtyard, less than parade ground, used for mustering, returning salutes from a few soldiers along the way, a brief tap of the right fist to the chest.

As they strode past, Adelis spared a five-fold tally sign for the fort's temple, which faced his headquarters across the square. Pen, belatedly, copied him, waving his hand down forehead, mouth, navel, and groin, but spreading it properly over his heart, as this temple was dedicated to the Son of Autumn, god of comradeship and thus, alas, war. And then Pen's habitual extra tap of the back of his thumb to his lips, for his own god's ambiguous blessing.

The activity under the sacred portico suggested preparations for a funeral. Not unusual, given the population here, but still . . .

They angled around the rows of barracks to the back corner of the fort given over to its hospice. It had its own small gate leading to a colonnaded court, and just inside a shrine to the Mother of Summer, patroness, among other things, of healing. Rather the opposite of the aim of an army, Pen fancied, but he glimpsed what seemed to be an unusual number of supplicants perched on the prayer rugs spread out before Her shaded altar.

Treatment rooms, stores, an apothecary, and its own bathhouse and laundry ringed the sunny court. The quiet far side, under its colonnade, was lined with chambers for patients, each door in the row made—somewhat—private by a leather curtain. Four to ten cots per chamber, depending on demand, so the place,

Pen had been told, could accommodate up to two hundred sick or injured men at a time.

Adelis went to one of the leather curtains and pushed through, Penric on his heels, and the bright serenity of the courtyard was abruptly replaced with a shadowy scene of turmoil.

His eyes adapted quickly enough without Des's proffered help, though the details were no reward. Six cots set up, all occupied, five by groaning, restless men, one by a figure gone too still. Kneeling at its side a young man bent weeping, his shoulders shaking as he choked his grief into silence.

"Oh, no," breathed Adelis, stopping short. "Not Master Orides. I'd hoped you could save him at least, Pen."

Pen suspected Adelis hoped for a lot more than that, and flinched in prospect.

Orides was the senior physician of the legion. Pen had met him but briefly at the campaign celebration last year, finding the officer level-headed as only years of experience could bestow, a trifle dyspeptic—possibly also from the years of experience—but with a sly wit. The crow-visage jutting up from its pillow bore no humor now, humanity fled with life's warmth, the darkened flesh shrinking to its bones seeming prematurely mummified.

Des, Sight.

His demon lent him her spiritual perceptions only at Pen's request, because the dual vision could be overwhelming, and his reacting to things no one else could see alarmed those around him. Ghosts, for example, although when he'd last been out here the fort had not been more rife with sundered souls than any other building of like age. But Orides, it seemed, was already gone to his goddess, gathered up like the valued child he must have been to Her. The scent of that passing divinity was fading like a whisper of perfume. *That much grace, at least, in this graceless moment.*

The young man looked up at the sound of Adelis's voice and scrambled to his feet, visibly pulling himself together. He tapped his fist over his heart, and in a squeezed voice said, "Sir!"

There was this to be said for military garb; you could tell who a person was, or at least their function, at a glance. Temple robes likewise, Pen supposed. This one was a young medical officer, by his green sash and somewhat stained, sleeveless, undyed tunic. In his early twenties, perhaps? His coloration was typical of this region: dark coppery-brick skin, black hair, brown eyes; his build average, his height a little under Adelis's muscular middle stature. His drawn, exhausted face was not standard-issue, nor his heartbroken whisper: "You're too late."

Adelis flicked his gaze aside at Pen's wince and, perhaps wisely, elected to let this outburst pass unremarked. "Penric, this is Orides's senior apprentice, Master Rede Licata. Our second medical officer." First, now, apparently, and by Rede's indrawn breath he was just realizing the full burden that had fallen upon him. "Master Rede, this is Learned Penric kin Jurald, Duke Jurgo's Temple sorcerer. He and his demon, Madame Desdemona, have experience in medical matters, and I trust will be able to help us sort out this crisis."

Adelis did not, to Pen's relief, name him a physician

outright. Though the general's touch to the burn scars
marring the upper half of his face like red-and-white owl
feathers, which framed eyes that could again *see out*,
suggested he was tempted to. Des just preened a trifle
at the rare nicety of being separately introduced.

Only the continuing swipe of his hand through his hair
betrayed how harassed Adelis was feeling. With a chin-
duck toward the cot, he went on, "When did he pass?"

"Not half the turning of a glass ago." Staring down at
his late mentor, Rede rubbed the back of his wrist over
his reddened eyes, and finally thought to offer, "It was
probably already too late by the time you rode into
Vilnoc this morning."

Adelis hissed through his teeth. "I daresay."

The smell of death was a misnomer, and really didn't
apply till a corpse was well along, but the stink of
sickness here masked all else, despite the diligent efforts
to keep the chamber clean. An orderly glanced up from
holding a basin for another patient to weakly vomit into,
and called to Rede, "I'll help you lay him out next, sir."

Rede waved him back to his task. "He'll wait for us
now."

"That feels so strange. He was always hurrying us
along."

"Aye," sighed Rede. He made to draw the stained
sheet up over Orides's face.

Pen raised a stemming hand. "I had better take a close
look at him."

"Oh. Yes." Rede grimaced. "I think he would actually
appreciate that."

Adelis stood back, arms folded, face grim, as Pen,

Rede looking over his shoulder, bent to examine this most notable victim of the mysterious malady. He folded the cover all the way down and studied the corpse systematically from the toes up, neglecting no part.

Alive, Orides's skin had been the color of some warm wood or spice. It was darkened all over now to a grayish sort of blotchy purple. No external eruptions or lesions, though his pulpy flesh had started to break down at the pressure points where he'd rested on the cot, the bedsores looking like ones developing for weeks, not days. Eyes, ears, nose, and the inside of his mouth were traced with drying blood but not otherwise markedly different from any other dead man's. No special tell-tale stenches. The sunken flesh was similar to the parched state of several common diseases that rendered persons unable to keep any fluids down.

Sight again, please.

His soul is taken up.

Yes. But give me everything material you can.

The room faded away, and the weird, familiar sense of descending like a disembodied eye into a miniature somatic world replaced it. So, the empurpling *was* bruising, of a sort; not from blows, but as if the tiny blood vessels had disintegrated from the inside out, leaking their contents to coagulate and darken. The effect was apparent all through the body, not just at the skin, including in the lungs and gut. Pen extracted his extended senses as though pulling himself out of a bog. The sense of sticky horrors clinging to his skin was illusory, he reminded himself firmly, though he wanted to wash his hands at his first chance.

Mindful of the sick men in the beds nearby, Pen lowered his voice. "The victims vomit, cough, and pass blood?"

"Toward the end, yes. It's the sign." Rede's mouth tightened. "Master Orides knew."

"Had he performed any autopsies on the earlier deaths?"

"Yes, the first two." Rede's glance also went to the wary eavesdroppers on the nearby cots. "If you've seen all you can, Learned, perhaps we should take this conversation to the courtyard."

"Ah. Yes."

Rede covered his master's body once more, and made the holy tally sign with an extra tap to his navel. They shuffled back out to the bright courtyard, Adelis himself holding the curtain aside and exiting with alacrity. He was a brave man, Pen thought, but this wasn't the sort of enemy he could face with a sword or spear, for all that it was killing his soldiers in front of his eyes.

Rede sank down on one of the stone benches under the colonnade, squinting through puffy eyelids. In this better light, he looked even more strained, and Pen wondered when he'd last slept. Probably not last night. Adelis leaned against the nearest pillar, head bent with the labor of listening hard—not to their low voices, but to what they conveyed.

"I suppose I should begin with the obvious questions," said Pen. "What is the course of this thing? How does it first present?"

Rede shrugged in frustration. "At first, it appears as a common fever, the sort that passes off on its own with a few days of rest. Headache, and pain in the joints and muscles, loss of appetite. After a day or two, stomach pains start, with loosened bowels, again nothing unusual. The first certain sign is tiny spots under the skin, hard to make out. Then the skin starts to bruise, the spots growing to blotches and coalescing, as you saw. Then bloody or darkened stools and labored breathing. The descent into death is swift after that, three days or less. Altogether, from four days to a week."

"Have any men recovered on their own, or had milder cases?"

"Some are still alive after ten days, though I dare not name it recovered. Half, perhaps?"

"Hm. So, contagion, or contamination, do you think? Plague, or a poisoned well or the like?"

Rede's brows twitched up, as if the latter thought was new. By Adelis's jerk, it was an unwelcome idea to him, too. "I . . . Master Orides thought contagion."

I think Master Orides was correct, Des put in, thoughtfully. *Or at least on the right trail.*

Pen set aside the distracting memory of the famous possibly-poisoned well on the island of Limnos, which had historically destroyed an occupying army.

"Who were the first to fall ill? Is there any pattern?"

"Master Orides and I were puzzling over that. The first to die was our chief farrier, who'd been a strong man in excellent health. But the next was a quartermaster's clerk. Four foot soldiers. A cavalryman. A groom. Just last night, a laundress, the first woman. One of our own orderlies. And, now, our physician." That last seeming a heavier loss to Rede, and possibly to the fort, than all the rest combined.

"Any word of outbreaks in the village below?"

"The laundress was the first. I fear not the last. I've not yet had a chance to go down and ask."

"Someone should be sent for a census."

Adelis frowned, but nodded.

"So you . . . you are a sorcerer," said Rede, looking Pen up and down in perhaps justifiable doubt. "What can you do?"

So much. So little. Pen muffled a distressed sigh. "Have you ever worked with a sorcerer, or a Temple sorcerer-physician, before?"

"I'd never even met one. . . . Master Orides mentioned doing so once, but he didn't tell me much. Something about destroying the painful stones in the bladder."

"Ah. Yes. One of the easiest and safest procedures, and among the first taught. Much better than that thing with inserting the horrible spatula."

Rede nodded in a way suggesting he knew that ghastly technique first hand. Adelis, hah, cringed.

"The first thing you must understand is that my god-gift is *chaos* magic. It tends, and lends itself, most naturally to destructive procedures—downhill, it's dubbed. Of which there are more in medicine than one might think. But those can only clear the way for the body to heal itself, as the bladder cleans itself after the obstructing stones are rendered powder. Sometimes tumors can be destroyed." *Sometimes not.* "Intestinal worms also, though really, an apothecary's vermifuge does just as well." The wrenching urgent treatment for the fetuses misplaced outside the womb was the most delicate and advanced of all that downhill roster, and nothing Pen cared to discuss with the army physician. Or anyone else.

"So . . . is there then uphill magic?"

This boy is quick, Des purred in approval.

Pen nodded. "But it comes with a higher price than the downhill sort. A sorcerer can create order in, well, a number of ways, but then must shed a greater amount of disorder, somehow. If a sorcerer tries to do too much at once, or can't soon shed the excess of chaos, he or she is afflicted with a sort of heatstroke. Which can be as lethal as any other heatstroke."

"Oh. That, I had not heard of." Although from Rede's intent look, he understood and had undoubtedly treated heatstroke among the soldiers, no surprise in this climate. But then his nose scrunched up. "How in the world do you *shed chaos*? What does that even mean?"

Rede, Pen hoped, wasn't going to be a man baffled by technical vocabulary. He wouldn't have to water down his explanations.

"The area around the sorcerer suffers accelerated deterioration. Ropes fray or break. Metal rusts. Wood rots. Cups slip and spill or shatter. Sparks burn holes or set things alight. Wheels fall off, saddles slip, mounts go lame. The events aren't, usually, inherently unnatural, just their concentration and speed. Which is why an untrained hedge sorcerer is ill-advised to travel by ship, by the way." And then there were the tumors arising in the sorcerer's own body, which probably killed more inept sorcerers, in the long run, than uncanny heatstrokes. "Half my Temple training consisted of learning tricks to direct my demon's chaos safely outward to theologically allowable targets."

Rede was still listening intently, not interrupting this flow. Pen took a deep breath.

"The first magic my demon ever showed me was how to kill fleas and other insect pests. It turns out that the swiftest, most efficient sink of chaos is killing: the fall from life to death is the steepest slope of order to disorder that exists."

And the climb up it, as life built itself freely from matter in the world, its equally miraculous reverse. As Florina had just brought home to Pen most profoundly, but really, miracle was to be found in every breath and every bite of food he took, if he was mindful.

"So if I'm called upon to do much healing, I'll soon need to find some better sink for the chaos than a few bedbugs. We can deal with that later. The point is, my uphill magic doesn't cure or heal in a direct way. It fosters improved order in another's body so it may more speedily heal itself.

"So the other limiting factor, besides the need to find a chaos sink and the hazard of heatstroke, is how much help a body can accept at a time. I can no more force an injury to heal all at once than a man can eat a month of meals in a sitting. Repeated small applications are required.

"It follows that if the sickness is progressing faster than the body can digest my help, my attempt will fail. If the disease has gone past the point of no return, my magic will be wasted."

"You healed me," Adelis protested uncertainly. Rede

glanced up at his commander's sober, scarred face, and his eyes widened in realization.

"I can heal a man. I can't heal an *army*. If many people end up afflicted, rationing my efforts is going to be required." Pen frowned unhappily at Rede. "We may be forced to choose my patients wisely and cruelly. As a legion's physician, you must know how that one works."

Rede rubbed his brow. By his matching unhappy frown, he was following this better than Adelis. "I've not yet attended on a battlefield, but Master Orides would sometimes speak of that problem, yes. If we could get him in his cups."

Pen nodded. "From the outside, my results look random, even though they're not. But when fears and hopes rule in such a hectic mash, it can generate unfortunate misunderstandings about my sorcery."

"You sound as if you speak from experience," said Rede. "Like Master Orides."

Pen gave a capitulating wave of his hand. "Two of my demon's prior riders were active physicians in the Mother's Order. Counting their whole careers both before and after they were gifted with a Temple demon, it adds up to something like ninety years of medical practice." Leaving aside his own fruitful, fraught five years of attempting the trade back in Martensbridge. "Given I'm only thirty-three, the effect can sometimes feel . . . odd."

Adelis's eyebrows rose at this. Had he never done the arithmetic?

An officer entered the far side of the courtyard, spotted Adelis, and headed determinedly toward him.

Adelis shoved himself off the pillar to meet him partway; they conferred in low tones, then the fellow stood aside and waited. Adelis turned back to the pair on the bench.

"I need to attend to this. I'll leave you two to get on with it, for now, but report to me as soon as you have something substantive to add, Pen." For all the world as if Pen were one of his soldiers—score to Nikys.

Desdemona seized control of Pen's mouth. "Adelis, a word before you go."

"Hm? Is that you, Madame Desdemona?"

"Aye, boy."

Rede looked startled. "The demon speaks through his mouth?"

"Yes," sighed Pen.

Rede looked to his commander. "You can tell them apart? How?"

"Practice," said Adelis wryly. "I grant, some days I just give up and think of them as my sibling-in-law."

"Howsoever," said Des, for once unamused. "I'm going to let you conscript him for this, because halting him now would be hard. But you have to make me a promise in return."

"Oh?" said Adelis, with due caution.

"You've set him onto this road, so you have to tell him when to step off it. Because he won't be able to stop, and then we'll end up having another bloody argument about it. Shut up, Des." Pen closed his mouth with a snap. But she muscled in for a codicil: "You're the man in the saddle here, General Arisaydia, which even Pen must concede. This must be your load to lift."

"I am not much inclined to let a chaos demon

dictate my duty, but I do take your point, Madame Des. We'll see."

"Evader," she muttered to his back as he trod off.

"But honest," said Pen. "One of his better traits, surely."

"Hah."

Rede had watched this exchange with increasing . . . not mistrust, exactly, nor disbelief, but maybe the wondering air of a man waiting for more evidence. True to his trade, that.

Pen clasped his hands between his knees, contemplating what must come next. First. Next-first. "Des, in your two centuries have any of you, physician or not, seen this particular sickness before?"

"Plagues and contagions, yes, but . . ." She shrugged with his shoulders. "There are only so many ways disease can break a body down. So the array of symptoms are for the most part familiar. That dire all-over bruising is the one new thing. Very diagnostic."

"The most urgent," Pen began, "no, the most important is to find out how it passes from its source to people, or from person to person if that's what it's doing. Right now, I need to test how much simple uphill magic can do. Which we'll only find out by trying it." He unfolded to his feet, Rede, after a tired moment, shoving up from the bench likewise. Pen added to him, "When we go back in, don't introduce me as a sorcerer. Just as a learned divine brought in by their general to pray for them. Which actually won't be a lie. But it would be very bad to raise false hopes at this stage." He added after a moment, "Or false fears. Some people have wild ideas about magic. And not just Quadrenes. I'm usually pleased to tutor anyone who will listen, but now isn't the time." And after another, "Except for you. You need to know."

"Yes," said Rede heavily, "I do. Show me."

Rede led him to the door of the next chamber past where his dead mentor lay. Pen thought to ask, "How many men brought into your care do you have still alive?" How far was he going to have to stretch himself?

"About thirty, at last report. Two more brought in this morning. Less one, now." His face set, doing this mortal summing.

Rede lifted the leather curtain, and Pen took a breath and forced himself across the threshold.

Six cots, again. One man was still able enough to be helped to the commode chair by two orderlies. Three of the afflicted were quite young soldiers, the others older but not old. Five times Pen knelt by cots and said, "Good day. I'm Learned Penric of the Vilnoc Temple, sent to pray for you," which was accepted without undue puzzlement, and once with a feeble smile and thanks. He made the tally sign over them, laid a palm on each flushed chest, murmured more rote blessings, and quietly let as much uphill magic as Des could produce wash into them.

The sixth man, skin purpling, his breathing labored, was bleeding from his nose and swollen eyes, being sponged clean by a worried orderly. He did not react to Pen's greeting. After a brief glance within his rotting lungs and gut by Sight, Pen just knelt and prayed.

Sweat was trickling down his back and beading at his hairline when Pen arose and motioned the closely watching Rede to follow him out. He headed straight for the fountain at the end of the court, where he washed his hands with the lump of sharp-scented camphor soap and, after a dubious glance at the much-used towel on its hook, shook them dry. He likewise passed over the common ladle hanging beside it, leaning in to guzzle straight from the bright stream, heedless of the splash on his garments. And then stuck his head under it, letting the flow cool his scalp. He was still panting when he straightened up again.

"And now," he wheezed to Rede, "I need to go find something to kill."

"I beg your pardon?"

"Stores. Grain stores would be good, or the stables. Or the midden. Anywhere rats or mice gather, or other vermin. Flies. Crows. Seagulls in a pinch, if any fly in this far from the harbor."

"Sometimes," said Rede. His stare was still doubtful.

"I don't need help for this part, if you need to get back to your tasks. Or some sleep."

"I . . . no. I want to see what you're doing."

To his patients as well, Pen guessed. "There won't be much to see."

Rede opened his hand. "Nonetheless."

"All right, then. Follow me."

Rede ended up leading, to the middens outside the most-downwind postern gate of the fort. The gate guard let the physician through without demur.

The manure pile lay to the left of the pathway, the kitchen waste to the right, both spilling down the slope of the fossa. The manure pile was much smaller than Pen would have expected for the number of horses, mules, and oxen kept within. He saw why in a moment—a villager at the bottom of the trench, shoveling up a load of good army rot into a hand barrow, to take off and spread on his garden or crops. Probably garden; if he'd wanted to manure a field he'd have brought a wagon. The flies were abundant on both piles, though no rats slinked about on this bright afternoon. He'd have to come back at night for those. Though a few crows and seagulls were picking over the kitchen trash, good.

Pen waited for the villager to turn away and start dragging his cart up the well-worn path on the far side of the big trench, then waved a hand. The faint buzzing over the pile died away. The flies dropped like, well, flies.

Rede stepped forward and stared down at the sprinkling of tiny, shiny black corpses. "That's disturbing."

"It took some getting used to for me as well, but I've had to feed my demon for fourteen years, now. It feels almost housewifely." *Feed* was a misnomer, the directed shedding of chaos being more a sort of elimination, but Pen had discovered that term went over much better with listeners than more messy material metaphors, all just as inaccurate.

That had been a lot of flies, but their tiny lives were not going to be enough for this. Also, Pen was now fresh out of flies. Glumly, he selected and dropped a crow as well, which fell over in silence. And without pain, there was that consolation. A couple of its curious comrades hopped over and stared down at it, understandably perplexed. Did crows grieve? Their god did, Pen knew. He tapped his lips with the back of his thumb in apology, to what or Whom he was not sure.

"That will do for the moment." Pen wiped his wrist

over his cooling forehead. "But show me where the grain and food stores are, while we're over here."

Reentering, they were delayed by the gate guard demanding news of his sick squad mates. Rede, to his credit, gave a clear and honest, if brief, summation, though Pen wondered what distortions it would acquire when it came back off the soldier's tongue in barracks gossip tonight.

"I hope those idiots will bring themselves to me at once if they begin feeling ill," said Rede, looking back over his shoulder as they continued on to the grain stores. "The half who aren't malingerers to start with tend to claim they're just fine, no problems, sir, till they fall over. Master Orides says"—a hitch of breath—"said they annoyed him far more than the first sort."

Pen made five more trips between the hospice and the middens and stores before the late summer sunset. He examined, treated, and prayed over every sick man once, but by the time he visited the first chamber for the second time, the courtyard was dark and he was reeling and famished. Without demur, he let Rede guide him to the hospice staff's mess, where he wolfed down plain but abundant army food, and to a spare cot in the chamber where the orderlies slept. He wondered if it had belonged to the one who'd died.

"Is this helping them?" Rede asked bluntly as Pen flopped down on the wool-stuffed mattress.

"It's too soon to tell. Though sometimes you can only tell if it's too late. If a man dies, then it wasn't enough. If he recovers, would he have done so on his own?"

"Mm."

"I feel like a bucket brigade of one man, running back and forth from a well trying to put out a fire," Pen complained. "I need a bigger bucket. Or a closer well. A pump and hose. More men."

Could he get more men? There was only one sorcerer-physician he knew of in Orbas, serving the Mother's Order at Duke Jurgo's winter capital, but a more junior sorcerer might be conscripted for this, under Pen's supervision. The treatment was simple enough; not like the insanely finicky reconstruction of Adelis's acid-boiled eyes. Demons did not work well together, but they might be made to work in parallel.

I could manage to tolerate one, for this, Des told him. *How the other demon would fare, I can't guess.*

Gods, that was right, Pen needed to send a report on all this to his Order, and to the Mother's Order, in Vilnoc. It could be copied by scribes there and sent on to outlying chapterhouses. He should get up and go hunt quill and paper. He should.

"Has this thing broken out anywhere else, do you know?" he asked the shadowed ceiling. "Through army couriers or the like?"

"Not that I've heard. Master Orides was going to write to—oh, I should look through his papers. I don't know what he sent out before he was stricken himself."

Had Rede slept at all? Was he going to?

Pen compromised: "Have an orderly wake me at midnight. I'll make another round."

In the morning, after not enough sleep, Pen discovered that while the soldier who had been too far gone to treat had continued his journey to his god—though no others had died, yet—three more sickened men had been brought in. With such arithmetic, he wasn't getting ahead, here.

Also, one of Master Rede's orderlies had deserted in the night.

Rede swore in fury when he was told this over their hasty breakfast in the staff mess; not, it turned out, at the disloyalty or cowardice, but at the chance the fellow might have carried the contagion off to wherever he had fled to hide.

When he ran down from this muted tirade, he leaned his head back and asked either the plastered ceiling or Pen, "Which leads to the question, is this something a person gets only once, like some of the poxes, or is it something they could get over and over, like a catarrh or lung fever, with a chance of dying each time? Because if it's the first, I could safely press those who have recovered into service helping those who have fallen ill. Otherwise . . ."

Pen could only shake his head in equal doubt. Des, for once, had nothing to add.

Pushing himself up from the table, Pen began, again, the wearying round of prayer and magic alternated with hunting around in odd corners of the fort for more allowable vermin to slaughter. The manure-bred flies would take a few days to renew themselves, but seagulls, it appeared, flapped in routinely from the nearby coast, which might prove a reliable daily delivery. A seagull was worth a bit more than a rat, each of which was worth several mice, each of which was worth a few hundred insects. But if this went on much longer, he was going to need something more. Larger.

In between he ate, drank, and wrote urgent but frustratedly inconclusive notes to as many authorities as he could think of, for Adelis's military couriers to deliver. Adelis, when Pen handed these over to him in his headquarters map-room-and-scriptorium, had some disturbing return news carried by this same service. It had been sent from the fort and town at the far western end of the long east-west road spanning the duchy, which guarded the three-way border between Orbas, Grabyat, and Cedonia.

"From the description," Adelis said heavily, handing over the note for Pen to peruse, "it's the same Bastard-accursed thing we're having here. No disrespect intended to your god," he added as an afterthought.

Pen absently tapped the back of his thumb to his lips. "I think He accepts curses the way most gods accept prayers, really." He read the fort commander's terse description of their affliction, phrased less precisely than Pen would have put it but recognizable all the same.

Spurred, he sat down at the staff officers' writing table and composed a note to go with the next courier, to be given to the western fort's physician: briefly summarizing what had been happening here at Vilnoc, recommending they find a local Temple sorcerer if there was one, and giving his best guess so far of what such a mage might do to help.

"I wonder if this evil thing has turned up in Cedonia," Adelis remarked from his stool beside Pen, where he'd been watching this composition and giving unsolicited advice. He propped his elbows on knees and glowered at his sandals as if he could threaten them into an answer. "And how we could find out, or how soon."

For all that his natal country had so brutally exiled the general, Pen thought, pieces of his heart still anchored him there. Not, to be sure, with the Imperial bureaucracy, but rather with Lady Tanar and her household near the capital of Thasalon. Adelis's courtship of the young noblewoman had been disrupted by his arrest, blinding, and flight three years ago, but not, apparently, extinguished. A few secret letters had been smuggled across the border between them, Pen knew, because Adelis had shown them to his sister and mother.

"This isn't a hazard your sword arm could guard her from even if you were there," noted Pen.

"Is that supposed to be consoling?" said Adelis dryly.

"I suppose not. Though it's true."

"Hnh."

Pen's magic might help, but he had households much closer than Thasalon to concern him. "Have there been any reports of cases from the village besides the laundress?" Who had worked in the hospice. "Or from Vilnoc?"

"Not Vilnoc so far, five gods avert." Adelis made a less perfunctory than usual tally sign. "Some carters from the village, I'd heard."

Such men also frequently worked for the fort. Was there a connection? "I'd better go down and look at them, too."

Adelis frowned. "My men should come first."

Pen gave him a side-eye. "I serve my Order, and the archdivine. Not the army."

"They all owe allegiance to Duke Jurgo."

"The white god doesn't. Nor would the duke be wise to wish Him to."

Unable to gainsay this, Adelis just grunted.

A soldier came to the map-chamber door and called, "Sir, they're ready."

"Right." He rose and swung his red cloak over his shoulders; the soldier helped him set the bronze cloak-pin.

Pen followed them out, to discover that the reason for Adelis's military finery was the funeral just setting up at the temple across the main courtyard.

"Services for Master Orides," murmured Adelis. "Shall you attend?"

"I think my presence would distract your fort's divine, and Des would disturb the sacred animals."

Would not, protested Des. *But I suspect even Orides would prefer a more effective use of our time.* "We know he's gone to his goddess already," she added aloud.

Adelis glanced aside, as if trying to parse which one of them had spoken, then just shrugged.

Pen spotted Master Rede and a couple of his orderlies, who had also donned their military uniforms for this, trudging in from the direction of the hospice. Pen waved a hand at Adelis by way of farewell and angled toward them. Rede motioned his subordinates on, stopping by Pen.

"I'm about to walk down and take a look at any sick in the village," Pen told him.

"Oh. Good." Rede squinted in the bright sunlight. His eyes were bloodshot, but Pen trusted that was just fatigue and not a symptom. "Anything you can learn, bring back to me. I had a chance to look at Master Orides's papers. He'd been working on making a kind of list or grid of all who had come down with this thing, laying out everything known about them and looking for a pattern. I'm going to try to continue it later this afternoon."

"Sensible." Pen glanced across to the temple portico, where the sacred animals that signed which god or goddess had taken up the soul of the deceased were being brought out by their soldier-grooms. "You inter your dead whole here, yes?" A military cemetery lay outside the fort's walls, in the opposite direction from the village. "Should those who've died of this be cremated, instead, d'you think?"

Rede grimaced. "I just don't know. The weather is dry, so there should be no ground seepage from the cemetery. And wood is dear, if much would be required."

"In the cantons and the Weald, wood is abundant and cheap, but people still mostly bury." Des added as a cheery afterthought, "Except in certain special cases where burning is required to prevent spirit-possession of the corpse."

Rede looked taken aback. "That's real? Not a tale?"

"Death magic? Very rare, although dealing with it does fall as the duty of the Bastard's Order, so I was taught about it. Nothing I'd expect here."

"Glad to hear it."

Pen tapped his lips in either a blessing or a gesture of

averting—with the white god, much the same thing—
nodded wryly, and turned to make his way to the front
gate.

It was a short walk downslope to the dusty village of
Tyno, which hugged, and hogged, the riverbank. It
would have been shorter, but Adelis, when he'd taken
over here two years back, had spearheaded one of the
periodic removals of buildings that had encroached upon
his defensive perimeter. This had not made him popular
with the villagers, but since then his stern fairness, not
to mention some compensation from Duke Jurgo's
purse, had won the new general a grudging respect.

The main east-west road that—along with the river
approaches to Vilnoc—the fort guarded ran through the
upper outskirts of the village. Here clustered the taverns,
Tyno's most lucrative trade; a few attendant inns, mostly
for more modest visitors who couldn't afford lodging
within Vilnoc's walls; and the brothels—prostitutes were
among the Bastard's flock of human oddments, so in
theory under Pen's care as a divine. A livery and a smithy
also stood convenient to the road and its travelers.

Either would be tied into the town's gossip net. Smiths
could run to either taciturn or usefully garrulous, but in
either case were like to be busy. Liverymen, on the other
hand, had to talk to their customers, and would also know
where to find the sick carters. Pen strolled through the
broad, open doors into the shaded stable. He left Des to
snack on the available flies without his oversight.

A man advanced from the aisle between the straight
stalls, propping a pitchfork aside and wiping his hands

on his trousers. Ostler or owner, it didn't matter. "Good afternoon, sir," he began. "Whether it's a good riding horse or a nice, calm cart cob you're wanting, you've . . . five gods." He stopped short and stared wide-eyed at Pen, whose height, bright blond hair, blue eyes, and milk-pale skin were unusual for Orbas, if common in the cantons.

Or it's your pretty face, love, Des quipped.

Hush.

Thanks be for recognizable Temple vestments, or at least mercantile manners, because instead of falling into the usual wearying interrogation about Pen's looks, he recovered himself and went on, "Uh, learned sir? May I help you?"

"I hope so, although not to a horse, sorry. My name is Learned Penric, of the Bastard's Order in Vilnoc, and General Arisaydia asked me to examine the people who have fallen sick here lately of the strange bruising fever. A couple of carters, I was told, and perhaps others by now. Can you tell me names and where to find them?"

Arisaydia's status was even more useful here than the Order's, Pen guessed, because the man merely said, "Oh," and gave Pen directions to a house a street over.

"This bruising fever isn't one of our usual summer sicknesses," the liveryman added, swallowing uneasily. "Very fast and frightening, striking down grown men, not just the old or the infants. Does the Bastard's Order suspect a curse?" Holy or otherwise lay implied.

It wasn't an altogether unreasonable question, but it could be a dangerous rumor to let get started. "No," said Pen, more firmly than he felt. "It's a nasty disease, but there's nothing uncanny about it."

Agreed, said Des.

"But wouldn't a divine from the Mother's Order . . ."

"The fort's physicians are working hard," Pen diverted this. *True enough.* He decanted what the man knew of other sick folks here—three more households already, gods—and made his escape before he had to field further awkward speculations.

The carters' place, belonging to two brothers who lived together, lay in a row of houses that turned plain, whitewashed stucco faces to the street, not unlike a reduced village version of Pen's home. Pen knocked on the green-painted wooden door; waited; knocked again. He was just contemplating the horrid possibility that there was no one left alive inside, and if it would be acceptable to use Des's powers on the lock to intrude and check for corpses, when the door squeaked open.

An exhausted-looking middle-aged woman stared blankly up at him. "I . . . what?"

"Good afternoon, ma'am. I'm Learned Penric of the Vilnoc Temple. General Arisaydia asked me to look in on the ill folk here in the village." All right, not quite what Adelis had said, but there was no harm in making him sound charitably concerned.

She looked Pen up and down. She evidently knew enough to read the details of his garb, for she said in some bewilderment, "Why did he send a sorcerer? If the Vilnoc Temple is trying to help, I want someone from the Mother."

Des put in, before Pen could speak, "I'm married to his twin sister."

"Oh," she said, her inflection somehow combining

surprise and reassurance. She opened the door to admit him.

What's Nikys got to do with it? he asked Des, a little bewildered himself.

It worked. She'll trust you across her threshold. Don't complain.

Wouldn't dream of it.

Fibber. You complain all the time.

Turnabout, fair play . . .

The carter's wife led him into the usual inner courtyard, ringed by the rooms of the house and used for every task from dining to sewing to washing, leatherwork, or minor carpentry. Right now, it was converted to a chamber for the sick, judging from the two beds of fine straw laid out on the flagstones. Upon them lay two men of sturdy build, but weak and flushed, glazed of eye. One redder than the other but not darkened to bruising yet; maybe Pen could still help? A basin of water and washrags, and another for vomit, sat between them.

"Is it only you to care for them?" Pen asked.

"My sister-in-law took all of our children to her mother's when we realized this was that thing from the fort."

"That . . . seems prudent." Or else it would spread the sickness to yet another household, but the deed was done and there was no benefit to worrying this woman further. It appeared the villagers had not, yet, taken to exiling the sick or their families beyond natural seclusion in their own houses.

Aye, plagues can get ugly far beyond their medical courses, Des remarked. From experience, Pen feared.

Contagion. Let's just call it a contagion, in front of people.

May be wise, for now.

While the woman knelt between the pair and took it in turns to bathe their faces with a wrung-out cloth, Pen sat cross-legged and asked all three about their recent activities.

The carters' latest venture out of Tyno had been to take an oxcart piled with the possessions of a retiring fort officer back to his home village, up a valley lying next-south from Vilnoc's. The trek had taken a week, but that had been nearly a month ago. Since then, they'd been busy locally, hiring themselves, their cart and their beasts to construction up at the fort.

"Could we have brought this thing back with us as hidden cargo?" asked the younger brother, the less feverish of the pair, uneasily. His elder winced.

"Given how recently you've been stricken, I don't think it," Pen reassured them. Truthfully, he hoped. "You should have been the first if that were so. No one else in your household has come down with it yet, right?"

They both looked at the woman, wife of the elder, in worry. She shook her head. This nurse would not desert her post, but it didn't mean she wasn't frightened. She added, "I wondered about the sheets. Because of the laundress." She gestured somewhat helplessly at the straw bedding. "This, we can burn later, but it's not what I like."

"Boiling the soiled sheets should suffice," said Pen. For the sheets and their next users, anyway. For the washerwoman handling them, it was less clear. "But there's nothing wrong with this straw arrangement, in this warm weather." Clever, actually; he'd have to suggest it to Rede.

The set of her shoulders eased at this endorsement.

Really, I am no authority to her, thought Pen, discomfited.

Do not waste our advantages on pointless humility, chided Des. *We may need every one before this is over.*

Mm.

Duly reproved, Pen merely smiled, and moved on to kneeling at each straw-bedside. There, in a spirit of theological redundancy worthy of a bridgebuilder, he performed a prayer to all five gods, while covertly inserting as much uphill magic as they would take into each body. *Performing* seemed all too apt a term, but the audience, all three, seemed pleased enough with his delivery.

He wished he knew whether it was enough. He'd better not promise to come back, given the uncertainties up at the fort, but he wanted to try.

I know you do, said Des uneasily, *but this had better not become another hillside for you to die on.*

I am advised, he returned vaguely.

The sense of a snort.

"This is so strange," said the younger carter, frowning at the flush on his forearm discernible even through his sunbaked skin. "Do you think it was brought by those accursed Rusylli?"

Scowls all around at this conjecture.

"Have you heard of any sickness in their encampment?" asked Pen, alert. No one at the fort hospice had mentioned any, but then, their plates were full. Another place to check while he was down here? Adelis's name would not provide a glad welcome there, though his authority would get Pen in.

"No, but I haven't been out to the market for a few days," said the carter's wife. "My sister and neighbors have been leaving food at our door."

The older carter, peevish in his fever, growled, "I've told the youngsters not to go over there, but I know they do, when our backs are turned."

Pen's lips twisted in doubt. "But the Rusylli have been here, what, a year? If this was something they brought, it should have shown up much sooner." He drove home the point with, "Just as if it was something from your cart trip, it should have shown up later."

This was taken in with brooding looks, but no one tried to argue.

The batch of Rusylli prisoners of war from last year's campaign lived in an odd limbo, here at Tyno. Too important to sell off as slaves; not high enough to be held close as key hostages by Duke Jurgo's ally-in-law the High Ohan of Grabyat. How Adelis had allowed himself to be lumbered with them, Pen was not sure. Nevertheless, several hundred Rusylli—lesser tribal leaders and their immediate families—had been dropped downriver of Tyno and anchored there in a makeshift village by the expedient of the military engineers removing the wheels from their big house-carts.

Some people, Pen knew, romanticized the nomadic warriors. But then, some people romanticized *pirates*.

Pen was not one of them, pirates on horseback seeming no more appetizing to him than the seafaring sort. As long as the Rusylli clans contented themselves with raiding each other, Pen had nothing to say to it, but when they took to preying on their settled neighbors, in western Grabyat and southwestern Cedonia, trouble started. Which kept men like Adelis employed, he supposed.

Des, in her prior lives in Cedonia, had not much encountered them. So even if not suffering from this malady, they might know something more, or at least other, than her long experience provided. Putative enemies, yes, but disease recognized no borders or boundaries. Rather like gods, that.

Pen hauled himself up and took his leave with a few more harmless sops of blessings all around, for which everyone seemed more grateful than Pen thought justified. He did not allow himself to frown in new thought until he had been seen out by the anxious wife and turned down the street, heading to the next stricken household on his list.

The sun was low by the time Pen emerged from the last of these, and he was overheated, fretful, and fatigued. The other families had offered the same maddeningly random assortment of victims, including one child. Pen had poured all he could into the boy, fearing it too little. He must squeeze time for a repeat visit to that household tomorrow, if no others. He hoped Rede would be able to make more of his observations than he did, so far.

He paused at the corner, needing to make a decision, which seemed slower in coming than it should.

That's because you need to decide to go eat, Pen.

Likely so. What he *wanted* was to go talk to the folk in the Rusylli encampment. But should he grab some bite from one of the nearby taverns, exposing them to whatever contaminations he might now bear, even if he ate it out of hand while walking down the river road? He wasn't sure if visiting the Rusylli after dark was a good idea. They'd be wary enough of him in daylight. Tomorrow morning might work better.

Return to the hospice mess, then, where they could all be contaminated together. He also very much wanted Rede to show him Orides's notes. He headed uphill in a weary trudge too like how his magic was starting to feel.

To Des's maternal approval, he got himself around some solid and abundant army food—*all the olives you can eat* wasn't that many for Pen, and he still could not like the dried fish planks, but the ox jerky and barley cakes were good, and the harsh red wine, once watered, more than acceptable. Sustained again, he tracked Rede down to Orides's writing cabinet adjoining the treatment rooms. Now Rede's writing cabinet, as the new commander of this careening disaster, though Pen wasn't quite sure if the man had assimilated that yet. Perhaps the funeral would have helped center him.

At Rede's beckoning, Pen sat down in the yellow lamplight of Orides's desk to share perusal of the late master's half-written reports on the autopsies and other case logs.

"Is an autopsy something you'd wish to repeat for yourself?" asked Rede, as Pen squinted at the inky scratches. He'd worked with worse handwriting on ancient manuscripts, but really, what was it about physicians? "Because we have a fresh body. The catapult sergeant died about two hours ago."

"Oh. I thought he might." Pen made the tally sign. "His internal disintegration did seem too far advanced to make anything of my help." Though Pen had tried, Bastard help him, in his last cycle through that sick-chamber. Just in case . . .

"But with Des's Sight, I don't need to open or even touch a body anymore to find out what's going on inside. Although my anatomical training, and Helvia's and Amberein's, were invaluable for putting a foundation to my understanding. Spirit-sight is not a match for what you'd see with your eyes or a magnifying lens, and it takes some practice to reliably connect the meaning of all those moving colors with their material substrate."

Rede sat back and stared at him with frank envy. "It sounds a wonderful skill for a Temple physician to possess."

No denying that; Pen shrugged. "Also, curiously, Des can tell contagion from poisoning, even when the gross symptoms are similar. Each can be diffuse, but there is something *alive* about contagion that poisons don't share. I keep thinking about that. Too diffuse for Des to separate, or it might be possible to kill the disease but not the person, the way I can kill fleas on a cat but not the cat. I like cats," he added muzzily. Gods, he was getting tired. Soon he'd be making no sense at all. This day felt a year long, and he still wanted to make another pass through the infected chambers.

Rede, charitably, ignored this last haphazard remark, unless he was growing as tired as Pen. But his black brows drew together in new thought. "Could such a thing have to do with how the saints of the Mother effect their miraculous cures?"

Pen's heart lifted at this rare sign of understanding. "I've had that exact notion. A task too fine-grained for a man or even a chaos demon should not be too fine for a goddess. If ever I run across a saint of the Mother again, I want to ask"—if Des could refrain from going into conniptions at the divine proximity— "though it's possible the saint may not know. It's emptiness, not knowledge, that allows a person to channel a god. Howsoever, the Mother's Order in Vilnoc does not possess such a blessing, that I've heard." Although might the letters he'd sent off earlier today turn something up? It was too distracting a hope. "For now, we're on our own."

Rede nodded reluctant agreement.

Pen tapped the papers scattered across the table. "You've been observing this for longer than I have. Any thoughts? Speculations? Wild guesses?"

Rede scrubbed a hand through his scalp, spiky black hair overdue for a military haircut. "I don't think this disease starts in the lungs or the gut—those symptoms come last. It doesn't seem to travel in the breath, or people would have it in batches, especially in the barracks. Instead, it's one man out of dozens. Given all the vile things sick men emit, you'd think it would move in soiled linen, or vomit, or feces, but we've all been handling those, and only a few have taken ill. One laundress dead in three days, the rest fine, though several have refused to come back to work. I need to ask General Arisaydia to find us volunteers to help scrub. If there are not enough, conscript some, though that won't go happily."

"Mm."

"I've been thinking about the blood," Rede went on. "Master Orides would have been more exposed to that than anyone, during the autopsies."

"Did you assist at those?"

"I'd been detailed to other duties."

"Did anyone else, and have they been among the ill?"

Rede shook his head. "Once they'd set things up, Orides ran his helpers out. He said no one else needed to get that close."

Pen grimaced. "If you're asking if this disease is *in* the blood, yes, to be sure—the gross symptoms tell us that. Whether it starts there . . . I'll try to attend more closely to that question as I make my way around. Blood is peculiar stuff. Do you know it's still alive when it leaves the body, till it dries?"

Rede's brows flicked up in interest. "Oh?"

"I learned a lot about it, even beyond what most Temple physicians know, back when I took a year to train with the royal shamans of the Weald. Who use blood and the sacrifice of blood routinely in their magics, as demons use chaos and order. We had debates about connections, generally in their dining hall over late-night beer, but I can't say we found conclusions.

"I'm not sure where in my body my chaos demon is domiciled, but the shamans' Great Beasts definitely live in their blood. This has been known for a long time, which is why the execution of a shaman back in the days of the forest tribes used to involve hanging him upside-down and butchering him like a hog. They believed it drained him of his powers with his blood."

"That . . . would work on anybody, really," Rede pointed out.

A spurt of laughter escaped Pen's lips. "True. Anyway. This bruising disease does seem alive in the blood, not unlike those lethal infections that sometimes follow wounds. . . . Though the shamans would be quite offended to have their Great Beasts dubbed a blood disease."

"I'll keep that in mind, should I ever meet one." Rede had a dry humor hidden in there, if battered at the moment.

They turned once more to Orides's writings, coming to the end too soon, like their author. The case notes, meticulous in the beginning, grew ever more abbreviated. *Bastard's teeth, another one*, read one of the last. The physician's observations seemed keen to Pen, but included nothing he hadn't seen for himself by now.

Pen bit his lip and sat back. "Were you able to make anything of that comparison-grid he'd started?"

"I added the newer cases to it. They're all over the map, or at least all over the fort. I ranked the numbers by company. There may be a slight bias to the cavalry, but that doesn't explain the laundress. Or the people in town. Oh. I should include them." He scratched in Pen's accounting from the village and handed the page across to Pen.

Indeed, any clustering seemed slight. "I suppose more numbers might make it clearer, but that's not something to wish for."

"Five gods avert," said Rede. And then, after a pensive moment, "Do They?"

"Not that I can tell," sighed Pen. "I've sometimes wondered if the gods regard death not as a dreaded ending, but as a welcome beginning."

"Of what?"

"I am deeply not sure. Which doesn't stop people from making up a thousand tales." Or maybe the gods provided a thousand versions, tailored to each soul. Pen wouldn't put it past Them. "There doesn't seem to be any need to rush to find out, though. The gods wait all the same."

Rede signed himself; Pen didn't bother. They both shoved up to return to the sick-chambers.

Pen washed himself the next morning at the hospice courtyard fountain, stripping to the skin and applying the camphor soap liberally, including his hair. His summer vestments, much the worse for the past two days, he tossed into a bucket for Des to deal with. The price of even a few insect lives for his laundry seemed dimly wrong to Pen, but this was a special case.

Even with Des's help, he didn't think he could wash *enough* to risk returning to his Vilnoc home, and Nikys and Florie and Idrene, not until they'd come to understand how the bruising disease passed from person to person. When he'd answered Adelis's plea for aid, Pen had not anticipated so profound an exile.

He shook out the de-bloodstained whites for Des to speedily steam dry, trusting the passing orderlies would be too distracted by their duties to notice his odd activities, redonned them, and fastened his hair back in a simple switch. Slipping on his sandals, he clipped off to find Adelis.

He tracked the general down in his quartermaster's office. At Pen's wave, Adelis interrupted his business and came to the doorway. Pen led him out under the colonnade.

"Have you heard of any cases of the bruising fever in the Rusylli camp?" Pen began. "Master Rede hadn't."

"Hm. The quartermaster's grain deliveries to them are made weekly, and one of their tasks is to report back to me on the state of affairs there. So not unless something has popped up in the past few days, no."

"I'm going to walk down there and see if they know anything about this disease that we don't."

Adelis shrugged. "I shouldn't think they'd be very willing to talk to you, but I suppose you can try. Hold a moment, and I'll detail you some guards."

"I don't need them, surely. I mean . . . *we* don't."

"I don't underestimate your ability to defend yourself, Penric. Yourselves. But the presence of a few of my men will reduce the temptation to ambush you, avoiding the problem in the first place."

"Mm, and doubtless make the Rusylli even more closemouthed. I think not."

Adelis plainly misliked this plan. "Then take my translator. The Rusylli have several of their own Cedonian speakers, but at least you'll be able to know if what you're told is what is actually being said."

"Same problem, and also not needed. All those Cedonian language lessons I gave to Rybi the Rusylli girl last winter didn't just go one way."

"Really?" Adelis's brows rose. "I thought you inherited your gifts of languages from Madame Des."

"I did, but I haven't let them lie fallow and uncultivated. Also, it turns out languages are like children. Once you have six, adding a seventh hardly makes any difference. Or so my mother used to say." He added after a moment, "Me being her seventh, you know."

"I'll take her word for it." Adelis's mouth ticked up at the corner. "Report back to me if you learn anything new."

"Of course." Pen escaped before Adelis could come up with more objections. To be fair, the man wasn't just being a fusspot. He'd been ambushed by Rusylli a *lot*.

Pen made his way out to the main road and turned right, thinking about Rybi. Adelis had dumped the pregnant Rusylli girl upon Pen's household—well, upon Idrene, whom he knew would be sympathetic to her plight—late last fall. She'd had a drearily familiar story: a soldier-lover from the fort, forbidden trysts, predictable consequences. Accusation on her side, denial on his, and a family who had beaten and forcibly ejected her. The uproar had worked its way up to Adelis, who didn't have any more luck sorting out the truth than anyone else. Pen thought he and Des might have, given some time with the boy, but the Father of Winter, not the Bastard, was the god of justice, and Adelis's army was not any responsibility of Pen's. Although somebody had to be detailed to clean the latrines, and Adelis, for so many reasons not appreciating the ruckus one bit, had made sure the soldier's officers knew who.

The anguished girl had slowly recovered over the ensuing months, bruises both physical and mental fading under Idrene's and Nikys's care. The Rusylli had no writing, so Pen had weighed in with lessons in both the Cedonian language, and reading and letters, in return for all those household chores. She'd given birth to a healthy boy about a month before Nikys had delivered Florina. Nikys had no need at all for a wet nurse, so Pen had found Rybi a place doing that at the Bastard's orphanage in Vilnoc, where she and her child were well-fed, safe, and very welcome. She still returned to Pen's house once a week for language lessons—not just hers, but his.

Rybi had taught him quite a bit about the nomads' lives and customs, along with their vocabulary and peculiar grammar. Sadly, nothing about it led Pen to believe that mentioning his care of her would be of aid in the encampment, and more likely the reverse.

I think you're right, said Des. *Also, if they offer you a translator, it might be wise to conceal your command of their tongue, as well as how you acquired it. For much the reasons Adelis said.*

Eavesdropping, Des? It was a ploy that had served Pen well a time or two before, true. *We'll see.*

After a ten-minute walk down the road, a somewhat denuded grove of trees hove into view. It sheltered a collection of huts, formerly wagons, fifty or sixty of them. On this clear morning, the shafts of light filtering through the branches and the bright sun-dapple spangling everything made the place look more idyllic than it likely was.

Pen turned in past the cursory guard post kept there, just four soldiers. At least one of them recognized not only his vestments but Pen as the general's sorcerous brother-in-law, because he braced and gave a military salute, saying nervously, "Learned sir. Sir." With Adelis's army brutes, Pen was never sure if this intimidation was from the brother-in-law or the sorcery part.

Pen returned a tally sign, and murmured, "Five gods' blessings upon you all. I'm on an errand for Adelis," and marched past, avoiding delays for interrogations, gossip, or anxious inquiries about what was happening in the hospice that he really couldn't answer.

A few people were about, tending to chores in the shade. An occasional goat, chicken or pig wandered among them. A dog scratched itself and lay back down with a tired whuff. The army had seized their hostage-prisoners' draft animals—oxen and beloved horses—for much the same reason as they'd removed the wheels from their traveling huts, but had left the smaller food animals. Pigs, ill-suited to keeping up with wide-ranging herds, were not normally a steppe meat, so Pen presumed they'd been added later. The Rusylli had no other objections to pork, being happy enough to steal it while raiding outlying farms, though horses and young women were more prized. At least they didn't eat the last.

Pen's arrival was noticed at once. Pen was inured to being stared at in the street, but not usually with such hostile suspicion. Though it wasn't for his coloration; particularly in the far south, the Rusylli clans had their share of blonds and redheads, possibly a legacy of all those stolen wives.

A half-dozen sturdy men assembled on the rutted entry road. Bows and swords had been taken from them, of course, but the army had perforce left them knives and butchering tools. And cudgels, Pen knew, could bash sorcerer skulls just as well as they did ordinary ones. The men weren't heavily armed; they just looked as if they wished they were. They wore a motley combination of traditional dress—well-fitted, bright-patterned weaves, leather straps, metal ornaments—and Orban army castoffs, variously mended.

Des commented, *I wonder if their reputation for screaming into battle dressed in nothing but riding chaps and tattoos is less bravado than their wives and mothers objecting to the wear, tear, and bloodstains on their shirts?*

Not in the steppe winters, they don't. Which Pen understood could get even more bitterly cold than his mountain cantons.

Around the encampment, a scattering of young women and girls whisked or were whisked into the huts. The old crones kept working, though they watched the proceedings narrow-eyed. A few young boys took up idle poses, and didn't even pretend not to stare in curiosity.

Pen wondered if they included some who'd sneaked out to play with the carter children along the riverbank.

Pen really wanted to talk with the old women, but apparently these mature men were who he was going to get. They were all here in the first place, Pen was reminded, because they were leaders who were disinclined to make peace.

"Good morning," Pen began in Cedonian as they all stopped within speaking range. "Five gods bless and keep you." He offered a tally sign, which was taken in with neither delight nor offense. The vagaries of Rusylli theology were a whole other dissertation, but they did recognize Pen's god as one of the Five, not an abject reject of Four as the Quadrene heresy would have Him. Or Her, or Him-Her, depending on the tribal region; for a bodiless, if vast, being of pure spirit, Pen granted that the assignment of sex was arbitrary. These men could decode Pen's Orban vestments, anyway. "I need to talk to someone."

One of the group shouldered forward. Middle-aged—by Rusylli standards, which probably meant he was about as old as Pen—missing his right arm, so not a bowman or warrior. Anymore. He lifted his bearded chin at Pen.

"I'm Angody. I speak Cedonian."

"Thank you." Pen bent his head in a polite nod. He gestured to a circle of stumps and logs around a nearby cold firepit. "May we sit? This might take a bit." Once seated, Pen would be harder to eject.

Angody glanced to another man, taller and with brown hair and beard in ornamented braids, who nodded permission. So, the translator was follower or retainer, not leader. They all shuffled over and settled themselves, not comfortably, but that wasn't due to the makeshift furniture.

"Should I get a woman to fetch drinks?" another man, more warrior-like or at least still in possession of all his limbs, asked the leader in low-voiced Rusylli.

"No. Maybe he'll go away sooner."

A nod of understanding, and the fellow sat cross-legged and straight-backed, frowning at Pen. Guests were normally plied with food or drink in Rusylli camps; Pen, having heard vivid descriptions of these treats from Adelis, was just as glad to be spared the need to politely choke down, say, fermented mare's milk.

Which they don't have anyway, since their mares were taken away, Des pointed out. *We're safe.*

Hm.

"My name is Learned Penric. I serve the Bastard's Order in Vilnoc," Pen began. He paused, but no return introductions were forthcoming. As they seemed to be skipping opening pleasantries, he continued directly: "Master Rede, the physician at the fort, wanted me to ask around. A number of his men have been taken with a strange fever, unknown in Orbas. Or Cedonia, or anywhere in the countries easterly, for that matter."

He paused while Angody converted this to Rusylli, with tolerable accuracy. No reaction from the other men. Pen went on, "It begins as an ordinary fever, but then progresses to bleeding, under the skin, in the gut and lungs, and finally even from the nose, ears, and eyes. The skin all over darkens like a bruise—well, it is a bruise, technically—toward the end. It's very painful."

Angody's brows went up, and he repeated this, more rapidly. *Now* his listeners all flinched back.

"We've started dubbing it the bruising fever, for lack of any other information, but it must have a name *somewhere*. Wherever it comes from. Is this anything the Rusylli know, or that you've heard or even heard rumors about?"

"The blue witch," muttered one man. "Her curse has come *here*?"

The braid-bearded man motioned him to silence.

"What should I tell him?" Angody asked the leader.

"Tell him nothing. Tell him we know nothing. Those army curs are always willing to believe that."

"I don't think this one is that stupid," said Angody. "And not army. These eastern templemen are bookish fellows, aren't they?"

"That doesn't make them any less witless," put in another man, the eldest if the sprinkling of gray in his beard was anything to go by. "Just more nearsighted."

"Maybe we'll be lucky and they'll *all* be cursed," another said with venom. "The demon general first."

A moment of weirdly respectful fear slithered through the circle at this mention of Adelis. When Adelis had come back from his blinding as if risen from the dead, face exotically scarred and eyes turned garnet red, both enemies and allies found him newly alarming. Never a man to waste either time or an advantage, Adelis accepted this addition to his command mystique and let the fantastical rumors proliferate. His private feelings, no one witnessed save his sister and mother. And Pen, as his intimate healer.

"Yes, let our wicked foes be punished," agreed the ill-wisher's seatmate on his log, in piety of a sort Pen supposed.

"Now you're talking foolishness," said Gray-beard. "The blue witch has neither friends nor mercy. She takes men as blindly as a madwoman picking flowers."

Braid-beard nodded grim agreement. "And if she's *there*, she could come *here*."

Pen kept his expression bland and mildly inquiring as he looked to Angody.

Angody blinked at his leader and said to Pen, "It sounds very frightening. But we don't know it."

"You've had no such sickness here in this camp?"

"No," said Angody firmly. Not lying about that, at least. A man could make the five-fold tally as well with the left hand as the right, and Angody did. Although if the gods could avert any of this, Pen had seen no sign of it.

Des's sly ploy had paid off, Pen had to grant her that. He wouldn't be getting the half of this if the Rusylli knew he understood what they were saying. And he had the main information he'd come for; that the bruising fever hadn't broken out here at all, let alone first.

Should he interrogate them further, revealing his eavesdropping? It sounded as though their understanding of the disease was shot through with wild tales, which however interesting to Pen as a scholar were of little use to him as a physician.

Perhaps not, said Des in doubt. *Though odd clues do turn up in strange dress sometimes, in diagnoses.*

Pen wanted more, but either coercing or tricking it from such reluctant informants would take him time and energy that thirty-five men in the hospice and a little boy in town could not spare. He contented himself with a, "Well, if you think of anything else, or hear of anything further, please send a message to me at the fort by way of one of the gate guards. They'll be able to find me. I'm very interested. And *especially* if anyone here comes down with it. That would be a matter of utmost urgency. I can help."

Which . . . was not yet proved. Upon Angody translating this, it didn't look as though they believed him anyway.

Pen rose and took his leave of the Rusylli men with another polite blessing. They walked him almost to the road, seeing him out. Or off.

He was, to no surprise, now accosted by the gate guards wanting news of their comrades in the hospice. Trying to strike a balance between reassurance and honesty was awkward, but at least Pen was able to put in an authoritative word or two absolving these Rusylli of having anything to do with it, which might help prevent future trouble.

Pen strode back toward Tyno wondering if that was really true.

"Hey. Hey. God man," he was hailed in a sharp whisper from the verge.

He wheeled and paused. The speaker crouching half-concealed in the weeds stood up. A Rusylli woman, by her dress and ornaments; older, a near-crone, work-gnarled but still hale, by the way she sidled up to him. She was guarded, or dogged, by a thin hound, its muzzle gray to match her head. It leaned into her skirts, watching Pen as anxiously as its mistress. Her hands flexed, as if wanting but afraid to grasp him.

"Rybi. Rybi. Demon general took. Alive? Dead? *Rybi*," she said in broken Cedonian.

Bastard be thanked. Making an instant decision, Pen returned in reasonably smooth Rusylli, "The girl Rybi? Who left your camp last fall? Who are you to ask after her?"

At hearing her language, a look of relief crossed the woman's worn features, and she came back with a term in Rusylli that meant something like a maternal sister of an older generation; *great aunt*, Pen decided, was close enough. He'd get the nuances from Rybi later. She went on, "They say the general took her away. They say she died."

"She's alive."

"Where? How?" If Pen's summer tunic had possessed a sleeve, he thought she would have tugged it in her urgency.

"Given that her brothers half-killed her, while her father egged them on and her mother did nothing, I'm not sure I should tell her family where to find her to finish the job."

Taking this in, she nodded grimly. "It goes that way, sometimes."

That particular flavor of sexually charged brutality was by no means unique to the Rusylli, although whether the neighbors condoned or condemned it varied from people to people. Pen was glad his god was implicitly on the side of *condemned*.

"I gather that she crawled off to die in front of the fort

gates by way of reproach, which is how she came to General Arisaydia's attention." He'd near-tripped over her, by the tale he'd told Idrene and Nikys. "I can tell you she's recovered, doing well, and in a safe harbor." Should he mention the healthy infant, or would that just multiply the targets?

"Can you speak to her?"

Cautiously, Pen chose, "I might be able to relay a message."

"Then tell her, her Auntie Yena cares for her still. Tell her, live and be well. Don't come back. Don't look back." She nodded decisively.

Rybi had pretty much figured all that out for herself by now, Pen thought, except for the part about her aunt's regret, so he merely said, "I will."

A huff of relief.

Pen, murmured Des. *Don't waste this opportunity.*

God-given or no, right. "I didn't come out here about Rybi. I came to ask about a disease that has turned up in the fort, that I hear is known to the western Rusylli people. The men wouldn't speak to me of it. Will you?" She stood poised, tense, but not running off, so Pen again went on to describe the bruising fever. "They named it the blue witch, or the curse of the blue witch; it wasn't clear how they thought of it. Though I can say with confidence that there's nothing uncanny to it. It's just a disease, if a gruesome one."

Yena scowled, taken aback. "Is that so, god man? I've never seen it myself. I've met folk who lived through it."

So, people were known to survive it; encouraging. "Oh?"

"Sometimes it killed whole camps, they say, out in the far west. Sometimes only one or two folk. But only in the summer. Other sicknesses kill us in the winter. The survivors are shunned, so they stay with each other, as best they can."

Alone on the steppes was a good recipe for *dead on the steppes*, Pen had no doubt. "I see. Important question: do you know if people get it just once, or more than once?"

Her brow wrinkled. "I've never heard of anyone stricken with the blue curse twice. If they're weakened enough, they sometimes die of other things later." She shrugged. "As do we all. Though the warrior lads don't want to hear of it, as if death in battle is the only one that counts."

"The five gods count them all, Auntie Yena."

"Do they, now." Her first worries quelled, she stared him up and down with more open curiosity.

"I'm sure of it."

Her lips pursed. "The red-eyed general—do you know him?"

"Uh, yes?"

"Is it true he commands demons?"

Not exactly. There's only the one, though she'll do him favors now and then. If he asks nicely and she feels like it. Probably more detail than Yena needed. "No. He's not a sorcerer. Temple or hedge." Did she not realize that Pen was? He was becoming unsure, but it would explain her boldness.

"Huh." Her gaze flicked toward the grove, and back. Her voice dropped to a rough whisper. "Will he ever let us go?"

Adelis, Pen knew, would be delighted to be rid of the Rusylli clan—actually, portions of four different clans—dropped on his doorstep. It doubtless wouldn't do to say it so bluntly. Pen temporized, "It's not up to General Arisaydia. He obeys Duke Jurgo, who keeps you as a favor to his ally Grabyat. If your countrymen ever stop raiding across the Uteny River, maybe the High Oban will relent." *Not up to me, either*, Pen hoped she understood. If not, time and people being what they were, a century from now this encampment might be just a village of Orbas with a population that spoke an odd dialect.

She grunted at this unhelpful, if true, answer, then looked over her shoulder, as though afraid of being spied out from the grove. Granting Pen a short nod—half salute, half thanks—she scurried away into the scrubby trees, her skinny old dog at her heels.

Pen walked on, his mind churning.

The little boy in the village was still alive this morning, Pen discovered to his relief when he diverted to stop in and check him. If uncomfortable, whiny, and restless, possibly a good sign; he'd been panting and quiet yesterday. Another prayer-treatment seemed to be smoothly absorbed. Because she was right there, he went on to minister to his feverish servant mother, and then, unable to forbear, made the rounds of the three houses he'd visited yesterday. If only to examine and record what changes his simple magics had produced so far, he persuaded himself.

No one had died in the night; no one was obviously

on the road to recovery. In the course of this, he learned
about a fourth household stricken, a family of tanners,
so he visited them, too. By the time he made his way
wearily back up the hill to the fort, body too hot and
demon too tense, it was past noon, much later than he'd
intended to be. Arriving at the hospice, he discovered
that Rede's thirty-five patients had grown to forty.

I can't do *this*, was his first dismayed thought.

Or, came his second, not with what scant vermin
remained in the fort from his prior hunts. It was time to
arrange a more reliable chaos sink. Which was going to
be awkward at best and at worst did not bear thinking
about. He trudged off to find Adelis, who, for a change,
was actually in his headquarters.

"How did it go with the Rusylli?" Adelis asked at once.
"I see you still have your ears." One of the less grisly
trophies Rusylli warriors took from their enemies; more
portable than heads, Pen supposed.

"Oh, yes," sighed Pen. "As you guessed, they were
not forthcoming, but I was lucky." He detailed his visit
and its unexpected codicil with Rybi's aunt. Adelis
planted his elbows on his writing table, folded his fists,
and rested his mouth against them, stemming
interruption till Pen was finished.

"The upshot," Pen concluded, "is that the bruising
fever may have come from the Rusylli tribes, or at least
from the far western steppes, but not from your Rusylli.
It is named, but not explained. By the way, I suggest we
call it something other than *the blue witch*. That's the
sort of thing that could get perfectly innocent black-
haired hedge mages murdered by their neighbors."

"I see." Adelis frowned.

"There were two more cases in the village last night," Pen went on, "and five more of your men reported in to Master Rede. If I'm to go on, Des must have a better way to shed our discharge. Your fort cooks kill far more animals in a day than I ever could. I need you to order them to let me do some of their slaughtering."

Adelis's forehead wrinkled like some wine-inked topographical map. "As you do for my sister in her kitchen?"

A few times a week, depending on the menu, Pen relieved the scullion of the chore of killing the chickens, ducks, pigeons, or rabbits bought live in the market and destined for roasts or stews, depending on the age, price, and stringiness of the meats. Adelis had on occasion watched with fascination. He'd had the theological lecture often enough that he'd stopped asking Pen, somewhat enviously, why he couldn't do this to enemy soldiers. "Yes, but scaled up."

"I must say, I was impressed by that thing Des does with the feathers. One pop, and you have a bag of feathers and a naked bird to hand to the cook. Very efficient."

"I am not using my demon to pluck chickens for your army, Adelis." *Thank you*, murmured Des. "Time is of the essence here, or at least, my time is. The point is, people who are unaccustomed to me and my magics can get very disturbed by my processes. I had a special arrangement with a Martensbridge butcher, back when I was practicing medicine regularly there, and even he kept my visits, well, not quite secret, but private from his customers. A kitchen that serves several thousand meals a day being what it is, there's going to be nothing private about this."

"Yes, the place is a maelstrom." Adelis's eyes narrowed. "Hm. I think I have a solution for that. Let's go."

Pen found himself trotting after the general's quick tread, threading through the fort to the side that housed the soldiers' mess and the kitchen courtyard. The latter was much less serene than the hospice courtyard, crowded with its own fountain, an array of brick ovens, several firepits for slow-roasting large carcasses that were smoking aromatically, and a lot of scurrying men, shouting and swearing.

A pool of startled attention formed ahead of Adelis, closing to uproar again as he passed through, like water around the hull of a ship. He tacked off to the colonnade, under which they found an open chamber filled with writing tables, invoices, accounts, and a harried mess-master and clerks.

"Sir!" The mess-master rose and saluted Adelis. He was a swarthy, scarred, and grizzled fellow who'd come up through the ranks of army cooks, Pen guessed.

"Good afternoon, Sergeant Burae. This is my brother-in-law, the Temple sorcerer Learned Penric. I've assigned him the task of slaughtering the chickens and whatnot for the officer's mess tonight. I've watched him do this at his home. The animals that die serenely and calmly in the arms of his god taste much superior to those which die struggling in pain and terror."

No, they don't, said Des. *They're all the same.* Though

Pen was just as glad that his food didn't have to suffer further for its sacrifice to his table.

"Mind, these are to be reserved for officers only," Adelis emphasized. "Don't get them mixed up with the men's mess."

Burae looked confused but impressed. Pen muted a grin, and Des said, *Ah. Clever lad. By tomorrow, they'll be begging you to kill their poultry, and sneaking it away for the kitchen rowdies to sample.*

"I'll leave you two to get on with it," Adelis finished. "Penric will tell you what he needs."

"Sir!" The mess sergeant saluted again as Adelis took his leave. He turned more uncertainly to Penric. "Learned sir . . . ?"

Burae led Pen through an arch in the colonnade to the kitchen's slaughtering space, a tiny courtyard open to the sky, paved with flat stones angled toward drainage channels. A pair of kitchen lads were engaged in dispatching crates of doomed poultry through the traditional method of grabbing the bird by the head and swinging it vigorously around, snapping its neck in the instant, until the body flew apart from it, wings still flapping wildly for a minute or so. Even for young rowdies like these boys, the novelty of this entertainment had clearly faded after the first few thousand chickens.

"This fellow is the general's tame sorcerer," Burae told his lads, evidently all the introduction he thought they needed. "He's here to kill the chickens for the officers' mess. Somehow." His stare at Pen was very doubtful.

To make it apparent to his agog observers that he was actually doing something, Pen made the tally sign, tapped his lips, and waved his hand beneficently over the remaining birds. Three dozen chickens fell over silently in their crates.

Ohh, said Des, a very corporeal-seeming sigh. *Oh, that helps* so much. Pen controlled a perfectly imaginary urge to belch.

More? Pen inquired.

Bastard avert, no. How would you feel if you ate that many chickens at a sitting?

That seemed all they could do on one visit, then. *How long do you think it will last us?*

A hesitation. *Maybe not forty men.*

Or however many had turned up at the hospice by now. *Understood.*

"That's all I can do at present," Pen told Burae. "I'll be back later this afternoon. Please save me some work if you can. About that much again."

Bewildered but, thanks to Adelis and habits of army discipline, pliant, Burae nodded and saw his visitor out. Pen winced to imagine the garbled kitchen and barracks gossip that was going to arise from this episode.

He headed back to the hospice court. Really, if this worked out smoothly enough, he might not have to visit the fort's main abattoir, located outside the walls. There the large animals, cattle and pigs, were slaughtered; hides, horns and hooves removed and sent to the tannery and other local workshops, dismembered joints carted up to the fort ready for the cooks to further break down into the dozens of ways every bit of an animal was used. Skipping the slaughterhouse would be fine by Pen. He was keenly aware that he was good at this task, but he disliked it and was happy to leave such killing to other men. Rather like the practice of medicine, with which, for him, it was so weirdly, intimately bound. Not a useful thought right now, that.

Rede's forty patients had grown to forty-one by the time Pen, still not done working through the initial roster, had to break off due to overheating and Des's growing frenzy. Back at the fort kitchen, he discovered that its mess-master had found time to collect gossip and think.

"You've been working in the hospice." Standing up to Pen, Burae sounded scared but stern. "I don't want sick men in my good kitchen. No matter what the general thinks about his dinner."

"I'm not sick, but I appreciate your point," said Pen, startling Burae a trifle; had he imagined Pen would argue? But Pen needed his food animals, or some animals. "I can think of two compromises. You could have your lads bring the crates of creatures to the courtyard entry, and I wouldn't have to come within. Or, better"—from Pen's viewpoint, as he didn't want to be putting on a show for every passerby—"if there's a back entry to the slaughtering room, I can use it."

"There is," said Burae slowly. "I suppose at least you wouldn't be trailing through our whole working space."

"Good thinking."

Partially reconciled, the mess-master led out and roundabout to show Pen the delivery door. The lads had reserved him a couple of crates of rabbits, which would do nicely, rabbits being, for some reason, an even better sink than poultry. Someday, when he had time to think,

Pen wanted to work out a creature-ranking for this effect to see if it would reveal an underlying pattern, but today was not that day. By its end, he'd probably be too tired to walk, let alone think.

Des's burden relieved, Pen headed back to the hospice, wondering about scheduling. Slaughtering was normally a morning task for the kitchen, and it looked as though he'd be working the night around.

They start very early, said Des. *Still night by your scholarly standards. And even you must sleep sometime.*

I suppose . . .

The fort's officers having not fallen over poisoned in the night due to sorcerous meddling with their food, Burae seemed less worried the next morning, leaving his lads with Pen to carry on. As a result Pen spent a long, miserable, unimpeded day ferrying death back and forth across the fort. He was able to slip down to the village once, in the late afternoon.

One sick woman, an acolyte at the village temple and so better educated than most, twigged to the fact that Pen was delivering magic along with his prayers. Either Pen's forced explanation reassured her, or fear of the fever proved greater than her fear of sorcery. But the news, necessarily decanted in front of the sister who was caring for her, would be all over the village by tomorrow. Would the infected households turn him away in alarm? Pen wasn't sure what he'd do then.

Let 'em rot, advised Des, her crankiness hinting she was getting to her limit again. *You've no shortage of other work.*

You know we can't stop. If anyone I've touched or

even come near dies, they won't blame the disease for killing them, but me for not saving them. Or worse, as rumor chewed and spat out frightened nonsense.

Don't borrow trouble. The interest rate is much too high. One day at a time, here, Pen.

Or one hour. He shook his head and trudged uphill again.

Upon returning to the hospice court, Pen traced Rede to one of his treatment rooms, wondering what fresh bad news the physician might have to impart. He found Rede with a small pile of bandage scraps, scissors, and a flask of wine spirits, suggesting he'd just concluded some wound care, but standing scowling down into a high-sided wooden box on the table. Approaching to look over his shoulder at the source of his displeasure, Pen discovered it contained a large, elderly, and very sick rat.

The mangy creature lay on its side, panting in irritation, not even trying to escape. Some rats, if they were young and healthy, could be rather attractive little animals, bright-eyed and inquisitive. This . . . was not a cute rat.

"Is that for me?" asked Pen, a trifle confused. "Because I'm not looking for more rats, now that I've worked out my arrangement with the kitchen. But I can kill it for you if you like."

"No!" said Rede, with a sharp deterring gesture. "Don't. I want to save it."

"Er . . . did you want Des to heal it, then?"

Rede cast him an exasperated look. "Of course not. I want to save it to watch. Study."

"Where did you come by it? I didn't think I'd left a rat or a mouse alive in the whole fort."

"A soldier brought it in. Quartermaster's clerk. He'd been bitten. In the archives, where he'd gone to hunt up some record or another. Rats and mice lurk there—going after the old parchment, probably. He saw the beast was sick, so he caught it in a cloth and brought it to me along with his bleeding arm. In case I could tell anything. He was worried it might have given him some disease, maybe the bruising fever. I can't see if the wretched thing is bruised or not, though." He glanced aside at Pen. "Can you?"

"Uh . . ." The creature had dark fur, what there was left of it, and black skin, except for its pale feet. In the bruising fever, the extremities darkened first. *Des?*

Really, Pen. The things you ask of me. A pause. *Fevered, yes. Bruised, no. Apart from where it was manhandled in its capture.*

"Nothing distinguishing. Yet."

A short nod. "Which is why I want to hold it aside and watch it."

"I . . . huh. Had any other of the bruising-fever patients reported rat bites? None were mentioned to me. Rat bites seem the sort of thing people would notice."

"Not the rats," said Rede, his eyes narrowing. "Their fleas."

"Uh." Pen paused, taken aback. "That would seem to have the opposite problem. Nobody's been bitten by rats. *Everybody* is bitten by fleas." Well, not Pen. Nor anyone for a block around his house. "But not everybody has the fever. Thankfully."

"Blood. You were talking about blood being still alive once it's left the body. If you've ever managed to kill a flea that's just fed on you before the little bugger jumps away, it smears out blood. Just like a mosquito or a tick. If the blood is alive, and the contagion is alive, maybe the contagion is alive *in* the blood. At least until the flea digests it."

"That . . ." *is a brilliant idea*, Pen did not say aloud. It had to be flawed, somehow. "How in the world would you ever show if such a thing was so?"

"I'm not sure. How long would the blood, and the contagion in it, still be alive? Maybe a person would have to let a flea feed on a sick man, and then feed on himself." Rede's frown deepened. "It would have to be me. I couldn't ask this of anyone else."

"It most certainly could *not* be you!"

He looked up at Pen. "If I contracted the fever that way, could you save me?"

"I don't know. And that's just the first problem." How could he talk Rede out of this horrifying idea? "Anyway, it couldn't be you, or anyone else who has been up to their armpits in the sick. Because how could you tell if it was the flea bite, or your contact with the soiled linens or the vomit or the blood in the basins? It would have to be someone who was pristine with respect to this mess. Which is nobody in the whole fort, for a start. Or in the village, by now."

"Agh." Rede rubbed a weary hand over his face, shoulders slumping.

Pen sighed, hoping he'd thwarted this insane plan. "Anyway," he said after a moment. "If it really is the rats or their fleas spreading it around, new cases ought to tail off in a few days." Beguiling thought. "There being no more rats." Save this one, apparently, hidden out of the way.

"Or you've just destroyed all the evidence."

"I'd take that trade."

"No—well, yes—but . . ." Rede made a frustrated swipe. "Never mind."

"Have any new cases reported in here while I was gone to the village?"

"One. And the provisioner's ox-driver died."

Pen grimaced. He felt like a man treading water with no shore in sight to swim for. "I swear to all the gods, I truly don't know if I'm saving lives, or just prolonging deaths."

Rede looked at him in surprise. "Two men seemed sufficiently past the crisis that I moved them to the recovery wards."

"We have recovery wards?"

"Oh. I suppose I didn't take you in there. Yes, because we don't know whether a person can be reinfected. I try to move the ones who seem to be improving out with each other. And the ones who are better still, the same again."

Pen should have noticed. Realized. He'd been head-down among the dire cases . . .

"You're so pressed, I didn't think I should waste your attention upon men who are getting better, or who'd had milder cases and seem to be recovering on their own."

"Oh." *Oh, Bastard's teeth*. This was going to be just like the nightmare of Martensbridge all over again, wasn't it. Only the worst cases, *all* the worst cases, and never any easy victories. Because that would waste Pen's *time*, which was better directed toward . . . another worst-case. Inescapable logic. "I see."

And when had people started flowing under his hands as indistinguishably as the waters of a river? Except for those who'd died, sticking up like boulders with memory eddying around them in agitation. Pen had mainly been tracking the total of sick, the work set before him this hour, which had never gone down, only up. Had the population of their chambers turned over at least once by now? Maybe twice? Rede would know the numbers. Pen didn't ask.

A little silence, while two tired men stared at nothing much. The dark tunnel of their future, Pen supposed. "I'd best get back to it, then."

"Yes. Me as well."

But when Pen made his way out, Rede was still gazing speculatively down into his rat-box.

Penric, exiting the second sick-chamber of the following morning's round and wondering if Des needed to go back to the kitchen yet, found a man waiting for him just beyond the colonnade whom he dimly recognized as one of Adelis's headquarters clerks. The fellow extended a long arm with a letter held out delicately between thumb and finger. "This came for you, Learned Penric."

"Oh. Thank you." Pen accepted it, and the clerk nodded and skittered out without waiting to take a reply; understandable. Visitors to the hospice court were as few as could be arranged at present. Master Rede had forbidden the soldiers to come see their comrades ill with the bruising fever, a prohibition that had not been hard to enforce.

Pen opened it, scattering sealing wax on the tiles, and was both pleased and disappointed to find Nikys's handwriting. He'd been hoping for some—preferably helpful—replies to his urgent notes about the contagion. But this was fine, too, since it began, *We are all well here.*

I imagine you'll first want any news from town about the sickness out at the fort. She had that right. *Gossip in the marketplace is not yet too worried—most people seem to think it's some camp dysentery or summer fever. In which case you should have been home by now. As you are not, I conclude this is something more difficult. It is, as always, useless to expect Adelis to write, so please, if you're not returning to Vilnoc today, send me some news of you. Make him write it honestly, Des!*

If the sickness has come to town, I have not yet heard of it, but that's no surprise. I expect the Mother's Order would be the first to know.

Some small household news tidbits followed, including, *We did remember to feed your sacred pets. Lin even undertook to clean their boxes,* which made Pen smirk a little. Pen kept a small menagerie of rats for magical trials—young, healthy, tame, flea-free, non-biting rats, which last Pen had assured by the application of a bit of shamanic persuasion. He'd never been able to convince their housemaid that cleaning up after them was a holy task, or even within her duties at all, but apparently Nikys, or necessity, had better luck.

At least it's not dolphins, Nikys had once sighed to Lin. His wife had wholly disapproved of Pen's shamanic experiments with the harbor dolphins, even though Pen hadn't actually drowned.

Yet, muttered Des, who'd been on Nikys's side.

Reading on: *Your correspondence is piling up. Let me know if I should bundle it up and send it out to the fort, or hold it for your return.*

Florie has been a bit fussy—Pen frowned—*but Mother says it's too early for her to be teething. So maybe she just misses you, as I do. Come home safe and soon!*

Your loving Madame Owl.

Pen vented a hopelessly fond sigh, folded the letter back up, and tucked it away inside his sash. He had a chamber full of sick men waiting. And another after that. Maybe he could write a reply during supper, which he'd have to stop for anyway.

As he knelt beside his first patient in the next chamber, the man's hot hand wavered up and feebly clutched Pen's, halting its blessing. "No!"

"Let me pray for you, young man."

"You aren't praying. Bastard's necromancer. You're doing some magicky thing." He scowled, fretful, feverish, and frightened. "Maybe a curse."

He wasn't the first soldier to suspect the uncanny extras, as most who didn't already know who Pen was at least realized what the silver braid in his sash meant, but he was the first to object.

"Magic, yes, a little, but I assure you, it isn't any malediction. It's an aid against the fever." Pen knew better than to promise it was a *cure*. "Come now, I treated you last night, I know, soon after you came in."

But as Pen lifted his hand, the soldier muttered incoherent protests and thrashed away, falling out of his cot, which brought the attendant orderly trotting over. He shied again as Pen tried to help him up, and Pen stood back, frustrated. Was the lad a secret Quadrene, or just full of nursery tales about evil sorcerers? *Or both*.

"Try to calm him down," Pen told the orderly. "I'll come back later."

But Pen had been a subject of worried gossip and slanderous speculation in here already, he discovered when two more sick men refused his aid. He seriously considered knocking them all unconscious with that brain-trick he'd been trying on his rats at home, and treating them anyway, but that skill was . . . not perfected. Also, the household cat was growing finicky about eating his failures.

He knelt beside the last cot, whose occupant was beyond protest or even awareness of Pen and his magic. Pen made his ministrations quiet and brief. This one wasn't going to be a good example to point out to his chamber mates about the harmlessness of Pen's doings, Pen feared.

He needed one of their own authorities to back him up; Master Rede, probably. Pen reflected glumly that Master Orides might have had more clout than the younger physician, and maybe more old tricks tucked in his green sash for dealing with uncooperative patients. As a last resort, Pen might try dragging in Adelis, but if the soldiers were that sick and scared, even ingrained military disciplines might break down. Rede first, then.

He spotted the man he sought under the opposite colonnade by the apothecary's chamber, talking with an orderly. They both broke off as Pen clipped up, the orderly making a vague salute and heading away to his tasks. Pen hadn't yet crossed paths with Rede at his early breakfast, nor coming back from Des's feeding, either.

"Master Rede. I'm facing a mutiny among some of your patients. Mostly I suspect due to sheer ignorance on their parts, but I don't think they'll accept tutoring from me. You might have better—" Pen broke off, staring at the gauze bandage wrapping Rede's left arm; his hand shot out to grasp his wrist and turn it over. "*What* have you done?"

Des's Sight answered his question even as he asked it. The skin beneath the gauze was sprinkled with an array of tiny inflamed dots, recognizably flea bites. "I told you not to do that!"

Rede shrugged away. "It was then or never. The rat died the next hour."

"It should have been *never*. Sunder it! I *knew* I should have killed that thing on the spot last night. *And* the fleas that rode in on it." Upset, Pen pulled Rede's other arm out, searching for wounds. "Did you make it bite you as well?"

Rede brushed him off, grimacing. "We already have one man bitten by that rat. I've set him in a chamber apart, although he didn't want to stay here. We didn't need a second example, and besides, this way I might tell whether it was the rat or its fleas."

Too late, Pen groaned inwardly. Brave, determined,

desperate, deprived of sleep—no wonder Rede wasn't thinking clearly. It was a miracle—maybe?—that he wasn't down sick already, one way or another.

I don't sense any godly residue, Des answered literally the question Pen hadn't actually asked her.

Agh.

Keep an eye on those bites seemed a stupid thing to say, since no doubt Rede would be observing them obsessively. "Come find me at once if they appear to be doing anything that ordinary flea bites would not," said Pen instead.

"Of course," said Rede, in far too careless a tone for Pen's liking.

A bustle at the courtyard gate drew both their attentions.

One soldier supported another, limping. Two more were being transported on army stretchers, poles gripped on each end by bearers. Far too much blood was splashed around on the wrong sides of their skins. Pen was disturbed to recognize a couple of the Rusylli camp's guards he'd spoken with the other day.

"What's all this?" said Rede as he hurried up. "A fight?" He glanced beyond the gate, but no further parade of injured men followed.

The answer came from Adelis, striding in behind them. His scarred face was tight with that particular flavor of fury that masked furious worry.

"It was the Rusylli. Most of the encampment rose up last night, overpowered the gate guards, and fled down the road. They passed by the village quietly in the dark, thank the gods, but did stop to steal a few horses from our pastures along the way. The most of them are still afoot, though, so my cavalry can overtake them."

"They left their house-carts?" said Pen. Well, they'd have had to.

"They left nearly everything. We'd deliberately limited their provisions to short reserves, so they can only live off the countryside. How many farmsteads they'll raid along their route before we catch up will depend on how fast we move. They're heading up into the western hills, as nearly as we can make out."

Wild, rugged country; hard to live in, easy to hide in. Pen said uncertainly, "If they have their women, children, and old with them, surely they couldn't put up much of a fight?"

"Ha. You've never watched the Rusylli women, children, and old cutting the throats of enemies wounded on a battlefield. They creep over the ground like murderous gleaners picking up fallen grains. Penric—*what* did you say to those people day before yesterday?"

"Me!"

"They're not fleeing their captivity. They were largely reconciled to that. They're fleeing this bruising fever, their blue witch. More afraid of it than they are of me, which I'm going to have to teach them is an error."

"I didn't say that much," Pen protested, "apart from a bare description of the disease to find out if they recognized it. I suppose they could have picked up some marketplace gossip from the village—I know you let a few of them go in for supplies. Or from the gate guards, who do talk to them, to while away the hours if nothing else." Rybi's lover, or seducer, had been such a gate guard, Pen recalled. "And I know their children sneak away to play with the village children, who sneak away to play with them. Who knows how lurid their chatter was."

Adelis's lips tightened in vexation at these likelihoods.

It seemed doubtful that these rag-tag Rusylli could cross two entire realms and succeed in reaching the Uteny River, but the trail of bloodshed and destruction they'd leave while recklessly trying was horrible to contemplate. As much as Pen sympathized with their fears, he sympathized more with the hapless Orban farmer families who'd be caught in their path. Worse, they already might be carrying the disease with them, spreading it as they traveled; more lethal to more people, ultimately, than their warriors.

To be honest, murmured Des, *that's just as likely to come from Adelis's troop.*

No better.

Aye.

A couple of alert orderlies had arrived during this exchange. Rede motioned the whole lot of them toward his treatment rooms, but then wheeled back to Adelis.

"General Arisaydia. Especially if we're going to need more sick-chambers for wounded, I'm thinking we could shift all the fever convalescent to one of the barracks, if it could be cleared out for them."

Pen blinked. *We've treated a whole barracks' worth of patients so far . . . ?* That was upwards of a hundred men. No wonder everyone was exhausted.

Adelis, listening, made a motion of assent. "You have

that many recovering? Good. See my second. The barracks closest to the hospice would be best, I suppose."

"Yes, please." Rede made a hasty salute and hurried after the injured men.

Adelis's irritated gaze fell on Pen. "Riding out after Rusylli had not been in my plans for today, but here we are. Do you think your translation skills, or, er, other skills, might help convince them to surrender?"

Pen threw up his hands. "You have other translators. You don't have other sorcerers." At least unless someone from his Order answered his pleas for help. Maybe he should dispatch more notes. More strongly worded. "If I'm *here*, doing *this*, I can't be *there*, doing *that*. Pick one, Adelis!"

Adelis snorted out breath through his nose, in his version of concession. ". . . Stay here."

He exited the gate, the aide at his heels already taking orders for the cavalry expedition.

Pen turned back toward the sick-chambers.

In the late afternoon, Pen plodded uphill from his rounds in the village, mulling. In the very extended family of tanners, another man and a woman had fallen sick. One household had refused Pen entry. The little boy and his mother were still alive. The younger carter seemed on the mend, but his elder brother was worse— could Pen come back tonight? He glanced up at the fort gates to find himself following a sedan chair across the drawbridge, its bearers wearing the green tunics of servants to the Mother's Order in Vilnoc.

Pen sped his steps, catching up as the bearers set the chair down in the middle of the hospice courtyard and helped its occupant clamber from the wicker seat. Doffing her wide-brimmed hat, she tossed it onto the cushion. She was a slight, aging woman in a simple tunic dress, but belted with the green sash of a senior physician. Pen's heart lifted in hope. Had someone sent them help?

Rede appeared from the door of a treatment room, wiping his hands on a cloth, and his lips parted in what Pen guessed was the same hope. He hurried out to the chair. Pen's quick glance by Sight at his left arm showed the flea bites under the now-grubby wrappings healing at about the usual rate for flea bites, for what that was worth.

The woman clutched what Pen recognized as one of his notes from . . . however many days ago that had been. Not a speedy response, but definitely something. At last.

Turning, she took in his summer vestments. "Ah, you are Learned Penric?" She waved the note.

"Yes, Master—?"

"Tolga."

"And this is Master Rede Licata, senior physician in this fort."

She gave Rede a solemn nod. "I'd heard about Master Orides. He was a fine physician and a good man. I am so sorry."

"As are we all, ma'am." The two healers eyed each other with professional interest, evaluating.

Rede evidently passed her muster, for she nodded again and turned to Pen. "We received your letter. What we think might be the first case of your bruising fever turned up on our doorstep this morning. I've come out to see your patients for a comparison."

Faint disappointment crossed Rede's features, but he murmured, "Of course," and gestured toward the sick-chambers. "We have, unfortunately, plenty of examples for you to look at."

This was not a tour Pen needed to take. "Des and I must pay a visit to the kitchens," he told Rede. "I shouldn't be long."

"Right."

As he strode off, he heard Tolga saying to Rede, "So what exactly is this sorcerer *doing* for your men?" and Rede replying, "Well, let me show you . . ."

His routine in the killing room having become practiced and efficient—chickens again—Pen returned to find the pair of them emerged from their inspection and perched on one of the stone benches in the shade of the colonnade, talking with a serious air. Rede saw him and motioned him over, shifting to give him room to sit.

Pen sank down with a tired breath, eyeing the Mother's woman across Rede. "Can your Order send us any help out here?"

She shook her head in polite regret. "In fact, I'm hoping I might take you back with me to look at our case."

Rede sat up, frowning. "We have all he can do right here. You have one"—he waved at his row of sick-chambers—"we have forty-eight."

It had been forty-seven a while ago . . .

"Plus however many in the village," Rede continued.

"Two more today," said Pen.

Tolga grimaced. "I'm not naïve enough to think our first case will be our last, and neither are you."

All the more reason, Rede's expression suggested, though he bit back saying so aloud. "In any event, General Arisaydia called him out to the fort. Only the general can release him, and he's not here right now."

Tolga turned more directly to the pair of them. "I'm sure that is not so. As a divine, his own Order must have his first allegiance. A senior sorcerer, even more so— they go where they will, I've heard."

"That," said Pen, "is more-or-less true, yes. And I came here." Leaving the conclusion to her. But . . . *town*. The menace was now inside Vilnoc's walls, it seemed, with Nikys and Florina and the rest of Pen's little household.

"I could lend you my chair. Or send one for you."

That was nearly tempting. In a sedan chair, he might doze on the way, getting double use out of the time. But Pen shook his head. "I can borrow a horse from the fort. It would be faster."

"You're going?" said Rede uneasily.

"I think I better had. To be sure what's going on."

"Only so long as you come back."

Pen rested his elbows on his knees, and his forehead in his linked hands. "Even with all my magics, I can't be in two places at once. If we could scare up another Temple sorcerer, *any* Temple sorcerer with a reasonably well-tamed demon, I'm sure I could train him or her in this one basic technique in a few hours." He frowned at his feet, adding with muted vehemence, "Even a *hedge* sorcerer."

Tolga asked, "Have you heard from any?"

"Not so far." Pen sat up. "I sent out letters at the same time I sent yours. Orbas is not all that rich in Temple sorcerers—there were more at my old chapterhouse back in the cantons, for all that its archdivineship wasn't a quarter the size of this duchy. Are there any stray mages you know of that I don't?"

"I don't see how I would," said Tolga, looking at him askance. And . . . covetously? "My Order isn't hiding any away. We don't even have a petty saint right now."

"More's the pity."

"Aye," she agreed ruefully. Her chin lifted in determination. "You'll come today?" she urged.

"Yes," Pen reluctantly promised. "I have a round of treatments to complete here, and then I should wash up before I start out. But I'll ride in before nightfall."

She gave a sharp nod of acceptance, and victory. Rede's shoulders slumped.

"I must away, then, and carry the word back to town." She rose and motioned her bearers, who'd been sitting warily in the scant shade of their vehicle, as far as they could get in all directions from the hospice colonnades. They jumped to their feet, as ready to be gone from here as their mistress, if for other reasons.

The green-sashed physician swayed out by the gate she'd entered. Pen and Rede still sat.

Watching her go, Rede asked, "Why are there so few Temple sorcerer-physicians?" His brows tightened in fresh mystification. "It's becoming plain to me how valuable you can be. I'd think the Mother's Order would be set on making as many more as possible."

"And so it is, but candidates don't grow on trees. Though they do have to be grown, even more slowly than trees." Pen considered how best to explain this. "It takes at least one full generation, sometimes more, to tame a wild-caught demon to be fit for the task. Which is done by yoking it with a responsible Temple divine, one who can imprint or pass to it the necessary . . . knowledge of life, I suppose you could say, of living it well. And the recipient must be a strong-minded person, too, preferably already disciplined in the physician's arts. Medical magics include some of the most powerful and subtle skills known. Handing that knowledge off to an innately chaotic demon that could ascend and run off with its possessor's body is a very bad idea."

Rede vented a thoughtful noise, taking this in.

Pen rubbed his stiff neck. "Many Temple demons are lost along the way, through time's accidents. Some are taken back by the god. Some are spoiled by bad riders, or just unsuitable ones. Also, the transfer is tricky, since the candidate must be brought together with the old sorcerer exactly at their deathbed." *Or on a roadside . . .* Pen had long wondered if his pivotal encounter with the dying Learned Ruchia and her demon had been as chance-met as it had seemed at the time, though it had certainly not been arranged by the *Temple*. "As you know, people seldom die to schedule."

"So . . . why aren't you working for the Mother? You could be brilliant. You could help so many!"

Pen smiled grimly. "*Many* turns out to be the problem. I did try my hand at the trade, back in Martensbridge. Des thinks the problem was that I was not well supervised, the Mother's Order there being inexperienced with sorcerer-physicians."

I think the problem was that the greedy gits ran you into the ground, grumped Des. *And you refused to learn to say no, till the end.*

"In any case, I found it was not my calling, so I declined at the last to take oath to the Mother's Order."

To put it mildly, said Des, shuddering.

"That seems impossible. It's *clearly* your calling!"

"Many cases entailed many failures, especially as all the most difficult ones became funneled to me. Fine when I was credited with healing, not so when my losses outraged. You saved *her*, why not *him*? It grew wearing."

Rede made a frustrated, negating gesture. "Every physician gets that."

"To be blunt," said Pen to his sandals, "when I tried to kill myself as the only way I could see to escape, I knew it was time to find another way to serve. Or Des did. I'm good at translations, you know." Oh, gods, how had that admission escaped his teeth?

Because you are too cursed tired, Des opined. *And because this one is a* good *physician. Remember how your patients used to confess to you?*

"Sorry," Pen choked.

Rede sat back, his arguments abruptly muzzled. "Ah," he said after a moment. "That."

He wasn't baffled? *Bless him.*

Rede's gaze lifted as if to count down the row of sick-chambers. His voice took on a new diffidence. "So . . . how are you holding up?"

"Oh," said Pen. He straightened and waved a hasty

hand. "That's no longer a hazard for me. I had fewer attachments back then." He'd still been reeling from the deaths of his mother and his beloved princess-archdivine in such close succession that year, Pen supposed at this calmer remove. His life in Orbas, his new family, held more hostages against him now, blocking that form of flight. He trusted he would not become so desperately pressed over this business that he'd come to resent that fact.

Past time to get off this subject. "How are your flea bites?"

"They itch." Rede rubbed at his arm wrapping. "If anything else is going to happen, it's likely too soon to know." He glanced across at Pen. "Can you tell?"

"No. Which is either good or, as you say, too early. Let's hope for the first, eh?"

"If I start turning purple, I'm not sure if I would be frightened or relieved. I want an *answer*, not this, this . . ." His fists clenched. "*Any* answer!"

"Only the true one, I daresay."

"Well, yes." He scowled across at the patient chambers, and his voice fell. ". . . What do we do if it doesn't stop coming?"

Pen chose to take that as a rhetorical remark, because the answer, *Then we don't stop, either*, was too appalling to voice. But Rede had the right of it. As long as they didn't know how this disease was getting around so randomly, they were fighting blind. Pen needed an Adelis-brain, all tactical.

Except not actually Adelis's, said Des, *because the man is useless in the sickroom.*

Howsoever. Pen grunted to his feet. "Maybe I'll find some new clue in town tonight."

"You *will* come back," said Rede. Question, or demand? Or fear . . .

"It depends on what I find there. If this thing is loose in Vilnoc, my priorities could change."

"Physicians can't choose their patients."

"Unethical, yes, I know. Between Amberein and Helvia and me, I've had the training three times. But I've never taken the oath to the Mother's Order, and I've never been sorry. Apologetic, maybe, but that isn't the same." The white god's more, ah, *fluid* approach to bestowing tasks upon Pen and his resident demon suited him better, despite its occasional seeming-lunacy.

. . . But was this one of them? He was ironically betrayed, if so.

Rede's mouth opened, and shut, on some further protest. "Let's hope you can learn something new in Vilnoc, then."

"Aye."

It was almost sunset by the time Pen rode the army plodder he'd been lent through Vilnoc's western gate. The main chapterhouse and hospice of the Mother's Order lay at the opposite end of town, and he looked around as he threaded his way through the winding streets. Nothing seemed amiss, residents drawing in to their homes for the night in the usual rhythm. He passed the corner of his own street, and shuddered with longing to be one of those contented residents. *No*.

The main marketplace was almost deserted, the last few vendors giving up and taking in their wares, apart from a few horses and mules tethered for the night at the far end devoted to livestock sales, heads down munching desultorily at a wispy drift of hay. One nickered in curiosity at Pen's horse, who returned the greeting. Competing for their fodder, their unsuccessful owner was setting up his bedroll on a hay pile, ready to try again in the morning. A couple of other men camped to guard their more bulky goods, such as the stack of large ceramic storage jars.

Around a few more corners and small squares, up a slope, and the Mother's Order hove into Pen's view. The Vilnoc chapterhouse was an old merchant's mansion bequeathed in someone's will a generation ago, and its hospice the former warehouse, gradually refitted to its new purpose. Penric had not been inside before, his own household having no need to call on its services.

At the gate, he found the porter just raising the oil lantern that would burn all night over the open doorway. He recognized and respectfully saluted Pen's vestments—new-laundered, but more frayed with every day of this crisis, like their wearer—took charge of Pen's horse, and directed him on to Master Tolga's lair.

He found the Mother's physician in a writing cabinet she shared with several others of her Order, most of them evidently gone home for the night or to dinner— Pen's dinner had been a handful of bread and meat jerky eaten while riding in. She rose at once when he knocked on the door jamb.

"Ah! Learned! You did come!"

"I said I would."

She shrugged. "Things happen."

"Aye. Have any more things happened here?"

"Unfortunately, yes. Another feverish girl—I'll take you to see her, too, if you would be so kind."

"As long as I'm here."

She nodded and led him out onto her second-floor gallery, down, and through an archway to the former warehouse turned holy hospice. It was laid out as another colonnaded rectangle around a central court, its own well dug new and deep; just the one level, as the old merchants would not have wanted to hoist their goods up and down stairs. The big gate at the end that could admit wagons was now closed and barred. The chapterhouse's front door would remain open at all times, mark of the Order's vow to turn no one away. This resulted, naturally, in the hospice filling up with the indigent sick and injured, such that anyone who could afford it preferred to engage a physician privately to visit them at home.

Every cot in the sick-chamber was occupied by more routine residents, although the bed of Pen's prospective patient was shoved a little aside. A small barred window, pierced through the far wall as part of the conversion, let in air and, now, dusk. A dedicat lit an oil lantern hanging from a central hook, and Tolga took up a candle in a glass vase, holding it above the cot. Pen didn't bother to tell her he didn't need it to see his work, because the fellow laid out, feverish and restless, needed to see him.

A quick examination by sight and Sight told Pen that Tolga had not misdiagnosed; the tell-tale mottled flush in the man's hands and feet was starting. Luckily, he wasn't so far along that he couldn't speak or answer questions. Struggling to prop his shoulders up against the headboard, he regarded Pen with fever-blurred curiosity.

The fellow turned out to be a merchant's clerk from Trigonie, sailed into the port ten days ago with a load of mixed goods. He'd not been outside of Vilnoc's walls since, and his sickness was too recent for him to be suspected as any sort of source; he must have contracted it after he'd arrived. His master had brought him here, not unreasonably preferring not to share his inn room with a deathly ill retainer, but paying in advance for his care, good man. So, not indigent, merely very far from home and unhappy about it. The clerk's work had kept him mostly around the harbor, but he had walked all about the town to see it in his off hours.

As usual, he'd never met a sorcerer before. Though his expression betrayed bewilderment, he accepted Pen's prayers and magic, again explained merely as a help against fever, like some sort of spiritual willow-bark decoction. Pen finished with a few reassuring platitudes about the excellence of the Mother's Order in Vilnoc, which gratified both of his listeners and wasn't untrue. Pen did not promise he'd come back.

"Well," said Pen to Tolga, rising and shaking out the knees of his trousers. "Let's see your other suspect."

She guided him around to a chamber devoted to women.

The girl in the cot there, a servant much like Lin from a house in town, was very feverish and distraught. The fever had been the familiar sudden fierce onslaught. The distraction was from being turned out onto the street and told to make her own way to the hospice; summarily discharged, Pen gathered, more to save her employer the expense of her illness than to protect the rest of the family from infection. He bit back a scowl at this. She had not been outside the town walls in months, despite running errands hither and thither within them—she could not remember all the places, although the list she did give him was maddeningly long, and did not include the port.

Pen summoned all his charm for her, and also as much uphill magic as he could force her body to accept. For whichever cause, she was weakly smiling when he left. This was an early case; if he could come back for more treatments, her prognosis should be good.

Pen had hoped the new examples might offer him some clarity, but they only increased the fog. Also his worry for Nikys, but he didn't need to discuss that here. "Let's go talk somewhere," he told Tolga.

They settled on a bench by the well in the darkening courtyard, the flickering candle-vase between them.

"Was she another of the same sickness?" Tolga asked.

"Yes. Well-spotted. You should see the flushing in her extremities by tomorrow, unless my early treatment helps push it back."

Tolga nodded in a mix of satisfaction and frustration. "Exactly how is that working?"

"Have you dealt with a sorcerer-physician before?"

"Once, some years ago in the winter capital, but briefly, and I can't say as I understood what she was doing."

So, not quite as untutored as young Rede, but almost. Pen ran down the same account of the limitations and uses of his uphill magic that he'd given to the army physician, which made her frown, though not, Pen thought, from lack of understanding.

A burly male dedicat came out to draw up a couple of buckets of well water, by a clever foot-wheel mechanism which Pen would have been glad to examine. If he ever again had time.

"Do you think we can expect more of these fevered?" asked Tolga bluntly when the creaking died away.

"I truly don't know, because I still have no idea how the accursed thing is getting *around*," said Pen. "If it follows the same pattern as in the fort and Tyno, then yes." A sprinkling, and then more, and then . . .

"Can you stay?"

"Of course not."

". . . Can you come back?"

"I don't know. There seem to be more sick out at the fort every time I turn around." And adding in a couple of hours of travel, even if he visited the Order only once a day, would put Pen further behind schedule for all the sick he already owned. At what point would his treatments, already slipping from optimum to minimum, become so attenuated as to be useless?

Anything to add, Des? His demon had been oddly silent, not even offering tart quips. *Observations, memories?*

Nothing helpful. Carry on.

Was she growing as wearied as he was? He'd been using her hard, and more continuously than ever before.

He knew better than most that *powerful* was not the same thing as *invulnerable*.

Pen continued to Tolga, "Send a message to the fort describing them if you get new cases, though. I especially want to know where people have been, what they were doing, before they contracted this." He huffed a breath. "Although I know quite a lot already, and it's not helping."

Tolga let him go with great reluctance, although she could hardly kidnap him. He could tell she was tempted, though. He didn't tell her exactly how she might accomplish it.

He remounted his horse outside the chapterhouse's door and turned its head toward Vilnoc's western gate. He must write to Nikys again tonight, he decided, warning her of these new developments in town without the distortions of marketplace rumor. He'd fumigated his first note to her the other day with burning sage before he'd sent it off, but he wasn't sure that the smoke had done anything other than make the paper smell odd.

He passed his own street again with a pang. The scholar's life he had achieved with such trouble—the wife, the child, the peaceful study, the cat, the well-run modest household—could all be lost to him, he'd always known, any time he rode out for the duke or the archdivine, by some misadventure happening to *him*. He'd never pictured his refuge being stolen away from him while his back was turned, but his well-stocked imagination now supplied him with several versions of just how that could occur.

And it was not just his own immediate family at risk.

Rybi and her son at the orphanage, Lencia and Seuka and the other young dedicats at his own Order's chapterhouse, all his other Temple friends there and at the curia of the archdivine, right up through Duke Jurgo's own household—in a mere three years of residence, how had he acquired such a huge array of friends vulnerable to fate in Orbas? And Adelis, well, Adelis was always at hazard by his choice of trade, but this was not any hero's death he might have imagined for himself.

Pen rode out to the fort road slowly—he could see in the dark, his horse could not—and did not turn aside.

The next three days passed in an increasing blur for Pen. He looped back and forth from the hospice to the kitchens, to Tyno, to the kitchens again, and a daily ride into town which qualified as his sole break. There, Tolga had acquired five more fevered people, none with any relation to another that Pen could determine. If there were more sick tucked away privately in their own houses, they'd not yet been brought to Pen's attention, and he wasn't going to go looking for them.

Arriving back from the most recent of these evening excursions to Vilnoc, he encountered Rede having an equally late dinner in the staff mess. Pen thought he recognized the dead-rabbit bits in the cooling hash Rede was shoving around absently with his fork. The page of scratchy notes Rede was studying was new.

Pen thunked down opposite him and tried to work up more enthusiasm for his own meal. He was hungry enough; just tired.

"Any more men arrive sick while I was in town?" Pen asked.

"Yes, two. But I moved one more man to the convalescent chamber, so he's off your list."

Two steps backward, one forward? It was still a march in the wrong direction. "What do you have there?"

"A roster of the sick, and when they arrived, stripped down to just days and numbers. Including Tyno and Vilnoc. There is something odd about the way they are progressing. It feels strange to say it, but they aren't coming fast enough."

Pen rubbed his neck. "Have you run mad? Any more, and I'll be overwhelmed." If he wasn't already.

Rede waved his worksheet in impatience. "It's just that if people were giving it directly to each other, cases should be doubling and redoubling, because that's what contagions *do*. But after the initial burst, it's settled in to a steady supply. Increasing, yes, I'm afraid so, but not . . . not in that way."

"I can hardly be sorry, I suppose."

"Yes, but d'you see, this suggests . . . I'm not sure what. That everyone is getting it from the same source?"

"In the fort, and Tyno, and Vilnoc, *and* that border town a hundred miles west?" The first three, maybe, but surely not the last. Pen glanced at Rede's left arm, where the flea bites were almost healed. "But not from rat fleas, apparently."

"You, ah, see nothing going on in me with your magical vision?"

"I have looked at, and into, so many patients by now, in every stage of this thing, I could diagnose it in my sleep." And so he was, in his more unpleasant dreams. The waking nightmare was bad enough; he didn't need the even weirder versions. "You have no incipient bruising fever. Offer your thanks to the god of fools and madmen. Which would be mine, I suppose."

"Hah."

Pen addressed his plate. "The elder carter in Tyno died this morning. Add him to your list." His wife—now widow—had been distraught, with that extra edge that hope disappointed gave. No matter how little Pen tried to promise, how briefly explain, people built up expectations of his magic that crashed down hard with its failures. Worse, he sometimes thought, than if he'd never tried at all. "His brother is getting better, though."

Rede nodded. Not patients he'd seen, touched, talked to; he could maintain his composure.

"I don't . . . I'm starting to wonder if I'm actually doing anything, or just deluding myself." And everyone else.

Rede tapped his notes. "Oh. That's really interesting, too. Among the first wave of men who came in with the bruising fever, what, three weeks ago now, one died in two. A few days after Adelis brought you, that dropped to one in five. Now, one in ten. With occasional setbacks. I'm certain that improvement is your doing."

"That's . . . not good enough. My uphill magic is getting stretched too thinly. Even you will be able to tell within a couple more days, because that mortality will start to rise again. I *can't* work any faster." He glanced up at Rede. "When that moment comes, *you* have to choose which people I will keep treating and which I will abandon. I won't be able to." Would Rede put his soldiers first, as Adelis had wanted? It was where his sworn loyalty lay, after all.

"I . . ." Rede scraped his hand through his scalp, ducked his head, grimaced. "All right."

Army men. Pen wasn't sure whether to be grateful or horrified.

Doesn't matter. He washed down his hash with a not-very-watered beaker of fort wine, and pushed off to the sick-chambers.

Penric made his way back from the kitchens the following afternoon—late, he was always late these days—wondering whether it would be more efficient to go down for his rounds in Tyno before he washed up and rode into Vilnoc, or after. Crossing the entry court inside the fort's front gate, he was stopped short by the sight of a new and unexpected figure.

The old man standing with his old horse's reins twisted around his arm, talking with a gate guard, wore a road-grimy, home-cut version of Bastard's summer whites, lacking decorative embroidery. A tarnished metallic braid circling the tunic's standing collar stood in for the formal torc. The silver braid in his sash was merely cheap gray cloth, but the demon inside him, much younger than himself, was entirely genuine.

"Bastard bless us," breathed Pen, and strode toward them in fragile hope.

The fellow looked to be on the high side of sixty. Likely stouter when younger, much like his bony farm horse; his skin had grown loose with age, wrinkling. In coloration, he was of the Cedonian type, but hewn from a lighter wood, like fresh oak. His hair was cut in a military style overdue for scissors. Once black, it was gray with white streaks that reminded Pen of fog over thawing snow.

The gate guard looked over, and said, "Oh, there he is now."

The visitor followed his glance to Pen, and his gray eyebrows climbed. He started to step eagerly forward; the young demon within him recoiled in fright at the dense presence of Des, resulting in a sidewise trip, till he frowned sternly and righted himself. "None of that, now. Behave yourself," he muttered.

The demon settled like a dog cowering before a stern master, and no wonder; it had been a dog, or rather been in a dog, at one time, Pen was certain. The new-hatched elemental had found its early way through lesser animals before that, maybe, but mostly it was doggish. This man was clearly its first human rider, Temple-approved and with luck trained by the white god's Order. And if he wasn't, he was about to be . . .

The other sorcerer looked up at Pen and blinked in surprise. "You are really Learned Penric of Martensbridge? And Lodi? I was expecting someone older." He waved a familiar note clutched in his free hand, which explained his presence, but not his form of address. Pen had signed his urgent missives *Learned Penric of Vilnoc*.

"I was at one time, but I owe allegiance to the archdivine of Orbas, now. Via the Bastard's chapterhouse in Vilnoc." The functionaries there paid his stipend, anyway. "And you would be . . . ?"

"Oh. Learned Dubro from the town of Izbetsia. Although I'm afraid I'm not very learned, by your standards." He gave a self-deprecating and somewhat nervous chuckle. "I was Brother Dubro there for years, a dedicat serving the Son of Autumn." He gestured a tally sign, ending with his hand spread over his heart. "But then there was this demon, which forced many unexpected changes in my life." He tapped his lips apologetically.

"Yes, they do that," agreed Pen. "If you'd pledged yourself to Autumn, how did the white god's Order come to gift you with a demon?"

"It was the other way around. I acquired my demon more-or-less by accident, and the Temple decided I should keep it."

"Ah. Sorcerers are made that way more often than is commonly realized. I shall like to hear more about that, later. But I see you have one of my letters about the bruising fever?"

"Yes, the Vilnoc chapterhouse forwarded it to me in Izbetsia. But did you really want help from just any sorcerer? Because I have no physician's training at all."

"I can remedy that," said Pen fervently. "You came. That's the only qualification needed."

He nodded in uncertainty, still staring in some wonder at Pen. Though not in doubt; he could sense Desdemona as readily as Pen could sense his doggish passenger.

Pen directed the gate guard to offload the saddlebags and stable Dubro's horse. A polite contest over who was going to carry the bags was won by their owner. Pen led his welcome guest through the fort to the hospice.

"I'm bunking in with the orderlies," Pen told him. Maybe not a good moment to mention that some had come down sick with the fever themselves? Pen didn't want to scare this godly gift away. "We'll find you a spare cot. Try not to wake up anyone who's sleeping—they probably have night duty."

Pen had Dubro set his bags on Pen's bed before following him to the courtyard fountain for a wash-up.

"How far a ride is it from Izbetsia?" Pen asked, eyeing his travel dirt. He suspected he'd have to look at one of Adelis's larger-scale maps to find the town marked.

"Two days, at the best speed my old horse and I go," said Dubro, scrubbing industriously.

"You came quickly?"

"After I got the note I took a day to think about it. And to pray."

"It is a frightening disease."

"Oh, that's not it." He waved a negating hand, also shaking the water off. His splashes evaporated from the sun-heated tiles. "But I wasn't sure we could be of use."

"It's a very young demon to be set to such a task, though I've been thinking about how to make it as straightforward as possible. Let's go find out."

"Right now?" He straightened, startled.

"Oh, yes."

For all his claim to bravery, Dubro did hesitate at the door of the first sick-chamber, but gulped and followed Pen into the dimness and stink. Pen wondered if he should have diverted for some medical lecture first, but really, this was going to be easier to show than describe. He picked a soldier who was too woozy with fever to complain or comment, and had the older sorcerer kneel alongside him.

"Just watch, for the first few."

Pen had dispensed with the disguising prayers a few beleaguered days ago, but he did make a salute of a tally sign before commencing the first application of uphill magic. Dubro squinted his eyes in concentration, though following this with inner more than outer vision.

"I've only worked with downhill magics, before," he murmured. "Small and safe."

"Not unwise, if you've had no mentor. Er, have you been all on your own in Izbetsia?"

"We've a senior Temple divine who is my supervisor, but he trained with the Father's Order. It's not a big town."

Supervisor, or wary watchman? Pen would wager the latter. So likely not an encourager of experimentation or exploration. Pen could see how being made responsible for something one could neither understand nor control could make one a touch rigid, even without the typical tidy-mindedness of those attracted to the Father of Winter's service.

You are too charitable, Pen, reproved Des. *If this fellow has had his dog for as long as it looks, it's been a waste of opportunity.*

Dubro's glance shifted aside. He wouldn't be able to make out Des's silent speech, but that she spoke, he sensed.

I don't imagine the dog's been very chatty, she added. *Ha. Unlike the ten of you . . .*

My first human rider Sugane found the speechless

imprints of the mare and the lioness extremely confusing,
I'll grant. But back then she had no Temple support at
all. This Orban country man seems luckier.

Pen worked his way all around the six patients in the
chamber, then led Dubro out again.

"And now, on to the kitchens."

"The kitchens? I admit, I'm a little peckish."

"We'll get to eat in the orderlies' mess, later on," Pen
assured him. "But I have an arrangement with the cooks
for dumping Des's chaos, which I'll demonstrate shortly.
Also, I didn't think your first trials with transferring
uphill magic should be on people."

His brow wrinkled. "All right . . ."

"Follow me."

Dubro chuckled as they exited the hospice court. "I
already know my way around this fort, or rather, it's
coming back to me. I served here, oh . . . over forty years
ago, because I remember the celebration when young
Duke Jurgo was born."

The duke was now a hale man in his mid-forties, so
that dated it with precision. "You were in the Orban
army?"

"Aye. I joined at age sixteen, all young and hot—I
couldn't wait to get out of my home village. Funny, after
my twenty years, I couldn't wait to go home. I took my
veteran's allotment of land as close to my birthplace as I
could get it, outside Izbetsia. Married a widow I'd known
as a girl, had two youngsters of my own before her womb
closed up—that was a good time. They're both grown
now. I helped out with the town temple on holy days as
a lay dedicat."

"You didn't have your demon then?"

"No, that came later. As a surprise all around. I had a good old farm dog, Maska. One night he killed a weasel that was trying to get at our hens. We figured out much later that the weasel had picked up a demon elemental from a wild bird it had killed, probably a quail. I thought for a while the dog had run mad, or fallen sick, and I was going to have to put him out of his misery, but after a week or two he settled back down. He was never quite the same, after, but he was still loyal to me."

By which Pen concluded that the distressed Dubro had been putting off that unpleasant duty to which, as either soldier or farmer, he should have been steeled. Also that the stronger personality of the dog had overcome the influence of both the demon and its prior animal possessors, which was unusual and most interesting, theologically speaking.

"I kept old Maska for over a year after that, till he died of a tumor. In my arms. And then I got the demonic surprise. It gave me the cold grue later to realize he might just have likely died with my wife or my youngsters, and given the demon to one of them. My wife thought *I* had run mad and sick, maybe over grief for the dog, and I was wondering myself."

Pen put in, "My demon, at least, had been in several humans before, and could explain itself." *At great length.*

Now, now, murmured Des in amusement, as fascinated by this tale as Pen.

"Ah? That would have helped a good deal, aye. It wasn't till our divine took me to a Temple sensitive in Vilnoc that I was rightly diagnosed. They sent me on to

Trigonie, where there was a special saint who was supposed to have the gift of removing demons, but after looking me over she decided instead I should keep my demon and tame it for the Temple. They swore me to the white god's service and held me there for a year, training me up as a divine of sorts. I wasn't very happy about it at the time, but as I behaved myself and did what they told me to, they did let me go back to my farm."

"Have you farmed there ever since?"

"Aye. My wife left me for a while out of fear, but she came back, good old girl. She passed on to her goddess about four years ago. Our boy has taken over the farm for me, in the main."

"I see."

They came to the delivery entrance to the killing court, and Pen ushered Dubro inside. His demon was still very wary of Des, so there was a brief tussle between Dubro getting close enough to his new mentor to hear and see, and his demon trying to get as far away across the room as possible. Dubro won. Des controlled her natural irritation smoothly.

The lads had saved Pen out a crate of chickens for emergency night rations, as was become routine.

"You say you've worked downhill magics? Killing vermin, fleas and rats and the like?"

"Yes, I did learn to do that, early on."

"Poultry for the table?"

"Not so much. I taught Maska *firmly* as a pup not to worry the chickens, so he gets edgy over that. I just kill them in the usual way, at home."

"You think of your demon as Maska? You've named him?" Pen smiled in approval.

"Keeping his old name seemed easiest. Eh, does your demon have a name? Or names?"

"Eleven of them, one each for her prior human riders, and one I gave her for all of her together. Desdemona, or Des for short. Naming your demon is a very useful thing. A lot of sorcerers don't figure that out, so good for you."

"Huh." He stared at Pen. Or through Pen at Des, maybe. "It—she?—is so dense and deep. Yet she doesn't ascend? You aren't afraid?"

"We, ah, came to an understanding early on, so no." Pen turned back to their more immediate problems. "Divesting the excess chaos that will accrue to your demon from the, as it were, uphill donations to the sick men will be exactly the same as killing vermin, directed to precise targets, so I don't have to teach you that part." *Thanks be*. "Right now, I want you to try placing a bit of the uphill magic just as I showed you in the sick-chamber, but into a chicken."

"Ah, I get it." Dubro opened the crate and expertly removed one chicken. He stroked its feathers, frowned, and concentrated. The blast of uphill magic was well-directed, at least. The chicken squawked, flapped its wings wildly, and, as nearly as Pen could tell, died of a heart attack.

"Oh," said Dubro, daunted. "That wasn't good." Gingerly, he set down the feathered corpse, which stopped twitching after a few more moments.

"Actually, it wasn't bad. Just too much at once. Also,

still too much to try to put into a sick person at one go. You had the right move. Now let's work on finer control."

Three more chickens died before Dubro caught the trick of it, but then he did, in that odd sudden way so familiar to Pen of breaking through to a new skill. He didn't quite seem to believe Pen's praise, but they worked through the rest of the crate, saving a couple of fowls at the end for Dubro to practice divesting the accumulated disorder, after calming Maska's inhibitions.

Pen ruthlessly slaughtered the survivors, because he next had to walk down to Tyno. Or, at this hour, jog down to Tyno. This left two sorcerers sitting on the stained flagstones surrounded by a dozen dead chickens, and Dubro shaking his head.

"Is this really going to work?"

"Yes," said Pen firmly, because confidence was important in dealing with demons. And humans. He scrambled to his feet and helped the older man up. After shouting into the kitchen for the lads to come collect their next plucking job, news not received with joy, Pen led back to the hospice.

"Will it be all right with the Temple authorities for me to be doing this kind of magic?" asked Dubro in lingering doubt. That first chicken had unnerved him, Pen thought.

"I'm the senior Temple authority for sorcery in Vilnoc, so yes."

Dubro's lips twitched. "Aye, I've known officers like that . . ."

"Just wait till you meet Adelis. Uh, General Arisaydia."

"That will be a marvel." He nodded without irony.

In the ensuing patient chamber, Pen picked a less badly off soldier for Dubro to try. Were their two magics going to prove compatible? Or should Pen work up separate rosters for each of them?

Separate if you can, advised Des. *I could handle it, but that dog has enough new things on his plate.*

Leaving Pen to assign himself the worst cases; it was obvious enough how this had to go. Again.

The sick soldier eyed the elderly sorcerer with more confidence than he usually bestowed on youthful-seeming Penric; Pen did not try to correct this misapprehension. Dubro knelt, gulped, prayed—more for himself than for his patient, Pen suspected—pressed his spread hand to the fevered chest, and let a dose of magic flow.

"Very good. Stop."

He hauled Dubro back out to the courtyard, where he blinked in the too-westering sunlight, shaken. His demon was a little twitchy with the new demand and the inflow of disorder, but not at all out of control.

"That was perfect," Pen told him. Or close enough. "While that's settling in, let's go get Master Rede and introduce you. Senior fort physician. He runs the show in the hospice. It's been a hard month for him, but you'll find him a good man."

While Pen *wanted* to toss Dubro straight into the bottomless pool of need, here, it would be a very bad idea. Young demons were very vulnerable to mishandling. The little time spent training would be repaid later.

They found Rede in a treatment chamber just

finishing setting a soldier's broken arm, because life went on in the fort. The majority of its denizens remained unaffected by the bruising fever except by fear, thank the gods, and *why*? The pattern of those who hadn't contracted it was as mysterious as that of those who had.

Rede sent the soldier off with his arm in a sling and instructions to rest, and turned to his new callers. His tired face lit when Pen introduced Learned Dubro and explained why and how he'd come.

"I've just acquainted him with his medical duties. I'll leave you to get him settled in. He's had a long ride today, with a pretty abrupt tutorial at the end, and hasn't had dinner yet." He eyed Rede. "Have you had a break?"

Rede stared blankly, as if Pen had spoken in Darthacan. After a moment he offered, "Funerals. I went to some."

"So no, I see. I have to run down to Tyno." Literally, if he wanted to be back before darkness fell. "Then Vilnoc." For the best result, he should be visiting each patient more than once a day. Maybe Dubro could make the difference?

"Any more cases down there?"

"I'll find out soon. Learned Dubro has some interesting stories to tell. And he should hear all you've learned about this disease he'll be helping treat. I'll see you both when I get back." Pen strode out, waving without turning around.

Penric returned to the fort from Vilnoc long after dark, to find Rede and Dubro talking earnestly in the lamplight of Rede's writing cabinet.

"Oh, good, you're back." Rede seemed to greet Pen's every return with relief, as if in fear Pen might abscond somewhere, or more likely be abducted and held prisoner by the Mother's Order. Pen imagined Tolga had thought about it. "What's new to report?"

Pen swallowed his last bite of probably-ox jerky—it had lasted his whole ride—and answered, "Three new cases in the village. One in town. No one else died this afternoon. Although a couple of people at the Order are in a bad way. I'd like to see them twice tomorrow if I can." Actually, he'd *like* to see them three times, or maybe four. More than four treatments in a day, he'd discovered in his prior career, were in general too much for the patient to absorb, and so the effort was wasted. Three or four were ideal, but he wasn't going to be able to do that many, so there was no use brooding about it. Or rather, it had been out of the question before Dubro's arrival. Pen's arithmetic might be about to improve. He smiled at the other sorcerer in much the hungry way that Rede and Tolga smiled at him. Dubro smiled back in uncertainty.

Pen's eye fell upon an unexpectedly familiar slim codex open on Rede's table between the two men. It was Pen's own translation into Adriac of Learned Ruchia's primer on the basics of sorcery, printed three years ago in Lodi by the archdivine's press. "Oh! However did you come by that?"

"Ah, so you *did* write it?" said Dubro. "I thought you must be the same man, but then I thought you were too young. It was sent to me last year by a friend in the Trigonie Temple."

"You read Adriac, then?" Pen asked, pleased.

Dubro shook his head in regret. "No. Our town divine reads a little, and helped me go over it, but I don't really think he understood the sorcery parts."

"Which would be . . . pretty much all of it, oh dear."

"Even so, I could see it was clearer and plainer than some of what I'd been taught when I first got Maska." Dubro tapped the open page.

"Yes, Learned Ruchia was very good. It was the first volume that ever fell into my hands about my craft, and still the best, so I was lucky."

Dubro frowned. "She still lives on in your head, doesn't she?"

"Her imprint, yes, that was very helpful, too. Although she can get tart with me when I'm slow. When I first ran across her book back in Martensbridge, written in our native Wealdean, it only existed in a few manuscript copies, horrifyingly rare and vulnerable. One of my first tasks as a young divine was to transcribe it for printing. Oh, making printing plates by sorcery—I'll wager that's another skill I could teach you. Although not this week."

"Ho, I saw that in the codicil."

"Yes, that part I really did write. Since I made up the technique."

Intent, Rede asked, "Is it true there's supposed to be a second volume about medical sorcery?"

"Yes!" said Pen happily. "I finally finished making all the wooden plates and shipped them off to the archdivine of Adria last fall. The book is three times as thick as this one, in both senses, so it took a while. Completing Volume Two for him was part of the bargain I'd struck for releasing me to the service of Orbas, when I moved here. I very much wanted to finish it anyway, so it was an easy promise to make. They're supposed to send me copies soon. I hope."

"I see."

"Do you read Adriac?" Pen inquired in hope.

"Ah, not well. I have better Roknari—army men tend to learn the languages of their enemies. But there is not likely to be a work on medical sorcery in that tongue."

"You'd be surprised what gets handed around in secret. But no, the Roknari writings I've read on sorcery were odd and obscure, by Ruchia's strict standards. Partly to hide what they were writing, which . . . rather defeats the purpose of writing, partly I think because their understanding was distorted by Quadrene theological teachings." Pen could go on at length on the topic, but now was not the time.

Dubro said tentatively, "But will there ever be a translation to Cedonian? That I could read, maybe?"

Pen gave a vigorous nod. "I've been working on one under the patronage of Duke Jurgo. Revising as I go, since every time I've translated it, it seems I've learned more. It keeps getting longer, so, slower."

You're going to have to put your name on it as a co-writer, if this keeps up, said Des, smug. Or was that Ruchia? Someone in his head was pleased with his progress, anyway. After the Wealdean, the Darthacan, and the Adriac translations, Des usually just complained about the tedium of sitting through it all *again*.

"How many times have you translated it?" asked Dubro, staring at him.

"Uh, four? Counting the Wealdean in as one. Four and a half with the Ibran, but that was interrupted before I'd got very far. I want to get back to it someday."

"I'd like to see that second volume in Cedonian," said Rede.

"I'd love to have you do so. The first draft needs checking by someone well-up in current Cedonian medical usage. Before I recopy it for the printing plates. I'm hoping to be able to use metal plates for Jurgo's edition—I'm working with his court printer on that. More durable than wood, able to make many more copies before wearing out."

Rede and Pen gazed at each other in a moment of mutual rapacity, before Rede sighed and said, "After this is over."

"Aye." Pen stretched, preparatory to the effort of standing. Up. Again.

Rede fingered the volume, a thoughtful look on his features, then gently closed it. "This could be quite important. Instead of sharing your knowledge with one apprentice at a time, you might reach hundreds. Perhaps people you'll never even meet."

"That's my hope, anyway. Why I crouch over my writing table for months on end."

Fibster, murmured Des. *You love your writing table*.

More than he loved this nightmare in which he was presently embedded, to be sure. But maybe, now, not alone? "Ready for another trial in the sick-chambers?" he asked Dubro.

Dubro gulped, ducked his head in assent, and followed him to his feet.

Rede went along to watch them work their way through the next chamber full of men. Frustrating for him, since there was nothing for normal human eyes to see but a mismatched pair of templemen kneeling by cots, moving their hands a bit and conversing in low tones. Dubro and his dog perceived much more. The rural divine might have come late in life to being a lettered man, but Pen doubted he'd ever been a dull one.

By the time Pen led back to the kitchens for the midnight slaughter, he was hoping he might leave Dubro to work unsupervised as early as tomorrow afternoon. Which was insanely faster than any normal tutorial, but this wasn't a normal situation. The Trigonie saint seemed to have judged the supplicant sorcerer's strength of character correctly, back at his beginning.

Or her Master did, said Des.

Let's pray so.

Penric didn't know whether it was the former disciplines as a soldier or as a farmer that had fitted Dubro for his new challenge. Both involved relentless routines dutifully carried out, daily without a break, the latter even more than the former. Keeping animals and plants alive and healthy, not to mention children, year in and year out, was certainly a more complex task than garrison guard.

Howsoever Dubro had been prepared, by noon the next day Pen thought him ready to try a roster of patients under Rede's eye, including the fellows who had recently resisted Pen's sorcery. To Pen's dark amusement, Dubro's local origins and reassuring age, grandfather laced with sergeant, seemed to overbear the soldiers' prior superstitious fears, although the fact that they were growing sicker and less able to object doubtless played in.

The young demon Maska was a keener concern, but his inherited canine loyalty to his—evidently once equally loving—master granted an edge over his underlying chaotic demon-nature. The skill Pen taught was an advanced technique, but it was only the one, and by the time anyone had repeated a task that often, that close in succession, growing adept was almost an inevitability. Demons, Pen knew too well, tended to become bored and cranky with repetition, but there appeared to be no end to the number of times a dog delighted in fetching a stick.

Pen watched until he felt confident he could let the pair get on with it, then cantered off to Tyno and Vilnoc and his other two rosters of patients for the first, but not the only, *ha*, visit of the day.

Meanwhile, Pen had a demon nearer than Maska to concern him. By the time he rode back from Vilnoc, where in his relief and hope he'd poured all the uphill magic he could muster into Tolga's now-ten patients, following directly from Tyno's now-seventeen, Pen's tunic was dank with sweat and Des was mute, brimming with unshed chaos. And it wasn't the good sort of silence from her.

Pen diverted his horse around the fort's downwind side to the slope where its abattoir was situated. The small building had its own aqueduct branch running into it, used in keeping the pavement rinsed in its dismembering courtyard, but the initial killing, skinning, and quartering of the large animals was done in a yard outside, cluttered with hoists, cranes, chutes and carts. The reek that rose from it was intense, and Pen's horse snorted and shied.

Pen had participated in butchery in his own rural youth, on the farm at Jurald Court and on hunts, but the cantons were much colder than Orbas. This was a rare moment for Pen to appreciate that. The fort butchers wasted very little of their animals, but the residue of offal raked off to the side still made an unsavory daily banquet for crows, ravens, stray dogs, and flies. Pen decanted a splash of chaos upon the flies on his way in, like a libation spilled from an overflowing drinking vessel, but it wasn't going to be enough.

A small shrine to the Son of Autumn was set up at the side of the killing yard, in mindful gratitude for His creatures sacrificed here. The sergeant in charge no doubt led his men in a brief prayer before it as they commenced each day's work, mitigating the unavoidable brutality. As a usually unthinking beneficiary of their labors, Pen was heartened at the vision.

He sought out the workmen, finding them inside with a lot of very sharp tools turning an ex-ox into cutlets. Sergeant Jasenik proved a stringy old buzzard, an Orban army veteran cut from the same cloth as the fort cook Burae. Since a couple of his own men had come down with the bruising fever and passed into Pen's care, his anxious interest in their fates overcame whatever fears of sorcery he might have harbored. The rumors of Pen's activities in the fort hospice and kitchen had already come to his ears, if garbled, so Pen's explanations didn't have to start from scratch, quite. Pen went into more detail about how he'd used to work with that butcher in Martensbridge, which set up a strange sort of professional camaraderie between them, or at least made Jasenik decide Pen wasn't just a typical town-bred fool.

"We do most of our killing in the morning," the sergeant told Pen, to no surprise. "But there's one pig still left today."

"That would certainly do. I can only handle one large animal at a time."

"Ho. We're the same, so maybe we can match up all right."

He rounded up four of his men and led them back outside, where a surly hog waited in an enclosure. Their prayer at their shrine was more perfunctory than Pen had fondly imagined, though they seemed to appreciate him adding his own official-Temple-divine blessing. The hog did not cooperate with its doom, but after a practiced tussle the crew had it hoisted for killing.

Which Pen quietly accomplished. The screeching sensation along his nerves from the overload of chaos died away along with the animal's squeals.

Oh, wheezed Des in a profound relief that Pen frankly shared.

Everyone stepped back in surprise at the unaccustomed silence. "Is that . . . all right . . . ?" asked one man.

"It died without pain," Pen promised him.

They accepted this in a hesitant sort of faith. Although they stood a little farther from him, after.

All right was a broader question, theologically

speaking. Domesticated animals were considered to shelter under the cloak of the Son of Autumn, not a part of the Bastard's motley collection of vermin, so Pen was encroaching a trifle on another god's territory, here. More critical was the sheer size of the victim. Killing large animals wasn't just a little like using magic to kill a human would be; it was exactly like it. Knowing not just in theory, but in repeated practice, precisely how easily he could do it was always an uncomfortable piece of self-awareness for Pen to confront.

But only the once, said Des. *Then the white god would seize me back through your target's death.*

You and I both know that's not invariably true. The exceptions in medical sorcery were fraught indeed, and Pen *wished* he only knew them in theory.

Be that as it may. He would set aside all the chickens in the kitchens for Dubro and Maska, and keep the visits to the abattoir and its ambiguities to himself. And not from greed. Breaking a promising young demon that might serve the Temple for generations yet, here at its very outset, would be a huge, if wholly invisible, loss to that future.

Speaking of his other charges, it was past time to go check on them. Pen thanked Jasenik and his now-wary men, made arrangements for tomorrow, collected his horse, and hurried back up to the fort.

Penric's evening was brightened by the receipt of a note from Nikys, gingerly handed to him by one of Adelis's clerks. Eager and anxious, he carried it out into the last light of the hospice courtyard and tore it open.

It was all benign domestic news, nothing unexpected or worrisome, and his heartbeat slowed to calm as he read it and read it again. Nikys had a nice turn of phrase when describing Florina's infant tricks.

"All's well, then," he muttered to Des. Nikys hadn't added *Wish you were here*, but maybe Pen was wishing that hard enough for both of them.

Yes, observed Des, reading as usual over his shoulder, or through his eyes. *Nothing in it to distract you from your duties, to be sure. It's what good wives do.*

Pen hesitated. *Does it seem too cheerful? Do you think she's leaving out anything?*

Mm, probably. I suppose if anything truly dire occurred, she would ask you for help. But, you know, army widow. Their notions of an emergency are not trivial. She'll be keeping her fears to herself.

Pen wasn't sure whether to be grateful or distressed. *I expect she'd prefer grateful.*

"I suppose . . ." He wanted to be his wife's buttress and confidant, not someone she thought she had to coddle or tiptoe around.

Pen tucked the note in his sash. With luck, he'd get a moment tonight to dash off a reply. He wanted to tell her about Dubro, among other things. He tried not to think too much about his unfinished Cedonian translation of Ruchia's second volume, which he'd left scattered in bits all over his study, in an order understood only by him. He should remind Nikys to restrain Lin from attempting to tidy them up.

Meanwhile, it was time for another pass through the sick-chambers. He'd tightened the interval between rounds by curtailing the prayers to a tap to his lips for his god and the bedside manner to a tap for the magic. The parts he could not reduce were on the other end, the travel between fort and village and town, and the running back and forth from hospice to kitchen to wherever to find poor creatures to kill. He hoped the abattoir would improve his efficiency, if Des could bear the larger loads of disorder between visits.

Urgh, from Des. As a rule demons relished chaos, but she was not enjoying this version any more than he was.

The next few days and nights blurred together without much distinction, except, while Dubro treated the lesser cases over and over, Pen was able to hit Vilnoc twice a day, Tyno three times, and the worse-off men in the fort sometimes four. Between one visit and the next, and more between one day and the next, Pen could *see* his labors having an effect, not just delaying but pushing back the fever and bruising and pain. It felt like the difference between watching dry mountain grass roots stubbornly survive the winter, and eager bean sprouts break ground in the spring.

The abattoir remained useful and its crew helpful, although after that big-eyed, tame, and unusually friendly calf, which had nudged Pen's hand as if looking for its mother's milk, Pen remembered why he'd gone off eating meat for a while in Martensbridge.

He fantasized about burning his fraying vestments when he finally reached home. The women of the household would likely object to this disposal of their prior labors, wanting at least to make them into kitchen towels or, the last refuge of rags, braided rugs. He hadn't read a letter from his correspondents in other realms or a book, new or old, in . . . weeks, yes, it had been well over two weeks this had been going on. Was there ever to be an end, or was he to toil on endlessly as if caught in some centuries-long curse from a nursery tale?

His moaning to Rede in the mess, as the one man likely to understand his need to vent his frustrations, produced an unexpected reply.

"Well, of course. Whenever you start to get ahead, you don't rest; you just add in an extra pass. I'm going to start forcibly taking the improving men away from you soon. I can see the difference too, you know. More men are recovering, and recovering faster, since Learned Dubro's arrival allowed you to increase the frequency of treatments. You said that would be so, and so it is."

"The opposite would also be true, you realize, if we get more sick in. How many today?"

Rede's lips stretched in a weird white grin. "Here in the fort? None."

"What?"

"None."

"That . . . can't be true. It's probably an artifact of chance, and tomorrow we'll get double, or some such." Pen added, as if he were a moneychanger attempting to balance his scales, "There were two more sick in Tyno."

"How many there no longer need your magics?"

"It's so hard to tell when it's safe to stop."

"I see."

But there were no more new cases in the fort the next day, either. Nor the following.

"Are we actually *beating* this thing?" Pen asked Rede, more than rhetorically.

"Maybe? Or it's burning out on its own. Contagions do, sometimes. Well, always, eventually."

"Preferably not because there's no one left alive. Sunder it! It was getting around, now it's not getting around, and *why*?"

Rede shrugged helplessly. "If you find out, tell me."

"You'll be the first to know, I promise."

There were no new cases in the fort the next day, either, nor the next; a much more welcome mystery than the disease's arrival, but still maddeningly obscure. Though for the first time, Pen found himself waking in his cot looking forward to his tasks. It wasn't even that he might anticipate an end; it was that he could see that he was making a difference, that his effort was receiving its due reward of success at last. Most heartening.

. . . And then Adelis rode back into the fort with thirty wounded, forty deathly ill cavalrymen, and two dozen sick Rusylli.

Over the next two days, Penric could see all the progress he, Des, and Dubro and Maska had made slipping through his hands.

The fort hospice was designed to take in the sudden aftermaths of battles, although the sole clash near Vilnoc for over a decade had been at the port with a raiding fleet. With more cots set up, the patient chambers absorbed their new load but only just; by crowding, Rede was still able to assign the wounded and the sick each to their own wards. Not that the former couldn't turn into the latter overnight. The Rusylli were sent back to their camp to be cared for by each other, and Penric had a sharp dispute with the exhausted Adelis as to whether he should go in after them.

It was settled only by the Rusylli themselves, who assembled in a frightened, furious gang to turn Pen back at their gate; this, after having to argue with the greatly augmented Orban guard troop to let him pass within. Pen retreated walking backward up the road shouting instructions in Rusylli for how to send him a message should they change their minds, although he was very much afraid that by the point they did, he'd be unable to break away, the time for today's visit being stolen from Tyno, and Tyno's from the fort. He'd not been able to ride into Vilnoc at all, and his imagination had plenty of material to envision the relapses that must be taking place there, because they were taking place *here*.

Atop it all, the fort was generating new cases again, at first from Adelis's returned cavalry troop and grooms. Either they'd acquired the bruising fever a bit later than some of their comrades, or it took different periods to brew up in different men, or both. Pen was not optimistic enough to believe it would remain limited to that still-too-large pool of men.

On the third morning, Dubro reeled in to report to Penric, "Maska won't come when I call!"

Pen looked them over. Maska cowered within his rider a little like Des in the presence of the Divine, but rather more like a whipped dog hiding under a bed. It was almost the opposite of a demon ascending, for a creature with no other way to retreat or escape. Pen could sympathize.

"Your demon is spent," Pen told him bluntly. "Take the rest of today and tonight off. Tomorrow morning, I'll check him again."

"I could do more," said Dubro, his aged face pinching. "We need to do more!"

"I know, and you can't."

"I could at least help out in the hospice? You know I'm not afraid to get my hands dirty."

Pen nodded with respect, but said, "Rede can get Adelis to conscript him more men for that." At some cost in increased desertions, perhaps. "You need to stop and take care of your demon, which cannot be replaced." Pen would filch a few minutes later to write more begging notes to his chapterhouse for sorcerers, any sorcerers, but he'd done that twice already, and Dubro had been the sole result.

"What about your demon?" Dubro squinted in worry at Pen, although with Maska in this hysterical state, his Sight was unavailable to him. "Is she all right?"

"Over two hundred years old. She has more endurance than I do, and has probably seen worse plagues."

Indeed, murmured Des. *Still not fun.*

"She truly cannot ascend and make off with you? I'd swear she seems powerful enough."

"She could."

At our first acquaintance, yes. But you've been growing more powerful yourself, Pen. So, not such a foregone conclusion as it once was.

Haven't you been growing with me? The proportions should be keeping pace.

Hah.

"But she won't," Pen finished firmly. Collapse from fatigue, maybe; could a demon do that? He didn't want to find out.

Then there was nothing for it but to get back to work, from the sick-chambers to the abattoir and around again, with some side-trips to the kitchen's killing room to pick off the poultry that Dubro would not be getting to today.

That evening, he received a note from Tolga in town. She sounded frustrated and angry, either begging or commanding him to return, though futilely in either case. She went on to detail the progress, or regress, of his worst-off patients, confirming his imaginings.

Pen stuffed the note into his sash, where it burned like a coal.

Maska was somewhat recovered the following morning. Pen gave Dubro a strict ration of a dozen patients to treat, and no more. For Maska's sake it should have been half that, curse it. For the fort's, double. This didn't really buy Pen enough time to visit Tyno, but he went down anyway.

There, not at all to his surprise, he found that some of his patients had backslid, one from the tanner clan into death. Which got Pen shouted at by her weeping husband.

"Why didn't you come back? I thought she was getting better! Why didn't you come back sooner?"

There was nothing to say to this but a useless if true, "I'm sorry."

Pen escaped from the grief and recriminations as

swiftly as he could, and stood blinking in the half-deserted village street. The abattoir—he should march up there on his way back to the fort, see what poor innocent beast they'd saved out for him next. And then kill it.

Instead, he found himself turning aside at the village temple.

The Tyno temple was a neat little building just off what passed for the main square. Stone-built, with whitewashed stucco on the outside, its sturdiness hinted that it had been designed and built with the help of the local army engineers. Its six sides supported a concrete dome with a round oculus in its center. The streetside face was devoted to the entryway under a portico. One leaf of the pair of wooden doors was hooked open for the day's petitioners to enter and pray or, with luck, leave offerings.

Penric ducked into the dome's cool shade and made the tally sign. The pavement was mere flagstone, but rendered interesting with a clever pattern of subtle colors fitted together. The five altar-walls bore the familiar profusion of frescoed images associated with each god, more earnest than artistic. On the central plinth, the holy fire had burned down to coals, aromatic with incense. Pen fed it a fresh stick from the wood-basket in passing.

A couple of villagers rose from their prayer rugs before the Mother of Summer's altar, set them in their stack, and nodded warily at Pen on the way out. Nearly all of Tyno knew who he was by now. It didn't, unfortunately, follow that they trusted him.

Pen considered the Mother's altar for a moment, then cast it his usual apologetic touch to his navel. He turned to the Bastard's altar instead and pulled out a rug, made and donated by some devout village woman, to lay before it. He sank to his knees, then, after a moment, prone, in the pose of utmost supplication, arms outflung. It seemed less piety than exhaustion.

What should he pray for? Forgiveness? Not the white god's specialty. More sorcerers, he supposed. Far more people begged the gods to do something for them than ever offered to do something for the gods, and he wondered if the Five ever grew tired of it. Maybe They were too vast, and so prayers fell like raindrops into the ocean. Pen tried not to bother his god more than he was absolutely forced to, not because he thought the Bastard wouldn't answer him, but because he feared He might, and then what?

He tried to compose his seething mind into a proper mode of holy meditation, open or baiting, he wasn't sure. Slowly, he settled. There seemed more danger that he would simply fall asleep.

Yawning and about to give up, he became aware that Des had shrunk within him to a defensive ball. Deprived of Sight, he extended his ordinary senses to their utmost. Nothing but the musty scratchiness of the rug beneath his cheek, the faint snap and scent of the plinth fire, distant echoes through the door and the oculus from the village life outside.

A tickle on the back of his left hand.

He turned his head to blink owlishly at a horsefly feasting on a drop of blood. The tiny wound did not hurt or itch; could the creature somehow subdue the pain in its victims to give it longer to feed? How, and was it something Pen might learn how to use . . . ?

As horseflies went, it wasn't as big and ugly as some; its body and wings were a pretty iridescent blue.

The connections fell in all at once, like a tower crashing down in an earthquake. *Blood. Rede's flea theory. The blue witch . . .*

Pen spasmed up, grabbing for the fly, which circled through the air and out the oculus. *Sunder* it.

"Des! Was that accursed thing an *answer to my prayer*?"

I don't know, she gasped. *I couldn't watch*. Slowly, she unfolded again.

Unhelpful, Des!

Pen shouted in frustration to the oculus, "You could stand to be less *obscure*, You know!" He ran outside and looked up, but the fly was long gone. Not that he could see such a speck at this distance anyway.

No matter. Where there was one fly, there were bound to be a thousand more somewhere. If not up at the fort right now. He tried to think if it was of a kind he'd ever seen before. Perhaps not? Certainly not in the cantons, where he'd been enough of an outdoors boy to observe such things. The blue color was very distinctive.

His brain picking at the problem, he walked distractedly back up to the abattoir.

As he trudged past the building to the killing yard, raised voices reached him along with the reek. Jasenik had a good sergeantly bellow. The other's was sharper and more whiny. He rounded the corner to see an overgrown bull-calf waiting in a chute, presumably Pen's current ration, Jasenik, and a groom from the fort holding the lead line of a trembling horse.

"I *told* the cavalry not to send those sick beasts here with my good food animals!" said Jasenik, irate. "Take it straight down to the tanners."

"Well, nobody told me!" complained the groom.

"What's this?" asked Pen, coming up to the group.

Jasenik wheeled. "Ah, Learned Penric. This here's a beast you can kill with my good will. Except not here. Let it walk itself down to the village, if it can."

"What?" said Pen. It looked to be a shaggy steppe pony, normally an incredibly hardy breed. Not now; its eye and coat were dull, its head hung down, and its legs shook. Blood was crusted around its soft muzzle.

"It has the bloody staggers," the groom informed him glumly. "We've been getting a string of them. We separate them out and put them down in a pasture by themselves as soon as we're sure, and some of them come around again, but this one isn't going to get better."

Des, Sight.

If Penric hadn't been head down for weeks at the closest range to an endless parade of people with the disease, he wasn't sure he could have recognized it in an animal. But he had been and he did, near-instantly.

"That's not the bloody staggers. Well, I'm sure you call it that, in horses. It's this accursed *bruising fever.*"

Both men jerked back. "What?" said Jasenik. "People don't get horse diseases!"

Pen was shaken by a moment of doubt. It was a new idea to him, to be sure. Was it too wild, too desperate?

Des, after a moment, offered, *Thrush. Amberein once treated a poor fellow with a thrush infection in his mouth. Though I doubt he got it from licking the frog of a horse's hoof, so I don't insist on the connection.*

Really . . . ? Pen fought off the distraction; also the repulsive image. "How long ago did you have these sick horses show up at the fort?" he demanded of the groom.

The fellow squinted in thought. "A month ago? No, two? Not more'n two."

Within days of the first outbreak, then. "Where did they come from?"

"Well, this lot"—he jerked his thumb at the trembling horse—"came in with a string of war prizes from Grabyat. But, y'know, any horse seems to get it. And one mule, so far."

"Oxen? Other animals?"

"Not so far as I know. Just horses. The cavalry master is fit to be tied."

"And *nobody* thought to tell Master Orides, or Master Rede?"

The groom stared. "They don't treat horses."

"Brought down the western road from Grabyat?" Past the border town and fort that also reported struggling with an outbreak of the bruising fever? Nothing so likely as for such live battle booty to be set to rest a while at such a fort before being sent on to walk the breadth of a duchy.

"How else? Nobody's going to ship them all the way around the Cedonian Peninsula by sea."

"*Where* do you sequester—keep apart—your sick horses?"

"Up t' road"—the groom pointed upstream—"at the farthest pasture, beyond the woodlot."

"I have to see them." Pen turned, turned again. "Don't give that horse to the tanners. It has to be buried whole and untouched someplace away from people, deep enough the dogs don't get to it. No one should get its blood on them. . . . I might be able to get back to kill it bloodlessly for you by the time you round up some men and get a trench dug somewhere."

"What, nobody's going to do that on my say-so!" said the groom, startled by Pen's vehemence.

"Not yours. Tell the cavalry master Learned Penric ordered it." That Penric was nowhere in his chain of command wasn't something to point out just now. "I'll be back later to explain it to Adelis. And everyone. If I can prove what I think is so."

As he turned again toward the road, Des moaned, *Pen, please*.

Oh, right. He waved at the bull calf, which dropped in its tracks. Des sighed relief.

Then he just ran.

Pen strode and jogged and didn't stop till he reached the far pasture, which turned out to be a good two miles up the road. He leaned on the gate and caught his breath, studying its occupants. The equine equivalent of the hospice, Pen supposed.

About a dozen disconsolate horses, and one mule, drifted listlessly about, or stood with their heads hanging down but not grazing. One gelding lay on its side, clearly at its last gasp. Pen let himself in and started hunting strange blue flies.

Normal horseflies tended to swarm in their damp breeding places, disgusting enough for anyone encountering them. If one fly was repulsive, dozens of the big buzzing things stooping at you was dozens of times worse. For a few minutes, Pen wondered if he'd flown off the handle about this theory, but then he began to spot the blue intruders, in shy singles clinging quietly to the horses' undersides, or in the inner shadows of their loins. In a few minutes, he'd collected and killed a whole handful. He plucked out fabric in his sash to make a temporary pocket, and tucked them gingerly within.

He then set Des to slaying every fly and parasite of any kind in the pasture, and picked out the least-sick horse there, a black mare that would have been quite comely when well. Pen transferred the biggest blast of uphill magic to the mare that Des could manage. The mare snorted and shied, but thankfully didn't drop of a heart attack; he dumped the chaos into the dying gelding, speeding its demise. Following this up with a strong shamanic compulsion upon the mare to obedience, which he was going to pay for with a nosebleed shortly, Pen shoved her out the gate and scrambled aboard boosted by a foot to the fence. He grabbed mane and kicked her, bridle-and-saddleless, to a canter down the road.

He didn't stop or turn aside at Tyno, though the mare briefly tried to dodge toward the fort; cavalry mount, right. She probably wanted to go home as much as Pen did. He kept her moving at the best pace he could force until they reached the guard post at the Rusylli camp. He was just as out of breath and disheveled as if he had run the whole way, his face and tunic smudged with blood, but at least he'd got here faster. The mare stood puffing, sweating, and trembling as he slid off her bare back, but nudged him and tried to follow as he strode up to the gate guards. Who stepped back in alarm.

"Let me through," Pen snarled, and didn't wait for a reply. A dozen heavily armed soldiers recoiled out of his path.

No unwelcoming committee greeted him this time. Everyone in sight whisked out of it, into the huts or the trees.

Pen, after a frustrated moment, stood in the middle of the clearing and bellowed in Rusylli, "If someone doesn't come out and talk to me *right now*, I'm going to burn every one of your huts to the ground!" He illustrated this empty—probably—threat by setting alight a small, innocuous shrub that straggled nearby. Summer-dry, it went up with a satisfyingly menacing roar. It died down just as fast, but Pen kept an eye out to be sure the conflagration didn't spread.

After a couple of minutes of skittish silence, a familiar figure emerged from one of the huts: Rybi's aunt Yena. Her gray-muzzled hound, whining and cringing as he neared the incendiary Penric, nonetheless faithfully followed, and Pen thought of Maska.

Bravely, Yena straightened her shoulders. "What is it, god man?"

Pen thrust out a hand with a few iridescent dead flies in it, and demanded, "Is *this* the blue witch?"

She drew nearer and peered, then glanced up at his wild-eyed state as if fearing for his sanity, or possibly for anyone in range of his insanity. "I don't know . . . ?"

"Do you know anyone who might? Likely an older woman, or someone from the western clans."

Her lips compressed in thought. "Maybe. Wait here."

She vanished into the grove. Pen jittered in impatience and anxiety.

In a few minutes, *more* minutes, she returned with an even more aged woman. This one was a proper crone, rheumy-eyed and hobbling on a stick, and Pen wondered if she'd been one of the weak ones left behind when the encampment had tried to escape. Adelis had mentioned such, though only to speculate why they hadn't been killed or suicided when their kinsmen fled, a dreadful defiance sometimes practiced among the Rusylli at war.

Pen asked her, "What do the western Rusylli call this kind of horsefly?"

She squinted shortsightedly into his palm, then jerked back and made an averting hex sign, of no actual magical value. "Those evil things! We called them blue witches when I was a girl. Give you a nasty bite. We killed them wherever we saw them."

"Bastard's tears." Pen scrunched his eyes in something like a prayer of gratitude; drew a deep breath. "*Thank you.*"

He shoved his sample flies back into his sash and ran for his horse.

❖ ❖ ❖

Penric found Adelis in his map-room-and-scriptorium, sitting at his writing table with his arms folded atop it. The groom from the abattoir and a wiry, leathery-faced man whom Pen recognized as the fort's cavalry master, Captain Suran, stood before him. All three men looked around as Pen panted through the door.

"Well, here's the mage himself," said Adelis. "This should settle the matter." He raised his eyebrows in curiosity at Pen's hectic state. Pen dug half-a-dozen dead blue flies out of his sash and cast them across the table. Adelis leaned back, startled at this abrupt, bizarre gift.

"*Here* are our killers. Or at least the contagion's couriers. These are what the actual western Rusylli dub blue witches."

Adelis frowned in surprise. "Not a sorcerer or a ghost or a demon or a nursery tale? I thought that was what you were thinking."

"I was. I'm fairly sure that's what my first Rusylli informant thought, too. But you know how that goes. One person recounts an observation, the listeners misunderstand, mishear, or just embellish it according to their fancy, and three relays down the line it is changed out of all recognition. Sometimes just one relay."

"How, couriers?" said the cavalry master. "What can horseflies have to do with this bruising curse?"

"Cursed, certainly by me, but not a curse. The fever's not uncanny, however ghastly. The contagion is carried in the blood. Rede guessed it right, though it wasn't rats and their fleas to blame after all. From horse to human, apparently, through the cuts made by these blood-sucking flies. One bit me down in the Tyno temple a while ago." Pen didn't add his theological speculation about that event.

He held out his left hand in evidence. A trickle of blood still spun over its back, although Pen expected that was mostly a side-cost of his shamanic persuasion upon the mare. It would only confuse his audience to stop and try to explain that right now, and the demonstration was, ahem, handy. Usefully dramatic, supporting the unwelcome news he was going to impart next.

"Mine isn't a guess, Adelis. I went to look at the horses in your cavalry's hospice pasture. I collected these flies there, some from directly off their hides. I could *see* the disease within them. Five gods know, I've been studying it deeply enough in people for the past weeks. Bloody staggers be sundered, it's the same sickness, and why didn't anyone *tell us* . . . ! The infected horses act as blood reservoirs for it. They need to be slain and buried at once. The flies, well, Dubro and I and everyone else can go after them, but we're much more able to *find* the horses. I still don't know if ordinary horseflies or houseflies can also act as blood-couriers, once the sickness is established in an animal, but I doubt anyone will complain if we kill them too." Pen paused for breath.

The groom made a harried gesture at Pen as if to say, *See, there was what I was trying to tell you all!*

The cavalry master had drawn back in repugnance and dismay. "*All* our horses?"

"Gods, I don't know. I hope not. The ones who are far into it, displaying obvious symptoms, you can identify for yourselves. You already have. The ones in the early stages, Learned Dubro and I could likely tag for you, and so spare the clean ones. If we have time." Pen was already *so late* getting back to his next round in the hospice. But, since it was a matter of perception, not the more taxing magical manipulation, maybe he could let the bulk of the task fall on Dubro and Maska? "I don't know yet if horses that appear to have recovered can still act as blood-reservoirs or not."

"If you call for our well-seeming mounts to be taken out and killed, it's going to cause a mutiny among my men." And the cavalry captain looked as though he didn't know which side he'd be on.

Adelis was equally appalled. "Must they be? Can't you heal them as you've been doing for my men?"

"In theory? Maybe. It would have to be tested. But right now, over in the hospice, we're having to choose which *men* to save. If you dump a hundred horses onto my roster as well, I'll be able to save no one." He added in reluctance, "Once all the people, here and in Tyno and Vilnoc, are past the crisis, maybe Dubro and I could try. Something."

"But if you have your way, my horses will be killed by then!" With a gesture at Pen, Captain Suran demanded, "Do you believe this wild tale, General?"

Adelis's hand drifted to touch the burn scars framing his eyes. "Yes," he said heavily. "In matters of his craft, Learned Penric is unequalled in my experience."

Since Adelis's prior experience of sorcerers, Temple or hedge, was almost none, this wasn't as ringing an endorsement as it sounded, but the horse-master nodded unhappily.

"And the Rusylli," Pen added. "I must treat them, too, if they will let me back into their camp."

Adelis looked as though he'd rather put his cavalry horses first, but this time he didn't try to argue. To be fair, the Rusylli were sufficiently horse-mad, they might have agreed with this.

". . . Which makes me wonder if the Rusylli encampment will be protected from new cases by its distance, as it seemed to be at the first outbreak. I think the blue flies can't go too far without their horses, or the disease would have traveled east from the steppes long before this." Pen paused, shaken by a horrific notion. Could he himself have carried the disease into Vilnoc, hidden within his borrowed army mount?

It was already there by then, Des chided him. *Calm down, Pen.*

Oh. Right. But that it had traveled somehow from the fort to town, quite possibly in or with a horse or its flies, as it seemed to have hitched its ride from Grabyat, was a logical-enough speculation.

"Were any sick horses or mules taken into town, do you know?" Pen asked.

"Of course not," said the cavalry master, and "Uh . . ." said the groom.

All three men looked at him. He went mute, frightened.

"Spit it out," Adelis growled, "or it will go badly for you."

The groom gulped. "Maybe . . . somebody who was told to take a few down to the tanner might have taken them into the town market and sold them, instead?

Not me!" he added hastily. "He didn't get much for them, if so."

The market. All sorts of people from all over town might have gone to the market on the dangerous days that the sick horses were present, explaining the random distribution. And, as Pen had just experienced, the bites of the flies were hardly noticeable, and so not recalled a few days later when the first fever symptoms showed. Other horses as well, probably, and oh gods someone was also going to have to trace *those*.

Adelis rubbed his face in uttermost exasperation. He pointed to his cavalry master. "Find out if this is true. If it is, secure the man or men and report back to me."

"Yes, sir," said the daunted Suran.

"Gods, I will hang them," muttered Adelis.

"I'll help," Pen told him through his teeth.

"I thought you weren't allowed to kill."

"By demonic magic. Ropes are not included in that. Executioners are in the white god's flock, come to think. I'll at least give the hangman my learned blessing, if this proves out."

Adelis shook his head. "I do wonder about you some days . . ." He sat up, gathering himself to issue the necessary, unpleasant orders, and called for his aides.

Before he left the scriptorium, Pen seized quill, paper, and ink to write a hasty note to Nikys, warning her of the newly discovered danger.

. . . At once devise a covering, cheesecloth or gauze, for Florina's cradle. Fasten it firmly around the edges so no fly can creep through. If the cloth can be found, make tents for everyone's beds as well. In the tighter wooden

houses of the cantons, Pen thought a person might stretch and tack cheesecloth across the windows for insect-proof screens, but the open Cedonian-style architecture in Orbas would make this unfeasible. Still. *Tell our neighbors with children this trick.* He thought a moment. *Better, tell them all. Kill any fly you see within the house, but not with your hand. I'll be back as soon—* he scratched this last line through. *I don't know when I will be back. Things are about to get even busier for me here, but we may be able to find our way to the end of this thing at last.*

And then another letter to the medical officer at the border fort, describing Pen's new findings, the blue fly, and his drastic recommendations for containing the contagion. He trusted they'd found themselves their own sorcerer by now to endorse his advice, not to mention carry it out, or it was going to sound like raving. *And—* Pen stifled a moan—someone was going to have to examine the entire track through Orbas that Adelis's cavalry had taken chasing down the Rusylli . . . He finished with a shorter scrawl to Tolga, who at least required less explanation.

He shoved all three notes into the hands of Adelis's clerk with a demand to dispatch them instantly, and hurried to the hospice.

Rede and Dubro were coming out of a sick-chamber together when Pen jogged into the hospice courtyard.

"Where have you *been*?" Rede's voice was edged with the sort of anger only fear lent. "We expected you back hours ago!"

Pen danced up to him, grabbed him by the hands, and spun him around. "And time well-spent it was! Rede, I've *cracked* this nut!" Well. In theory. Practice was going to be harder, but wasn't it always?

Rede shook him off and stared at him as though he'd gone mad, which Pen supposed he looked. *Elation* hadn't been anyone's face around here for a while.

Eagerly, Pen dug out his sample flies and repeated his explanations. The two men drew close, ex-farmer Dubro nodding understanding sooner than Rede did. Hesitantly, Pen added to Dubro, as he had not to Adelis, a fuller description of his and his demon's experience before the Bastard's altar in Tyno.

Dubro's eyes went wide. "Do you think you were god-touched?"

"The Bastard being what He is, I never quite know. But Des reacted the way she does to the Divine, which is to retreat." Cower, to be precise.

No need to be rude, she sniffed.

"And the fly bite"—Pen waved his left hand—"would be typical of His humor."

Rede captured his hand and squinted at the wound, which was finally crusting over, in professional curiosity. Glancing more closely at the bloodstains on Pen's tunic, he frowned. "That's your blood? Not a patient's?"

"Shamanic magics are a whole other discipline, which I will be delighted to describe to you in detail—"

"I daresay," murmured Rede, who was beginning to know him.

"But not right now. First I need to take Dubro—no, first I need to—no, first I need . . ." Pen paused and took a deep breath, holding it for a moment, then began again. "First I need to take a pass through here and tap my worst-off patients. Then I need to take Dubro to the cavalry stables and show him how to discern the sick horses. This isn't going to make us popular over there, so I have to make sure everyone understands the onus falls on me, not him."

"If anyone complains," said Rede grimly, "take their names. I'll draft them as relief orderlies. That should educate them in a hurry."

Pen nodded agreement, gathering that this wasn't in the least a joke.

"May I treat more patients?" said Dubro. "I think Maska could, now."

"No. Well, maybe. If there is going to be an end to this thing, I may not have to guard your demon's endurance as closely. But separating the sick horses and eradicating the flies comes first for you, because that will stop new cases from coming."

"How soon?" asked Rede, intent.

"Not wholly sure, but I realize now it had already started to happen, before the cavalry came back with all their sick—men and mounts and parasites—and began it all over again." *And the Rusylli, never forget them.* "I must have killed all the blue flies in the fort along with the others, around when I was first divesting chaos. However long it takes for the disease to brew up in the last man bitten, that will be our end-point."

Until other flies flew in, from whatever pockets they were breeding at—odd corners of Tyno, up and down the river valley, and oh gods, Vilnoc. Infected animals in the village and town were going to be a thornier problem than in the fort, as no one was going to be willing to give up their valuable beasts if they weren't obviously very sick.

General Arisaydia having no direct authority to order such compliance among civilians, Penric would have to call in Duke Jurgo on that problem. Adelis, bless him, had been fielding inquiries from the duke right along, not to mention shielding Pen from demands that he attend on the palace, giving the very just excuse that Pen had been up to his elbows in the sick and shouldn't enter there. If any of the duke's family, retainers, or servants had come down with the bruising fever, Pen had no doubt his priorities would have been abruptly rearranged for him. Persuading Jurgo to support the slaughter out of his purse, *argh* that was not going to please his patron duke; add that to Pen's list of chores. Next-next.

Rede's breath drew sharply in. He grabbed Pen's left hand again and bent to stare at the scab. "Last man bitten. Is that *you*?"

"Uh . . ." In the excitement of his discovery, Pen hadn't even thought of the disease being included with the holy gift of inspiration. Might the white god have made sure that Pen could not possibly miss the point by sending him an infected fly? Pen was afraid the answer was *Absolutely*.

Be careful what you pray for, sighed Des.

"It's too soon to tell," Pen told Rede and the freshly anxious Dubro. "But in any case, Des can cure me just as we cure others. She once healed me of a fractured skull, and trepanned me for the clot to boot. Of course, the problem was I had to stay *conscious* through it all . . ."

"Mother's blood," swore Rede. "I want to hear that tale."

"Later," Pen promised. "Best over a gallon of wine. Oh." He turned to Dubro. "This may not have come up in your training, but one sorcerer cannot heal another. Incompatible demons. Before you go home, I must teach Maska some more tricks for keeping you well."

Dubro's eyes were still wide. "Thank you . . . ?"

Pen grinned at both men. Compelled by his momentary euphoria, they smiled back, rare and welcome expressions. "All right. Let's get to it!"

After his pass through the sick-chambers, Pen put the most important tasks in train as quickly as he could. In the cavalry stables, Dubro proved able to sort out the diseased mounts almost as readily as Pen. Leaving Captain Suran to deal with the uproar in their wake, Pen led his colleague down to Tyno for the first time, through orienting visits to his sickest patients, and on to the tannery. Pen was unsure if the heavy outbreak of fever in that clan was from fly bites or the infected blood to which the tanners had been exposed in their work, but then, he was still unsure whether Master Orides might have picked it up from those first autopsies. In any case, they found alien flies in the smelly work-yard. Blue witches, indeed.

Maska dispatched them handily. Evidently, the dog-demon relished hunting deadly blue flies quite as much as hunting rabbits or weasels back in his farm days. So Pen was confidently able to leave the pair to quarter the village and its environs looking for more. Any sick horses or mules would have to be left until someone with more authority could get here, but with the flies gone, they wouldn't be such an immediate hazard.

He circled back via the abattoir, where some sheep that he'd have to greet on his plate tomorrow awaited. Really, he was going off meat. He explained about the imported horses and the invading steppe flies to Sergeant Jasenik and his men; Jasenik was both horrified and smugly validated in his views on sick livestock. In any case, neither sheep nor flies of any description were left alive behind Pen when he slogged up to the fort.

Where, in the westering light of the entry court, a distraught cavalryman attempted to run him through with his lance.

Pen was so tired by now that even with Des's startled aid he almost didn't dodge fast enough. The spearpoint, which the man had been trying to drive into his back, ripped through Pen's tunic and skin and skittered over his ribs under his left arm. The shaft burst into sawdust and the point spun away, a moment too late to spare him the blow.

"Bastard bite it!" Pen swore, turning around and preparing to disable the fellow's legs through his by-now-practiced nerve twist. But a couple of shocked gate guards had run up and tackled the cavalryman for him.

"Oh," wheezed Pen. "Good." He dabbed at the red wet on his side. It would start to really hurt in a minute, he supposed.

"Learned sir! Are you all right?" A passing officer grabbed him anxiously by his arm.

Do I look *all right?* Scarlet was seeping through his

torn tunic and down his trouser leg, which would have to be mended and laundered now, blast it. Irritated, Pen shook him off. "Don't get my blood on you. It might be contaminated."

The man recoiled.

"Learned sir!" called a guard holding the struggling would-be assassin. "What should we do with him?" The cavalryman was still swearing at Pen. And weeping. Had they already started the sick-horse slaughter, and with his beloved mount? Evidently.

The cavalryman was quite a young soldier, Pen saw, though past being a boy. Years younger than Pen. As the last in his family, not to mention bearing a centuries-old demon that would make anyone feel a child, Pen still felt awkward with seniority and the duty of care that came with it, for all that it could only become more common in his future.

"Just take him to Captain Suran," Pen sighed. "Tell him what happened. Maybe he can rule it a temporary madness." *Unless it happens again*. Pen hoped not. "I don't have *time* to deal with this."

"Can I escort you to the hospice, sir?" asked the anxious officer.

Pen stared glumly at him. "I know my way by now, I promise you."

Oh, said the outraged Des, still a little frenzied from the sudden attack and defense, *we could be a lot more sarcastic than that! Let me, let me!*

Settle down.

Well, he'd wanted to report in to Master Rede anyway. Pen put his unwashed-since-the-abattoir hands behind his back to keep them there as he continued his trudge to the hospice. He wasn't dizzy. Was he? Not from this shallow if ragged cut . . .

Rede greeted him with interest and then, as he took in the gory details, horror, and rushed Pen to a treatment room. Pen sat gratefully on a stool and let himself be fussed at, although Des was already stopping the bleeding. *That tunic's done for*, Pen thought as it came off at Rede's hands and landed in a heap.

"Does this hurt?" Rede asked, coming at him with a sponge of wine spirits.

Why did people even *ask* that? "Like a bitch," Pen gasped as the cleansing fluid hit. "It was all right *before* you got your paws on it."

"Aye, I don't think so," said Rede, swabbing grimly as Pen flinched. "Do you *know* you're in shock, Master Not-really-a-physician?"

"Am I?" said Pen doubtfully, and "Yes, you rather are," put in Des aloud.

"I see this in my army idiots. I don't expect it of you."

"Ngh." Pen added after a moment, "I was going to try to ride into Vilnoc tonight."

"And now you're not," said Rede firmly. His hands didn't stop working.

The room was turning. *Then* the nausea hit. Pen countered it with deep breaths.

"Your demon was right when she told the general you wouldn't know when to stop," Rede complained on. Pen didn't argue with him. There were very few people in the fort that poor Rede could vent his feelings upon at the moment, just Pen and, well . . . Pen. And Des, maybe.

"This is why medicine can't be my calling," said Pen dimly. "The demand is endless, and I've learned I am not. Only the gods could deal with all the world's pain, all at once, all the time. It's a wonder *They're* not driven mad. Unless They have been, which would explain some things. Theologically speaking. Even a sorcerer can't be a god, not all by himself. Although desperate people will try to make him so."

"Nor can a physician," sighed Rede.

"Aye."

The *all by himself* problem was partially addressed for both of them, late the following morning, when a large traveling coach rolled up to the fort gates and disgorged, of all the people Pen had stopped expecting, the senior sorceress-physician from the Mother's Order at Jurgo's winter capital. Along with a crew of her aides.

Learned Master Ravana was a small, aging woman radiating the dense presence within her of a demon at least four generations old. For once, Des had no sly jibes about the rival. Pen had the sense of exquisitely polite bows exchanged between high-level diplomatic enemies being escorted to a negotiating table. In any case, after Pen and Rede came dashing out to welcome them all, Ravana's demoness did not interfere with her rider's determined and efficient introductions.

There followed the fastest tour through the sick-chambers that Pen could arrange, along with a clipped description of all that they had discovered. By Ravana's pertinent questions, she had little trouble understanding events. Then Pen ruthlessly commandeered her and her coach to drive them into Vilnoc where he could toss her to the beleaguered Master Tolga.

Given their many commonalities, Pen thought the two Mother's physicians might get along well. For one thing, Tolga wouldn't start already angry at Ravana as she was at Pen for not coming lately, even though he'd been there and the sorceress never had. Because people were illogical like that. Some days, Pen really preferred demons.

Why, thank you, preened Des.

Hush.

Pen might even be able to set the senior sorceress on *Jurgo*, now wouldn't that be a boon. She'd worked for the duke much longer than Pen had.

Pen tucked himself into a corner of the coach, grateful to be sitting down. "Apologies for being so close, Learned." His vague gesture took in their two powerful demons, each studiously ignoring the other like two strange cats.

She waved this away. "It can't be helped." She sat back, her eyes narrowing at him. At them. "So, you are the one Duke Jurgo has told me about. I'm pleased to finally get a chance to meet you, though sorry the occasion is so fraught."

"And I, you." It had been Pen's second summoning, she'd told him earlier, backed by a note from Jurgo himself that had torn her out of her own sticky matrix of responsibilities in order to travel to Vilnoc. That, plus the very real possibility that if the bruising fever should jump to the winter capital, she might well find herself dealing with it there, and she'd wanted to be beforehand.

She'd been very frank about that, for which Pen was grateful.

Ravana took this chance to ask a few more shrewd questions about the fever, while the aide who'd accompanied them, herself a physician, listened closely. Pen was just glad for a chance to sit down, though as the coach rocked through a rut, he touched his ribs and winced.

Ravana nodded to his side. "And just what happened there? The wound looks fresh, even with uncanny healing."

Pen was wearing his old house tunic this morning, but she'd recognized his status instantly upon meeting due to his dense demon. His injury was doubtless as bare to her Sight beneath the cloth and bandages as anyone else's would be to him and Des. He sighed and recounted the incident with the murderously upset cavalryman.

Her lips twisted in resigned understanding. "So sad about the horses. But I have to believe you are doing the right thing in removing them as swiftly as possible. Poor young fellow! Will they hang him?"

"I've asked them not to. His captain, though furious, was sympathetic to his plight, so I think they'll listen to me."

"I see." She frowned out the window, tapping her knee, then turned a more considering gaze upon Pen. "So. Your Darthacan translation of Learned Ruchia's two volumes on sorcery came to my hands last year," she went on. "Duke Jurgo kindly sent it over."

That must have been the version printed back in

Martensbridge several years ago, which had traveled as far as Pen had; possibly one of the very sets Pen had gifted to his patron. "Ah! You read Darthacan?"

"Not as well as I'd like, and most of my apprentices, less. I understand from Jurgo that you are working on a translation into Cedonian?"

"Oh! Yes." Pen brightened. "The first volume is done and waiting for me to recopy onto the metal printing plates. The second, I am still translating."

"The one on medical sorcery, yes?"

"Yes. It's a much thicker and more complicated volume, and so is taking longer."

"Such a work would be a boon to my apprentices."

"That's my hope. When I was in seminary at Rosehall, the scarcity of texts was a source of much contention. And once, a lurid stabbing. That was what first inspired me to develop the plate-making method. Which I describe in the codicil to the first volume. Although not the part about the stabbing."

"I read that." She sat back and favored him with a peculiar smile. "I want copies for my students. And myself."

"You should be able to extract them from Jurgo. It will be his ducal press producing them, if all goes well."

She nodded firmly. "Pray do not let anyone else run you through before it is finished, Learned Penric."

Accidentally implying they'd be welcome to turn him into a pincushion after? Pen, remembering the state in which he'd left his study, could almost endorse the sentiment. He returned a sheepish grin. "I'll try not, Learned."

Then the coach arrived at the Mother's Order, and all was urgent bustle again. The harried Tolga greeted this relieving force with all the joy Pen had hoped, and even spared a smidgen for him as he detailed the story of the sick horses and the blue flies. It was quickly evident he could leave the women to get on with it, so he begged the loan of a chair and bearers to carry him back to the fort.

It wasn't exactly malingering. The spear cut still throbbed, and he could lie back, close his eyes, and extend Des's range and sensitivity to its maximum to slay a swath through every biting insect along his route through Vilnoc to Tyno. After this was over, he never wanted to kill another domestic animal in his life, but he thought he could cheerfully make this bug-slaughter a routine wherever they traveled. It was a start.

In five days, new cases trickled down to none. By ten, Pen and Dubro and Rede were able to move the last of the victims from the sick-chambers to the recovery barracks. With fewer deathly ill men to spread the magics upon, they healed faster and faster. This left Pen more chances to circle Tyno, with a similar result. Ravana and Tolga reported a matching course of events from the Mother's Order in Vilnoc.

In the middle of all this the Rusylli encampment *finally* sent for his help, and he took Dubro along, not solely in case of more angry spears. To his bemusement, the sick Rusylli responded to the older sorcerer, who spoke not a word of their language, with more trust than they gave the more powerful but younger-looking

Penric—Pen was reminded of his obstreperous patients in the fort who had yielded to that same grandfatherly air. It would have been better, always better, if they'd been able to start the treatments earlier, but with the source of new infections cut off, they at least stood a chance of catching up, and within two days Pen was able to leave the Rusylli to Dubro as his special charge.

This also gave him ten days to be very, very sure Des had managed to clear the disease from his own body, because, yes, of *course* that horsefly in the Tyno temple had been infected. Pen wasn't even surprised when his fever began. But since soldiers persisted in eating, no doubt to the dismay of the army ledger-keepers, there was a never-ending parade of beasts in the abattoir to divest chaos upon. Pen added his own body's incipient disorder to the discharge, and his ailment passed off with no other symptoms.

Thirty-six days after he had left home for a two-hour visit to the fort, Pen stood before his own front door once more.

Had its cheerful red-orange paint been peeling this much before? Pen had barely time to wonder if he should get someone on that before it was flung open and Nikys bolted into his arms.

"Oh, you're back, you're well, you're alive, you're *here*!" she cried in excitement, pulling him into the atrium.

Pen let himself be hauled, helpless against his spreading grin, and her. "Hey, hey, I sent you a note yesterday, it shouldn't be a surprise . . ."

"We've been watching out for you all morning. I promise you, I didn't let Lin touch your study."

"It doesn't matter. I can't remember what I was last doing there anyway," he assured her. For all that he wanted to cling to his writing table like a barnacle and never be scraped off again.

"You've grown so thin!" She unhanded him just enough to scowl down the length of his body. "You could hardly afford that. Des, didn't you make him eat?"

"Army food and general madness," Des defended herself. "Not my fault."

"Well, you'll find neither here."

"Five gods be praised," Pen told her. Footsteps and a faint mew drew his attention beyond her, where Idrene stood holding Florina and smiling. "Oh my word. Her head's grown so much!"

"They do that, about the fourth month," said Idrene placidly.

"Well, yes, I knew that, or Des did—six of her prior riders had been mothers, did I ever say? Before they contracted a demon, of course." His reach toward the sleepy infant was briefly thwarted by Idrene stepping back. "No, I'm clean, I wouldn't be back here if I weren't."

He pried his child away from her and fixed her on his shoulder, stroking the fuzzy head in wonder. "It's just . . . marvelous. To marvel at. You are a marvel, yes you are . . ." He was fairly sure his expression was completely foolish. He was fairly sure he didn't care.

His glance around the atrium found it all . . . exactly the same, clean and serene, and when had that become a miracle? He spared an arm to snag Nikys. "I have so much to tell you."

She choked on a laugh. "I have so little!"

"No...no...everything here is marvelous." He breathed in her curls. "*Everything*."

EPILOGUE

"SO," SAID REDE, fingering the metal rectangle. "This is what a magically finished printing plate looks like."

"You can pick it up," Pen said cordially. "It won't break."

Endlessly curious, Rede separated it from its stack and did so, tilting it this way and that in the bright light from Penric's study window.

"That's still the Cedonian translation of Volume One, which I'm well along with, but I broke off to add a chapter on the bruising fever to Volume Two," Pen told him. "I will be very pleased to have you read the first draft and check it for accuracy, as there's scarcely anyone with more expertise on that subject right now than you, hard-won as it was."

"You," Rede pointed out. "And Master Tolga and Learned Ravana."

Pen nodded concession. "But you're here. Anyway, my plan is to first make it a separate little chapbook, for the palace printer to send around to the relevant Orders in Orbas. Because it seems more locally urgent."

Rede said wistfully, "Do you think all the blue flies have really been eradicated?"

Pen grimaced. "I've been murdering ordinary flies for years, and haven't made a dent in their legions yet. More to the point, wherever the evil things came from, out there among the western Rusylli tribes, they're likely still there. As long as the western Rusylli press on the eastern, and the eastern on the borders of Cedonia, Grabyat, and countries south, they're bound to turn up again."

"Let's pray not for a long time," sighed Rede. Pen vented an agreeing hum, more in hope than belief.

The sounds of Lin admitting a visitor drifted up from the atrium and through Pen's study door, open to catch whatever draft might relieve the heat of this early autumn day. "It's important," said Pen, "but not actually what I invited you here to talk about today. And here's my other guest."

Pen rose to greet Learned Dubro as Lin ushered him into the study. Dubro looked around with great interest. "Ha. This looks a proper scholar's lair."

Pen grinned. "I'd apologize for the mess, but I'm not in the least sorry. Here, sit, sit." Pen cleared a chair of scrolls and pulled it close to Rede's.

The two men exchanged what Pen was fairly sure were mockeries of military salutes. "Good to see you again," said Rede, and, "You as well," said Dubro. There followed a short, social delay while Lin brought in a pitcher of cooled tea and a plate of spiral cakes, curled around spices. Dubro seemed to find their delicacy somewhat alarming, and sat more carefully on his chair as he consumed them.

"So." Pen took a swallow of tea and cleared his throat.

"I've been thinking about this for some time. And I've concluded that Master Rede would be an ideal candidate to receive Learned Dubro's demon, upon his passing, and so become Orbas's next sorcerer-physician."

Rede made a taken-aback sound.

Dubro seemed less discomfited. "Don't look like that, young fellow. We all have to go sometime. And I'd be pleased to know I was leaving Maska in such good hands."

"But—you'd have to die."

"That's the way it works, aye. There's more than one reason the Quadrenes call us Temple sorcerers necromancers. I wouldn't volunteer to leave early, mind you."

"You and I"—Pen nodded to Dubro—"both acquired our demons by accident, if not necessarily by mistake. Receiving one in a planned fashion doubtless feels a much stranger event when the donor-sorcerer isn't a stranger." Pen turned to Rede. "Because it wouldn't just be Maska you'd be receiving. In effect, if the transfer was successful, your head would be haunted for the rest of your life by an image indistinguishable from Dubro's ghost. And human images *talk* to you."

"Maska communicates," Dubro objected. "In his own fashion."

Pen waved allowance.

"It wouldn't be his sundered soul?" asked Rede uneasily. "Cut off from his god?"

"No, not normally. Although in certain botched transfers—well, that goes into technicalities that need not delay us here. Plenty of time to learn about it all later. I've never liked the term *image* for the shape a demon takes from its rider's life, because that would seem to imply something static. Within you, the demon still lives and grows and learns and changes, and will bear all those memories to its next rider. After a few transfers, a demon becomes something of a layer cake. Underneath the ten women who make up Des, that first wild mare and the lioness that killed her still linger. They send me odd dreams now and then."

Dubro nodded. "I get little fragments from the weasel and the quail, sometimes, though Maska looms larger. Dog dreams aren't very colorful, but they smell amazing." Dubro's lips twisted. "I've no idea what Dubro-dreams would be like, though I wouldn't wish some of mine on anyone else. I suppose you'd end up knowing more about me than my wife or mother ever did. But so would whoever inherited my demon. Maybe once your soul is gone to your god, you don't care about embarrassment."

"I think, at that point, the donor-souls have a vaster and stranger world to absorb them," Penric agreed. "The recipient does have to get over the shock of the intimacy." Des snickered. He asked her dryly, *Anything to add from your position of expertise, here?*

No, carry on, she said. *You're doing fine so far. But— layer cake, really?*

I could come up with less appealing metaphors, but I'm trying to sell the idea, here.

Merchant of demons? Peddling demon-flavored cakes, ah, I see.

Stop. You'll make me laugh, and then poor Rede will be even more confused.

She settled back to watching smugly.

"You have a while to think about it," Pen told Rede. "Maybe years."

Dubro eyed his knobby hands, dusted with age spots. "Or maybe not, eh?"

Pen tilted his head in acknowledgement. "Today would be merely a declaration of intent, a preliminary contract."

"Like some peculiar sort of betrothal?" said Rede, which made Dubro, lifting a cake to his lips, snort a laugh, then cough on crumbs. He restored himself with a gulp of tea.

You have no idea, thought Pen. "More a betrothal on one side, a will on the other. But chances happen. It may be that some other Temple demon becomes available first. Or that this one might be lost, Bastard forbid. Although . . . the white god is the god of chances, good and ill. If He approves, he has unexpected ways of helping make things occur." Pen surreptitiously rubbed the back of his left hand. "Sometimes very subtle." And sometimes less so.

"There would be a spate of required theological study," Pen went on, "which I doubt intimidates you. And Temple oaths, which cap all others. Including military ones, but if you undertake to go on as an army physician, there won't be any trouble negotiating that. You're already adept at balancing your oath to the Mother and your oath to Orbas. You really do have a calling in Her craft."

"This seems a very direct solution to the shortage of sorcerer-physicians that I was complaining about," Rede said ruefully.

"The only one I know of," said Pen. "With the white god, you learn to be careful what you pray for."

Rede puffed a laugh. "So it seems." He set down his tea, took a breath, turned to Dubro, and extended his hand. "Well, Learned Dubro. If it chances so, then, I would like to try this."

Dubro's seamed face curved in a smile as he gripped back. "Master Rede. White god willing, so should I."

The memory of a moment on a spring roadside in the cantons drifted through Pen's mind, curiously doubled. *Let me serve you in your need*, and, *Accepted*. He'd had much less notion than Rede what a wide new world he'd been getting into, back then.

You didn't, no, Des agreed. *I had much less than I thought. But One other guarded us both, I think.*

And we've done all right so far, haven't we, Des?

Aye.

"White god willing," Pen prayed sincerely.

OUTRODUCTION

❦

I'VE PUT THESE REMARKS in the order in which the novellas were originally composed in 2019 and 2020.

THE ORPHANS OF RASPAY

I had long wanted to see what would happen to each side if Penric encountered pirates, toying with several ideas for story-starts including one for Pen's first meeting with Nikys and Adelis, perhaps captured and thrown together when the siblings were fleeing Cedonia after political persecution. I had a better idea for that one, and the pirates were shelved for a time, but they sailed back over my horizon eventually once I had Penric placed in his later context in sea-coastal Orbas.

I don't buy into the romantical glamorization of pirates—real ones, over the long worldwide history of sea theft, included some deeply unpleasant folks, and it should not be overlooked that in many instances part of their loot was human beings kidnapped to be enslaved. "Pirate!" may be a term that inspires imaginative identification from my fellow modern couch potatoes; "Slaver!" generally does not, but they were often one and the same. I wanted to explore and de-romanticize this aspect.

I've read a lot of history, and have picked up bits and pieces over the years about the brutal practices of pirates from a wide range of places and times, from Roman to Scandinavian to Japanese as well as the more familiar Caribbean, but the medieval Mediterranean model was closest to my fantasy-world-story needs. A book I first read a couple of decades ago, and revisited while booting up the needed setting and economic and political background for this story, was *Pirate Utopias: Moorish Corsairs and European Renegadoes* (1995) by Peter Lamborn Wilson.

Wilson seems a romanticizer, though he dresses his pirate-fannishness in some rather anachronistic 19th Century politico-philosophical clothing, but his account of the short-lived pirate city-state of Salé on the Moroccan coast, with its government of, by, and for the pirates, proved chock-full of telling details to ground my setting of Lantihera. Wilson glorifies his anti-hero subjects as dedicated to proto-modern political rights and freedoms that I'm pretty sure were not in their minds at the time, and gives short shrift to the destroyed freedoms of their many victims. Granted that the other tyrannical governmental authorities of Salé's day were just as awful, I preferred my tale to side with the victims, of which my titular orphans and their fellow captives were fair representatives. Though probably not Penric, heh.

THE PHYSICIANS OF VILNOC

As I've been explaining ever since its e-publication in May of 2020, what became "The Physicians of Vilnoc" was conceived and begun at the end of 2019 before the coronavirus pandemic appeared on my horizon, although it was finished very much during. Any reader of history, the history of science, or especially the history of medicine is well aware that the recent pandemic year brought nothing new to humanity, and all my springs of inspiration for this story were from older models, which were plenty enough.

Probably the oldest was a book I read back in fifth grade, one of those kids' chapter-book biographies, this one of Walter Reed (yes, the one the famous hospital is justly named for) and his work in the tropics as a young army doctor figuring out the real vectors of the deadly yellow fever. I don't remember the name of my fifth-grade teacher or any of my classmates (this was sixty years ago) but I vividly remember that book's account of Reed's experiment. He and a crew of equally determined volunteers locked themselves in a well-screened cabin for a couple of weeks with a lot of horribly soiled bedding and other waste from fever victims who'd died, but no mosquitoes, thus dramatically proving that the disease was not spread by personal contact, which was the prevailing theory at the time. The characterization of Master Rede in my story is inspired by him.

Turning to Penric's personal history, real physician

burnout is I hope better understood these days than it used to be. It has parallels with burnout from any other demanding professional or indeed personal task, but especially those where the practitioner is trying to do a good thing that can and sometimes does go horribly wrong—teaching and parenting, for just two examples.

As for the emotions of it, I suppose this aspect of Penric goes back to the period of my twenties that I spent working at a major university hospital as a drug administration technician, a sort of nurses' aide whose job it was to give the medication to all the patients on a ward, under the supervision of the hospital pharmacists. Looking back from long after, I can see that a bookish, introverted, vaguely dissociative person who lived mainly up inside her own head was not especially well-matched with the job, and by the end of the decade I couldn't *wait* to be out of there. I haven't had nightmares about it for a while now, but it still surfaces now and then.

I was unconscious at the time of just how very much human observation of all sorts I was putting under my belt, to the great benefit of the writer I eventually became. Scaling it up to Penric's much, much more responsible and difficult medical duties is a typical creative move that writers do all the time, small experiences writ large.

MASQUERADE IN LODI

I did a lot of research reading on the city of Venice back when I had completed my first fantasy novel, the stand-alone *The Spirit Ring* (1992). At the time I was toying with an idea for a sequel that would take my two young protagonists to their alternate-our-world-with-magic version of that canal city, in pursuit of a maguffin in the form of heroine Fiametta's mother's stolen death mask. That vague notion was set aside in favor of more Vorkosigan series—*Mirror Dance* (1994) came next, so, good call—and I never got back to it.

Penric's world is of course full of late medieval European roots, including an analogue of Venice. The city of Lodi was previously established as the home of one of Desdemona's earlier riders, the flamboyant courtesan Mira, and as a place where Penric had served the Temple for a year or so in a period of his career my tales had skipped over. But really, it seemed too splendid a setting to totally pass up, plus I already had all that source material squirreled away in my head and on my bookshelves.

It's always tricky inserting an earlier story written later into a fictional timeline, since it raises the question of why, if it's important enough to write about, do the characters never think about it in their "later"? One of the ploys is to make the story small-scale, tucked in a natural sort of time pocket. Another is to hang it off some throw-away line or lines. Another is to put it in a different or out-of-the-way setting, to have been visited by only one or two of the "current" cast of series characters. I deployed all three tricks for what became "Masquerade in Lodi."

The famous Carnivale of Venice linked up irresistibly with the series-established idea of the Bastard's Day midsummer celebrations. A family trip in 1965 that included a day in Venice gave me some somatic memories not from any book. Learned Iserne first appeared in a throw-away line in "Orphans," as an otherwise undescribed Lodi Temple contact of Penric's. So how had they become such good friends that Pen could call upon her for favors . . . ? Her family spun out naturally from her, and my villain from her victim-son and my reading about Venice's complex seagoing mercantile customs. Ideas about magical fun with dolphins also came up during the earlier-written "Orphans," and from a memorable paddle in a kayak out among a pod of them during a visit of mine to Florida.

Blessed Chio floated in on her own and seized the oars as I was already writing the opening sections—logic dictated the city must harbor a saint of the Bastard, so who might this person be, different from the first one we'd met back in "Penric's Demon"? Chio was almost as much of a surprise to me as she was to Penric, though I did have the experience of once being a bright, frustrated, somewhat discounted teenage girl to draw upon. Though I most certainly never channeled a god of chaos . . . I don't think.

—Ta, L.

AUTHOR'S NOTE:
A BUJOLD READING-ORDER GUIDE
~~~

THE FANTASY NOVELS

My fantasy novels are not hard to order. Easiest of all is *The Spirit Ring*, which is a stand-alone, or aquel, as some wag once dubbed books that for some obscure reason failed to spawn a subsequent series. Next easiest are the four volumes of *The Sharing Knife*—in order, *Beguilement*, *Legacy*, *Passage*, and *Horizon*—which I broke down and actually numbered, as this was one continuous tale divided into non-wrist-breaking chunks. The novella "Knife Children" is something of a codicil-tale to this tetralogy.

What were called the Chalion books after the setting of its first two volumes, but which now that the geographic scope has widened I'm dubbing the World of the Five Gods, were written to be stand-alones as part of a larger whole, and can in theory be read in any order. Some readers think the world-building is easier to assimilate when the books are read in publication order, and the second volume certainly contains spoilers for the first (but not the third). In any case, the publication order is:

> *The Curse of Chalion*
> *Paladin of Souls*
> *The Hallowed Hunt*

In terms of internal world chronology, *The Hallowed Hunt* would fall first, the Penric novellas perhaps a hundred and fifty years later, and *The Curse of Chalion* and *Paladin of Souls* would follow a century or so after that.

The internal chronology of the Penric & Desdemona tales is presently:

> "Penric's Demon"
> "Penric and the Shaman"
> "Penric's Fox"
> "Masquerade in Lodi"
> "Penric's Mission"
> "Mira's Last Dance"
> "The Prisoner of Limnos"
> "The Orphans of Raspay"
> "The Physicians of Vilnoc"
> *The Assassins of Thasalon*
> "Knot of Shadows"

"Demon," "Shaman," and "Fox" are collected as paper volumes in *Penric's Progress*; "Mission," "Mira" and "Limnos" in *Penric's Travels*; and "Lodi," "Orphans" and "Physicians" in *Penric's Labors*.

OTHER ORIGINAL E-BOOKS

The short story collection *Proto Zoa* contains five very early tales—three (1980s) contemporary fantasy, two science fiction—all previously published but not in this handy format. The novelette "Dreamweaver's Dilemma" may be of interest to Vorkosigan completists, as it is the first story in which that proto-universe began, mentioning Beta Colony but before Barrayar was even thought of.

Sidelines: Talks and Essays is just what it says on the tin—a collection of three decades of my nonfiction writings, including convention speeches, essays, travelogues, introductions, and some less formal pieces. I hope it will prove an interesting companion piece to my fiction.

The Gerould Family of New Hampshire in the Civil War: Two Diaries and a Memoir is a compilation of historical documents handed down from my mother's father's side of my family. A meeting of time, technology, and skillset has finally allowed me to put them into a sharable form.

❖ ❖ ❖

THE VORKOSIGAN STORIES

Many pixels have been expended debating the "best" order in which to read the Vorkosigan saga. The debate mainly revolves around publication order versus internal-chronological order. I favor internal chronological, with a few adjustments.

It was always my intention to write each book as a stand-alone, so that the reader could theoretically jump in anywhere. While still somewhat true, as the series developed it acquired a number of sub-arcs, closely related tales that were richer for each other. I will list the sub-arcs, and then the books, and then the duplication warnings. (My publishing history has been complex.) And then the publication order, for those who want it.

Shards of Honor and *Barrayar.* The first two books in the series proper, they detail the adventures of Cordelia Naismith of Beta Colony and Aral Vorkosigan of Barrayar. *Shards* was my very first novel ever; *Barrayar* was actually my eighth, but continues the tale the next day after the end of *Shards*. For readers who want to be sure of beginning at the beginning, or who are very spoiler-sensitive, start with these two.

The Warrior's Apprentice and *The Vor Game* (with, perhaps, the novella "The Mountains of Mourning" tucked in between.) *The Warrior's Apprentice* introduces the character who became the series' linchpin, Miles Vorkosigan; the first book tells how he created a space mercenary fleet by accident; the second how he fixed his mistakes from the first round. Space opera and military-esque adventure (and a number of other things one can best discover for oneself), *The Warrior's Apprentice* makes another good place to jump into the series for readers who prefer a young male protagonist.

After that: *Brothers in Arms* should be read before *Mirror Dance*, and both, ideally, before *Memory*.

Komarr makes another alternate entry point for the series, picking up Miles's second career at its start. It should be read before *A Civil Campaign*.

Borders of Infinity, a collection of three of the six currently extant novellas, makes a good Miles Vorkosigan early-adventure sampler platter, I always thought, for readers who don't want to commit themselves to length. (But it may make more sense if read after *The Warrior's Apprentice*.) Take care not to confuse the collection-as-a-whole with its title story, "The Borders of Infinity."

Falling Free takes place 200 years earlier in the timeline and does not share settings or characters with the main body of the series. Most readers recommend picking up this story later. It should likely be read before *Diplomatic Immunity*, however, which revisits the "quaddies," a bioengineered race of free-fall dwellers, in Miles's time.

The novels in the internal-chronological list below appear in italics; the novellas (officially defined as a story between 17,500 words and 40,000 words) in quote marks.

> *Falling Free*
> *Shards of Honor*
> *Barrayar*
> *The Warrior's Apprentice*
> "The Mountains of Mourning"

"Weatherman"
The Vor Game
Cetaganda
Ethan of Athos
Borders of Infinity
"Labyrinth"
"The Borders of Infinity"
Brothers in Arms
Mirror Dance
Memory
Komarr
A Civil Campaign
"Winterfair Gifts"
Diplomatic Immunity
Captain Vorpatril's Alliance
"The Flowers of Vashnoi"
CryoBurn
Gentleman Jole and the Red Queen

❖ ❖ ❖

Caveats:

The novella "Weatherman" is an out-take from the beginning of the novel *The Vor Game*. If you already have *The Vor Game*, you likely don't need this.

The original "novel" *Borders of Infinity* was a fix-up collection containing the three novellas "The Mountains of Mourning," "Labyrinth," and "The Borders of Infinity," together with a frame to tie the pieces together. Again, beware duplication. The frame story does not stand alone.

Publication order:

This is also the order in which the works were written, apart from a couple of the novellas, but is not identical to the internal-chronological. It goes:

> *Shards of Honor* (June 1986)
> *The Warrior's Apprentice* (August 1986)
> *Ethan of Athos* (December 1986)
> *Falling Free* (April 1988)
> *Brothers in Arms* (January 1989)
> *Borders of Infinity* (October 1989)
> *The Vor Game* (September 1990)
> *Barrayar* (October 1991)
> *Mirror Dance* (March 1994)
> *Cetaganda* (January 1996)
> *Memory* (October 1996)
> *Komarr* (June 1998)
> *A Civil Campaign* (September 1999).
> *Diplomatic Immunity* (May 2002)
> "Winterfair Gifts" (February 2004)
> *CryoBurn* (November 2010)
> *Captain Vorpatril's Alliance* (November 2012)
> *Gentleman Jole and the Red Queen* (February 2016)
> "The Flowers of Vashnoi" (May 2018)

. . . Three decades fitted on a page. Huh.
Happy reading!

—Lois McMaster Bujold

The Saga of the Skolian Empire
THE RUBY DICE
HC: 978-1-4165-5514-8 | $23.00 US/$26.99 CAN

DIAMOND STAR
PB: 978-1-4391-3382-8 | $7.99 US/$9.99 CAN

CARNELIANS
HC: 978-1-4516-3748-9 | $25.00 US/$28.99 CAN
PB: 978-1-4516-3849-3 | $7.99 US/$9.99 CAN

Skolian Empire: Major Bhaajan
UNDERCITY
TPB: 978-1-4767-3692-1 | $15.00 US/$18.00 CAN

THE BRONZE SKIES
TPB: 978-1-4814-8258-5 | $16.00 US/$22.00 CAN

THE JIGSAW ASSASSIN
TPB: 978-1-9821-9196-2 | $16.00 US/$22.00 CAN
PB: 978-1-9821-9276-1 | $9.99 US/$12.99 CAN

Dead Man Walking

TPB: 978-1-9821-9243-3 • $17.00 US/$22.00 CAN

When a rogue secret agent is murdered in detention, Ishmael Jones and Penny Belcourt are called in. But then the agent's body goes missing . . . and more people start dying. Has the murdered agent risen from the dead to get his revenge? Secrets are revealed and horrors uncovered. But with the bodies piling up, Ishmael and Penny have to wonder if there will be anyone left to reveal the solution of the mystery to.

Very Important Corpses

TPB: 978-1-9821-9273-0 • $18.00 US/$23.00 CAN

The twelve most important business people in the world are having their annual meeting. But one by one, they're being murdered. It's down to Ishmael Jones and his partner in crimes Penny Belcourt to get to the bottom of things. Of course, it doesn't help that this is all taking place at a hotel near Loch Ness.

Haunted by the Past

HC: 978-1-9821-9228-0 • $25.00 US / $34.00 CAN

Ishmael Jones and Penny Belcourt specialize in solving cases of the weird and uncanny. They're called to one of the most haunted old houses in England to solve the unexplained disappearance of a fellow compatriot. They say that something prowls the house in the early hours, endlessly searching. They say . . . it crawls.

Available in bookstores everywhere.
Order ebooks online at www.baen.com.

Explore the Liaden Universe®!
Space Opera on a Grand Scale by
SHARON LEE & STEVE MILLER

Omnibus Editions - Full Liaden Universe Novels in One Volume

The Dragon Variation 9781439133699 • $12.00 US/$15.99 CAN
The Crystal Variation 9781439134634 • $13.00 US/$15.00 CAN
The Agent Gambit 9781439134078 • $12.00 US/$14.00 CAN
Korval's Game 9781439134399 • $12.00 US/$14.00 CAN

Exuberant praise for the Liaden Universe® series:

"Every now and then you come across an author, or in this case, a pair, who write exactly what you want to read, the characters and personalities that make you enjoy meeting them. . . . I rarely rave on and on about stories, but I am devoted to Lee and Miller novels and stories."
—Anne McCaffrey

"These authors consistently deliver stories with a rich, textured setting, intricate plotting, and vivid, interesting characters from fully-realized cultures, both human and alien, and each book gets better." —Elizabeth Moon

". . . sprawling and satisfying. . . . Space opera mixes with social engineering, influenced by Regency-era manners and delicate notions of honor. . . . it's like spending time with old friends." —Publishers Weekly

". . . delightful stories of adventure and romance set in a far future . . . space opera milieu. It's all a rather heady mix of Gordon R. Dickson, the Forsythe Saga, and Victoria Holt, with Lee and Miller's own unique touches making it all sparkle and sizzle. Anyone whose taste runs toward SF in the true romantic tradition can't help but like the Liaden Universe." —Analog